TO FRANCO THE MAN WAS A DEVIL—
BUT EVEN THE DEVIL KNEW BEAUTY . . .

The unveiling was over, the sun had gone down, and the church was dark and empty. Franco climbed the steps to St. Anthony's two at a time. He was in an ebullient mood. When he reached the red front doors, he found the handles chained together, but he took his hammer and broke the chain. Then he entered the church and lit a match to see his way up the center aisle. Yes, there it was, the statue. He burned his fingertips, threw down the spent match and struck another. With this one he lit a few votive candles so he could see.

The statue stood white and bloodless on a new altar that had been especially built to hold the great weight of the stone. Franco crossed himself. It was only a statue, but you never knew if the Blessed Mother would be hovering nearby. Not that it really mattered. He would go to confession next Saturday and the whole matter of what he was about to do would be forgiven.

He swung over the brass communion rail, then climbed up on the altar itself. His hand touched the marble. It was very cold. He looked into the statue's face. For a moment he hesitated. It was such a lovely face—how could such features ever have been conceived by his uncle's unfeeling heart? Franco unconsciously turned his mouth down in a sneer. Even the devil knew beauty.

He took a breath, listened to the harsh hiss of his own laughter echo in the empty cavern of the church, and began to swing his heavy hammer into the Virgin's face.

E.A.
TREMBLAY

Miles Standish Press

Published by
Miles Standish Press, Inc.
353 West Lancaster Avenue
Wayne, Pennsylvania 19087

Dell ® TM 681510, Dell Publishing Co., Inc.

ISBN: 0-440-04180-5

First printing—November 1984

4   3   2   1

Printed in the United States of America

For Jeanette and Nicholas

ACKNOWLEDGMENTS:
In loving memory of Pietro and Maria Buttone
and with many thanks to Ed Claflin
for his support and enthusiasm.

BOOK I
THE OLD COUNTRY

Chapter 1

Italy, 1909

"Go to America! What the hell do I care?" Giorgio looked up angrily. On the old pinewood table in front of him sat a cracked porcelain bowl filled with lentil soup. Rising steam plastered the straw-colored wisps of his adolescent beard to his cheeks. A lock of light brown hair fell over his eyebrows and he brushed it back. His eyes were gentle and blue, like the Mediterranean, but when he was angry they glistened and narrowed contemptuously.

Across the table sat a burly man of twenty-four. He twisted one end of a giant black mustache between his thumb and forefinger. "What do you want me to do? I'm a poor man and there ain't no work here. Teresa's pregnant. I got to make some money."

"We got bread and wine and plenty of *pasta fazool*. We ain't no worse off than anybody else."

"Agh, *fan' gool*, you got a head as hard as a marble block. Everybody in Italy is going to America. Maybe you want us to be the only ones left here."

"Sure, then I can be the king of all of Santa Barbara and to hell with the rest of the sons of bitches who go to the other side of the world, like a certain older brother whose name I won't say, Sebastiano.''

''And to hell with you too. Fourteen years old and already you got a mouth like a sewer.''

''Where do you think I learn?'' Giorgio turned his head away in disgust and propped it up with his hand. ''I got a good teacher.''

Sebastiano pushed his chair back so violently it flipped over as he came to his feet. ''I'll show you what you got.'' His face was red as sunburn and his shoulders trembled with rage. He grabbed a small carving knife from the table and shook it at his brother. ''I don't let no damn little kid with a runny nose talk to me like that.''

''That's right, kill me! Then you got nothing to worry about.'' Giorgio stood up also, stuck his chin out and pointed to himself with both hands. ''Maybe you'll cut my throat, eh? Or cut off my scalp like a cowboy-Indian.'' He threw his hands up extravagantly. ''It don't matter if you kill me or not. I ain't going to America.''

''You come if I say you come. I didn't take you out of no damn orphanage so I could leave you a beggar in the street.''

''Who asked you to take me, eh? I was doing fine with the nuns.'' He rose to his feet and began to pace, shaking his head in agitation. ''Anyway, that was six years ago. What the hell, don't you ever forget what you did six years ago? I ain't no little kid anymore. I can take care of myself.''

Sebastiano made a grunting sound that was meant to be a laugh. He continued to shake the knife in the air as he spoke. ''How're you going to take care of yourself? You're just a kid.''

''I got hair between my legs. I'm old enough to work.''

''You're old enough to do what I tell you.''

"What am I going to do in America? I'm learning to be a mason. They don't build nothing out of stone over there."

"How do you know what they build?"

"I heard. They make everything out of wood, even their gravestones. All they need is carpenters, like you."

"So? I'll teach you to be a carpenter."

"I don't want to be no damned carpenter. I want to cut stone. That lasts forever. With wood you turn your back and it's gone. Wood is shit. No wonder you got no work. Who needs you in Italy, where everything lasts for two thousand years?"

"You insult my work?"

"Your work is shit."

Sebastiano's eyes grew wide, his head began to twitch in nervous little tics, and before he realized what he was doing, he drew back his hand and flipped the knife through the air. Giorgio saw it coming. He jerked his head out of the way just as the blade hissed past him. It stuck for a moment in the plaster wall next to him, then fell to the floor.

From across the room came a shattering scream. A young woman standing in the doorway dropped a basket of bread to the floor, then pulled her black scarf away from her face and began to beat Sebastiano over the back of the neck with it. "What's the matter with you?" she shouted. "You try to kill a little boy, your own brother, your own blood! Have you gone crazy?" Again and again she whipped him, and when he covered his head with his hands to protect himself, her rage grew. She dropped the harmless scarf and began to beat on him with her fists. "What kind of man are you? What kind of man did I marry? Is this the way you will treat my baby when he comes?"

Giorgio stood out of the way in a corner, trembling, trying to disappear into a shadow. His eyes were wide, his lips apart; he was panting like a frightened dog, looking for his moment to bolt away. Sebastiano shouted and howled at his wife. She shouted back unintelligibly and began to use her sandaled feet on his shins. His patience with her completely gone, Sebastiano took her by the shoulders and shook her like a child.

"This is my house and I will be treated with respect."

"Respect? Who can have respect for a man who would murder his own blood? Even the Sicilians don't behave like that."

"He insulted me and my work."

"I too insult you and your work!" Teresa freed her hand and slapped him hard across the face. He did not turn with the blow, but took its full force, then raised his clenched fist and threatened her.

"You want to hit me?" she said, standing fast. "Go ahead, hit me. Then see if I give you a son. See if I go to America with you."

"You are my wife! You go where I say and have all the sons I want you to have." He pushed his fist into her face.

Giorgio could stand no more. He stepped out of his corner, took a deep breath and shoved his brother from behind. Never before had he done such a thing. He was certain he would be dead in a moment, but Teresa had stood up for him so bravely; how could he not do the same for her? Sebastiano lost his balance and shuffled to regain it.

"Don't you dare hit her," Giorgio said in a voice that came out in a loud squeak. "You want to hit somebody, hit me. I ain't afraid." He craned his head forward to make his face a better target. "Come on, if you're going to do it, knock my nose off. Do it right. Give me a scar I can brag about."

Sebastiano glared and snorted like a racehorse after a

sprint. Teresa covered her mouth with her hand to stifle a sob and tears came to her eyes. "My family," she cried piteously, "what has happened to my family? Brother against brother—"

"It's because I have an idiot for a brother," Sebastiano said, but now his voice shook with regret and tears came to his eyes also. He hesitated only a moment, then threw his arms around Giorgio. "Sometimes, as much as I love you, you make me think in circles, both of you." With one hand he gathered Teresa close, and they all embraced and sobbed into each other's shoulders.

Giorgio felt exhilarated. He had been brave and lucky. Sebastiano, after all, was a big man—big enough to knock down a tree with his fist—big enough to kill a bull with a slap.

Never before had Giorgio recognized how much his sister-in-law cared for him, though he suddenly realized she had given him many hints, often telling him what a handsome and clever boy he was. It felt good to be admired by such a pretty woman, and at the moment it seemed to him that there was none prettier.

She had eyes the shape of almonds and the color of espresso. Her black hair she kept braided and modestly tucked up on the crown of her head. Her face was round and easily broke into laughter or tears, and her bosom— Madonna, he thought, it made him want to bite the back of his hand. Now that she was pregnant, the slight swell of her belly made her all the more beautiful to Giorgio. This confused him. Lately many women looked beautiful to him, when only last year they all seemed ugly and useless.

"I don't know what the hell comes over me some- times," Sebastiano carried on, "but a man has his pride. What's he got if he ain't got his pride?"

"It's all right," his wife cooed. "Sometimes you

behave like a jackass, *mio caro*, my sweet, but you're a man, after all. What can you do?''

Her acquiescence annoyed Giorgio. Of course it was her duty to smooth matters over with her husband, and Giorgio had no desire to see his brother suffer further, but the cloying predictability of her words seemed to deflate the room of its fire too quickly. Besides, he had to admit he would rather have her bestow her time and sympathy on himself.

''What could any man do with a kid brother like him? Giorgio, why do you make me so angry? Why do you insult me that way? Ain't I always been good to you?''

Giorgio shrugged. ''Sure, you always been good to me. I just ain't going to America, that's all.''

Again Sebastiano's cheeks began to grow crimson, but Teresa whispered into her husband's ear, ''Go outside. Find some friends to have a little coffee with. I'll talk to him.''

Sebastiano frowned, but his wife immediately threatened him with small signs that her temper was starting to boil again—an arched eyebrow, one hand on a hip, a leg slightly bent at the knee—and she indicated with a movement of her head that if he didn't go at once, there would be another crisis between them. Sebastiano set his jaw, shook his hand in the air with exasperation and left the boy alone with her.

''Sometimes I don't think you love your brother,'' Teresa accused Giorgio as she went to the black iron pot on the stove to ladle out a little more soup for him.

When she brought it over, he shook his head and waved her away. ''I ain't hungry.''

''You can eat it, I know you can. You're a big boy with a big appetite. *Mangia'*.''

He accepted the bowl as a matter of protocol; he

knew he would have no peace until he did. But he only stabbed at the steaming food with his spoon.

"Even if you don't love your brother, he loves you, Giorgio, and it's your duty to respect him."

"Who said I don't love him?" he replied resentfully. "I love him just fine. But that don't mean I got to love America."

"Oh, you're going to be a big shot, right? You're going to stay here and maybe grow up to be a criminal like your father."

Giorgio slammed his spoon down. What had happened to the beautiful woman who stood up for him only a moment before? He had heard all the stories about his father in the street. Why should he have to hear them again in his own home?

"My father wasn't no criminal," he mumbled bitterly, but the words sounded hollow even to him.

"You don't remember. You were too young, but I know. I was just a kid, but I remember what everyone said when he and your mother were killed. Your father got himself mixed up with the wrong people over in Naples. Murderers, kidnappers, who knows what? Maybe the Camorra or even the Mafia. There was a killing in Caserta and someone put the finger on him. The *carabinieri* found both him and your mother in a lime pit. Their bodies were all burned up. You're lucky you and your brother weren't killed too."

"It's lie. You don't know what you're talking about. My father was killed in a construction accident and my mother died of grief. Sebastiano told me." This he believed. He had never heard anything about a murder.

She wagged her finger at him. "Your brother told you a story. He thought you were too young to know about these things. Mark my words, if you stay here, you're going to end up no better than your father. Sooner or later somebody with a big mouth will tell you who killed your parents, and then you'll swear a vendetta and probably get yourself killed, and there won't even be anybody around to wash your body or kiss your wounds."

"Sure, I'll swear a vendetta. I swear it right now, before you and God." He kissed the thumb of his right hand and with it made little crosses on his forehead, his lips and his heart. "I got my honor to defend and the honor of all the Farenzas. I ain't going to run away to America. I got a responsibility. I swear my parents' blood will be paid for in blood." His eyes were intense, and his lower lip, which was almost always relaxed into a pout, was sucked in behind his teeth. "You know who killed them?"

Teresa made a frustrated looping motion with her arms. "No, I don't know who killed your mama and papa, little boy, and if I did I wouldn't tell you. You think I want you to go out and get your throat cut?"

"To hell with my throat. I know what I have to do."

Teresa shook her head and laughed out loud. "What are you going to do? You're fourteen years old. Someone could step on you like an ant."

"Agh, Teresa, you drive me crazy, both of you!" Giorgio kicked the table and turned his back on his sister-in-law.

One wall of the apartment opened through a pair of tall French doors onto a small balcony that overlooked the street. Giorgio stormed out and leaned against its crumbling stone railing. As always, there was enough noise below to drown an orchestra. The street, a narrow gorge between ancient water-stained stucco buildings, was crowded with cinnamon vendors, bakers, shoemakers, women balancing flat baskets full of bread on their heads, old gossips dressed in black, unwashed farmers, magicians, priests, laborers, crooks, and of course prostitutes, who could always be identified by the way they wore their hair long and loose down their backs.

Down there, he knew, was the real reason he wanted to stay in Italy. This was his home. What place could be better? Would the sky be any bluer somewhere else? Would the food be any cheaper or taste any better? Would it be easier to make a living where the barbarians couldn't even speak Italian? No, here was where he belonged. You didn't have to go hungry if you were clever and willing to work—or willing to steal when there wasn't any work. Maybe he was only fourteen, but he'd been hanging around the quarry for five years and he'd learned a few things about making a living for himself.

At first the masons paid little attention to him except to slip him an occasional cigarette in order to get a good laugh out of his hacking and coughing and tearing. When he saw how much he entertained them, he coughed the mightiest honks a nine-year-old could bring up.

After a while they let him carry sand and wash tools and sweep up at the end of the day. The foreman had decided to pay him—sixty lire a week, a few cents.

Over the years his responsibilities increased. Now he went out on jobs. He mixed mortar, sometimes helped with the pointing and was even learning to cut stone. He made two hundred lire a week, enough to pay his own way. He had it all figured out. Even in the winter, when there was no work and hardly anything to steal, he could live off charity from the church.

As for avenging his parents, it was expected of him. He had to do it. Still, Teresa was right. It would be dangerous, and he wasn't nearly so eager to do it as he had pretended. A vendetta could wait. Such a responsibility had a way of finding you in its own time. Actually, he didn't remember his parents, though he had dreamed about them all his life. In his dreams neither his mother nor his father had a face. He knew them only as shadows, as voices, always together as a presence with no more definition that a ghost's, but always his dreams wrenched and twisted and wrung out something inside him, until an unquenchable longing to know them made his eyes burn and his head ache and his heart feel sore.

Teresa stepped up behind him. "Giorgio, a boy has to have a family. You think you're old enough to care for yourself, but I know better. Listen to me. I know what it is to be an orphan. I have no parents either. It makes you lonely. It makes you empty. Maybe you don't want to go to America, but we want you with us. We love you, boy. We are the only family you have, and what is more important than a family, eh? Maybe you love us and maybe you don't, but at least you need somebody to cook for you and mend your clothes."

He bowed his head in shame. She took it to her bosom and stroked his hair. "I know," she crooned. "I know how you feel."

How kind she was, he thought, and how merciless in her kindness. She was wrong; she didn't know how he felt. She thought he was weak and a child, but he would get along fine without a family. Others had, and he was cleverer than most others. There was no use going on like this. He must get out now and stay out, or she and Sebastiano would persuade him or even drag him along.

"I need time to think," he said, "time to be alone."

"What's there to think about? I told you what you will do."

He gently took her arms from about his head. "I'm sorry, Teresa, but no one can tell me what I will do." He pushed past her without looking up and went out the door before she could stop him. He took the worn marble staircase two steps at a time. Teresa appeared on the landing above to curse him and tell him never to come back. He cursed her back out of love. Then he rushed into the street.

He wandered about for hours. There was nowhere to go. It was Sunday and no one would be at the quarry. He stopped at a stall and bought a persimmon, a Chinese apple, as everyone called it. It was barely ripe and the tartness made him pucker his lips, but he liked spitting out the seeds and watching them go dancing across the mossy cobble of the street. Blackbirds alit around him, quickly nibbled up his leavings and flew off again before anyone took serious notice of them. Birds of any sort were prized delicacies, and they seemed to realize it.

He bought a fresh pack of cigarettes at a stall outside St. Anthony's, a little medieval church that sat just outside the plaza at the center of town. Nearby was a grotto that he had helped to build the previous summer. It was a tough job; the priest who commissioned it was a tough old crow, and the masons had twice torn down their work and redone it to please him. At the center of the grotto stood a life-sized statue of Our Lady of Good Hope, cast in concrete and left unpainted. Giorgio sat in her shadow on an old iron bench, crossed himself twice—once to show respect and once to bring himself luck—then lit a cigarette.

"I hope the smoke don't bother you," he said to the Virgin. He half expected her to reply, so kind and lovely was her face. It was a face he imagined his mother might have had. In fact, in this quiet moment, in the shadow of the statue and surrounded by cypress trees, it seemed to him a face not unlike Teresa's. He swallowed hard and coughed as a bit of smoke dried his throat. He would make it a point from now on to avoid this grotto. He didn't need to be reminded of people he would never see again.

Suddenly he was aware that he was no longer alone.

A girl with a pink rosary dangling from her folded hands stood just a few yards away. She looked to be about his own age. At first she seemed to be praying, but he noticed that her eyes were glancing impiously away from the statue to him. What did she want? he wondered with annoyance.

He stared at her boldly and she immediately let her gaze fall. Her lips formed the Ave Maria and her fingers nervously pinched and rolled a rosary bead. Still he felt uncomfortable, though he couldn't say just why—something about her appearance.

Maybe it was her large black eyes or her pale skin. Or it could be the dress she was wearing—it had little blue violets printed all over it—or her shoes, which were made of beautiful soft white leather and were buttoned up over her ankles. How did she dare to wear them in the filthy streets? he wondered. Whatever it was, he found himself unable to take his eyes off of her.

So engrossed was he that he hardly noticed when the ash fell off the end of his cigarette like a twirl of cut crepe, but then the ember burned his lips, and when he took it between his fingers it burned them as well. He was sure the girl would laugh, but she only lifted her eyes to heaven and seemed to pray harder. He threw the stub down, stamped it out, then lit a fresh one. At that her eyes turned angrily from heaven to him.

"Who taught you to be such a pig?" she demamded.

Giorgio let his fresh cigarette dangle from his lips. The burning smoke made his eyes water. "What do you mean? What have I done?" Whoever she was, she obviously came from money, and people with money in his experience were always accusing other people, who maybe didn't come from money, of terrible things.

"You're making a mess at the feet of Our Lady," she

replied haughtily, indicating with the barest of nods where he had squashed the butt.

He felt his cheeks burning with embarrassment, but he took a long, sucking draw of smoke and blew it out toward the sky. "What goes on between Our Lady and me ain't none of your business."

She smiled sweetly. "You talk like a peasant. Is that what you are?"

He stood up and shook a fist in her direction. It was the only bluff he knew. "I speak the way I speak. Who asked to have a conversation with you? Who are you, anyway? Nobody, that's who."

She took two steps forward. "Now what's the matter?" he demanded.

"You're very nice-looking for a peasant, aren't you?"

At first he glanced at her suspiciously, then kicked the ground with his toe. "Sure, I'm a pretty good-looking fellow." It was his turn to smile, and he did it in such a way that his face seemed to grow ten years older in a single moment. It was an expression he had learned from grown men, one every boy learned as part of his birthright.

Now the girl seemed to be inching closer and closer in timid, shuffling little steps. "What's your name?" she asked him.

He considered a moment. Everyone talked to each other on the streets, rich or poor, friend or stranger. That was natural, but this asking of a person's name was another matter. There was no telling what a stranger could do with such information. You could find yourself kidnapped or murdered. Worse, you might be cursed by a witch; a name was a powerful tool of magic. He stalled. "Tell me yours first."

A cloud passed over her face. She seemed to be cautioned by the same considerations. "Perhaps I will tell you when I know you better," she said.

"Me too."

"Who taught you to smoke?"

"I taught myself," he said. "I don't need nobody to teach me."

This seemed to impress her. By now she was close enough to touch him and he felt a curious urge to back away. She reached out and tapped his breast pocket. "Can I try one?"

He laughed. "Get the hell out of here. You're a girl. Girls can't smoke."

"Why not?"

"It's indecent. Didn't your father ever tell you anything?"

"If it's indecent, he wouldn't dare bring it up."

"You know what I'm talking about."

"How would I? I'm a girl. Girls don't know anything."

He knew she was toying with him, but he didn't seem to care. He felt himself growing disoriented, intoxicated by an unusual scent she seemed to give off—the smell of violets, like those on her dress. It was obvious that her rosary wasn't made of the usual olive stones; now he observed that it was carved of clear pink stone, round beads for the decades and larger faceted ones for the paternosters. It was not strung on the usual wool cord but on a fine gold chain. There was no doubt about it. Whoever this was, she was rich.

"Maybe I'll sell you a cigarette," he said. "You got any money?"

"I was right before," she said. "You're a peasant." She made a little wrinkle in her nose to show she was offended and waved him away with her hand. As he didn't move, she turned to walk away from him. He watched her curiously. She was a strange one, but she interested him.

"Maybe I would take your rosary beads for a cigarette," he said. "They're very pretty—like you."

She stopped at the edge of the grotto and turned

sharply. "You'd better watch the way you speak to me or my father will have your throat cut."

This made him smile. "Your father must be a big shot if he can cut somebody's throat just for saying something nice to his daughter."

"I will get him to show you what kind of big shot he is if you want," she snapped.

Giorgio warded off her threat with a little shake of his head. "I'm sorry, signorina," he said with as much conviction as he could muster. "I didn't mean to insult you. Here." He drew a cigarette from his pocket and held it out to her. "You want one? No charge."

"I don't want anything from you," she said, but with a sideways look that told him she was interested.

Giorgio lit the cigarette with his own and sauntered over to her. "Here, try it."

"I thought it was indecent for girls to smoke."

He grinned. "What the hell do I know? I'm just a peasant."

She held the cigarette prissily between her thumb and forefinger, as if it was something dirty. When she raised it to her mouth, she shut her eyes tight, puckered her lips and blew on the end, which made the ember glow brightly and shot sparks of hot ash off it.

"No, like this," Giorgio said. He carelessly took the cigarette from her hand, inhaled the smoke deeply, held in it for a moment and then let it escape in a long satisfied sigh, very much a man of old habits.

"I know how to smoke," she said rather sharply, standing up and down on her toes with impatience as she waited for him to pass it back.

He wondered about her more and more. Where were her parents? Why was she allowed here alone? Even the poor of the district never let their daughters very far from sight, and a girl like this, even at her age, could cause a family much grief if they weren't careful to watch her. She was clever enough to cause trouble.

When she took the cigarette from him again, she smoked it exactly as he did, even down to the squint of her eyes. It made him laugh, but it also made him wary. He wasn't used to clever girls.

At first she coughed harshly and didn't seem to like the taste of the thing, but she smoked on like a steam engine, Giorgio thought, in quick regular puffs and with too much noise. Once he tried to take it away from her, but she slapped his hand down as if he were reaching for her person.

"Hey, come on. It belongs to me."

"You have plenty," she said. Her voice was weak and scratchy.

"Agh, you're getting sick, aren't you?" Her pale skin looked pasty to him, and her haughty eyes were rimmed with red. He hadn't thought about this possibility. At first he was annoyed, then sympathetic. After all, she wasn't getting sick on purpose, and he was getting to like her looks, which made sympathy much easier to come by.

The only thing he couldn't figure was why he liked her looks. She was only a girl, useless, but she seemed to capture his eyes. Why? First Teresa, his own brother's wife, and now a complete stranger. Something was happening to him, something in the pit of his belly that he could not name, a feeling that he was rising and falling in a boat with the swell of the waves, a frustrating, pleasureful giddiness in his loins. It seemed to have something to do with the presence of women.

Suddenly she reeled to one side and rested her arm on his shoulder for support. She was very sick, he could see that now, and almost at once she began to cough and retch. He stiffened and began to push her away. He didn't want her throwing up all over his pants since they were the only ones he owned now. But she pressed her cheek against his neck and the warmth of it caused a violent tingle to weaken his back and legs. He stiffly put his arms around her and she cuddled into his embrace.

"I think you've poisoned me," she managed to gasp. "I'm going to die. Blessed Mother, pray for my soul. Intercede with your Son for me."

This tempted his bravado. "What are you talking about? You ain't going to die. You just ain't used to the smoke, that's all."

"I don't think I want to get used to the smoke," she whimpered.

But in a while her retching calmed, and because he thought it was the right thing to do, he put his hands over hers in a paternal way. Hers were very cold and damp. His were very hot and damp. Suddenly she came viciously alive in his arms, twisting until she freed herself from his grasp. Then, before he realized her intention, she turned and slapped him.

"*Managia*, what did you do that for?" he said, stroking the sting in his cheek.

"Because you were trying to take advantage of me," she replied matter-of-factly.

"I don't know what you're talking about. What do you think, I want to steal something from you?"

She faced the statue of the Virgin and lowered her eyes. "Sure. You're a man, aren't you? You're all the same. You all want to steal something from the girls."

Now he was completely confused. "There ain't nothing you got that I want," he said to her.

"Leave me alone and let me pray." Again she was holding her rosary in her finger tips. "Hail Mary, full of grace—"

"What is it that men want to steal from you?" he persisted.

She gritted her teeth and closed her eyes in annoyance. "If you don't know, I'm not going to tell you."

"Why not? I want to know." He was beginning to suspect that she didn't know either.

"Then ask your mama, bambino."

He flushed with resentful embarrassment. Who did she think she was, calling him a child? She was trying to look so superior in her white leather shoes and her pretty dress, and praying with a rosary made of something strange and expensive—who was that going to impress, the Blessed Mother? She was probably so rich she didn't appreciate the beauty of the beads. If he owned such a rosary, he would feel unworthy even to pray with it.

"I don't know why I bothered with you," he mumbled.

She didn't bother to turn when she answered. "Why don't you go away? I'm tired of hearing your peasant's voice."

He almost kicked her, but he thought better of it. Instead he reached out and snatched away her rosary. Then he was off. She came dashing behind him, shouting for someone to stop him, but the race was soon over. He was up one alleyway and down another, around a corner and up a flight of street steps before he looked back and saw her a hundred meters behind, sitting on her haunches with her sobbing face buried in her hands.

A guilty smirk touched his lips. "It serves you right," he crowed, and as he went his way, he examined the prize he had captured. He realized now that the beads were made of rare, flawless deep pink rose quartz, and they sparkled like jewels in the bare sunlight. The crucifix at one end was carved of walnut wood. Despite the gold chain and the quality of the stone it was the workmanship that gave the thing its beauty. He imagined the girl's plump little hands holding the lovely stones, and he thought of her sitting in the street crying after her lost treasure, but he was glad he had taken it. It gave him something to hold near his heart that night as he slept under a donkey cart in a gutter on the edge of the town of Santa Barbara.

Chapter 2

Sebastiano returned to the apartment to find Teresa on the bed crying. Shards of broken clay bowls were strewn through a puddle of cooling soup on the floor. He crunched and sloshed his way through the mess and stood there with his mouth open and his arms spread apart like a supplicant.

"What the hell has been going on here? Where's Giorgio? What's happened?"

Teresa sobbed bitterly without looking at him. "What do you think happened?"

Sebastiano put his finger up as if about to give his wife a warning lecture, then seemed to think better of it and sat beside her on the sagging mattress. He put an arm around her. "Did my brother make this mess?"

Teresa shook her head and sniffled. A tear fell from her chin and tickled her husband's arm. "No, I did it."

"You? But why? I don't understand what's going on here."

"Of course you don't. You don't understand nothing."

From her closed fingers she took a crumpled square of linen and dabbed at her sore red nose. She wished he would leave her alone. She wished everybody would leave her alone.

Tomorrow they would go to Naples and board a ship

that would take them across the ocean to a strange land. She didn't want to go. She wanted her child to be born in the land of his fathers, the land of his blood.

To go to America was to admit that poverty had beaten you. It was a shame on your honor. She had heard that in the old days emigrants always lied when they left for the new world, insisting to their neighbors and family that they were only going to the north of Italy to find work.

Now no one cared about honor. They bragged of the fortunes they would make among the barbarians. Some did get rich; most didn't. A few got themselves killed trying— and not just the crooks. There were accidents and sickness and for some just more killing poverty.

Oh, Holy God, she silently prayed, bless and keep us, especially my baby when he comes, and don't let us die among strangers. I don't want to go to America. I don't want to go.

She thought she knew exactly how Giorgio felt and she had wanted to tell him so, but she could not betray her husband's authority. If there was to be a family—and there must always be a family—there had to be a man at its head, and his word must be law. So if Sebastiano wanted to go to America, it was her duty to obey, no matter how reluctantly.

Not that living here was easy. In the south, the *mezzogiorno*, life was hard in the best of times and other-wise nearly impossible. The *contadini*, the peasant farmers, were starving because there was no place to sell their crops, meager as the yields were. America was growing her own oranges and grapes these days, so much of the fruit market had dried up. Most of the peasants in the countryside lived in one-room stone shacks with dirt floors and no windows.

Like Naples, most cities were pits of filth and squalor where people had to live like rats, scavenging for garbage and cutting each other's throats for money. She had seen it herself. She'd been around. She'd even been to school when she was little and could read.

What she read in the newspapers made her want to weep. Everywhere in the south things were getting worse. Taxes were getting higher as the *latifondisti*, the major landowners like the Terasatti family, were gouging more and more money from the peasants while the government wasted money on wars in Africa.

But for all its troubles, the Campania was home, the land of her birth. The hills around Naples coiled up and embraced each other like snakes, and there was a great blue sky that everyone said was like no other, and the wine was sweet and the tomatoes plump and red and the olives black and bitter and wonderful in the mouth.

Teresa was proud of her country, even *Alta Italia*, the provinces the bastard northerners came from. Italy was the home of civilization, a place of churches and statues and ruins, a land over which the mighty Romans had built roads to march upon. Here the greatest artists in the world had left their paintings and incomparable operas were performed for an adoring public.

What had America to compare with all this? Dante left no great poem for America. There was no Garibaldi in the *Stati Uniti* to conquer the Bourbon kings. There were only, as Giorgio said, cowboy-Indians and the sons of the English—the very same English who came to Italy to escape from the miserable weather in their own homeland.

Why, then, did Sebastiano want to leave his home and his people? Maybe the farmers were starving, but he was no farmer. He was a craftsman and he always had enough work to survive.

No, it was the letters from his friends across the sea with all their bragging about money in the streets of Boston and New York and Philadelphia that made him want to travel halfway around the world and drag his family into misery. He didn't want to leave because his belly was empty, but because his pockets weren't full enough to suit him.

She felt his hand rub gently across the swell of her abdomen as if to reassure the child inside through her flesh, and she tingled with love and remorse. Maybe she was being too hard on him. Maybe he was doing it for the baby. Fathers never believed the world was good enough for their children, that there was enough food or clothing to keep their little ones strong. That had to be his reason. It was their unborn son who made Sebastiano willing to throw away the life he had made here.

She would have asked him about his motives long ago, but she knew he would laugh at her and make a meaningless answer intended only to quiet her. Teresa suspected that was because he wasn't sure himself why he wanted to go. Rather than admit that to her—Sebastiano was just like every other man—he could be counted upon to act like an idiot.

"Where is Giorgio?" he asked again now that her tears had dried.

"How should I know? He's your brother."

"I thought you were going to talk some sense into him."

"He went out."

"Then what's all this about?"

"He ran out and I got angry."

"You got angry. That's all?"

"That's all."

Sebastiano grinned incongruously. His teeth were yellow from too much smoking, but he had a simple, guileless smile that usually could disarm Teresa of her anger. This time it did not. She turned away and glanced at the letters hanging on the wall. If Sebastiano noticed, he said nothing. She felt him nuzzle her neck and his warm breath annoyed her. She shook him off, shrugging impatiently. She knew he wouldn't bed her while she was pregnant, but she didn't want to be touched at all. He looked crestfallen and she felt a little twinge of regret.

"Get me my knitting," she said.

The opportunity to do something for her cheered him, as she had calculated it would. He leaped across the room in two bounds and took a tiny white woolen shawl, a skein of yarn and the needles from a chair. He brought them back with such a bright look that she could almost see his tail wag and his ears prick up.

"You must go and find him," she said gently.

Sebastiano frowned. "Why? He knows where he lives."

"I know that boy. He don't plan to come back."

"If he don't come back, I'll break his neck for him."

She began to knit, counting stitches with a tiny part of her attention. Knitting was hypnotic, rhythmic, and it always calmed her. "Listen to yourself. Always you're going to break somebody's neck. Next time you go to confession, you tell the priest all these terrible threats you make."

"It's not a sin to make threats. Besides, I can do what I want and say what I want. This is my house."

"Maybe you can," she conceded, "but still, you should confess it just to make sure. When was the last time you went to confession?" He blushed and she knew she had him where she wanted him. "Father di Martino is always asking me where you are."

Naturally, Father di Martino knew very well that Sebastiano had not been to confession in years. Maybe he had some terrible sin he was afraid to tell, but more likely, she thought, he was just too embarrassed to go back after being away so long.

"You should go tonight so we can leave in the morning with God's graces," she added. "I will come along if you like."

"I thought we were talking about finding Giorgio," he replied petulantly.

"I thought you only wanted to break his neck."

"That was a figure of speech," he mumbled, "a way of talking. Don't worry about it. I'll find him."

"Good. And when you come back we'll go to the church and see Father di Martino." She was smiling now so that he would know she was teasing, but he did not smile back.

"Go by yourself, and tell that priest to mind his own business," he grumbled. "I won't be long."

Sebastiano stomped out the door and down the steps. Teresa shook her head after him, then put down her knitting. There was a mess to be cleaned up.

Sebastiano spent two hours looking for Giorgio all through the alleys, in the piazza and along the *corso* that ran like a collapsing vein through the heart of the village. He asked about him everywhere.

The fruit sellers, who knew Giorgio well because they'd all lost their share of produce to his deft hands and quick feet, claimed not to have seen him since the previous day. The crones who sat cackling on old chairs in the street before every doorway brightened with curiosity when they learned he was missing. The street urchins, the *scugnizzi*, scattered like starlings when Sebastiano approached them. With every step he cursed under his breath, as if the sheer power of his temper could draw his brother back. Finally the air grew cool and darkness fell.

Now what would they do? He didn't want to leave the

boy behind, but he saw no choice. The landlord, Giuliatti, would expect them to be gone in the morning. It was too late to change their plans now. Sebastiano had resisted every plea to renew the lease, so other tenants had been found. If he and Teresa didn't leave for Naples in the morning, they would sleep in the streets of Santa Barbara tomorrow night.

What could he tell Teresa if he returned home without Giorgio? She was excitable enough already. The old women said it was the pregnancy that made her that way, but whatever the reason, he was tired of living his life at the top of his voice. He enjoyed a good row and a few tears as much as anyone, but enough was enough.

The streets were barely visible now. Darkness had fallen and the only light came from an occasional candle in an open window. Where the hell could the boy be? He wouldn't be fool enough to leave the village and sleep in the countryside overnight; at least Sebastiano hoped he wouldn't. There were plenty of cutthroats looking for unwary travelers, and they wouldn't know a kid from a king on a night like this.

Visions of Giorgio's neck opened in a bloody smile made Sebastiano's stomach twist. He didn't like to admit how fond of his brother he was because he felt more like a father to him than a sibling, and it was improper for a father to show too great an affection for his children; it might spoil them. Nevertheless, alone in the streets of Santa Barbara with only the sawing of the cicadas and the occasional braying of a jackass to break the silence, Sebastiano began to realize just how much he would miss the little son of a bitch if he had to leave without him.

Giorgio touched his heart from the very day Sebastiano came to take him out of the orphanage, he was so small and weak. The nuns were far from cruel, but they were even poorer than most peasants, and they were forced to feed the children with the little bit of money they made from donations—not much in times like these.

How big Giorgio's eyes were that day, how full of fear and excitement. Before then Sebastiano had seen him only a few times since he was a baby. After their parents were killed, there was nothing else to do with the boy but to put him in the nuns' care.

If he didn't go to visit his brother very often, who could blame him? It was shameful for a man, even a very young man, not to have the means to support his relatives, and he didn't need to be reminded all the time by seeing the little one too often. Sebastiano was only sixteen at the time and didn't even know how he would fend for himself. Until then his only responsibility had been carrying messages to shady characters for his father.

After three months of begging and gladhanding and piece working and just lying about with nothing to do, he finally found himself a job as apprentice to a carpenter. It took him nearly a full year, but when the day finally came that Sebastiano was able to support another mouth, he went straight to the Orphanage School of the Immaculate Heart, and hat in hand, begged the sisters to release little Giorgio to his care.

He was refused. A child needed a woman to look after it, they insisted. Who would cook the meals and clean the clothes and make a home for the boy?

He could not answer them. It occurred to him for a moment that he might do all those things himself, but he realized he would be away for twelve, sometimes fourteen hours a day on the job, and even when he came home, he would be too tired to meet the responsibilities of both a mother and a father.

What he must do became immediately clear. He had to find a wife, but how to go about doing that he had no idea. He had no family to arrange a marriage for him, and it was nearly impossible to meet decent young women without a formal introduction. He supposed he could find a woman of some sort. In Naples or Caserta he could buy a wife, but he didn't want to be stuck with that kind of woman for the rest of his life.

He began to ask around about eligible young women in the village. To his surprise he had more replies than he could ever have hoped for. He learned through a tedious parade of unmarried elder sisters and cousins that nearly everyone was willing to help him, not so much to solve his problem as to solve their own—the embarrassment and expense of having a spinster in the house.

Night after night he returned to his cold little rented room above the bakery on the Via Appuliana and rested his head in his callused hands to ease away the pain. All these harpies with their chattering or shy stuttering or false modesty gave him a headache. If these were all that could be found, then maybe Giorgio would have to remain an orphan all his life.

In a way it was Giorgio himself who provided the answer to Sebastiano's problem. There lived at the orphanage a fifteen-year-old girl, by rumor the illegitimate daughter of a sea captain and an opera singer from Milan.

She had become so much a part of life there that she was about to make her novitiate vows and join the Order of Saint Francis. She was a shy girl with a disarming smile and slender hands. Her slow way of sauntering away made Sebastiano turn red with embarrassment every time she went past; he was sure it must be a sin to have the feelings she excited in him, especially in front of the nuns.

She was especially fond of Giorgio and treated him with such tenderness that he might have been her own child, so when Sebastiano came to visit, she was often nearby. At first they rarely spoke, but gradually they found themselves catching each other's gaze—and fast averted their eyes, of course. It took months for them to become easier together, but finally, with the help of the love they shared for the little boy, they began to court, at first without even realizing it.

They were never alone, of course. There was always one of the good sisters nearby to keep an eye on them, but Sebastiano didn't mind. It was easier to let the nuns be his conscience than to depend on the one God had given him, and it was the only sure way to keep him from doing anything stupid. He didn't trust his own impulses at all.

If at first Sebastiano and Teresa were unsure of their feelings, the nuns never had any doubts; they subtly encouraged the relationship. They wanted Giorgio to have a family of his own. It was only right for the child. Besides, in the way of kindly older women, they wanted for Teresa what they could not have for themselves. A life of prayer and piety had its satisfactions, but it always saddened them when a youngster came to them having no knowledge of the world. So whenever Sebastiano rang the small bell at the entry, Teresa was sent to guide him inside.

Even after he came to understand his feelings, Sebastiano had to admit he had been rather stupid about Teresa for a long time, since it still didn't occur to him that he might ask for her hand. She had no dowry and she had already made her first vows. It was only when she began to express her sadness that she would lose Giorgio to another woman some day soon that he decided to make a proposal. Giving Giorgio a good mother was more important than a dowry, and novitiate vows were almost meant to be broken.

Her answer came slowly and hesitantly. He started to fear she was trying not to laugh at him for being such a fool. What ever made him think she would accept in the first place? What had he to offer such a pious and beautiful

young woman? Holy God, if she turned him down, how
would he ever come back to see his little brother?

However, she accepted him. She mumbled her answer as if giving her confession in the dark, appropriately,
it seemed to him, because they were standing in the *matins*
garden outside the chapel door. Permission had to be given
by the mother superior, but after a stern look and a lecture
about the responsibilities of family life she gave them her
blessing.

The engagement became official on the Feast of Scarves
in the spring, when the young maidens of the orphanage
traditionally formed a line in the chapel and one by one
presented their suitors each with a white scarf. The betrothal was binding.

Because neither had a family, Sebastiano and Teresa
did not follow the marriage customs of their village. There
was no kidnapping or ransoming of the bride, no pair of
shoes set before her door, no doll made to represent the
firstborn child.

Instead Teresa dressed in the simple bridal gown a
nun wears when making her final vows and becomes wife
to the church. A priest was called from the church of Santo
Tommaso just down the street, and only the sisters and
Giorgio were in attendance.

After that the usual things happened. They moved
into an apartment he had rented. The marriage night was a
disaster, as it so often was. Neither quite knew what they
were supposed to be doing, and both ended up confused
and frustrated, she in tears, he in grumbling protests. Time
cured them of their problems in the bedroom, though he
had to admit—if only to himself—that only Teresa's patience allowed them to succeed.

Giorgio was another matter. He was a charming child
with bright-eyed enthusiasm and curiosity about everything,
but Sebastiano soon learned that being a father was not at

all as pleasant or as natural as he had expected. He had to be stern when he wanted to be gentle. He had to be gentle when he wanted to be stern. He had to punish when he wanted to say to hell with it and go out to the cafe for a few glasses of wine with the boys from work. Teresa kept him in line, and he tried his best to keep Giorgio in line, and through the sheer power of habit, they all slowly assumed their proper roles.

Authority now came more easily to Sebastiano because he had come to like it. He liked being treated with deference and respect. He liked being obeyed. When he was denied those pleasures, he found himself losing his temper almost uncontrollably.

A few times he beat his little brother black and blue, though he was vaguely aware that his authority didn't necessarily permit such behavior, especially after Teresa began standing up for the kid. But there were also moments like this one, when he thought of Giorgio as he was at the orphanage—an innocent, a small child—and his heart ached with love.

He walked the streets awhile longer, smoking and muttering and straining his eyes to see in the dark. Every now and then he would call out his brother's name, but he had come to the realization that there would be no answer. Even if he searched for a month, he would not find him.

It was no secret. Giorgio had turned hard-headed and intractable lately. Once he made his mind up, nobody, maybe not even God Himself, could change it. Tomorrow they would have to leave for Naples without him. For Sebastiano and Teresa Giorgio was as good as dead.

They set out at dawn. Already the day was sultry with the hot breath of the sirocco blowing up from Africa, and the sky seemed dulled with a white glaze. They hired an old man with a donkey cart to take them to Caserta, the old capital of Naples, which lay to the west. Travel was slow along the winding, hilly road, especially on the way down the side of the plateau from Santa Barbara, and a swarm of pestering flies seemed intent on following them the entire way.

At least they were traveling light. There had been little to pack—just a few changes of clothing, some carpenter's tools, a chair Sebastiano had made from scrapwood and three bottles of water. The bed in the apartment belonged to the landlord.

Sebastiano left a little money with the landlord for Giorgio, though he was sure his brother would never come back for it. Teresa had not spoken a word since his return the night before. If the boy was gone there was nothing to be done, but she was not taking it well.

Her belly seemed to drag down upon her more than usual in the heat and humidity, and she indulged in sullen shuffling of feet all the way down the steps and into the cart. Even the driver, who was full of cheer and good-mornings—as who wouldn't be, charging a thousand lire—couldn't bring a reponse from her. Sometimes these women were enough to make a man run away forever.

By ten o'clock their clothing was soaked through with sweat and Sebastiano had fouled his mouth with half a dozen cigarettes smoked one after the other. He took a long sip from a water bottle, then offered some to his wife. She shook her head.

"Teresa, you got to drink something. Think of the baby."

She set her jaw at his presumption. He knew what she must be thinking; she said it often enough. What did he know about having a baby?

"If you don't drink, then I'll hold your mouth open and make you, and the driver will help me."

The driver made an agitated gesture with an upraised

hand. "Not me," he protested. "I don't do nothing but drive. If I start interfering with my customers I don't get paid."

"Sebastiano, if you lay a hand on me, I'll jump out of this cart and walk back to the village."

Though he was mortified that she should challenge him this way in front of a stranger, he didn't have the heart to argue. It was too hot, and he understood her sorrow. It was Giorgio, after all, who first drew them together. Where he used to be there would now be a place of emptiness.

Sebastiano knew full well how their life ahead frightened her. She never protested at their going, but Sebastiano was no fool, or at least, he thought, not a blind one. Whenever the subject of leaving for America came up, she had a way of hunching her shoulders and falling silent that seemed to close a door between them.

It would take time, he knew, but she would come around. Time was a great mother to all. She held you under her apron and stroked you moment by moment, day by day, until you could forget any pain. Giorgio was gone and so was their old home, but in time Teresa would make a new nest, raise her chicks and lose her love of this Italy. Sebastiano loved Italy himself, but she couldn't give a man half a chance. A man's hopes were soon buried in government corruption and criminal organizations and stinking poverty everywhere one looked.

Teresa didn't know he had to pay a kickback to the *padron'* for every hour of pay he made, but it was like that all over Italy. There was no getting away from it. He'd heard stories from fellows back from the north, and things were no different there except that the northerners looked down their noses at the poor laborers from the south, treated them like pigs and paid them worse.

No, this country was no longer any place to rear a

family. There was hope once, when Garibaldi marched
into Naples and freed it from the rule of the Bourbons
decades before, but that hope proved as brief as any
dream. Naturally men still talked of hope, still spoke of
the unification of the country with pride and determination,
but all was lost in petty feuds and corruption. As far as
Sebastiano was concerned, Italy was a rotting corpse.
There was no point in talking about hope for a cure.

The ride to Caserta, though the city was only eleven
miles distant, took most of the day. The driver was in no
hurry, and three times he insisted they stop by the side of
the road to eat. There was cheese and bread and a little
sausage, and of course the wine.

It was pretty clear that it was the wine that made him
want to stop so often. He would drink until his voice
began to slur and then cackle mirthfully that they should
be off to their destination. In the heat the drunkenness
wouldn't last long and he would begin to grow sullen.
Soon they would have to stop for another meal. Sebastiano
finally had to take the reins himself to get them to the train
station before dark.

Caserta held many relics of its onetime reign as the
capital city of the Kingdom of Naples. There was a great
garden there and a palace that was said to rival any in
Europe. The road into town was a long wide boulevard
lined on both sides with plane trees. The cross streets were
straight and evenly spaced, built with formal logic usually
reserved for architecture and gardens. The houses and
public buildings were tidy and well kept, and even the
train station, filled with throngs traveling from the countryside to Naples, was swept and polished.

By now Teresa's depression had begun to wear off
and even her weariness from the long trip on the cart lost
its edge. There were so many people, so much noise, so
much hustling and pushing and laughing and crying that

she felt at once disoriented and infected with excitement. She had made this trip before as a little girl, but her memories were vague and uncertain and didn't prepare her for the pandemonium in which she found herself lost.

Sebastiano tugged her along by the arm. With her other hand she found herself automatically protecting her child by stroking her stomach and pushing away strangers who rubbed up against her. The smell of tobacco and sweat and coal fire stuck to everything, and she imagined she could feel it seeping into her clothes and mixing with her own scent. She didn't like the feeling.

All around she heard people sobbing and crying good-byes, while above it the piercing arias of the platform conductors seemed to rush everyone a little more. Sebastiano looked grim and single-minded as he led her inch by inch to the ticket line. He carried their luggage in one hand. The chair had to be abandoned to the donkey driver; it was immediately apparent that they wouldn't be able to carry anything so unwieldy through a crowd like this.

The tickets used up another thousand lire, and she began to wonder how much money he had stashed in the little bag tied so tightly and kept inside his shirt. She was sure that if they kept spending money at this rate, they would be destitute by the time they arrived in America, but her husband seemed unconcerned, and as Teresa had no idea how much he had brought along, she would have to trust him.

It was a fight to get back across the platform and still another to jam themselves into one of the passenger cars that clattered and swayed into the station. A monstrous steam locomotive hissed and billowed a fog over everything. Teresa began to feel faint.

On all sides of her people were pressing and lurching with the movement of the train. Sebastiano was taller than most, and it seemed to her that he was lucky to be up so high where he could get some air, but some idiots were smoking cigars and she could see even from where she was that the atmosphere above was thick and white with smoke. Sebastiano began to cough, and with every spasm he shoved against her and crushed her to a grossly fat man standing behind her who smelled of goat cheese. She said a little prayer for strength and promised the Blessed Virgin that if she survived this part of the trip, she would spend one hour a day for the rest of her life saying a special prayer in honor of the Immaculate Heart.

She did survive, largely because the trip took less than an hour. When they pulled into the station it was dark. The doors opened and the crowd poured out like sand from the mouth of a bottle.

The city smelled like a sewer. The winds could always be counted on to lift such odors away from Santa Barbara, but here the streets were crowded and buzzing even after dark, humanity hustled and jostled like a herd of cows trapped in a ring of burning grass, and the stink of them settled and stuck to everything. The smell of garbage— fish and lemons and onions and garlic rotting in the shore- line humidity—mixed with smell of human offal to pro- duce a reek that burned the eyes.

They made their way on foot to the wharves. It was a long walk, always downhill through unkempt winding streets, and it seemed to Teresa that every corner was supplied with a prostitute who made some joke about her belly. She cursed them roundly, of course, but she was tiring quickly. It must have been obvious to the watchers, because soon they let up on her and taunted Sebastiano for being too cheap to hire a cab to carry his woman.

He at once turned to Teresa. "Are you too tired to walk?"

"No," she said, barely able to take in a breath of air, "I'm all right. I can walk."

"Okay, but if you get too tired, you tell me, you hear?"

"Yes, I'll tell you."

In fact, they weren't the only ones walking from the train. There were plenty of others, many of them large families who marched through the streets like a brigade. For a long way there was tacit agreement among the men that for everyone to walk was a matter of strength and pride. Finally, however, one fellow gave in to his wife and took a donkey cart for her and their three children, and it soon became necessary for all the others to do likewise. Sebastiano hired transportation for Teresa, and no mere donkey cart but a real cab drawn by a grey mare with paper decorations on her ears.

It was growing late. When they arrived at the docks, they discovered that there were no ships scheduled to leave until morning. The emigration agent had given them bad information, but at least their reservations were booked. There was nothing to do but to buy their passage and wait out the rest of the night at the emigrants' shelter, a complex of dilapidated old buildings across the coast highway.

At dawn they would board the *Stella Romana*, not one of the old sail-steamers but a new ship propelled by steam alone. Sebastiano had heard all about it from a crowd of men milling around its anchorage. He was very proud as he told his wife how they would sail to the United States in luxury.

She nodded miserably, thinking for the thousandth time about Giorgio. He was as homeless as they were; more so because he had no one to comfort him. A tear touched her eye. Sebastiano held her close and sang a tender song of love and partings in her ear. She kissed him gently on the cheek. They smiled uncertainly at each other. Please, God, she thought, send us home, or at least send us our Giorgio.

*   *   *

The only difference between the weather this day and yesterday was in the thickness of the air as it blew off the bay. Teresa licked her lips, dry as salt, and moved her stiff aching legs off the flea-infested bed. All over her tiny red bumps itched and burned where she was bitten. Scratching only seemed to make things worse. "*Managia*," she mumbled under her breath.

Sebastiano rose off the floor, rubbed his eyes and yawned ferociously. He reached into the linen sack and took out a piece of stale bread, half of which he offered to Teresa. She spurned it.

"Come on, what are you going to do, starve yourself? *Mangia*." He pushed a piece of crust into her hand, closed her fingers around it, then hitched his pants up around his stomach and adjusted his suspenders.

She nibbled at the bread to satisfy him, but she had no desire to eat. The farther they got from home, the more certain she was that they never should have left, and her worry over her little brother turned into a noose that strangled her stomach into a tight knot.

What was he doing? How would he live? She was beginning to think that Sebastiano, her carpenter husband, must have turned his own heart into wood, for he had done nothing but sing and try to amuse himself since they left Santa Barbara. Not once had he mentioned his own brother's name; not once had he even looked over his shoulder toward his lifelong home.

Now he was belching like a pig and clearing his throat, wearing a fat satisfied look on his face. How pleasant it would be to slap such a face. On the other hand he was giving her a kindly look, the look of a friend concerned for one's health. Madonna, who knew what to make of such a man?

Chapter 3

Naples receded slowly, high and jeweled in the Mediterranean sun. It was the last lovely vision of home Teresa ever would see. She felt empty, as if her insides were spilling out across the white churn of the ship's wake. The feeling reminded her of the story of the ancient Greek who had touched the sacred oak and was forced to run round it with his bowels torn out and nailed to the trunk.

White squawking gulls soared and glided in zigzags above the great smokestacks. The sound was annoying. She took a crust of bread from the food pouch, broke it into crumbs and threw them into the air. The birds swooped and snatched and circled, waiting for more. They saddened her when she reflected that they were as homeless as she.

Sebastiano stood next to her, staring silently and intently back toward the mainland. Though she couldn't be sure, she thought she saw the glisten of a tear in his eye.

The ship's whistle blew and Teresa started. It was a brutish noise, like nothing she'd ever heard. Sebastiano put his arm around her. She was touched by the show of affection. It was unlike him and it didn't last long. After a moment he took his arm away and stuffed his hand into the pocket of his trousers. She wished the whistle would blow again.

That the luxury trip would not be so luxurious was apparent as soon as they boarded. In steerage men and women slept in separate quarters whether they were married or not. The cabins were small, dark, cramped and crammed with a dozen berths each, and they were well below the water line, so there were no portholes and little ventilation. The constant grating pulse of the engines made the metal walls vibrate, but that was a minor discomfort. In Teresa's room a bull rat had already staked out a corner for himself.

The smells were unbearable. Many of the emigrants were farmers who reeked of manure and sweat. A few peasants tried to bring livestock on board and had to be physically restrained when their animals were taken and given over to the port authority.

Teresa felt a twitch in her abdomen; the baby was kicking. She hummed a little lullaby under her breath. There were many dangers for an unborn child on a trip like this. Who knew what diseases had been carried on board? Malaria, scarlet fever, even plague might develop.

There were other dangers, both natural and supernatural. The water frightened her. What if the boat should sink? She knew nothing about swimming and she might be eaten by fish. The boat could catch fire. There was obviously a flame kept alive somewhere on board; billows of black smoke poured out of the huge howling chimneys.

And of course there were people of every description on board, so she had to be very careful whom she looked at. She had already seen a man with a harelip. She would have to make a special effort not to stare too hard at him lest her baby acquire the same trait. Such things had been known to happen. Worst of all was one she did not like to admit even to herself. A change of climate sometimes caused miscarriages.

Still, Teresa must not allow her fears to overwhelm

her or she would give birth to a fearful child. It was a very difficult job, being pregnant, but if she had to leave her home, her country, her people, then her baby was the only thing left that mattered.

The aft deck was getting more and more crowded as people fled from the conditions below. There were a few chairs about, but not nearly enough to go around, so Sebastiano decided to find one for her before they were all taken.

"I'll be right back," he said. "Don't go away."

"Where am I going to go? I don't know how to swim."

No sooner had he walked away from her and disappeared into what had now become a mob than she felt a gentle tap on her shoulder. She turned abruptly. Standing before her was a short, slightly built man with slick black hair, a pencil-thin mustache and a wide grin crowded with large pearly teeth. He wore a black vest and leather boots that appeared to be too expensive for a steerage passenger. Under his arm he held a collapsed wooden folding chair.

"The signora would like to rest?" he said.

"My husband is finding a chair for me," she replied tersely.

"All the chairs are gone. Please. You would do me a great favor to accept."

"What favor? What are you talking about?"

"To serve a beautiful woman is one of the few pleasures life can afford a lonely man."

Was he crazy? Couldn't he see she was pregnant? "Go away. Leave me alone."

"It's only a chair, signora." He offered the object, unfolded it and touched her arm to urge her into it.

She grew hot with embarrassment in her cheeks and arms. "All right, I will take your chair. Now go away."

But she knew from his pleased look that she was not rid of him yet.

"I am Don Carlo Federigo. I am pleased to make your acquaintance."

He held out his hand to take hers and she stared at it as if he had produced something dead at the end of his arm. Nonetheless, she was tempted to take it. After all, he talked like a man of quality, and who knew what was considered polite among people like that?

Before she could make up her mind, he withdrew his hand. "I see I have offended you."

Now what had she done? He was obviously insulted, and he had only showed her a little kindness. "No, no, signor, there's no offence, but I am a married woman—"

"And soon to be a mother, I see."

She nodded cautiously. "Soon enough."

Don Carlo sighed. "I have always wanted a son of my own. Your husband is a very fortunate man."

"You don't have any children?"

He shrugged. "None that I know of."

She knew she was blushing outrageously, and as always when she was flustered, she defended herself. "You should watch your language around me. I'm not a street woman, you know."

Again he looked apologetic. "Of course. You obviously have the most delicate of sensibilites."

What did that mean? she wondered with a frown.

"I would like very much to know you better, signora. Perhaps we can share a bottle of wine some evening on the way over."

His tone was solicitous, but she couldn't figure out what he wanted from her. Maybe he was just one of those crazy idiots who was attracted to pregnant women. "Would you like me to ask my husband for permission?" she said with an edge to her voice.

"Do you think he would be willing to give you up for an evening?" His smile turned to an ironic smirk.

Sebastiano provided the answer. He appeared from the crowd and lifted the fellow by the back of his vest. "I will give you up to the end of my goddamned foot," Sebastiano bellowed, administering a hard kick as if to score a goal with a soccer ball.

Don Carlo Federigo tripped forward, tumbled over and violently careened into a circle of four men who by their looks were brothers. Delighted to be part of the action, they cursed and prodded him with their boots while he doubled up and covered his head with his arms for protection. They didn't keep him long, for he wasn't much sport. After a moment they let him up to hobble away.

The scene was just beginning. Sebastiano had Teresa by the hair. "You shame me!" he shouted. The men in the crowd urged him on, telling him to beat her or to rid himself of her. "All the time since we leave home you hardly speak a word to me—me, your own husband—yet you take up with the first stranger who comes along!"

She fought him hard, slapping and scratching at his cheeks, all the while protesting her innocence, but he refused to listen, and so she turned sarcastic and insolent. "I was enjoying the trip, just like you said. A *scatapina*, an adventure, just like you wanted. Isn't that why you left your own brother to be a scavenger in the streets and dragged your wife and unborn son across the world? For a little diversion, right?" All the women around screeched in her favor.

He released her hair and shook her by the shoulders while he made his plea to the crowd. "Listen to this, listen! Is this what a man works all his life for?" He shook her harder. "You don't talk to no son of a bitch when you are married to me."

"You want to kill the baby? Go ahead, shake me

some more." She tried to pull his hands off her. "Yes,
that's it, more and more. Murder your son."

She hollered the same thing again and again until it
sank in and he released her. The crowd, which had been
having a glorious time, opened a path for her. She headed
straight for the stairs that led belowdecks. Sebastiano was
right on her heels, and though he wasn't laying a hand on
her, she screamed bloody murder; he bellowed like the
ship's whistle. She finally escaped him by dashing past the
steward who stood at the entrance to the women's quarters.

The steward was a stocky, powerful looking Britisher
with a pitted, scrambled face, deformed by devasting burns.
He wore a bleached white linen uniform that had been
pressed free of every wrinkle. "Sorry, guv'nor, can't let
you in there," he said in English.

Sebastiano stared at him stupidly, then tried to push
his way past. Teresa, who was standing just inside the
zone of safety, backed away a couple of steps. The steward was as unbudgeable as a stone slab. "I said you can't
go in, *capisch*?" He shook his head firmly to make his
point and manhandled Sebastiano backward.

Sebastiano tried to explain that it was his wife, but
the man couldn't understand him, and he doubted it would
make a difference anyway. Finally he gave up on the
steward and spoke directly to Teresa. "Come out here at
once. I'm not finished with you."

"Hah, why should I?" she cried out haughtily, but
she knew her voice trembled too much to fool him.

Sebastiano cursed and pleaded with her until the steward patted him on the chest and said, "Why don't you just
move along now?" He didn't have to speak in Italian to
make his point. The tone of his voice was that of a
policeman prodding a vagrant with a night stick.

"All right," Sebastiano said harshly to Teresa, "if
this is what you want, this is what you will get. I don't

need you or the child. In my eyes you are nothing. I spurn you. If I ever see you again, I will turn my face and I will not know you."

He turned away angrily, hunched his shoulders and strode off. Teresa dashed after him. She grabbed hold of his arm and cursed at him for a fool and an idiot, but he ignored her, and when he reached the metal steps, he shook her off without a word and left her staring at his back.

What had he said? What had he done? Oh, what a *cafone* he was. He pounded his head with the side of his fist. There were men on both sides of him slapping his back in admiration and offering congratulations. That was the way to handle a woman, they assured him on the assumption that he had beaten her.

He smiled with an effort, accepted their good wishes and wondered if he had lost his wife forever. He could not apologize. He had left himself no way to do that without losing face, not only with Teresa but with everyone on the boat. On the other hand, he knew his wife too well to expect her to come to him.

Why had he been so jealous, so outraged? Teresa was a good woman and a loyal wife. Never had she so much as looked at another man. But the ship was full of strangers, and in America it would be even worse. Who knew what might happen? There were more men in the world than the ugly fools who lived in Santa Barbara, and if he lost Teresa, what would he have left?

Why hadn't she come to him? Why had she stood behind the Englishman? Never before had she done such a thing. She knew he wouldn't hurt her. He would be incapable of such a terrible crime. Though he had threatened many times, he had never once struck her. But he had been so angry, so frightened; maybe she was right. Who knew? He hadn't stopped to think. She made a fool of him in front of the barbarian and there was nothing to do but turn away from her.

Someone shoved a bottle of Chianti into his hand and he took a long swig. He wanted so much to make her happy and he had ruined everything. What a fine carpenter he was, to build a house and then ruin the foundations. Life was a curse, he thought as he drank again. Love was a curse. It would be better to be a priest or maybe a hermit and live all alone on a mountaintop.

He drank again and again until the bottle was empty. Another appeared. They were laughing, celebrating a tragedy, he thought miserably. What kind of people were these? The deck seemed to heave violently under his feet. He was drunk and he wanted to get drunker.

"Teresa!" he called, and the only answer was the laughter of the crowd, so he called again. "My wife!" He hardly recognized his own voice. It sounded muffled and scratchy, like a saw biting into wet wood. Dear Lord Jesus, he thought, let her forgive me. Please let her forgive me.

Teresa lay on her cot in the dark with her face buried in the crook of her arm. To hell with him, she thought. He could not turn her away; she had left him first. If he did not want the baby, then so be it. Such a man was not worth having for a husband.

She felt heavy, weak, like a sponge that had soaked up too much water. Of course she knew what made him behave the way he did. She had spoken to a stranger in public. To make matters worse, she had publically defied her husband. Such things were not done. They were terrible sins against *la via vecchia*, the old ways of the family. Arguments were be kept private. Appearances must be kept up, for without appearances there was no dignity.

But she had no home. He had dragged her away from it, and nothing gave him the right to do that and then turn his back on her and his own child. Well, there was nothing to do about it. Somehow she would have to salve his pride and swallow her own. No matter what, he was her husband, the head of the family. It was her duty to forgive and mend. She could not raise a child without him. She had to get him back. Only, what was she supposed to do? An apology would change nothing. He was too proud.

Over the next two days they did not speak to each other, though they brushed shoulders on deck often enough. Sebastiano replaced his heartlessly stern expression with a wounded look, and Teresa wondered if an apology might not be enough after all, but when she approached him, he turned and walked away.

She shook her head and found a seat upon which to rest. She was getting tired of the game. The scorching sun was unforgiving and seemed to beat her to weariness. She was hungry all the time.

Though the ship's kitchen offered two meals a day, the only course was watery soup made of poultry stock and rice, and it smelled rancid. She had seen dozens of other passengers take sick, and she was uncertain whether their illness was seasickness or food poisoning, so she allowed herself only a little of the bread from home.

By the fourth day she had begun to feel torpid with hunger. Everywhere she turned there were people—stinking, loud, violent, sick, puffing on huge cigars or vomiting in their berths, trapped together like livestock in a railroad car. Why was she here? Why had Sebastiano done this to her? And now that she needed him most, why wouldn't he let her make peace?

Don Carlo Federigo had been watching the rift between them grow. He seemed always to be standing in a

corner nearby or at the rail just across the deck, like a
hungry wolf watching a rabbit. Teresa wanted to slap him,
to kill him, to spit on his grave, but she kept her distance.
She knew that Sebastiano would be watching from the
corner of his eye. He could not help himself. No matter
what he had said, she was still his wife.

On the morning of the fifth day three people died.
One was an old man who collapsed to the deck clutching
at his chest. The other two were young men who had
gotten into a fight over something or other. Knives appeared;
there were screams, then two cut bodies doubled over on
the deck. This seemed to make everyone sullen. To die
among strangers—what a fate.

Teresa was determined to have her husband back this
day, and he let her approach him, but he silenced her with
a hostile look when she tried to speak. This was no place
to settle matters, he seemed to be saying. His look only
made her angry and she walked away again.

Something was coming over her, something that got
inside her head and wanted to burst it open. She wanted to
moan as if sick, to tear her hair like a crazy woman. She
wanted a home in which to be safe, to be far from the sea
and to lie in the arms of a husband who cared for her.

She walked in circles around the deck. There were
many others doing the same. Some were mumbling
incoherently. Don Carlo caught up with her. "Your husband spurns you," he said with a hopeful smile.

Teresa turned her head away without answering.

"I would not spurn such a woman as you."

"Why don't you leave me alone," she spat. "It's you
who have caused all this."

"I paid for whatever I caused," he said bitterly. He
still limped from Sebastiano's kick. "Maybe I paid for you
too, eh?"

"Your sister's ass," she said, "that's what you paid for. I'm married and I'm pregnant. Leave me alone."

"I like married women. I like pregnant women." Again he grinned. "I want to be a family man, just like everybody else."

She slapped him. "May your soul rot in hell." She glanced furtively across the deck to Sebastiano, who was leaning against the railing and drawing smoke from a cigarette he had scrounged somewhere. Yes, he was watching, but coolly; he didn't move.

She was perplexed. Why hadn't he come over? Was he testing her or was it true that he really had turned his back on her forever?

Don Carlo was also keeping an eye on Sebastiano. "I've seen this happen many times," he said. "You would think a jealous husband would kill a man like me, eh? But they only do that when you sneak around behind their back. When you do it right in front of them, they blame the wife. You know why he kicked me down the other day? For show, that's all. It's you he blames. And since he already kicked me once, and he don't want nothing to do with you, who knows what will happen between you and me?"

She stopped and faced him with a hopeless look. "Why do you want me?"

He shrugged. "Because you got a big sign on you that says I can't have you. The things a man can't have are the only ones worth the trouble."

"I ain't the only pregnant woman on this ship."

"You're the only one who accepted my chair."

She covered her eyes with her hand. This was ridiculous. This little man was ridiculous. She wanted to laugh. What was going on? What kind of people were there in the world? This man was strange, sick. She pitied him, but he filled her with revulsion and strange amusement.

A giggle burst like a bubble from her lips. "Signor, whoever you are, if you don't leave me alone, I'm going to find a knife and stick it between your ribs."

His eyes narrowed; then he reached out and boldly patted her stomach with the flat of his hand. "Go get your knife. Let's see."

She pushed his hand away and spat in his face. Another woman nearby also spat on him. Teresa went down into the hellhole that was her cabin to escape him. Sebastiano watched it all.

Don Carlo stood leaning over the railing, watching the white foam hiss away from the hull of the ship in the moonlight. He was disgusted with the day's events. These southern peasants were no better than animals. The woman had actually spit on him, and after her damn fool of a jealous husband kicked him in front of all the others. Jealousy in an animal! Who would have thought it? It was laughable.

Well, he would have what he wanted. She was just like any other whore in Italy. A country slut was no different from a city one, a married one no different from an unmarried one, and a pregnant whore the same as barren. He would find her price and buy her. At least she had a comely face, and she looked cleaner than the others.

When he was through with her, he thought with satisfaction, he would offer to buy her soiled child, and out of shame she would sell it. That was what he was after, merchandise for the white slavers, some of whom bought their prostitutes young and raised them right. There was always good money to be made from the filthy, bawling little animals, and he needed money. There were gambling debts that had to be paid.

*   *   *

Sebastiano watched in the dark as the short, wiry man standing by the rail lit a cigarette and threw the match into the wind. He hadn't let Don Carlo out of his sight since that afternoon, when the man started to pester Teresa again. The humiliation had been unbearable, as the swarthy little jackal must have known it would be, but Sebastiano forced himself to hold his temper. He didn't want the crowd in on things this time. There was no point in waiting. He would do what he had to do. He stepped out of the shadows.

"Hey you," he said. "Over here."

Don Carlo turned in surprise, and when he saw who had called him, his eyes grew wide with fear. "What do you want?"

"What do you think I want? Ain't you the one who been bothering my woman?"

"No, I wasn't bothering nobody," he stammered, beginning to glance around for an escape route. "I was just trying to be friendly." Federigo took a quick step along the railing, a nervous start really, but the movement was enough to enflame Sebastiano's instincts, and they propelled him forward like a bear lumbering after small prey.

The rest took only a moment. Sebastiano grabbed the little man and lifted him high in the air.

"You're gonna leave my goddamn wife alone forever," he growled. "You hear me? Forever!"

"Of course, signor," Don Federigo whimpered. "Forever, I promise, but don't hurt me. Please, I beg of you." His eyes were closed tight and his fists were clenched under his trembling chin, like a child afraid to see what was coming next.

Sebastiano was beyond listening. The sudden release of his anger consumed the sounds that came into his ears, the sights that came into his eyes, the feelings that clawed at his gut. With a grunt he pitched the smaller man forward. There was only a short, pitiful shriek as Don Carlo sailed in a short arc over the rail and plummeted down to the ocean, calm and silver-black in the moonlight.

"Justice be done," Sebastiano said and crossed himself. He slept well that night.

On the morning the *Stella Romana* was due to dock in New York Harbor, Sebastiano decided he could stand the separation no longer. Bowing his head very low so Teresa couldn't fail to notice, he found her on the fantail deck and took her hand in his.

"Am I forgiven?" she asked him.

"Yes, of course. Am I?"

"How could I not forgive the father of my child?"

Sebastiano swallowed hard, also for her to notice. He wanted her to know how difficult this was for him. "Teresa, I had no business making such a public spectacle. I have made this voyage a terrible trial to you, I know." He waved his hand to stop an objection she did not make. "I apologize for my horrible, insulting, unmanly and very mortifying behavior."

Teresa reached up and stroked his face. He had not shaved since the day they left home and his whiskers scratched her hand. How sad he looked. The trip had not been easy on him either. His eyes looked haggard, and underneath them the skin hung loose and wrinkled like wet parchment. He was pale and cool to the touch. Suddenly their arguments seemed like hardships of the road, to be left behind now that port was near.

"I too apologize, my husband."

It was good to have said it, but Sebastiano obviously had something more to add. He was still wearing his serious stare. She knew at once what the matter was—the

turd who had pestered her, the one who called himself a
don. Sebastiano was still jealous.

"You want me to tell you about that awful man?"

"I saw. You don't have to tell me."

"Do you think I've dishonored you, Sebastiano?"
She was worried. If he did, than apologies would never
heal all the wounds.

"Of course not. It's your own honor that concerned
me, and that has been taken care of."

Her expression clouded with doubt. "What do you
mean? What have you done?"

"Only what had to be done." He touched her lips
with his forefinger. "Ask no more questions. Your honor
has been preserved. That's all you have to know."

Holy Madonna, she prayed silently, please. My husband is a good man. I am afraid he's done something very
stupid. Intercede on his behalf with your Son for protection and forgiveness.

She reached up and with her thumb made a small
cross on Sebastiano's forehead.

Chapter 4

"Land!" a voice cried out. "America!"

Hundreds of apprehensive faces strained forward to get a look. The wind had picked up and the water was getting choppy. Overhead vaulting black thunderheads were gathering, but as yet there was no rain. Those who were standing against the rails could make out a vague purple silhouette that pressed upon the sea. The haze gradually cleared in the wind.

The ship was entering a broad harbor, not so beautiful as the Golfo di Napoli, for the water was a deep seaweed green and the city behind it looked dingy and claustrophobic even from here, but the architecture was as nothing any of them had ever seen before. Instead of rotting plaster and cracked, stained stucco, New York was a place of towers that pierced the sky like a battalion of cathedral spires. The harbor was crowded with great steam vessels, whereas at home there were mostly passenger ships and small, lazy fishing boats that sat upon the gentle waves like corks.

"Everything reaches up for heaven," someone muttered. "These Americans must be crazy. That ain't the way to get to heaven."

"How do you know?" another put in. "Maybe America is closer to heaven than Italy."

Teresa pointed to starboard and Sebastiano turned his head to see a great statue of a woman with her hand held high. "I've heard of this," he said. "She's called the Statue of Liberty. She's waving hello to everybody who comes to New York."

"If she's waving hello, what is she carrying in her hand? It looks like a brush."

"She's a painter, an artist, that's all. Like Michelangelo."

"Agh, what do you know about Michelangelo?" Teresa teased him good-naturedly.

"I remember from the books at the orphanage. You're the one who showed me."

She took his arm and snuggled against his shoulder. She felt him stiffen, but she ignored it. This was a moment to be close. "I wish Giorgio could see this statue. He would be very much impressed."

"What for? We got thousands of statues in Italy, more statues than trees. He's okay right where he is."

Teresa wondered if Sebastiano would ever get over his bitterness. "Maybe someday he'll come over and see us," she suggested, though she doubted it would happen. Giorgio was as stubborn as a priest.

"I don't want him to come over and see us," Sebastiano said quietly. "Let him live his own life. He is no longer my brother."

"As you said I am no longer your wife?"

"Don't start with me now. I was angry when I told you that. I'm not angry now. I know what I'm saying. Giorgio wanted nothing to do with us. He wanted a life only for himself. So to hell with him."

"Agh, to hell with him, to hell with this, to hell with that, to hell with everything. That's all you ever say. But I know you love him. I know you too well, Sebastiano. You don't fool me.''

He grumbled without answering.

They passed quite close to the statue and were nearing the dock when the rain began. At first it was fine as the spray off the ocean, but soon it began to fall in torrents, almost painful, drops the size of fists, Teresa would have sworn. All the waiting passengers on the steerage deck huddled and covered themselves with scarves and shirts as best they could, but no one ran for the safety of the cabins below. They wanted to be here when the ship came to port, when they made landfall in America.

The gangplanks lowered and the great mass of people began to spill down to the wharves, though there was a slight delay waiting for the first- and second-class passengers to disembark. Those few people were escorted directly to the immigration building; everyone else was herded up one wharf and directly to another, where they were loaded like cattle into long side-paddle ferryboats.

''Where are they taking us?'' Teresa asked her husband. She didn't like this, hadn't expected it. They had just come to the United States and already they were being shipped away again.

''How am I supposed to know?'' Sebastiano answered testily. ''I'm new here, same as you.''

Teresa was annoyed with him for not knowing. There was no reason why he should, but she relied on him to know everything about this trip. After all, it was his idea.

The ferryboats were jammed so full of passengers that it was barely possible to breathe. The closeness of other bodies unnerved Teresa, as it had so many times since they left Santa Barbara, but she was learning how to be stoic. She knew that if you folded your hands in front of you and extended your elbows just a little, you wouldn't be crushed.

That was harder to do on a boat that vibrated and lurched and pitched with the waves in the harbor.

However, she found that if she lost her balance, she needed only to lean against someone else and hope they hadn't lost theirs. Sebastiano was wonderfully dependable in this way. He was broad enough and sturdy enough to keep his legs in the worst conditions.

The place to which they were brought, a castle of some sort as far as she could tell, was situated on a small island out in the harbor.

"You think maybe the king lives here?" she murmured into her husband's ear.

"There ain't no king in America, only a President who lives in Washington, D.C. This is the place of immigration. Giovanni Morretti told me about it in a letter."

"You and your letters," she sighed. "I'm sorry I ever taught you how to read."

"You didn't teach me to read. I went to school."

It was true that he had learned to read in one of the government schools built under the Compulsory Education Policy, but she loved to tease him on this subject. It always made him angry, and he could always win, so there was no harm done.

Someone overheard them and remarked, "It's Ellis Island. That's the official name of this place. I heard from a cousin in St. Louis."

Sebastiano turned to the fellow, a tall man with bad teeth but an impressive head of dark brown wavy hair.

"What is this St. Louis? It's a good place?"

"Best place in America. You going there?"

"No. Philadelphia."

"Ah. Maybe that's a nice place too."

This was the first Teresa had heard of Philadelphia. In fact, she had never thought of America as a land with

many cities. It had always been just America, and when
you got there, that's where you were. She knew about
New York, since so many people on the ship had said the
name so many times, but Philadelphia—this she had no
concept of.

When Sebastiano ended his brief conversation and
turned back to her, Teresa detected uncertainty in his
expression, a kind of edgy something that showed he
wasn't quite satisfied. She didn't like his being uncertain.
It was worse than when he didn't know where they were
being taken.

"What is it, Sebastiano? I see your thoughts on your
face."

"Why didn't Giovanni ever tell me about this St.
Louis? If it's the best place in America, why did he tell
me to come to Philadelphia?"

"Maybe it's not the best place. Maybe that man is
wrong."

"Maybe," he allowed, but still he looked very unsure.

The ferry churned slowly along a line of pilings,
bumping now and then and causing the wood it touched to
creak violently. Mooring lines were thrown out and tied,
and the boat settled gently to a stop. Planks were lowered
and the passengers were led by immigration officers into
the castle of Ellis Island.

The first stop was a cavernous room called the registry.
Here the crowds were broken down into groups of thirty or
so and held in waiting pens that were fenced in with metal
pipes. From there they were led down pathways fenced off
with rope and more pipes, at the end of which were more
pens, smaller ones usually, and a few offices.

Here they were asked to give their names and ages,
whether they carried any disease, if they had a criminal
record, if they were anarchists or polygamists or agitators
of any kind. Translators were always present to help the

newcomers, but when a name was too long for an officer to be bothered with, he would change it arbitrarily. The family name, Farenza, was written in the registry unchallenged. Sebastiano, however, became "Jim."

"What kind of name is that—Jim?" he asked Teresa when they had a brief moment to speak.

She laughed. "An American name. The kind of name you always wanted, right?"

"I don't like it. It's too short for dignity and I can't even say it right."

"Don't worry. I will always call you by your proper name, Signor Farenza."

They were given a test to determine whether they were mentally fit, a series of questions that pertained to little items that hung on the wall of an office—a picture of Garibaldi, a flag of Italy, the names of a few politicians. It wasn't necessary to answer the questions correctly, only not to make a complete fool of yourself—this Teresa knew from Sebastiano, who had it from Morretti.

Finally there was a medical examination. They stood in a long line at the head of which was a doctor in a khaki uniform. He checked eyes and noses and mouths and ears and looked for signs of leprosy and venereal disease.

This part of the procedure mortified Teresa. For a strange man to put his hands all over her to inspect her made the blood run to her cheeks and gave her a funny tight feeling in her loins.

Through a translator, a young American who had obviously learned his Italian in the classroom and was almost incomprehensible to Teresa, the doctor asked kindly if she was having any difficulties with her pregnancy. She replied rather rudely that there was something unnatural about a man who would ask such an intimate question of a woman—maybe he wanted to be a midwife?

Sebastiano scowled deeply at her for speaking so

brazenly. After all, these men wore uniforms, which meant they had some power, maybe even enough authority to send her back to Italy. However, the young translator only blushed and stammered, while the doctor shook his head in frustration, then waved her through.

After this examination a few people were sent to a detaining room; they would be sent back. Others were kept in a little crowd off to one side.

There was only the loyalty pledge to take now, and when that had been done—they imitated the English words as best they could—they were given their visas and told they were free to go.

Once they were back out in the registry room, Teresa refused to budge. She was hungry. There had been no decent food in ten days. Yesterday she had no bread left and finally gave in to the unhealthful-looking soup aboard ship, but even though it hadn't made her ill, it hadn't done much to nourish her either.

Sebastiano threw up his hands. "What do you want me to do?" he asked her in a very loud whisper. "Do you think I carry meals in my pockets?"

She was too tired to rise to an argument. "Maybe you could ask someone if there is food," she suggested as civily as possible. The controlled timbre of her voice calmed him at once.

"I will see."

He found a security guard who could speak a little Italian. Yes, there was a mess hall, but it was only for detainees. Was there any way for a man to get his pregnant wife a little something for her empty stomach? The guard shrugged. Dispensing food was the responsibility of the steamship companies. Sebastiano brought the news back to his wife and she resigned herself to the gnawing feeling inside.

It wasn't only she who was hungry, she thought, but

the baby as well. She was supposed to be eating for two, and she hadn't even had enough for one, not for a long time. Her hunger seemed to buzz inside her ears and she found it difficult to distinguish it from the constant, irritating hollow din of the crowd. There must have been five thousand people in that room, and every one of them was speaking at the top of his voice in a language that was foreign to every other.

Sebastiano seemed to have no idea what to do next. He turned around in a small circle several times, then sat down on the steamer trunk with his wife. People shoved and jostled past them, and a few cursed and told them to move on, but he was too proud to ask just where they were supposed to move on to. No one had bothered to tell him.

At last there happened what seemed to Teresa to be a small miracle. A good-looking fellow in a serge suit and polished boots came over to them and extended his hand to Sebastiano.

"How do you do," he said. "I'm Rocco di Prospero from the Society of Italian Immigrants. You look as if you're lost."

Sebastiano took his hand and shook it. "I'm Sebastiano Farenza, from Santa Barbara."

Di Prospero offered no look of recognition.

"It's a small village outside of Caserta," Sebastiano explained.

"Oh, Caserta, sure," the man laughed. "*Napoli.*"

Sebastiano didn't much like being identified as a Neapolitan, but it was common for people from other regions to do so. "This is my wife, Teresa."

Teresa extended her hand. "How do you do, Signor di Prospero."

"Charmed, I'm sure," he replied, and Teresa blushed in spite of herself. "Where is your destination? Perhaps I can be of service to you."

Teresa was delighted that someone had finally come to their aid, but Sebastiano seemed suspicious.

"What is this society? You want money or something?"

Again di Prospero laughed. "No, no. We're just a few people who didn't like the way we were treated when we first came to America. We were lost and there was no one willing to help us. Some of us were treated badly. There are people in New York who will take all your money for a place to sleep and trick you into signing a contract to work for practically nothing in a labor camp."

A light dawned in Sebastiano's eyes. "Ah, crooks. Like the Camorra. Like the Mafia."

"The Americans are not so different from the Camorristi, you're right. At least a few of them aren't. But as I said, a few of us are doing what we can."

"So they are the crooks and you are the church, eh? Charity."

Teresa tugged at Sebastiano's arm. At first he just flashed her an annoyed look, but since she wouldn't be put off, he leaned over for her to whisper in his ear.

"Don't be a jackass now, Sebastiano. Now is not the time. Allow the man to help us."

He considered for a moment; then with exaggerated humility he said, "My wife hasn't had anything decent in her stomach for a long time. I would like to find her some food."

Di Prospero frowned. "Haven't you been to the commissary?"

"What commissary? The *carabinier'* said there was a cafeteria, but only for detainees."

"Ah, *stunad'*," di Prospero grumbled. "These bureaucrats don't care about anything or anybody. Come with me. We'll find you something to eat. And please, Signor Farenza"—this sign of respect had the immediate effect of making Sebastiano thrust his chest out like a pigeon—"please forgive these ignorant people. Not all *Americani* are so stupid."

At the commissary they waited in a long line, but it moved quickly, and they finally bought a small boxed lunch for a few cents. Inside was some rice, stewed beef, two apples and hot beans. Di Prospero waited patiently while the two famished people found a place to sit and ate their little feast. When they had finished, he prodded them gently to be off to their destination.

"Where do you plan to settle, signor?" he asked Sebastiano. "In New York City?"

"No, in Philadelphia," Teresa piped up.

Sebastiano shook his head and passed his hand over his mouth in exasperation. It wasn't her place to speak up now, she knew, but she was tired of being left out of the conversation.

"Ah, then you must buy a railroad ticket," di Prospero said. "Come. I'll show you."

As they followed along, Teresa suddenly found herself full of questions. "Is Philadelphia very far from here, signor?"

"Not very, just a hundred miles or so to the south, a few hours by train. Do you have family living there?"

"No," Sebastiano put in. "We have no family anywhere, only us."

"Where will you live?"

"I have the address of a friend, Giovanni Morretti. Do you know him?"

Di Prospero smiled in an ironic way that mystified Teresa. "No, I'm afraid I've never had the pleasure."

"He is a good man," Sebastiano said. "He will take care of us."

"I see. He knows you're coming?"

"I sent him a letter, but he didn't reply. I'll give him a good go-to-hell for that."

"Yes, I understand," di Prospero said. "But just in case arrangements don't go according to plan, perhaps I should give you the address of our society in Philadelphia."

"That would be very nice of you," Teresa said before her husband had a chance to turn the offer down.

There were ticket booths all along one wall of a long spacious room. Men wearing vests and small-billed blue caps sat behind wire mesh collecting money and giving information. Sebastiano stood in line while di Prospero wrote the address out for Teresa.

"I thank you for all your kindness," she said. "You've spent so much of your time with us."

"It is my pleasure, signora." He took her hand and gave it a slight squeeze.

She blushed as she realized why he had given them so much personal attention. He liked her; it was in his eyes. She did not find him objectionable, as she had the man on the ship. In fact, she liked the way her hand felt in his. It made her think of shelter, of safety. She also knew that his attraction for her would not result in anything more than that squeeze of her hand. When she smiled coyly in return, his vanity was satisfied and their flirtation was concluded.

"If ever you come to Philadelphia, please have dinner with us," she offered. It was a little bold of her, she realized. Asking a *stranier'* to sit at your table was the same as accepting him into your family, but after all, this stranger had done them great service and he would be nice to look at over a glass of dinner wine.

"I would love to, but I'm afraid I rarely leave New York City. It's a big enough place for a fellow like me."

An awkward moment passed and then Teresa asked the question that had been burning half-formed in her mind for many minutes now. "Are you married, signor?" The question had more than personal interest for her. It was a woman's duty to see that every young man found himself a good wife.

"I haven't had that good fortune so far, but who knows? Someday . . ." He parted his hands in a gesture of apology.

Doubts immediately flooded her mind, the old doubts one always had. What was wrong with him that he had no wife, no children? He was handsome, obviously educated, obviously a gentleman. A fine catch. Maybe he had no family to arrange a marriage for him, or maybe he was a sissy. Being a sissy was the most commonly accepted reason for bachelorhood beyond the age of eighteen.

"You must find yourself a nice girl and settle down," she heard herself say. "A man can't be too happy living all alone."

Her persistence brought a look of pain to his face, but he was saved by the return of Sebastiano, bearing two tickets in his hand.

"Now it's off to Philadelphia," he said merrily, as if once again they were just setting off on their journey. "Where do we find the train?"

Di Prospero led them outside to a huge barge that was about to cast off. The rain had stopped, but the wind still blew spray off the water. Sebastiano shook his hand heartily just before he and his wife went aboard.

"You're a good man, signor. If ever you need anything, you call on me, you hear? You will never find a better carpenter or a stronger back to help you."

"Best of luck to you both," di Prospero said, and then he was gone.

The barge pushed off like an old horse slugging through a mud bog and made its way across New York Harbor. It delivered them to a dock just across a wide cobbled street from a railroad station. Some of the immigrants were greeted by relatives and friends. Others, like Sebastiano

and Teresa, dragged their trunks and bags onto the dock,
then waited and looked around in bewilderment. A Slavic
woman with three round-faced children, all dressed in
layers of draped tunic and scarves, was the first to start
forward. The rest of the crowd followed.

A horse-drawn ice cart clacked slowly past behind
them when they'd reached the other side. The driver, a
dour-looking man with a black cap and thick grey sideburns,
gave the little crowd a halfhearted wave. Teresa was
bemused. A place where you could buy ice—she wondered what it might be used for.

The train they boarded was not so different from the
one to Naples, but the passengers were of many nation-
alities—not only Sicilians and Abruzzes', but people from
even farther away whose languages sounded to Teresa like
the gassy mutterings of a man with a sour stomach. Genuine barbarians, she thought, like the pilgrims to St. Peter's
you might meet in Rome.

Sebastiano looked taciturn, surly. She patted his hand
in a maternal way, and though he allowed it, he said
nothing, did nothing in response. That was all right with
her. There was too much to look at out the window of the
train to be concerned about her husband's moods. Whatever was bothering him would come to light sooner or
later.

The passing landscape was flat and covered with pine
trees. New Jersey, she heard a conductor call it. It was a
lovely place but a little strange. There wasn't a mountain
to be seen anywhere, and hardly a human dwelling except
for a few small towns through which the train passed along
the way—Newark, Trenton, Princeton—all places with the
same grey look as New York, though not as large, not as
tall.

She stretched her cramped legs out as far as she could
and absently mumbled prayers for good fortune to St.

Anthony and St. Gennaro as well as the Holy Virgin. Then she gave God a little compliment to get on His good side, because they were close to their destination now and she desperately desired His help. "It's nice, this New Jersey," she said to Him. "You did a nice job."

After three hours of jostling and shaking the train chugged into a bizarre bald landscape of factories, brick warehouses and decaying tenements. Everywhere, like burning pencils pointing into the air, smokestacks and metal vents gave off vapors.

The locomotive's whistle screamed and then they were in blackness, a tunnel. For the first time she noticed the dim naked electric light bulb screwed into the center of the ceiling. She wondered how it worked and hoped it was dependable. The absolute blackness that had suddenly come upon the world outside frightened her.

Sebastiano had fallen asleep. His head was tilted back and over on the seat, and from his open mouth came short snorts that rumbled with phlegm. She was tempted to awaken him, but she thought better of it. Why bother him? The trip had been no easier for him than for her, and he hadn't been himself since they left the *Stella Romana*.

The train emerged from the tunnel and began to slow. Teresa tried to get a good look out the window, but too many others were more aggressive and all she could see were brick buildings.

"Philadelphia, Broad Street Station," a conductor announced. "All passengers for Philadelphia." He went down the aisles repeating the station call again and again. It was a word that everyone should understand.

Teresa nudged her husband. "Sebastiano, wake up. We're here."

He stretched with his eyes closed, vigorously rubbed his mustache with his hand, then popped his lids open suddenly as if they had come unstuck. "What? What now?"

"We are in Philadelphia."

He elbowed his way to the window and took a good look, then swore with admiration. They were on the huge Chinese Wall, sixteen tracks across, as he later found out, riding along at least twenty-five feet above street level. The cross streets went under the tracks.

They pulled into a huge shed like a half-cylinder lying on its side and ground to a halt. The passengers began to debark; Sebastiano wanted to shove and bully and be one of the first off the train, but Teresa held him back so the baby wouldn't be jostled.

Out on the street Sebastiano turned back and looked at the station, a gigantic stone building—the largest train station in the world, if he had known—with turrets and towers and gingerbread and hundreds of arched windows. There was a colonnade running along ground level and art work everywhere. He whistled in awe and admiration, then noticed that a walkway was being built across Market Street at second-story level.

"Some builders, these Americans," he admitted grudgingly. "Makes a liar out of Giorgio; not a scrap of wood in sight."

Teresa tugged on his sleeve. "Sebastiano, look over there."

He turned around and his eyeballs nearly fell out of his head. There across the street was the largest, most magnificent castle he had ever seen. It was dominated by a tower with a statue of a man on top that rose forty stories into the air. The lower parts were so elaborate, so thoroughly decorated that it made Broad Street Station look ordinary. Most stunning of all, you could walk straight through it; dozens of people were.

Greatly daring, Sebastiano led Teresa into the central

courtyard and rubbernecked for a while; then she sat on their trunk while he inspected all four of the tunnels that led to the street in the cardinal directions. The north-south Broad Street walkway was the most impressive, full of carvings and gargoyles and odd little stairwells.

At last he sighed and led her away. Teresa tagged a few steps behind him. They were walking along a smooth white pavement such as he had rarely seen in the old country. It made stepping easier than it would have been over the rough street of small round brick, as he was dragging his steamer trunk behind him. It made an annoying grating sound against the concrete.

"You know where you're going?" Teresa called after him.

"Washington Street, to Morretti's place."

"Washington Street. Okay. Where's that?"

"How the hell am I supposed to know?" he growled back at her. He would find somebody and ask. That's how you got things done. He had been looking for a friendly face to approach without caution, but the people who walked past them all seemed to be in such a hurry that he was afraid he would be soundly snubbed if he tried to stop one.

Teresa was tired and impatient, he could see, and her face was too pale. He didn't feel so good himself, but there was nothing he could do. Anyway, why the hell was she always asking questions? He didn't have all the answers, and it embarrassed him that he didn't. She was dissatisfied about something. Sure, it was plain to see. But what was he supposed to do? He had already given everything for her, done everything for her.

An image of the night on the ship's steerage deck pressed into his consciousness, the memory of a man's weight pressing down on his arms, the sound of a terrified voice in a last scream of despair. He had killed in a rage of jealousy. Any man would understand, though it wasn't the kind of thing you talked about. No one would blame him if they knew.

Still, nothing could alter the fact. Never before had he done such a thing. Even if he was justified, now that some time had passed and he had given it some thought, he hated what he had done. The man begged him helplessly and Sebastiano ignored his pleas, as God would surely ignore Sebastiano's on the day of his judgment.

What have I done? Sebastiano asked himself again and again, though he knew the answer: something that couldn't be undone, God forgive him.

It was his wife's bold ways that started it all, he told himself, and because of that he resented her as much as if she had deliberately put him up to it. He was certain she knew about the death of the man or at least guessed, yet she said nothing about it. She was letting him simmer in his own juices.

The more he thought about that, the more he came to resent the fact that it was for her sake they had come to America. If only they had remained in their village, none of this ever would have happened. Ah, but too bad, Sebastiano, too bad for you. Now you are in America, a place to forget what happened before as well as all the years in the old country, the loss of a brother. He had lost the calm and peace that belong to a man who isn't too poor but just poor enough.

Do I know where we're going? What does it matter? We'll end up somewhere, girl, don't worry. Our son will have a home.

They found a Sicilian fruit vendor on Market Street, and with a little help from hand signs, repetition and shouting, they managed to overcome the difficulties of the strange dialect and learn where Washington Street was.

They started walking south. Sebastiano noticed a smart-looking young couple dressed in expensive clothes hail a passing carriage. The weight of the trunk was wearing him out, so he decided to try the same thing, but no one would stop for him, not even when he removed his crushed bowler and made a polite wave at a driver who slowed a bit, then flicked his horse on. Sebastiano heard him shout, "No dagos," though he didn't understand what that meant.

Finally Teresa asked if they could sit and rest. Sebastiano glowered. He didn't want to rest. Once you sat down you didn't want to get up again and the job got harder than ever. But Teresa was adamant, and whatever she wanted, she got. That was the way with a pregnant woman.

He wondered why he was not happier with her. For years he thought it was because they were barren, but when she finally got pregnant, he began to wonder whether he was the father. After all, what had changed between them? They did everything the same way they had always done it.

However, there was no one to suspect. In the daytime she sewed bonnets at the mill and at night she cooked lamb and pasta for him. She had no time for dalliance even if she wanted it.

At times he felt raw irritation in his gut, his love grappling with his jealousy, and most of the tender feelings he had for her came out as grumbling and complaining and arguing. He wanted all the time to please her, and yet he wondered if she had ever been pleased by him at all, or was it someone else who kept her content?

Why he felt this way he couldn't say. She had never given him any reason, and in his calmer moments he would almost weep with shame over his suspicions. Then sometimes within the space of only a few moments he would fabricate a horrific daydream of being cuckolded and he would fall prey to a rage that came near being murderous.

Finally on the ship he had been given his excuse, and he had done it. He had killed a man, God forgive him, he had killed a man . . .

They reached Morretti's place that night. Morretti had seven children, but three were grown and out on their own. That left one bedroom open, which he was most happy to rent to his old friend Sebastiano for a dollar a night.

The place was a tenement with crumbling plaster walls and broken windows, and the smell seemed to have eaten into the woodwork. Morretti's family was noisy and had little respect for the privacy of their new tenants, but Sebastiano had no idea where else to go or what else to do. It didn't seem at all like the paradise his old friend had described in his letters, but it was better than sleeping in the street.

Morretti turned out to be more helpful in another way. He found Sebastiano a job on the railroad, and a real carpenter's job too, not *bracciante* work that was meant for a ditchdigger.

They settled quickly. Teresa didn't seem happy living in a single room and sharing their lives with a tribe of strangers, but she didn't complain much. She kept the place as clean as she could, and on the insistence of Morretti's wife, a fat woman with tar-black hair and a large mole on the left side of her chin, she spent much time in bed, resting up for the impending birth.

Sebastiano didn't much like the work, but it was steady and it paid ninety cents a day. Nobody bothered him much, and it wasn't long before he had a reputation for being a reliable and thorough worker. During his lunch breaks—and he always managed to take an hour with no complaints from his boss—he would eat a sandwich and drink a little whiskey.

Whiskey was an American drink. He'd never even heard of it before Morretti gave him his first taste, but it took him no time at all to realize it was much better than wine for getting you a little drunk. Getting drunk was a good thing in America. It made you laugh, and if you didn't laugh you would cry, with the freezing cold weather and the filthy crowded slums and most of all with the memories of murdering a man.

Chapter 5

Giorgio found shelter in a tiny roadside chapel a few miles east of Santa Barbara. For the past week he had slept under the stars, in fields or along roadsides, but the bottomlands were always damp and full of mosquitoes, so he was finally forced to look for a roof.

The chapel looked as if it hadn't been used in a long time. He found a couple of broken beewax candles, which he lit and set with molten drops on a rusting iron communion rail. There was no tabernacle or altar cloth, and the only statuary was on the sanctuary wall, an unpainted, dust-covered melancholy crucifix. Carved from pine, it was worm-eaten throughout. Giorgio crossed himself and genuflected before the little stone altar, then took the crucifix down and cleaned it as best he could with the flimsy tail of his soiled cotton shirt.

There was always something magical and frightening about touching an icon. Many stories had he heard of a statue suddenly showing some sign of life—a nod of the head, bleeding from a wound, a single tear flowing from an eye. He wanted nothing to do with such marvelous events, though he was sure they often happened in the silence of a place like this.

What did one do if God gave a sign? Such a personal

communication at least meant that He had been watching you more closely than you might wish. It meant that anything at all might suddenly happen. Miracles were unpredictable. You might be minding your own business, or maybe even doing something a little questionable, like stealing an orange to live on, when some saint decides to pop in for a visit.

No, as far as he was concerned, let the statues remain statues and the spirits remain in heaven. But to stay on the right side, just in case, he would give this one a little polish.

He carefully, meticulously rubbed first the hair, then the crown of thorns, the face, the torso, the legs and feet. He examined the spear wound over the heart. Please, God, don't let it bleed, he prayed. It didn't bleed, but he cleaned it as carefully as he would a gash of real flesh. He examined it closely, then cleaned it again. He got so involved in the details of what he was doing that he forgot his fears.

Then he stopped for a moment to examine his work. The left side of the figure was too deeply grooved and riddled by woodworms to leave the piece much dignity. The face was intact, though, and there was an expression in the eyes, something in their terrible drawn suffering compassionate look that was so poignant that Giorgio wondered how the hands of a man could learn to carve such godlike agony.

He passed his forefinger along the cheek as if feeling the skin of an infant. It was warm and dry, almost like cork. He thought of the stone the masons cut. It was colder, harder, but smoother too, and somehow more delicate when shaped into small detail. He wondered if such wonderful eyes as these could be cut in granite or marble so that they would last a thousand years.

He had of course seen his share of statues; there was no place in Santa Barbara or anywhere else you could go without bumping into some kind of carved or cast figure. But none of them had ever seemed so lovely, so well wrought as this little piece of riddled pine.

He was tempted to keep the crucifix for himself. No one would miss it here. All the same, it seemed at home in this old church, and to steal a statue of God might tempt His retribution a little too much, so Giorgio returned the cross to its nail, then knelt and said a prayer.

"Holy Christ, I would like to make such eyes in stone, but I don't know where to begin. I don't know nobody around to teach me either, which is where You come in. Maybe You could give me a name or address, leave a message with Father Leonori in Santa Barbara. I would be most grateful for Your help. I'm not a bad guy to work with and I learn real fast."

Giorgio made as if to get up and settled back down. He added, "Now that we're talking, could You also help me to find a little food tomorrow? My belly is empty, and I don't think I should be stealing too much if You and me are going to work together."

He thought for a moment, then whispered as if in confidence, "I got one more request. Keep my brother and his wife from getting in too much trouble, okay? Maybe they deserve a little bit, because America is no place for Catholics. Who ever heard of a saint from America? But Sebastiano ain't a bad fellow, just a little crazy with the knives. So maybe keep an eye on him."

He shivered. It seemed to be a little cool, though the night was hot and muggy and there was no breeze blowing in through the splinters of stained glass in the arched windows. The insect bites that rose like pox all over him began to act up, and he scratched frantically with his jagged long nails until there were spots of bleeding on his arms and legs. "I hope this ain't Your answer, God," he mumbled to himself in misery.

The candles were beginning to flicker out. He tried lying on three different pews before he found one that was comfortable enough to sleep on. The smell of must in the wood was overpowering. He covered his nose and mouth in the crook of his arm like a pigeon nestling under its own wing.

Thoughts were grinding around in his head like grain on a mill wheel. He was lonely and he was broke. He hadn't been to work since the day he left home, just in case his brother hung around to look for him. In a way he regretted that he had not gone with Sebastiano and Teresa, but he didn't know America, didn't trust it. At least here he could get around, make his own deals, play his own game.

While his family was still here, it had seemed obvious that he was perfectly able to keep himself in food, clothing and shelter, but now he recognized that for an idiotic idea that had somehow leaked into his brain from some devilish place. What landlord would rent to a fourteen-year-old? And he didn't know anything about cooking or sewing. He could learn of course, but who would teach him?

He had to sit up slightly to roll over without falling off the pew, and when he did, he grew suddenly dizzy. He shivered again, more violently than before. His clothes seemed damp. What was going on? He was sweating terribly. Oh, God, was he getting sick? What was he supposed to do if he got sick?

He looked up at the sanctuary wall. The candlelight was gone and only a speckled swatch of moonlight made the shadow of the cross visible. It seemed to waver like the air over a baking highway. He was hungry, that was all—hungry and tired.

He didn't like the feeling and he tried to sit up straight so he could shake it out. His body would not obey. It shivered. His teeth chattered. How long had he been lying here? He tried counting off time like a musician, marking his breathing in his mind: one, two, three, four, what time was it?

Visions of America flashed into consciousness, a place full of wild cowboy-Indians with carving knives. The insect bites on his legs seemed to be on fire, but when he tried to scratch them, his fingers slid over a film of sweat and it did no good. His teeth chattered uncontrollably, biting his tongue and cheek.

Somehow he managed to come to his feet. He staggered to the altar, reached up and pulled down the crucifix, then clutching it to his breast like a bedtime toy, he fell to the floor. I done You a favor, Holy Savior, and now it's time to return the favor. You got to help me out. I don't feel so good.

Maybe God didn't want to help him, though, because suddenly he thought of the girl in the grotto and the rosary he had stolen from her. He still kept it in his pants pocket.

His legs had no strength left. He would have to wait, to gather his resources. He drifted off and the chapel spun around and around, though he could not open his eyes to see it. The world spun and spun away—

The next thing he was aware of was a gruff voice repeating the same words over and over. "Hey kid, come on. Drink some soup." At first Giorgio couldn't make any sense of what was being said. He felt heavy and groggy. His eyes didn't want to open and his flesh was sticking to the prickly matress under him.

"Come on, kid. The doctor says you got to eat."

"What doctor?" Giorgio mumbled, his mouth still turned half down into a straw-filled pillow. "What are you talking about?" Saliva dribbled from the corner of his mouth and over his chin, then made a wet spot under his cheek. It burned uncomfortably. He managed to open one eye, then turned over and wiped the moisture from his face.

The pitched ceiling above was made of roughly cemented slate—it was the underside of a roof, thick with cobwebs and smoke stains. The light seemed bright enough. There must have been a window open someplace. The voice belonged to a round, unshaven, worried face with a sharp hook of a nose and lips the color of brick.

"What am I doing here?" Giorgio asked the man.

"I told you a thousand times already. I found you sick on the floor of the old shepherd's chapel across the meadow. The doctor says you got to eat and drink more of this." The man held up a bottle of clear liquid.

"What's that, some kind of wine?"

"No, it's quinine. You got the malaria."

This worried Giorgio. He had seen plenty of malaria. People turned yellow as squash and sometimes they died. "I'm pretty sick, eh? The doctor came out to see me?"

"No, the doctor don't come to see nobody unless you got a lot of money. You got money?"

Giorgio recognized the sound of thin hopes in the voice. "No, I'm broke."

"Ah," the man mused, "too bad. The one time in all my days I get to help someone and he turns out to be a beggar."

"I ain't a beggar, I'm a mason." Giorgio cleared his throat and looked around the one-room shack with petulant resentment. "I thought you said the doctor gave you the quinine."

"No, the apothecary gave me the quinine. First I searched for the doctor and tried to get him to come and look at you, but he wouldn't unless he was paid extra. So I told him how you were sweating and hot and rolling around like you were out of your head or possessed by the devil—I also bought a charm to exorcise the evil spirits—

and he said you had the malaria and sent me out to buy the quinine. You're going to owe me a little money when you get better.''

"Suppose I don't get better? What are you going to do then?"

"Feed what's left of you to my pigs, I suppose. You can save me a little money that way."

Giorgio answered in a shrill, brassy voice. "Nobody ain't going to feed me to no pigs! I'll get better. Give me the quinine and whatever else you got there."

The man let him take a little drink from the bottle, then fed him broth with a deep round spoon. The quinine was bitter, but Giorgio wasn't about to end up inside a piece of pork. He had no doubt the man was as good as his word. These livestock herders—for that's what the man seemed to be by his manner—weren't like everybody else. They were as unpredictable as wild asses and had crazy ideas from who knows where. Their animals were more important to them than wine or money, and there were many tales of herders and shepherds cutting each other's throats to avenge the death of one of their beasts.

The broth wasn't bad. It was hot and tasted faintly of poultry. Giorgio was comforted by the way it burned in his throat and chest and through his stomach, for he still felt a chill from the illness. He weakly took the bowl from the man's hands and put his lips to it.

"It's about time," the stranger said. "You haven't eaten in two days."

Giorgio looked at him suspiciously. "What do you care if I eat or not? I told you, I don't have any money."

The man gestured with his hand as if flicking away a piece of insignificant dust. "Someday you'll be rich and pay me back. It's the way I invest my money—just like the Americans do."

Giorgio shook his head. "Americans, Americans—

that's all I ever hear about anymore. Don't anybody know about anything but America?''

The man smiled. He had a gold tooth in the front. Otherwise his teeth were only slightly stained and were perfectly regular, broad and square, like pieces of mosaic. ''What do you know about America?''

''I know I got a brother and sister who went there to get their scalps cut off.''

''What are you talking about?''

''Cowboy-Indians.''

''I been to America and I ain't never seen no cowboy-Indians.''

Giorgio gulped the rest of the broth in one swallow. ''How come you been to America? Ain't you got all your animals here?''

''Animals? Oh, the pigs. They belonged to my wife, but she's dead now. She had the typhus. I think that's worse than the malaria. Every year I go to America for work. When the work ends, I come back home.''

''You ain't a shepherd, then?''

''No, I'm a stonecutter.''

Giorgio brightened. ''Yeah? Me too. I never seen you around the quarry.''

''I only come home in the winter, when there ain't no work. My wife took care of the house until this year. Maybe now I'll stay all year around. Somebody got to take care of the pigs. Or maybe I'll slaughter the pigs and go to America for good.''

Giorgio's interest was piqued. Here was someone at last with firsthand information about the mysterious place across the ocean that was eating up half the people of Italy.

''What's it like over there?'' he asked as casually as he could. People always teased you and held back information when you seemed too eager. It was a lesson he had learned early.

"It's a place. Like any place."

"Lotta work for a mason there?"

"Some. They don't got the same kind of buildings we got here. They like to build big, but it ain't always so beautiful."

"Aha!" Giorgio croaked gleefully, "I knew it. America is a place for carpenters and *contadini*."

"They got lots of money, though. The people ain't poor like they are here—except for the immigrants, of course. It takes a while to make your money, but you can get rich there."

"I don't care about rich. I want to build buildings of great beauty, not the kind they build in America."

The older man looked sadly amused. "Yeah, me too. I was making all my money for Gina—that's my wife. We don't have no kids. I wanted to buy her nice things, give her a nice place to live in, maybe down in Positano. I wanted to retire. But now—what's the difference? Here or America, it's all the same."

"If you were making so much over there, how come you asked me if I was rich?"

The old man shrugged. "I'm not looking for money, kid. I'm looking for luck."

This made Giorgio think of the crucifix. Hadn't he held it in his arms that night in the chapel? This fellow must have taken it away. He asked about it.

"I put it back over the altar where it belongs," the man said with a scowl. "Did you intend to keep it?"

This embarrassed Giorgio, because he had in fact almost given into that very temptation. "No," he protested too strongly. "I just wanted to see it again for luck, like you're looking for. There was something in the eyes—"

The man nodded with a faraway look. "Ah, yes, the eyes."

"They are the best carved eyes I have ever seen," Giorgio asserted. "I wonder who carved them."

"Probably some peasant with a knife and a few hours to spare." He left the bedside and from a cloth pouch hanging on the wall by the door he took an old nicked and battered hand-carved pipe, tamped in a pinch of tobacco and lit it. "Somebody who knows about suffering, eh?"

"I would give anything to able to carve like that in stone."

The stranger laughed. "You're too sick to get out of bed, but you want to be Michelangelo."

"Who's Michelangelo?"

"He made some statues and a few pictures for the pope," the man said wryly. "A big shot."

"You know this guy?"

"No, he's dead. Been dead a long time."

Giorgio threw one arm into the air. "Son of a bitch. What did he have to go and die for?"

"What do you care?"

"Maybe he could have taught me to cut stone, eh?"

"He was dead before your grandparents were born. Don't worry about him. You want to learn to cut stone like that? Maybe I'll teach you."

"Yeah, and what do I got to do, go to America with you? To hell with that."

"Maybe I won't go to America yet. Maybe I'll hang around for a while, make you my apprentice."

"What for? What's in it for you?"

"What's in it for you?" the man imitated in a harsh, squeaky voice. "I need somebody to feed the pigs, that's what." His expression softened. "Listen, kid, I got nobody. No family, nothing. I spent all my life learning to cut stone, and when I die, there's nobody left to know what I know. I got a book up here." He tapped his head with a stubby, cornified forefinger. "I got a hundred books up here and nobody to teach what's in them. What the hell is the good of that?"

Giorgio lay back down on the bed and supported his head with his hand. "What are you talking about, books in the head?" he asked doubtfully.

"Never mind. You want to be the greatest stonecutter in all Italy?"

"Sure, but how do I know you can teach me?"

"Well, maybe one time I was a peasant with a knife and a little free time."

"You?" Giorgio's interest was captured.

"I'll give you a bed and we'll share the food." The man shook his finger at Giorgio and sucked harshly on his pipe so that swirls of smoke played at his lips as he spoke. "But once you ain't sick anymore, you better not be a lazy bum. You want to learn, you got to work. Otherwise I'll throw you out and to hell with you."

"I ain't no lazy bum," Giorgio said, incensed. "I'm the best damn worker you ever seen."

"We'll see."

"Yeah, mister. We'll see."

BOOK II
GABRIELLA
1917

Chapter 6

"Hey, Giorgio, what's the matter, you crazy? Come down off there. You're going to kill yourself."

He was balanced atop an unfinished stone wall that stood at the edge of a cliff. It was twenty feet above the ground on the plateau side and twice as high on the other. In his hand he held a heavy stonecutter's mallet, which he raised above his head and angrily shook like a banner. A dozen workmen watched with amusement both from the ground and from the rusty iron scaffold against the wall.

"I don't build with mortar that will crack and fall off in a month," he shouted down to them.

A portly old man whose eyes were rheumy from too much smoking looked up indifferently from his work. "All right, Giorgio, we'll add a little sand," he said patiently. "It will be lovely mortar. I will let you personally supervise the making of it."

The old man's name was Enrico Scarfeticcerio, and he it was who had nursed Giorgio back to health so many years before. He spoke in a rough voice made of gravel and whiskey but completely without irony. He was short and had a prickly grey stubble on his cheeks. To protect the sensitive bare skin at the top of his head he wore a grey felt hat, and he held his trousers up with maroon suspenders.

Most people thought his name, of which he was most
proud, was too long to be bothered with. Instead they
called him Scarfo.

To Giorgio he was father and teacher and friend.
There was no one like him from here to Naples—maybe
not in all Italy. When he handled stone, his jaws would
clench, his nostrils would flare, and a look so determined
would come to his old brown eyes that it could easily be
mistaken for anger. He could take a shapeless piece of
granite and strike his chisel through it with such precision
that the faces of the resulting halves would look as though
they had been sliced with a knife.

Even after years of working with him Giorgio would
feel a startled tensing in the stomach every time the old
man's mallet struck home and kicked up a shower of
sparks and dust. It made a ringing through the soul that
shook its foundations. No other sight, no other sound
seemed to Giorgio so beautiful. Scarfo was more than a
mason. He was a sculptor, a master with the chisel.

But he had his failings. If a job fell down after two
months, he didn't care, so long as it looked lovely when it
was finished.

"Look! Look at this!" Giorgio swung the hammer in
a short arc and easily knocked a large piece of granite out
of place. He gave it a shove with his foot and it tumbled
off the far side of the wall to a dirt road forty feet below.
"How can you make a wall with this kind of mortar?"

"It's the weather," Scarfo said. "What are we supposed to do? The damp makes the mortar too thin."

It was autumn and the rains had come, but the work
at the Villa Vichierri could not stop for the rains. The wall
had to be finished. Soon the grassy hills of the Campania,
burnt to straw and rubble by the summer heat, would turn
green and lush, and the gnawing chill of winter would
drive the peasants of Santa Barbara behind the doors of

stone hovels to wrap themselves in knitted shawls and huddle around meager fires in homemade brick stoves.

There would be no working in winter, and if the wall was not finished, there would be no pay. Don Antonio Terasatti never gave money for a job half done. Even on days like this, when black clouds twisted and braided and rushed by so low you could grab them, the workmen only stopped when the rain drove so hard that they had to cover their mixing tubs with canvas.

"It won't hold the stones. The wall will be as ugly as that pig of a building." He pointed back toward the main house. It was a pink and cream monstrosity that had been erected only three generations before at the request of the King of Naples. There were two other buildings on the property: a stable a few hundred yards to the east, and just below the wall where the masons worked, a family mausoleum.

Scarfo's laugh strangled into a hacking cough. "The masons who set the stones would love to hear you speak so kindly of their work."

"Their work is shit. You know it as well as I do."

The sight of it always sickened Giorgio. He wondered what kind of people would build such a place. Every wall of it was marred with poorly applied stucco, and there wasn't a pillar or a balcony that didn't look like a nose where an ear should be. It was a face without a redeeming feature, a leper's face.

At least the garden, which extended from just beyond the mausoleum to the main house, had been properly designed, a formal maze of hedges as perfectly symmetrical as the carved swirls on a headboard. On either side of it was a small grove of cypresses, and at the far end, just below the terrace that extended like a stretched lip from the back of the villa, stood a line of silver olive trees.

But the building, the damned building—the King of

Naples was no more, but his building would curse the plateau for centuries to come.

"I ain't going to have no damn snotnose journeyman mason calling my work shit sixty years after I'm dead," Giorgio said.

"All right then," Scarfo replied, "we'll have plenty of work to do in the spring, when the whole thing falls down and we have to build it again."

"I'm not going to work for that son of a bitch Terasatti in the spring. I'm never going to work for him again."

No one liked working for Don Antonio. As any gossip in the village would tell you, the men in that family had always been cut from the same stick. They were an intractable, stubborn, tight-fisted bunch, and any one of them would cut your throat without even bothering to swear a *vendetta*. But they had power.

Don Antonio owned all the land from Santa Barbara to Caserta—maybe to Naples as far as anyone knew—and he owned all the *contadini* who lived on it as well as everything they produced. In the eyes of the law every piece of stale bread, every bottle of homemade wine, every pomegranate or chestnut that found its way to the tables of the *contadini* was the property of one man. His grip on the province was so tight that even the Camorra, the local crime sydicate, couldn't penetrate into his territory.

Don Antonio had become the sole male survivor of the family back in '95, when his only brother, Pasquale, was found gagged, bound and burned almost beyond recognition in a lime pit near Capua. No one was surprised at this turn of events. After all, the fellow did business with Sicilians.

Now the don held more power than any of his forebears, and if he wanted his wall rebuilt a hundred times over, few men in the province would refuse him no matter how much they despised him. Giorgio, however, considered himself an exception.

"What are you going to do then," Scarfo said, "join the army and fight the Austrians? Who else is going to hire you?" He fluttered his hand impatiently near his cheek. "Sometimes I think you are the stupidest jackass in all of Campania, maybe in all Italy."

Giorgio raised his free hand and pointed to the sky with rhetorical flourish. "Maybe I'm a jackass, but I won't let Terasatti ride on my back." Again the hammer swung and another stone went flying.

"I give up. To hell with you," Scarfo said. He went to his haunches and troweled off a loaf of wet mortar from his pallet, then began carefully to point, or finish, the cracks between the newly set granite.

Giorgio broke off another stone. Scarfo ignored him, but now the other men were growing impatient at seeing their work battered apart, and they began to shout at him.

"Hey, you idiot, why don't you come down off there and get to work so we can finish this job?"

"Yeah, Farenza, that's my work you're fooling around with up there. I cut those stones myself."

"You should cut your throat for doing this kind of work," he called back. "Don't you have any pride? Don't you have any dignity?"

"How you going to eat dignity? Maybe you can feed my wife with it."

"He don't know nothing about family. He ain't got a family, not even a mother."

"Agh, *facia di mamma*," he said, and another stone went tumbling.

Then the cursing began between him and the others, and the shrugging and finger signing and agonized grimacing. With so many voices Giorgio found it glorious, like an opera, like *Don Giovanni*. Even Scarfo couldn't resist adding his voice to the chorus.

God Himself joined in. Thunder began to vibrate the western sky, and the rain and wind gathered force. Giorgio balanced like a goat on his ledge and waved his hammer harmlessly while he cursed the workmen, their ancestors, their descendants, their relatives and their livestock.

Then something caught his eye. Coming up the road from the valley below was a flatbed cart drawn by an emaciated old donkey and driven by a skinny, one-eyed peasant from Abruzzi named Mario la Scuola. Next to him was seated a smaller figure, that of a young woman, who protected herself from the rain by holding a corner of a canvas tarp over her head.

"It's the daughter," Giorgio cried out. The other men became silent.

Gabriella Terasatti was the only child of the family. It was to protect her privacy that this wall as being built. She had returned home from a convent school in Milan only a week before. There had been rumors she would come, even though her father had left the villa for the time being.

Her mother was sick with consumption, and everyone in the district expected the old lady to die soon. At night you could hear her coughing all the way down the *Corso L'Itella*. The servants tended to her with with soup and wine and hot soaked towels.

Don Antonio, claiming he could not bear to see his dear wife suffer, had retired to Naples. He lived there quietly—with his mistress—to await the inevitable end. The entire affair was a public scandal, and Gabriella, who had always been pious and shy anyway, wore a veil over her face in public to hide her shame.

This delighted the villagers, who had not seen her since she was little. They suffered exquisite, burning curiosity about her looks and were almost religiously grateful to have a new subject for gossip. Most insisted that she must be ugly as a pig—that was the real reason she covered her face like an Arab and the reason she needed a wall twenty feet high to hide behind.

In fact, the wall had been intended by her father as a peace offering. If her mother died there would be no question about her returning to her quiet life at school. The villa would need a mistress. Don Antonio didn't relish presenting her with that possibilty, so to salve his own conscience as well as her feelings he promised her a private grotto where she could go to meditate on the memory of her mother and to say her rosary—and what more obvious spot than right at the mausoleum?

As it turned out he needn't have worried about placating her. The Franciscans had taught her well. She was unquestioningly obedient no matter how hurt or disappointed it might make her. She accepted the change in her life without a word.

As for Giorgio, he cursed her every time the rain doused his cigarette. Whether she was ugly or beautiful, she wasn't worth this kind of trouble and this kind of work wasn't worth the pay. All he wanted was a simple life—lots of laughs, good wine and beautiful stones to cut.

Of course he wanted to be rich. So did everyone in Italy. But nobody ever got rich climbing twenty-foot wooden scaffolds in the freezing rain. Unless you were a crook, a bureaucrat or both, like Don Antonio, you had to be satisfied with a simple life. And now he couldn't even have that. Goddamn the man and his ugly daughter anyway.

The wagon was making slow time up the plateau road. Rumor had it that the daughter had gone to Caserta to buy a funeral dress. She would soon be directly below the wall, where the road narrowed most along the face of the plateau's eastern cliff.

Giorgio leaned out to get a better look and had to

catch hold of a stone spar to keep himself from falling when a sudden breeze caught him unawares.

"You better pay attention to what you're doing," Scarfo warned him. "Maybe if you fell down and broke your neck it would teach you a lesson."

The other men had lost their reticence now. Why should they be silent and respectful if the don was away? She was only a spinster. If she was ugly, so what? She would get the same treatment as any other female would get who passed them. They started nudging each other and pointing. One fellow, a skinny Abruzzes' named Carossio, began making obscene gestures followed by suggestions at the top of his voice. The others took his example. The rain came down a little harder, which made them laugh. The drops hung from their mustaches and off the ends of their noses.

It didn't take long for her to understand what was going on. She looked up and stared at them for a moment. She was of medium height and she wore a magenta skirt with a shawl wrapped around her shoulders and a dark scarf over her head. All of her face but her eyes was covered with a black veil.

No matter how Giorgio felt about her, he wasn't about to be outdone by the other men. Since he was the handsomest among them, he told himself, he deserved all of her attention. Without hesitation he stood up straight and held his balance in the wind, then walked along the jagged spars of granite for several yards. A bolt of lightning cracked overhead and the earth shuddered and swung around a few times before he was secure again.

Scarfo stopped troweling, raised an eyebrow and point-edly looked Giorgio in the eyes. "What the hell do you think you're doing?"

Giorgio smiled to charm. "Impressing a lady. Don't worry, I know what I'm doing. You're the maestro of laying stone and I'm the maestro of laying everything else.''

"I'm the maestro of laying stone and you're the maestro of bullshit,'' Scarfo shot back sarcastically.

Giorgio glanced down out of the side of his eye. He had her attention. Very good. Now to make the best of it. He held his arms wide with the palms facing up, trying to look like Christ giving the Sermon on the Mount.

On their side of the wall the men were greatly appreciative. They clapped and whistled for his bravado. Only Scarfo remained sour.

"If I am only the maestro of bullshit,'' Giorgio shouted to all his listeners, "then why am I standing up here risking my life like a fool?''

"A very good question,'' Scarfo called back.

The wagon was directly below now and had come to a stop. The woman was silently looking upward. The driver seemed bored.

"If I am only the master of bullshit,'' Giorgio continued in a stentorian voice, "how is it I can perform great feats of terror for the lady down there?''

Almost faster than anyone could follow, he bent over and lifted himself into a handstand. The masons went crazy with delight. Such a show, and it hadn't cost them a dime.

Scarfo shook his fist and called out, "I'm not gonna live with no damn lunatic like you, Giorgio. Tonight I'm gonna pack my bag and move up to Rome, where the people got a few brains between their ears.''

Giorgio laughed. The rain came down harder. The wagon started to move on.

"Hey!'' he shouted at the top of his voice. "Don't go yet. The show ain't over.''

The woman glanced back up at him, though she was obviously having trouble keeping her eyes open in the rain now. He had to move quickly, before he lost her attention for good. He went to his knees, secured the toe of each boot behind strong spars and slowly tilted forward. With his hands he held the edge of the wall until he leaned so far out that he had to inch them down. Finally he was where he wanted to be—hanging upside down by his toes forty feet above the road.

The woman's hand went up to her face in shock. Giorgio smiled—it was an odd feeling, grinning upside down. It felt as if his cheeks had to stretch too far. Then it occured to him that he had no idea how he would get back up.

"Hey!" he croaked to the men on the other side of the wall, having no idea whether they could hear him. "Give me a hand."

"I told you you'd break your goddamn neck," Scarfo shouted, but Giorgio could hardly hear him.

The wind was blowing in his ears like a chorus of groaning men. The world seemed to be tilting in odd ways, and he suddenly couldn't make any sense of it. From somewhere came a scream, a woman's scream. Then he felt himself jerked upward as Scarfo and another man named Ferarella grabbed him by his ankles and pulled him back to the scaffold. He tumbled down on top of them and there was a moment of chaos before they untangled themselves, all shouting and cursing to beat the devil.

Giorgio scrambled to his feet and peered back over the top of the wall. The woman was on her way up the road, but she turned back once, and when she saw him looking, she yelled, "You're crazy out of your mind. Go see a priest."

"What the hell is the matter with you, doing a stupid thing like that?" Scarfo shouted in his other ear.

Giorgio only shook his head. He didn't know why he had done it. He must have been possessed, an instrument of the devil's work. Scarfo was right. He had to be an idiot, a lunatic to risk his life to impress a woman whose face he had never seen, especially a rich one who would never give him a second look. Despite himself even now he found himself wondering what kind of face that veil hid. His instincts told him it might not be such an ugly one.

"The don will hear about this," one of the workmen said. "She will tell him."

"Let her," Giorgio said with sheer bravado. His legs still felt rubbery and full of the shakes, while his heart was pounding mightily. "What's he going to do, fire me?"

The other men were silent. They didn't know what the don might do. He could do anything he wanted.

There was no more sign of her for days, but again and again Giorgio found his gaze drawn toward the house as if he hoped to catch sight of her. After a while he found himself growing angry with her. What was wrong with her, anyway? Didn't she ever go outside? Of course it was almost always raining at this time of year, but even in the worst weather it wasn't good to spend all your time indoors. It thinned the blood.

Ah, well, to hell with her. Why should he care if her blood was thin? She was nothing to him, nothing at all. Let her spend the rest of her life indoors.

Still, where the hell was she, anyway? Not that he cared, but he was curious. A man was allowed to be a little curious, especially about some crazy woman who didn't show herself in the daylight.

Besides, he wanted her to come out and see her wall, which he no longer thought of as the Don's gift to his daughter but as his own work of art. It seemed that every stone, every crack, every glint and glimmer of light reflected on it had somehow become the product of his hands.

Scarfo's work, which had before always seemed so perfect, now looked tawdry and sloppy to him. He began to cut more stone himself. His efforts were often slow because of the caution he took with each stroke of the hammer. He had something to prove. No rich, ugly daughter of a crook was going to call him crazy. He would build for her the most beautiful wall in the world, more beautiful than the walls of San Genero's cathedral in Naples, more beautiful than the walls of the Vatican, which he had never seen but had heard so much about. Yes, he would show her if he was crazy.

All of this drove Scarfo to distraction. It was getting late in the season, and although there were so many masons that Giorgio's slow work had little effect on the speed with which the job was getting done, every time the old man's cheeks turned red with chafing from the cold, he would turn to Giorgio and curse him. "We should be finished this job by now," he would grumble.

"I want to do it right. Why do it if you don't do it right?"

"Because we're getting paid to do it, that's why. What do you think, you're Michelangelo? Cut the stone and get it done."

"You mind your work and I'll mind mine."

"Agh, *gool' a' sor'*," Scarfo spat. Your sister's ass.

"Agh, *fang' gool'*."

Again and again they played the same scene up on the scaffold, and always out of the corner of his eye Giorgio kept watch for the daughter of the house, but she still stayed away and he was coming to be convinced that she was doing it just to torment him. His life became a misery. By day he was constantly frustrated, angry, tense, alert.

Every spray of cold rain, every bluster of wind he suffered made him more resentful.

At night, when he was alone with Scarfo in their tiny limestone dwelling down in the pastureland, he would take out an old mandolin Scarfo had given him years before, and sadly he would lose himself in its sharp, trembling tones. Sometimes he would improvise, letting the instrument master him and surprise him. Sometimes he would play old Neapolitan songs and murmur the words as if he only half knew them.

Scarfo would sit back in an old cane chair and listen quietly. Often he would pour himself a small glass of anisette and light an old pipe he had carved for himself out of a cow's bone. Only rarely would he take his brass trumpet from under his flatboard bed and play long doleful notes to Giorgio's accompaniment.

They never had harsh words when they were alone. They hardly spoke at all. What was the point? There was no one to hear, no one to take sides, no one to admire their anger. And of course there was no wall, no villa to taunt them. At night, when they were alone with their music, they knew each other well and did not have to speak.

Finally there came a time when the mandolin was quiet and Scarfo did speak. "This woman is no good for you," he said. "You know that as well as I do."

"What woman? I don't know who you're talking about." Giorgio simmered in the echo of his denial for a moment, then said, "Anyway, she's nothing to me. I only seen her once."

"Is that why it takes you an hour to cut one lousy stone—when you have the heart to cut it at all?"

"I don't know what's going on," Giorgio admitted. "I'm afraid I'm going to make a mistake, ruin every stone I touch."

"So what if you do? You ruin one, you get another one."

Giorgio put his hand to his head as if the dim firelight was suddenly too much for his eyes. "I don't know what's the matter with me. Nothing like this ever happened before. All of a sudden I want to make the most beautiful wall in the world. And why? For someone I don't even know. It's as if I'm carving a statue of her to make her immortal."

He considered for a moment, then looked at Scarfo. "You never taught me to carve that way, like you said you would. Like a sculptor. The eyes of Christ in the chapel, you remember?"

"Sure, I remember."

"What's the matter, then? Am I too stupid to learn?"

Scarfo tapped his chest with his fist. "You got to have it here, boy, before I can teach you. Marble ain't like granite. You got to be tender, you got to be like a lover to it—not the way you think about this woman, with your balls on fire, but a real lover, a guy who ain't afraid with every move he makes.

"How you gonna carve a stone if you're afraid of it? You gotta be brave and loving like a man makes you brave. *Managia*! Even that ain't enough. If you knew how to love, you still couldn't carve because you don't know how to use your eyes. You ain't suffered enough."

"What the hell are you talking about? I suffer plenty."

"Yeah? Maybe. Let me ask you, you want to make beautiful eyes in stone, right?"

"That's right."

"You ever seen any eyes in the world like you want to make?"

"No, of course not. It ain't the same thing."

"No? Then how come I see them eyes every place I go? You laugh, eh? I'm telling you, take a walk on the corso and you'll see a hundred eyes like that."

"I think old age is making you crazy."

Scarfo laughed. "Wait until you suffer. Wait until you been through the worst pain in your life. Then you'll know. Then you'll see beautiful eyes everywhere you look. Even in the mirror."

"To hell with carving, then. It's this Terasatti babe who's driving me crazy."

Scarfo sucked on his pipe and made a gurgling sound. "You ain't the first man ever to make a fool of himself over a skirt."

"Sure, but why this one? I never even seen her face. I could understand if it were Gina Raffetti, the miller's daughter, or even Lola Marelli—"

"The prostitute? Cut out your tongue, boy."

Giorgio shrugged. "She's beautiful, ain't she? With those hips she could give a man a dozen sons and not even get tired." Scarfo frowned, but Giorgio seemed not to notice. "But it's like I got a fever. I don't even think about those other ones. It's only this spinster daughter of a crook who sneaks into my brain all the time. What's the matter with me?"

Scarfo stood and turned to the embers of the fireplace. They were glowing orange and slowly cooling to ash. He let the moment grow heavy. He wanted his protege to listen. "Every time you look at a skirt, the woman who wears it falls down panting and sobbing, Giorgio. It's always been that way with you."

Giorgio didn't disagree. He had his pride, after all. In fact he had only made love once, and that was to a shepherd's daughter whom he never saw again. It was true, some seemed to find him attractive. It was equally true, though he often wished it were not, that many others found his charms quite resistible.

"You're crazy about this one because you can't have her," Scarfo explained. He made a dramatic turn toward

Giorgio and pointed his pipe for emphasis. "It is one of
the strongest and most terrible powers granted to women,
to make you crazy by doing nothing. It is a trick they all
know.

"I'm an old man, boy, and I've seen a lot, so you
take my advice. Forget about the signorina. She's not for
you. After your stupid trick up on the wall, she knows she
has you in her net, and she can have you for dinner if she
wants because you would go gladly. The trouble is that
you don't have the taste of money, so she leaves you
flopping around and gasping for breath while she goes
fishing elsewhere."

Giorgio did not argue with his old friend, but he was
convinced there was more to it than that—maybe a curse,
maybe a love charm. Yes, he thought, if he didn't know
better, he might very easily have concluded that he was in
love. Love was easy to recognize. It was the feeling that
made you want to beat your head against the ground, that
made you hang upside down from a wall and almost kill
yourself.

He did not want to be in love. Who on earth was
worth that kind of suffering? No, all he wanted was a
simple life, and he was determined to have it. He would
forget this little bird, and if he ever saw her again—well,
there would be no stupid stunts. He would ignore her.
How that would make her suffer! After all, everyone knew
that no female could stand to be ignored.

Chapter 7

Donna Maria Terasatti was dead.

Everyone came to the funeral. That night there was a reception at the villa. Only relatives were invited.

Gabriella Terasatti lay on her bed staring dully at the ceiling. She didn't want to go downstairs. The funeral that morning had been depressing enough. Her mother was dead, so let her rest in peace. Why rehash the final moments a hundred times with relatives who had only come for some free food and liquor? Gabriella's mother had allowed herself few friends, and blood relationships outside her immediate family meant little to her. She made herself a tough-minded woman, a little miserly, with only the barest flickering of sentiment for her husband and daughter.

Gabriella could remember receiving a kiss from her only twice: once on the day of her first holy communion, and once, curiously, after she bled the first time in womanhood. Still, Gabriella always gave her mother a special place of honor in her heart. She would not claim any great love for her, but she ardently admired her for a woman of strength and tried to take an example from her.

Gabriella did not cry at the funeral. Her mother would not have wanted her tears, she was sure. Her father broke

down into short, rasping sobs, fell to his knees at the
coffin and banged with his fist on the lid, begging his wife
either to return or to take him with her. Naturally Gabriella
did not take this behavior seriously. By tradition it was his
right and duty as a husband, but he had shown not a tenth
of this anguished devotion when his wife was alive. It was
proper funeral behavior, she acknowledged, but hardly
convincing in the circumstances.

Donna Maria would have expected no restraint from
him. She had never carried any illusions about her husband.
Perhaps he believed in all the sentiments he claimed on her
behalf, but she knew him for a tough little dictator in the
Campania and a constant philanderer besides. Still, she
had remained a dutiful wife, controlled his drinking and
his spending, kept an eye on his affairs and thus ensured
for herself a life that was comfortable if a little bleak.

Now the task of running Don Antonio's domestic life
would fall to Gabriella. She could only hope to do as well
as her mother. He could be a difficult, stubborn man.

There was the matter of the leaking roof. Since her
first night home Gabriella had suffered a soaking with
every storm, but he never listened to her complaints or at
least never took them seriously. He could always be counted
on to make an extravagant, sympathetic fuss over her, and
he would stroke her hair like a preening old hen, but he
had never parted with a lira unless her mother ordered it,
and her mother had never ordered anything unless she
could foresee some return on her investment.

She absently rubbed her feet together. They were still
damp from stepping in the cold little puddles that had
collected on the warped wooden floor of her room. Above
her in the flickering orange light cast across the ceiling by
her kerosene lamp she could see droplets forming along
spidery hairline cracks in the plaster and collecting into
brown coronas of water stain. There were too many leaks

to be caught in buckets, but that was just as well. Sooner or later the moisture would seep down into her father's room below, and then he would surely order the roof fixed. He was fond of his own comfort if indifferent to anyone else's.

She wished she had a cigarette. She had not been able to catch a smoke since she left school, and she was nervous and irritable, but there was no way for her to buy a pack around here without causing a scandal. If her father found out about her habit, he would kill her. Only men and prostitutes smoked.

She thought idly about the boy in the grotto so many years before who introduced her to cigarettes and stole her rosary. He often found his way into her thoughts. He was wild and arrogant, like a street urchin, and he liked her without even knowing who she was; of that she was sure.

Despite her mother's constant warnings that strangers would only care for Gabriella because of her family's wealth and power, that boy liked her enough to give her a smoke and to steal her rosary. Well, she argued to herself, maybe he stole the rosary to sell it, but she liked to think he had kept it.

The rain was beating hard to get in through the roof. This was by far the heaviest storm of the season. Good, she thought. By morning the rooms below would be soaked. Maybe her father would at last be convinced and order a few of the workmen to leave that silly wall for a day or two and do some repairs on the house.

The workmen. At the thought of them she rolled over and gathered her blanket about her ears, as if shutting out sound would shut out thinking, but she could not help vividly recalling the sight of the young man hanging from the wall her father was having built for her. What kind of a present was that for a father to give to a daughter anyway?

She shuddered, her shoulders hunched, and clasped

her hands under her stomach. Suppose he had fallen? Suppose the wind had blown him away like a leaf and plunged him to his death? She didn't understand why he had done it. She knew that men sometimes made fools of themselves over women, but she was a stranger to him.

Perhaps he was just crazy, or maybe all men behaved that way. Whatever the explanation, she was glad he hadn't fallen. She had never seen a violent death and she never wanted to. Her life at school had been calm, ordered, predictable, safe. She hoped for at least that much here.

She hadn't mentioned the incident to her father. He would blame her, she was sure. He would accuse her of being immodest. He trusted no woman, least of all his own daughter. He would call her a brazen slut, and then he would slap her until she cried. He had done it before. She assumed it was her fault, not because she was guilty of any sin of immodesty but because she was stupid enough to mention that a man had noticed her.

Other girls at the School of the Annunciation had had the same experience of their own fathers, and they spent many hours comparing stories and sharing confusion. Weren't young men supposed to be attracted to them? It seemed natural and sometimes so pleasant that it could make one giddy. There could be only one solution: some things you didn't mention to your father.

A knock came at the door; it was the maid.

"Signorina, are you coming down? Don Antonio is growing anxious."

"Please tell him I'm in the middle of my meditations. I'll be down in a few moments."

"*Pardon*?" The maid was a young Frenchwoman named Suzette de Chambeau. She had dark skin and black eyes and skinny legs. Bringing her here had been a whim of Don Antonio's. The French had once been masters in this part of the world, and the irony of retaining a French

servant appealed to him. She spoke a Sorrentese dialect of
Italian, which has the lisping quality of Castilian Spanish.
This combined with the heavy nasal quality of her Parisian
accent made her so nearly unintelligible that Gabriella
understood her only by a combination of listening hard and
guessing harder. The maid, in turn, understood Gabriella
not at all. She knocked again.

"Signorina, your father wants you. Are you coming?"

Gabriella realized with annoyance that the servant
would stolidly repeat the question until she heard the only
answer she was prepared to accept. "Yes, I'm coming,"
she sighed.

It wouldn't always be like this, she vowed. Once
Gabriella had established herself as mistress of this
household, there would be a few changes. She did not
share her father's sense of irony where the French were
concerned, and still less did she like being herded around
by the servants. She would have to scare them a little. She
had developed a killingly funny imitation of the overstern
mathematics teacher, Sister Maria Angelina, and with a
little anger and the natural Terasatti imperiousness behind
it, it would silence even the conveniently non-Italian-
speaking Suzette.

She allowed herself a moment to collect herself, then
rose from her bed and went to her dressing mirror. The
glass was old and a little warped, but she loved the gilt
frame of the thing and the way that in the half-light it
made her reflection look like an antique portrait. She
pinned up her hair in a bun, then slipped on a heavy black
mourning dress, which she had to button every half inch
from the floor up. It seemed a meditation to her, like
saying the rosary, and stilled her thoughts so that she was
most properly serene as she descended two floors of winding staircase to the reception below.

Relatives were crowded into the parlor, all draped in

black lustring coats, veils, hats and other tidy bits of funereal paraphernalia worn at just the proper angle and length, all cut and fitted so perfectly that the effect could be called fashionable.

Dorothea Scalini, an aunt on her mother's side, assumed the position of family matron by virtue of her age. She sat quietly on a blue satin couch bracing herself to meet the other family members, who were dutifully marching up to offer their condolences. She was a plump woman, especially at the hips, so that her flattened bulge on the seat pulled her black dress into tight creases. For the funeral she had covered her grey hair in a tight plain scarf and worn her special gold earrings, miniature crucifixes pinned through her lobes. Her eyes were wet and red.

So were everyone else's. None of them had seen Maria Terasatti more than once a year for the last twenty, but the death of a relative meant more to a family than the loss of an individual. It was more like the loss of an appendage, a disfigurement of the clan, a reminder of mortality. They were no longer whole. Something had been taken out of the heart of every person there.

Gabriella stood quietly on the staircase. No one noticed her at first, not even Francesco Speranza, to whom her hand had been promised at her birth. He was a gaunt fellow with too prominent a nose and a limp way of weaving his hands during a conversation that reminded her of the meticulous way a spider moves its forelegs.

She watched him for a long moment. Someone must have told him a joke, because he started laughing uncontrollably, though not boisterously because he never made any noise when he laughed. His mouth would hang open, and his eyes would tear, but only an occasional wheeze escaped his throat.

The sight offended her. It was obscene. How could they laugh when her mother had just died? Suddenly decorum deserted her and she cried in anger and frustration. She couldn't help herself. She buried her face in her hands. She didn't want anyone to see her.

There was a small crowd surrounding her aunt Dorothea. She formed a circle around herself, and the men, more reserved, stood back, uncomfortable in starched collars and cravats. Everyone sweated in the humid air. Young children, bored, impatient and confused, shifted from foot to foot and sucked their fingers.

Gabriella, standing at the foot of the staircase, dabbed at her reddened nose with a linen handkerchief she took from her sleeve. Dorothea and another sister, Tessa, were crying loudly at each other.

"She was such a good girl, Tessa," Dorothea cried. "She was the best sister a woman could have."

"God will take care of her, Dorothea," Tessa cried back.

"She was such a kind, dear, generous woman."

Gabriella did not remember her mother as being particularly kind or generous, except that she often made a point of insisting that she didn't mind giving her money to the church as long as it helped to guarantee her a place among the heavenly elect.

However, one had a right to say good things about one's own sister, even if they weren't true. It wasn't the elegaic lying that bothered her. It was the tone of their voices, the theatrical, exaggerated whine, affected to impress everyone with the quality of their mourning.

Funerals were full of women like these, full of men like Francesco Speranza and her father. To them it was all a show, a chance to act, no different from standing on a stage to make a wonderful display of their emotions, and Gabriella hated it all. There would be people like these at her own funeral, and the thought filled her with rage.

"I think she knew she was going to die, you know?"

Dorothea sobbed. "She said to me just last year, 'Dorothea, keep me in your prayers.' Why, Tessa? Why does God do these things? How can He take such a good girl from her family?"

Her mother wasn't a girl, Gabriella thought bitterly. She was nearly sixty when she died.

"God has His reasons," Tessa said sagely. "We just have to accept what He gives us. That's all we can do. We should thank Him that He has left us an image of our little sister in that beautiful child Gabriella."

"Oh, my poor Gabriella," Dorothea wailed. "All alone over there. Are you all right?"

Madonna, help me, Gabriella prayed, help me be civil to these people. "Yes, I'm fine," she said, shivering with tears.

"Why don't you come over and sit with us?" said one of the aunts.

Gabriella didn't pay attention to which mouth had spoken. "I'm all right. Thank you. I'm all right over here." Again she had to cover her face with her hands to cry.

"Dear Gabriella."

"Dear, dear Gabriella."

After all the relatives arrived and murmured their condolences, they moved into the huge dining room to accept a free meal under a wrought iron chandelier that held sixty-six candles—one was added every year on Don Antonio's birthday. The long oak dining table had been set with courses from one end to the other. The most popular of the hundred-odd dishes were fish soup, thin slices of stewed beef rolled up with pine nuts, pastas of every variety, sausages, bridal soup of escarole, meatballs and dumplings garnished with lacy egg-white in chicken stock— Gabriella had ordered it, but she could not remember it all, let alone eat it.

Only Aunt Rosa, Don Antonio's stepsister, remained in the parlor with Gabriella. She sat back with a long sigh in an old rocking chair and began telling her beads out loud.

Gabriella, though she tried not to listen, found herself silently reciting the Latin along with her aunt. After all, this was the only decency afforded the dead.

"Gabriella, why aren't you in the dining room with the family?" Don Antonio appeared from the library. He was a tall stout man with a goatee and slicked-down black hair liberally sprinkled with yellowish grey. He had an elegant aquiline nose and hands that seemed too big even for his considerable size. As always, he was dressed in a suit too elegant for his bearing.

Now, however, there was something much more unusual in his appearance. To his left arm a woman had attached herself. She was not dressed in the customary black, but in a high-color ruffled silk blouse and a shiny green skirt that didn't quite make it over her ankles. Her hair was ash blond, her eyes deep green, her bosom ample.

Gabriella had never seen the woman before but knew who she was. It was no secret that her father kept a mistress in Capua. Her own mother had spoken openly of this other woman with rather forced good-natured indulgence. Now her mother wasn't even cold in the grave and already her father had brought this slut home to warm his bed.

"Aunt Dorothea is seeing to the guests quite well, Papa," she answered stiffly.

The other woman was staring at her boldly with the smile one might give a shy child.

"Dorothea ain't the mistress of this house," he said. "You are."

"It seems I am not the only mistress in this house, Papa." Her spite was tempered with an involuntary sob.

"What do you mean by that? Come here and say what you mean."

Gabriella picked up her skirts and went over to her father without hesitation. She was afraid of him when he looked like this, his eyes wide so that the whites showed all around and the nostrils of his nose flared out like an angry bull's, but she would not show fear. If anything she would scorn him, make him angrier. He had no right to bring that woman into the house.

Aunt Rosa sat rocking with her eyes closed, droning Ave Marias. Her obliviousness to her brother's temper was not accidental. It had taken years of practice; she often said so.

"Are you talking about one of my guests?" Don Antonio demanded of his daughter. The woman on his arm seemed less sure of herself and her smile was faltering.

"You understand to whom I am referring, Papa. It is a matter of indifference to me whether anyone else comprehends or not." It always infuriated Papa to hear her talk like a schoolmarm, as he put it. Gabriella gave the woman a nasty look, impartially rude. They both had it coming.

Her father's voice became quiet but not gentle. "You better say you're sorry, girl."

"You degrade the memory of my mother and I cannot be sorry for anything but that circumstance."

Without warning he slapped her so hard that she spun halfway around, tripped and fell to one knee. "You are a monster and she is no better," she shrieked through her pain and mortification.

"My guest is Signorina Brigetta di Boromeo. You will take her hand and welcome her to our house."

"Antonio, please, the young lady is overwrought," Signorina di Boromeo said, but he paid her no attention. She was nothing but a prop.

"Gabriella, get up and face me. You will take the signorina's hand."

Gabriella put the back of her hand to her mouth and swallowed hard to keep him from hearing her sobs. She did not answer.

A man peeked in from the dining room. "Is anything wrong in here? Is someone ill?"

Gabriella recognized him. He was a second cousin who had come down from Rome. He rapidly took in the scene, hungry for gossip. Don Antonio made no explanations. "Get the hell out of here and mind your own business," he said. The young man vanished.

"If you think you can make me disrespect the memory of my mother by welcoming this—this signorina into our house, then you are very much mistaken, Papa. Better you cast me into the street and let that be my house."

"You are a foolish girl. Your mother knew Brigetta very well."

"Yes, they must have been the best of friends. They had so much in common." Gabriella turned and faced them both. "Maybe they shared you, but they did not share me. I am not this woman's daughter."

"No one said you were."

"No? Then tell me, is she not to move into the house? Is she not to become its mistress as well as yours?"

"Do you think I would bring a woman into my family without marrying her?" He was indignant, defensive.

"Does he plan to marry you, then?" she asked Signorina di Boromeo.

"We have made no decision yet, my dear."

Don Antonio's voice rasped and hissed as he spoke. "I have decided. I marry where I please. I don't take orders from no one. Do you hear me, girl? Brigetta will be my wife and you will accept her. I give the orders around here. I own this house, I own this land and I own you. I am king here, I am god! Whatever I want is mine and I want you to take the signorina's hand.''

Gabriella was shaken by his vehemence but determined not to be cowed by it. ''I will not accept her in this house. You have not behaved well at all. Because of you the Terasatti name has no dignity. We have no pride. You have made my mother and me as well as yourself look as common as she does. Look at her, dressed like a strumpet in a house of death. I would not shake hands with such a one in church on a feast day if she saved my life, let alone at my own mother's wake. What were all those fancy tears at the funeral if you were just coming back to show off your profligacy? If you think you own me, then do what you want to me, but you won't change my mind.''

''Please, Antonio, let me speak to her,'' the signorina said and placed her hand gently on his shoulder.

''Go ahead. Who's stopping you?''

''Go into the other room with your guests. Let the women talk.''

He was still seething, but he mustered calm enough to let Brigetta try where he had failed. ''Talk some sense into her head,'' he said, ''or I will beat some sense into it.''

Before he left the room, he jostled his sister Rosa, still praying. Her eyes opened with a start, as if she had been fast asleep. ''Come on, get something to eat,'' he said, hauling her from the room.

''Can we sit and talk?'' Brigetta suggested.

''I would prefer to stand,'' Gabriella said. She was slightly taller than the other woman, and standing, the signorina's age did not seem such an advantage.

''Well. At least you're willing to talk. It's a start.''

The signorina had lost the purring femininity she assumed with Don Antonio. Neither did she pretend to any overtures of friendship, as Gabriella half expected. She was courteous but to the point.

"Your father and I have loved each other for many years, Gabriella. You cannot change that. You may accept it or ignore it, but you cannot take it away from us."

Gabriella's eyes snapped with fire. "Why are you here? Why couldn't you wait? Why couldn't you even dress decently?"

"Your father needs me now. He has lost his wife. He needs someone to comfort him. And he asked me to wear colors to cheer him."

"I could comfort and cheer him just fine."

"You are a daughter. You cannot minister to him in the way he desires."

Gabriella turned her face away. "Your speech is full of filth."

"It is full of love for a man. Can't you understand that?"

"He is not full of love for you. You are his mistress. He pays for you, does he not? He loved my mother."

"He respected your mother. He honored her. But if he had any love for her, it was only because she gave him a daughter he loves very much."

This is nonsense, Gabriella thought almost in panic, absolute nonsense. What does this stranger know of my father's feelings for me? He dotes on me like a pet, in the same way as his favorite donkey. Has he spoken to her of me? To think so made Gabriella feel displaced, like a child who suddenly found herself in the care of strangers. This woman had no right to know anything about Gabriella. She was a trespasser.

"In a way your mother's death has been a blessing to him, though he would never say so, even to me. It was she who insisted you be sent away to boarding school. He missed you terribly."

"Of course she insisted. If I had remained at home, he would have kept me locked up like a Carmelite. My mother wanted me to see something of the world, to have friends, to learn.''

"Are you sure? Maybe you were simply a burden to her."

"Now you want to poison me against her. Is this what you have done to my father? You bring disease into our house."

The signorina made herself comfortable on a sofa. She had high, angular cheekbones and a mouth that seemed a little too wide. Her chin was small and round and delicate. Her eyebrows had been carefully painted in dramatic little arches, and her eyes in that light seemed as soft as a doe's.

Gabriella understood why her father had been attracted to her. By contrast her own mother was dowdy, a grey-haired matron with an ample bosom that sagged with age, broad pasta-fed hips and eyes of light green, furtive and best fit for seeking out a good buy.

"Your father, of course, was not telling the truth. Your mother and I were not friendly, though he may have convinced himself that we were. We despised and pitied each other. We both wanted the same man. We both understood what loving Don Antonio and not possessing him meant. But we were pulling, always pulling against each other.

"Gabriella, maybe I do speak ill when I should not, but I am afraid that your mother dead will come to be more of a wife than she ever was in life. So I am fighting for him. I love him and I want him and I will have him. If you do not wish me to live in your mother's house, then I will respect your wish for the sake of peace between us. I will remain in Capua and your father can live with me there. You cannot stop that. I will fight for him until I win.

"So you have a choice. You can accept me here and

keep your father or you can turn me away and your father with me. It makes little difference to me and perhaps it is less to you than your pride. But I promise you, it will make a great difference to Antonio. If he loses either of us, it will break his heart.''

Gabriella stood with her eyes cast down. Her cheek still burned from the blow of her father's hand. This di Boromeo woman was a vampire, a bloodsucker, a destroyer of families. She wanted nothing less than to become the heart of this household.

Gabriella realized there was no way to stop her. She was right. A daughter could not comfort a father in the same way a mistress could, and her father, as clever and powerful as he was, could easily allow his brains to be swayed by the arguments of his loins. If that weren't true, he would never have brought her here to parade in front of the entire family at his own wife's funeral reception. So what was there to do, step aside? Give up her rights, her place in the family?

Then another thought enraged her and seemed to knock the wind from her chest: this woman was still young enough to have children. A new family would be started. Gabriella would become an extra appendage, a reminder of another spirit, another time in this household. She would be resented or ignored. Not turned out, of course; her father wouldn't do that on purpose, but living here might be worse.

And then the thought concluded itself: she would not live here under these circumstances at all. All this nonsense was staged simply to salve her father's guilt. She had been promised to Francesco. Her father would marry her off and that would be the end of all his problems.

It was so easy for a man. There were any number of ways for them to slip and slide out of trouble. Women were always somehow trapped in their situations.

It was no different even for this ruthless mistress. She was making the best life for herself that she could because there was nothing else for her to do. What future did she have without Gabriella's father? Where could she go, what could she do? Her only way of protecting herself was to move from the outskirts of his affections to the center, to nest deep within the tree, where she could not be moved without cutting it down. There were no choices for Signorina Brigetta di Boromeo.

Gabriella's father was the only one with choices, the only one who depended on nobody's power but his own to live. If he called himself a king and a god he wasn't so far from truth. As with any king, there were voices in his ear. Gabriella was determined that one of those voices would be her own. If the signorina's predicament was understandable, it was still no more excusable in Gabriella's eyes. Let her go find another tree to nest in. Gabriella would not allow herself to be married off and be forced to give up her heritage and her birthright.

It is not my mother's ghost in my father's memory that you should fear, signorina, she vowed silently. I am my mother's ghost, and I will haunt my father's life and make him miserable until he throws you into the street where you belong.

"Well, Gabriella, shall we break his heart? Will he lose one of us?"

"You mean will he lose me, don't you?"

"I'm afraid it would end in no other way."

"Very well. Marry him. I won't stand in your way."

"I'm glad you've come to your senses."

People always think you've come to your senses once you go their way, Gabriella thought. She had the feeling that if she leaped off a cliff after this woman, she would have heard the same remark on the way down.

Don Antonio appeared in the doorway. "There are

two empty seats at the table. The guests have already started eating, but your absence has been noticed.''

"We are coming this very moment, Antonio."

"Has my daughter calmed herself?"

"Oh, yes, we are the best of friends now, aren't we, Gabriella?"

Gabriella swept past her newfound friend. "We have come to an agreement," she said and slipped past her father in the doorway.

Don Antonio shook his head. "Women," he grumbled, letting his eye roam over the fine, aristocratic features of his mistress, then down to her shapely bosom and over the curve of her ample hips. "Impossible, all of you. *Ma molta bella.*"

The dinner was noisy. The servants banged and clattered, the children were full of their usual fuss and the adults argued politics.

Italy had gone to war with the Austrians. Everyone was being inducted into the army, or so the young men insisted to impress everyone, though in fact only the sons of the poor had to go. It was easy enough to buy your way out of the draft or to get someone to go in your place for the right money.

Don Antonio had many connections in the government and could be very helpful in this regard if you were on his good side. It was due to these connections that the mausoleum wall was to be paid for with government funds, as he had managed to have the villa and the estate recorded in the registry of public landmarks. In the eyes of the beaurocrats the Villa Vichierri was no different from the Colosseum.

Francesco Speranza had already taken advantage of Don Antonio's influence. He had received his induction notice, but the good don had been kind enough to see to it that he was excused from service. The official reason: Francesco was supposed to have lost an arm in an accident when he was a child.

When he thought about that it had a strange effect on him. He began to feel at times just a little guilty for having all his limbs. He often held his hands in front of him and wondered which one was supposed to have been lost. He had not been told.

He believed that he really was not fit for service, but for a different reason. He had a very nervous temperament and was given to flights of fancy. The merest thought of going into battle frightened him so badly that once he wet his pants over it when he saw what a gun could do to a partridge during the annual bird shootings outside of Naples in the fall.

Of course he never confided any of this to Gabriella. He didn't want to her to think him a coward. He was in love with her, and desperately. He had done nothing to deserve her, he knew, but by a stroke of luck she would be his for the rest of his life through no effort of his own. It was this fact that made him religious. The idea of God and the Virgin and the rest of it all seemed ludicrous to him, but yet how could there be no God if miracles like his fortunate betrothal happened?

There was only one small shadow on this sunny future of his. Gabriella didn't seem to love him so desperately at all. During their few moments together since her return from school, she had seemed—though he hated to admit it—a trifle bored. When he tried to make a joke, she smiled, but her smile seemed to him to be suspiciously like a restrained yawn. If she thought so little of him now, what would she think if she knew that her father had bought his way out of the army?

Gabriella, who was sitting next to him, seemed to be making a point of talking to everyone but him. It annoyed him, but at least he felt under no obligation to think of clever things to say. He had to admit that he really was not very witty.

By the end of the meal Francesco, like most of the men there, was a little drunk. The wine cellars had been opened and the steward kept the crystal carafes filled. Inebriation didn't make him brave, but it did eliminate his judgment.

He wanted to say something that would capture Gabriella's attention, but nothing came to him. His mind, such as it was, was a blank. He didn't even know if they had any interests in common. What did a young woman do at a boarding school? Certainly she went to mass every day, and to class. She would have lunch. Did they serve wine to young women at lunch? Or milk? Wine would be natural. Who could have a meal without wine?

The nuns weren't supposed to drink it. On the other hand, he knew young women, or at least he'd heard about them. If they weren't served wine at lunch, it would be a perfect invitation for them to sneak some. Any farmer would sell them all they wanted. Yes, they would probably buy a bottle and keep it hidden under a bed, and at night, when they were supposed to be asleep, they would take a few sips and giggle and wrestle as young girls did.

Maybe they would then sneak out of their rooms and make love to the gardener. There was no telling what a young girl was capable of after a few too many sips of wine, but he had some idea. He had read Boccaccio, after all, and it was very pleasing to think about.

All these thoughts danced and hovered in his head like bees, though he didn't realize he was thinking them. When they escaped the hive, they came out in a question he didn't realize he was about to ask. "So, Gabriella, how was it at school? I hope you didn't fall in love with the gardener. I am given to understand all the young girls do.''

Gabriella spilled a little espresso from her cup onto the white linen tablecloth. She put the cup down and looked at him as if he had just cursed out loud in church. ''We do our own gardening.''

He frowned. ''Then who makes love to you when you get drunk?''

''I think perhaps it's you who are drunk, signor.'' She dabbed at her lips with her napkin, then excused herself and left the room. The ones sitting close enough to hear looked at him curiously and with amused compassion. He was obviously a little out of control, swaying in his seat like a wooden top beginning to slow down.

The minor commotion of Gabriella's departure attracted the attention of several others at the table. Voices fell away like dominoes. Soon the entire crowd was staring down the table at the young man.

Francesco only vaguely realized what he had done.

Don Antonio didn't know and didn't care. He laughed. ''Anyone who has such an effect on my daughter must be good for her.'' The others laughed as well. ''Maybe you better go and talk to her, Francesco. Whatever you did, she'll forgive you. Women always do. Take it from me.''

Francesco rose unsteadily and made for the archway into the parlor, but not before Don Antonio could give him a warning. ''Don't get too charming, and watch your hands.'' This brought a great silent laugh up from Francesco's belly.

Don Antonio was not smiling.

Chapter 8

There was a hard clack at the front door as someone used the stiff iron knocker. Gabriella heard it just as she came into the room. There was no one else to answer it. It was not always safe to answer a door. A man like her father made many enemies. They once had a butler killed by a shotgun blast. However, after what that fool Francesco said to her at the table, she was angry enough to do anything. She would sooner marry a jackass.

She yanked the door open wide, ready to meet another long-lost relative with the unfriendliest greeting she could repeat without having to go to confession. There under the front canopy was the stonemason, the idiot who had almost killed himself. She recognized him in spite of his changed appearance. He was dressed in a finely made brown suit with a bow tie and a folded collar. His shoes were so perfectly shined that the rain congealed into little droplets on them and rolled off in streams. He carried a huge umbrella.

"What do you want here?" she blurted.

He raised his head and stared at her for a long moment. At first he seemed to recognize her; then his expression turned blank.

"I have come to pay my repects to Don Antonio for the loss of his wife," he said.

"Don Antonio is sitting at his supper," she replied politely. "Come another time." She was unsettled at seeing him this way. He had already proved himself a crazy man. And there was something else, the sudden shock of seeing a creature from her dreams her waking world; although he was a man now, she realized at once that she had seen him before. He was the boy who stole her rosary.

"Please, signorina, I have walked a long way in the rain. I am a mason and work for him. I am working on the wall around the mausoleum. I only wish to offer my condolences."

Somehow she would never have expected this of him. He was talking like one of the parasites who were always finding ways of attaching themselves to her father.

Well, why shouldn't he? He was no different from anyone else. He had no more choices where the don was concerned than she or Signorina Brigetta did. If you wanted to live in the kingdom, you had to pay homage to the king.

"Gabriella, who is at the door?" It was Francesco, close behind her.

Even if he was a drunken clod, the sound of someone familiar nearby made her feel easier. "It's a man who works for Papa. He wants to come in and offer his condolences."

"Your father?" Giorgio said with surprise. "Signorina Terasatti?"

"Yes. Perhaps you were at the wall a few days ago when I returned from a trip to Caserta. I saw some workmen. I came up the plateau road in a cart."

"Oh, yes." Giorgio laughed nervously. "Some crazy guy was hanging off the wall making a fool of himself to impress you."

"Oh, is that what he was doing? He was doing it very well."

Francesco came up behind her and peered over his

shoulder. "How do you do. I am Francesco Speranza, Gabriella's fiance."

Gabriella was immediately annoyed. Once again she didn't like strangers hearing the details of her life. "Why don't you go back into the dining room, Francesco." Her tone made it a command. "I won't be a minute."

"Your father sent me out here to apologize to you."

"I accept your apology. It's very nice. Now go."

"But I haven't made it yet."

She turned to the door. "You may as well come in, Signor—?"

"Farenza, signorina, Giorgio Farenza." He made a few little bows with his head. "Thank you. It's very damp out there."

For many years his face had been fixed in her memory. That moment in the alleyway, that single moment of rebellion in her life, was for her a moment of magic. Even in the dizziness of cigarette smoke for once she knew the exhilaration of freedom, of following an impulse, even a slightly sinful one. This very man had given her that moment. She often wondered what had become of him and what it might be like to know him better. That afternoon on the wall he had behaved foolhardily, but she suddenly found that charming. Who else had ever behaved in such a way for her benefit?

Of course it was all nonsense. Though this fellow wasn't exactly a *bracciante*, he wasn't a *signore* either, a man of wealthy or noble family. He was hardly a proper subject for her dreams. She sighed.

At less distance she could see more resemblance between this fellow and the boy who once gave her a cigarette. He had grown into quite a handsome man. His eyes were still so light a blue you could almost lose yourself in them. His features were very fine, with a straight, narrow nose and lovely stern cheekbones, though he looked a little drawn, as if underfed.

"Now, Francesco," she said, "if you want to make an apology to me in front of Mr. Farenza, whom you don't even know, please feel free to do so. Otherwise I will consider it already done and you need say no more."

Francesco flushed and Giorgio looked embarrassed for him. Men are always on the lookout for each other, she thought with annoyance, though it was only a repetition of something she often heard from the girls at school.

"It was very nice to meet you, Mr. Farenza," Francesco said. Giorgio mumbled a complimentary reply but was beginning to look harassed by the whole situation. Francesco backed out of the room as if unsure he should leave them alone.

As soon as he was gone, Gabriella grabbed Giorgio's arm. It was an impulse. She no longer felt frightened of him; he seemed tame now, and she was curious to know more about him. And what a fine way to infuriate her father. "Take me for a walk in the rain, Mr. Farenza."

"We'll get soaking wet."

"You have an umbrella, don't you?"

"What about your father?"

"What about him? Francesco will tell him you're here alone with me and he'll be out in a second. Take me for a walk, quick, before he gets here. You're not afraid of Don Antonio, are you? Perhaps you're not as brave as I thought when you were hanging from the wall."

He rolled his eyes, shook his head and held the door for her.

Giorgio held the umbrella up for them both, though Gabriella had a difficult time keeping her hand off the shaft. She was used to doing things for herself. Every time a gust of wind sprayed her with a cold mist, she felt herself automatically reaching up to grab the thing, but etiquette proved more powerful than instinct, and she kept her impulse under control by folding her fingers together and holding her hands to her bosom. She was directing Giorgio down the cobblestone carriage drive at the front of the villa toward the gatehouse.

"Have we ever met before, Mr. Farenza?" she asked him as they walked along. She wondered if he remembered that day in the grotto of Our Lady so many years before.

He glanced at her briefly, shyly. "A man like me doesn't very often meet people like you, signorina."

"Then certainly you would recall if we had."

"I think so. Yes."

She smiled and gritted her teeth in exasperation. He had not answered her question, but if she asked him again, she would feel like an idiot.

Giorgio walked stiffly and quietly for a few steps before speaking again. "It was very strange what the fellow did up on the wall, you know? He could have killed himself."

"Yes, it was very foolish. But I was quite deliciously complimented even so."

"Were you?" he asked eagerly.

She looked at him with reassuring eyes. "Yes, I was."

"I wonder what your father would say if he heard about it."

"Who knows? He probably never will."

She found the look of relief that passed over his face slightly amusing, but she also found herself wishing her name were something other than Terasatti. It seemed to make men so fearful for themselves whenever they were reminded of her father.

They had hardly gone another three steps when through the hiss of the downpour Gabriella heard her name called out. It was her father. Giorgio stopped as if at the end of a chain.

"We should go back," he said.

His timidity annoyed her. "Why does my father frighten you so much? Because you might lose your job?"

"No. Because he might kill me for being alone with his daughter."

"Don't worry. I won't let him." She wished she could see his face more clearly in the dark. She had to bend her neck back to look at him at all. He was very tall and his shoulders were rather broad. The sudden realization of how small she felt next to him let her take ambivalent comfort in the sound of her father's voice angrily calling for her again and again. It was like having a watchdog ready to attack at her command. Still, for a fellow with such shoulders this mason might have been a little braver.

"I'm not a coward," Giorgio said indignantly, "but I ain't going to be the one to test a lion's appetite by acting like a piece of pork. Your father has a certain reputation."

"I know about his reputation. You think it's true?"

"Sure, don't you?"

"All right, then. Let's go back." Her voice was so full of ridicule that his veto seemed almost forced from his throat.

"Oh, now it's no. And why not?"

"Because I won't have you think I am a coward."

"How could you be a coward? I saw you hanging from the wall. You almost killed yourself." Even as she spoke she realized there was some truth in it, but she had embarrassed him by such a bald admission. In the darknesss she could almost feel him turn scarlet. Good. He deserved it. Let him stew for a little while.

After all, who was he to make fun of her because she had never smoked a cigarette? But that was years ago. What was wrong with her? They had been kids and he obviously didn't even remember. Perhaps she would remind him.

"All right, then. Into the gatehouse," she said, practically dragging him forward by the sleeve.

He resisted automatically and she gave him a yank that nearly pulled him off his feet. "Come on," she said, "or else take me back to my father and let him beat me."

He allowed himself to be pulled along now. "Beat you? What for?"

"For being alone with a man."

"What are you talking about? We only been out here a minute. What could we do in a minute?"

"Nothing, but he won't stop to think about that."

"He has no right to beat you."

"All right, then, why don't you stop him? Why don't you tell him what you think?"

"Maybe I will."

As much as she hated to admit it, he was probably right the first time. His instincts had been true. Her father could be a cruel man, even where his own family was concerned. He thought of himself as an emperor; in fact, he once commissioned a bust of Julius Caesar from a local artisan that had his, Don Antonio's, features on the face.

The gatehouse was a one-room dirt-floored hovel much like the houses of the contadini along the streets of Santa Barbara. Only the stonework of the walls made it distinct, and in that regard it was quite distinct. Every cornice and corner, every pitch and niche had been decorated with carefully set beach pebbles of a hundred different colors, none bigger than a pearl, and all set by hand. Giorgio lit a lantern on a broken-down table, the only piece of furniture in the room.

Don Antonio had not hired a gatekeeper in years. He didn't see the need. You couldn't pay a gatekeeper enough to ensure his loyalty. Bodyguards who lived in the house were a better investment.

"Why did you bring me in here?" Giorgio wanted to know.

"To catch a smoke," she said.

He looked at her quizzically.

"Excuse me," she said with an ironic little twist at the corner of her mouth, "but I thought you always carried a pack."

"Sure, right here." He reached into his coat pocket and pulled out a crumpled package of tobacco. He poured a little of it into a small square of brown paper, carefully spread it evenly along the plain edge, rolled it into a cylinder and licked the edge with the glue.

"Ah, you make your own now. You've gained some experience."

"What are you talking about?"

"You really don't remember me. I'm hurt."

Giorgio narrowed his eyes and looked at her more closely. "Should I know you, signorina?"

So he really didn't remember. She felt disappointed and foolish. What did she care what a stonemason remembered?

"Yes, you know me. You gave me a cigarette beneath a statue of Our Lady. It was many years ago."

At first it still didn't seem to mean anything to him, but a smile crept slowly into his expression. "On the day my brother and his wife left for America."

"I wouldn't know, Signor Farenza. I only know you taught me an excellent habit."

He shook his head and she smiled proudly. She felt she had kept faith with him all through the years. He held the cigarette out for her and she lit it, inhaled deeply, then let out the smoke with the long, slow, appreciative hiss of the connoisseur. There, let him think about that. She could see by the amusement and disapproval in his expression that he still didn't think a woman should have a cigarette. Good. That made it even better. Some things hadn't changed. Her dream about this moment had born fruit.

"Of course it was you," he said as if to himself. "The eyes are the same and the voice isn't too different."

"Here, share with me." She handed him the cigarette. It was a little intimacy that she should not, she knew, allow, but he had occupied her dreams for so long that it was really like sharing with an old friend.

"Does your father know you smoke?" he asked her without returning the butt.

"No, of course not. Don't be silly." She snatched it out of his hand and took a quick puff.

"I don't know if it looks very good on you." He took it back.

"That's not what you said before."

"Before! As if it were the day before yesterday." He cast the thing down and stamped on it.

"Hey, what did you do that for?" Her own foot stamped a little as she spoke.

"Because you make me feel like I've committed a terrible sin, making you smoke."

"You didn't make me. I liked it."

"Gabriella!" Don Antonio's voice was getting closer.

"Quick, the lantern," she said. Giorgio snuffed it. She reached into the dark to find him with her hand. She grazed his forearm with her fingertips and snatched them away as she realized she had touched him. "Perhaps you should go before he finds us here."

"What will you do?"

"I'll be all right. Don't worry about me."

"He'll beat you."

"No he won't. I lied to you," she lied. She had a feeling she wouldn't be able to get rid of him otherwise. "Now go. If he finds us together, not only will he beat me, he'll probably shoot you as well."

"Gabriella!" Don Antonio was headed straight for them by the sound of his voice. She gave the young man an urgent little shove, and before she could stop him, he leaned forward and put a tiny kiss on her lips, so light, so quick it could have been a hummingbird sipping at a flower. Just as quickly, just as deftly, her hand flew in a wide arc and slapped him across the cheek.

"Don't you dare, you son of a bitch," she growled at him, but he was already on his way out the window and didn't take time to answer. She was overwhelmed with shame and mortification and already trying to erase the sensation from her lips with quick little wipes of her fingers. No man had ever touched her in such a way before, and as far as she was concerned, no man ever would again except her husband.

That brought the face of Francesco to mind, that vacuous, nervous, overapologetic face that she knew she would one day have to wake up to in the morning. The thought sickened her. Men, why didn't they go to hell, all of them? She didn't want anything to do with them.

Maybe she would go into the convent. She had thought about it often enough; the nuns made sure of that. Maybe she would think about it more seriously. Other girls spoke of a religious vocation with horror, as of a fate like falling off a boat and drowning or being bitten by a snake.

To Gabriella, however, the religious life seemed like a rather simple way to pass away your days. There was a routine, the same every day—a little boring, true, but the sisters sometimes hinted at a religious ecstasy that went beyond the domestic satisfactions of a husband and children.

Ah, there was the real reason she had never made the final decision to take her vows—children. She was no different from anybody else. She was a woman, and what else was a woman for?

Nonetheless, there was a limit. Children meant a husband, and now she wasn't at all sure she wanted a husband. Men were always touching her—her father hitting her, Francesco pawing her shoulders, and now this mason, this peasant, kissing her.

The feeling wouldn't leave her lips. They felt as if they had been dried out and she couldn't moisten them again.

"Gabriella, where are you? Come to me right now or I'll make you regret it for the rest of your life."

Her father was carrying his cane, tapping it along the ground like a blind man. It was an affectation with him, like his Spanish cigars and satin cravats and pomaded mustache.

"I'm in here, Papa, in the gatehouse," she called out.

Don Antonio found the door and stumbled inside. He wasn't carrying a light. "Where are you? Show yourself."

"I don't have a lantern."

"What are you doing in here? Francesco said you left with a man. I'll break your neck. I'll break every bone in your body."

She felt oddly calm, as if her father's presence brought back order and predictability. She wasn't afraid of him at all, though she knew he might very well do what he threatened.

"Francesco is an idiot," she said. "Even if I am promised to him, I don't feel shy about saying so."

"Why would he lie about a thing like that?" He was still searching for her with his cane, though not so persistently. She moved away from the noise easily. She could make out her father's silhouette now that her eyes were used to the dark, and she stayed on the opposite side of the room from him. "He may be an idiot, but he's no liar."

"A man came to the door to offer his condolences to the family. I sent him away."

"What man? A man I don't know? If he's been

fooling around with my daughter in front of her own fiance, he's had it. I'll have his throat cut." He stopped moving now. "Ah there you are." His own eyes were adjusting too.

"He said he was a mason, Papa, one of the men working on the new wall. Why would I go anywhere with such a man?"

"Who knows why you do what you do," he replied testily, "the way you embarrassed me before Brigetta tonight."

"You should be glad I'm here to protect you."

"I don't need your protection. I choose whatever woman I want, just like I chose your mother. And I'll tell you something else. If I find out who this guy is, I'll have his balls on the mantelpiece in the parlor, you hear me?"

He swung viciously at her with his cane, but she was spry enough to duck safely away.

"Papa, stop, please. You'll hurt me."

"Yes, I'll hurt you. I'll cripple you." He swung again. She could see the thin malacca whip through the blackness and then she felt it strike her legs, heavy and brutal and burning. She staggered for a moment, then found the doorway. "Leave me alone," she screeched and she managed to hobble out into the rain.

He was right behind her. He had driven himself into a frenzy and he was swinging wildly. If he caught her while he was in this state, he really would kill her, she knew. The cane came down behind her and slapped the mud. He slipped to one knee and she gained a little distance, but she couldn't really run. Her leg pained her too much.

Don Antonio came on again, and once again she heard something go down behind her, but this time it was a much heavier sound. She turned just in time to see the figure of a man holding up a closed umbrella run into the darkness beyond the front gate.

"Papa, are you all right?" she said in sudden panic. She no more wanted him to be hurt than she wanted to be hurt herself. Who else did she have but him? And he loved her, she knew he did. Even if he did get into a mood sometimes, even if he did philander with a prostitute, he was her father and he loved her. Didn't he pet her and kiss her sometimes, and hadn't he told her stories about witches and haunted lakes when she was a little girl, and hadn't he taken her to church and made her go to communion every Sunday since she was six? He loved her, and . . .

"Papa, where are you? Are you all right?"

She limped and slipped and scrambled on one hand and both legs, then finally came upon him, lying huddled in the mud. There was a small cut on one side of his head, and it seemed to be bleeding, though the rain diluted and washed away the blood as fast as it appeared. She cried and took his head in her hand and kissed his wound, then cried again, and finally, in a panic, made her way to the house.

Who had done this? Who had hurt her father? It had to be the mason, Giorgio Farenza, the one who gave cigarettes to little girls and claimed not to be afraid of the don. It had to be him, and may God feed his soul to the devil. Men, they were all the same, violent filthy brutes. If they weren't beating women, they beat each other or went to war and shot guns at each other. She would be a nun. She didn't want anything to do with these so-called men.

Still, hadn't she wanted him to be brave, to stand up to her father? Yes, of course, but not to hit him from behind and not . . . Hadn't he done it for her safety?

She found her way to the flickering gas lantern that lit the villa's front doorway and stumbled inside, covered with rain and mud.

"Oh, dear child," Aunt Tessa cried, taking Gabriella into her ample arms.

"Pray for us sinners now and at the hour of our death," droned Aunt Rosa.

"Where's your father?" Francesco demanded. "He went out after you. What have you done to him?"

"He's hurt. He fell by the gatehouse and cracked his head."

Half a dozen men leaped through the door. Brigetta di Boromeo followed them, wringing her hands in a panic. Francesco remained. "It was that mason, right? He beat the good don over the head with a brick."

"What are you talking about?" Gabriella lashed out at him. "You're crazy. You're out of your mind. I sent the mason home."

"We'll take care of him," Francesco threatened. He was eaten with jealousy. "If he hurt your father, he'll be taken care of, you can be sure."

"But I told you, it wasn't him. I saw it all. My father slipped and hit his head on the cane he carries. It put a crack in the side of his head. It wasn't the mason. I saw it all!"

Francesco, dubious and disappointed, put a comforting arm around Gabriella. When she felt its awkward weight, she pushed him away in disgust.

"Take your hands off me," she said. "And let me tell you something else. I don't want you ever to touch me, even if we are married. You hear? Never."

Francesco grew flushed and angry, but this only made Gabriella haughty and spiteful. What was anger from a man like him? Nothing. Meaningless. Yes, she would marry him, but only for the privilege of chewing him up, or maybe smoking him like a cigarette.

Aunt Tessa was scandalized by her behavior. "Gabriella, he's to be your husband. You listen to him and obey him, you hear? Your mother would be horrified if she heard you go on like this."

"My mother would be horrified at everything that has gone on here today. Why don't you go home, all of you?"

No one pretended to be horrified by her remarks; instead they were amused. Young women were always a pleasure when their anger was aroused. The young men looked at Francesco and smiled with pity. He turned his face away in shame.

Aunt Rosa reached the end of her prayers. "Amen," she said.

Don Antonio's wound was not serious, though he nursed it in bed for three days, during which time Brigetta brought him broth and wine and a little venison to keep his blood red. Gabriella waited outside his door, but he would not see her. She begged Brigetta to let her in, and in fact Brigetta was perfectly willing to do so, but as soon as the door opened the first time, he thundered that she was banished from his sight and cast something large and heavy at her. She heard it strike the heavy maple door as she slammed it shut.

"I'm sorry, Gabriella," Brigetta said, sounding as though she meant it. "He'll calm down in another day or two. You'll see."

She knew he blamed her for his misery. He didn't know what had happened, so he had to take the word of his daughter, the only witness, as it was passed to him by others. She insisted it was an accident. He insisted that if it weren't for her, he would have had no accident. Of course he would never stop to consider that he might have killed her if she hadn't run away. That would only have occurred to him had he really done it. That was his way. What could one do?

Brigetta turned out to be right. Eventually he did calm his anger, and after Gabriella made an obeisant apology, forgave her—not in a kindly way, but almost as a matter of obligation that he reluctantly and resentfully dispensed.

Gabriella never went near the wall. It was nearly finished now anyway, and soon the masons would be gone for the winter, so she would not have to see Giorgio again. Her feelings about him seemed to rise and fall like the tides. One day she would try to remember the kiss, try to remember what it felt like and why it had made her so angry. To think about it was pleasant enough.

On the next day she would remember how it was his hand that had struck her father, and that because of him misery and blame had been cast on her own head. On another day she would grow strangely misty-eyed at the thought that he had risked his life for her twice now, and she had done nothing to deserve it.

Francesco began making a pest of himself. He came over to visit almost every day now, but he was always sullen and petulant. He spoke of their marriage as of an impending day of judgment.

Finally, as much out of pity for him as in consideration for herself, she ordered him to stay away unless he received an invitation to come, but he would not oblige. Her father, after all, was Don Antonio Terasatti. There was a certain decorum that had to be followed with the daughter of a man like that. If Gabriella guessed correctly, Francesco was trying to assert his own authority, not by exerting power or commanding respect, but by refusing to be an obedient little boy to the woman he wished to dominate.

She let him have his way. Why not, if he was such a fool? She let him come to see her and ignored him completely for hours on end. Sooner or later he would learn his lesson; at least she hoped he would.

Chapter 9

"Oh, God, what am I going to do? Tell me, please, what I should do," Giorgio mumbled over and over again as he stumbled through the dark to Scarfo's cottage. A small fire burning in the hearth made the place hot and smoky. He tore off his soaked clothing and hung it over a chair to dry; then, dressed only in torn grey cotton longjohns, he poured himself a cup of strong black coffee and sat shivering on a rickety old chair in front of the fire. Scarfo was lying down, resting but awake.

"Shit," Giorgio mumbled as he thought for the hundredth time of the trouble he was in. "Shit and double shit."

"What's the matter with you?" Scarfo grumbled from the cramped platform of boards he used for a bed. "You get yourself into trouble?"

"Me?" Giorgio smiled nervously. "No. Maybe tomorrow every crook and *carabinier'* in the country will be trying to kill me, but nothing you would call real trouble."

Scarfo's chest rumbled like a waterpipe as he laughed. "What the hell did you do?" He swiveled upright and coughed until his lungs were clear.

"I hit Don Antonio on the head. Maybe I killed him. I don't know. I didn't stick around long enough to find out."

Scarfo shook his head like a stunned bull. "Agh, *managia*, what the hell is wrong with you? What made you do it? Is that why you got all dressed up, to go and kill a man?"

"What could I do? He was beating his daughter with a cane."

"Oh, sure, the daughter. I knew she had her eye on you the first time I saw her. You gotta watch these damn women, boy. They get you into a hell of a lot of trouble."

Giorgio put on an appropriate hangdog expression, but he didn't want a lecture. He wanted help. "Scarfo," he said, "I need a place to hide."

Scarfo came to his feet and adjusted one suspender. He was freshly shaven. Once a week he stropped his straight razor and scraped the stubble from his brown old face. "Sure you need a place to hide, just like a bear in the wintertime. You need a place where you can play dead for a long time until someone can persuade Don Antonio to move to another country."

"Maybe I should go to Rome."

"Or to America with your brother."

Giorgio began to pace. Nothing seemed to him like a satisfactory answer. There was no place far enough that wasn't too far. He hadn't meant to hit the don, after all. It had just happened quickly in the rain, where a man didn't have decent judgment. And Signorina Terasatti might really have been hurt.

There was the real problem. Scarfo was right. He had been captured by her at once, in a worse way even than that day on the wall. She had put a spell on him.

Imagine, she had remembered him all these years, since he was just a little dirty boy in the street. How could he resist her? He had kissed her impulsively, without intent and without authority, and of course she was within her rights to slap him for it, but even the sting of her hand gave him pleasure. He would kiss her again just for the feel of it.

Still, what could become of the feelings she had awakened in him? Now her father would shoot him on sight, maybe with a shotgun, the way the hunters shot birds from the marshes in the fall. Or maybe the razor—that was more Don Antonio's style. That would be a lesson to anyone else who might raise a hand to such a powerful man. Giorgio couldn't blame him. In the don's position he would do the same. A fellow had to protect himself, after all, especially when he was so rich and had so many enemies.

Scarfo rubbed the deep sunburnt folds at the back of his neck. "All right, there's no reason to get crazy. Be patient. Stay here for the time being. Tomorrow I'll go to work and find out what I can. Did anybody see you hit him?"

"I don't know. Maybe not."

"Well then, don't get too worried. They've probably already forgotten who you are. You're just a peasant to them, not worth remembering."

A tear of fright came to Giorgio's eye. "I told the signorina my name, and her fiance heard it too."

"Her fiance? Hey, boy, when you do something, you do it very good, eh? If you laid stone that way, I'd kill you myself."

"What am I going to do?"

"Eat something. Let me think."

He ate a bowl of white kidney beans cooked in garlic and oil and drank nearly half a bottle of *Chianti*, but Scarfo came up with no brilliant ideas. The only answer was an obvious one. "You have to go to the caves," Scarfo said. There were many of them about in this part of the countryside.

"I'm not going to live in a hole in the ground like

some damn Calabres'," Giorgio shot back angrily. The province of Calabria had become so poor over the past one hundred years that thousands of people had been forced to make permanent homes in the caverns of that area.

Scarfo's face tightened into an expression of forced patience. "My father was from Calabria," he said. "My mother was from Calabria. I too am from Calabria. If you wish to insult the man who has given you a home and food and friendship all these years, I can't stop you. I can only wait for my heart to finish breaking—"

"All right, all right, I'm sorry. The Calabres' are wonderful people, all of them. Your family especially. It's just that I'm a little upset, you understand?"

Scarfo accepted the apology with a self-righteous nod. Giorgio, annoyed as he was at the old man for making him feel such shame, was in fact very sorry for what he had said. He had come to love the old son of a bitch and he wouldn't hurt him for anything, but sometimes a guy's mouth just got away from him.

To emphasize his contrition he said, "If you think I should live in a cave, I'll live in a cave. You're older than me. You know best."

Scarfo nodded sagely. "That's right. I been around."

"Maybe I could live in the old church. Nobody goes there anymore."

"No, it's too close by. They'll look there. Don't worry. We'll find you a nice little hole in the ground in the morning. But if you killed Don Antonio, you'll have to leave the country. His people will swear a *vendetta* and they'll never forget."

"To hell with that. I ain't leaving the country."

"We'll see, boy. We'll see."

"That's right, old man. We'll see."

*   *   *

There was no word at work for the next four days. That meant at least that Don Antonio hadn't died. Otherwise everybody would be buzzing with the news and cursing their luck for losing a patron. But Giorgio wasn't necessarily off the hook. He had still clubbed the man over the head. Scarfo asked around as subtly as he could, but suspicions among the gossip-loving workmen were whetted so easily that he soon decided just to keep quiet and listen.

Giorgio's absence was easily explained; his malaria often acted up at this time of the year. Since no one showed much interest in seeing him when he came down sick, Scarfo was free from worry about that.

However, there was one peculiar circumstance: a young fellow who looked like a bleached stringbean stopped by to have a look at the job every morning. Scarfo, who didn't bother much with anybody in town, didn't recognize him, but some of the other fellows knew who he was.

He wore beautiful kid gloves and suede boots, which everyone talked about and admired—it rarely occurred to anyone to resent the rich for their possessions—but they admired him even more because he had struck it lucky by getting himself engaged to the don's daughter. Even if she was a horror to look at (until they saw for themselves they wouldn't believe otherwise), it might be worth it to take her to wife if it meant having such a powerful man for a father-in-law. A fellow could always take a mistress, after all. The rich were liberal about that sort of thing.

Scarfo immediately disliked Francesco's oversensitive and sullen looks, and he went out of his way to make himself scarce whenever Francesco was around. If Don Antonio had shown no interest in locating Giorgio, there was no doubt that this effete young man had taken up the study.

By the fifth day Scarfo was beginning to worry about

Giorgio's health. They had chosen a little pouch of a cave deep in a hillside wood to the east. It was a good hiding place, well hidden and sheltered from the wind, but its cold damp could very well touch off Giorgio's illness and there would be no way to give him proper care.

Early in the morning of this day, when there was still fog drifting in tendrils over the scrubgrass and the daily rains had not yet begun, the daughter of Don Antonio herself eased Scarfo's fears when she came to the mausoleum to pay a visit to her mother's grave.

No one bothered her this time. Giorgio was the only one fool enough to test the don's temper, or his daughter's for that matter, and Signorina Terasatti was on solemn business. She stopped for a moment and quietly inspected the work they were doing. She was again wearing her veil, but after a moment she unpinned it and looked directly at Scarfo.

"Where is the young man who likes to risk his life to impress the young ladies?" she asked.

"I don't know who you mean, signorina," Scarfo said with exaggerated hemming and hawing as a sort of politeness.

"I mean Giorgio Farenza, the mason," she said more tersely. "He was kind enough to come to my mother's funeral reception a few nights ago. I wish to give him my appreciation for his thoughtfulness. Do you suppose anyone here can deliver that message to him?"

No one replied.

"Well, should any of you stumble over him on a rainy night, please give him my regards."

With that she pinned her veil and disappeared into the mausoleum. It was nearly an hour before she appeared again, and she made one last hopeful turn at the wall before quietly, slowly walking back up along the garden path to the villa.

*　　*　　*

"Didn't you hear me? I said you can come back to work. You can move back into the house."

"Yes, I heard, I heard," Giorgio said patiently, "but you must tell me again what she said—exactly. Here, would you like some beans?" He pushed a cold black cup toward Scarfo and offered him a slightly used spoon.

Scarfo wrinkled his bulbous, stippled nose and refused. "She said she wanted to screw you a hundred times. Now pack your cup and spoon and let's get home." Scarfo looked around warily. The cave was cramped and damp and the only light was the lantern he had left standing at the entrance. He wanted to get moving. There were bats in these places. If a bat flew over your head at night, it meant your imminent death.

"Come on, Scarfo, tell me what she said exactly."

"I told you before, and that's all I remember. She thanks you for your kindness. She sends you her regards. Maybe next time she'll send a few *lire* as well and we can buy some good cigars."

"I got to see her."

"That one is trouble. Forget it. You're lucky you ain't got your head blown off because of her already."

Giorgio smiled mischieviously. "Maybe you're jealous, eh? Maybe you think she's in love with me and she'll steal me away."

"Sure she's in love with you," Scarfo said. "She's young and stupid, just like you, and if she was only going to steal you away, I'd kiss her foot. But you only met her once and you're lucky you ain't got your head blown off because of her already. I'm telling you, if she ever bothers you, the first thing you do is pack up and move back to this hole where she can't find you."

Giorgio stared into the gentle flame of the lantern. A moment passed without sound. "Maybe she is in love with

me, Scarfo. I don't know. I only know I'm in love with
her.''

Scarfo shivered and grumbled and turned to crawl out
on his knees. "All this darkness is making you a little
dizzy," he said. "Let's get the hell out of here."

Giorgio wasted no time. As soon as they reached
home, he boiled some water and steamed the wrinkles out
of his suit. He was determined to go to the villa in the
morning. She had gone out of her way to ask for him.
What did that mean?

Perhaps she really was in love with him. Sure, why
not? He was a good-looking fellow. Lots of women in the
town threw themselves at him. Not exactly aristocrats,
maybe, but everybody was the same underneath, right?
Why should the daughter of a don be any different from
the daughter of a baker?

Because she was rich and beautiful and could have
anybody she wanted, he sternly reminded himself. He was
making a fool of himself over her. Scarfo was wrong. A
woman like that would never fall in love with a stranger, a
mason, somebody who could give her exactly nothing.

The fact remained, she had asked after him as well as
remembered him after all these years. Why should he be
surprised? Maybe he wasn't rich, but he wasn't a skinny
fool like her fiance either. He could give her beautiful
children, and what did any woman want more than beautiful children?

Hey, *stupido*—he slapped the palm of his hand to his
forehead—what are you thinking? You ain't even talked to
her yet, and already you're giving her a family.

He mumbled his thoughts on and on under his breath
as he worked. Once in a while would stop to make a
dramatic gesture. Scarfo said nothing, but he wandered in
and out of Giorgio's way and made little incoherent mur-

murs that sounded like a man talking in his sleep. Finally Giorgio was forced to notice him. What was the old man doing, anyway?

"Never met a kid so stupid," Scarfo mumbled.

Giorgio was suddenly so annoyed that when the old man turned his back Giorgio put up his hands as if to strangle him. It was always like this, he thought. If Scarfo didn't get his way, he would drive you crazy until you gave in. To hell with him. Scarfo hadn't noticed women in years. He had forgotten what it was like to stand in the gaze of beautiful eyes, to hear a feminine voice say your name as if it were a prayer.

He unconsciously felt at his chest for the impression made by the tiny crucifix that hung there. All these years he had kept the rosary when he could have sold it. He had been tempted a hundred times, but always the thought of that angry little face in the grotto of the Virgin made him smile. He had never used the beads for praying. He wore them like a hunting trophy.

He had never thought he would see her again, but now she was back, still beautiful as an angel, and he loved her. He'd come to that conclusion in a roundabout way, after a week of meditating alone in his cave like an anchorite. There wasn't much else to do. At first he was too frightened to think, but fear was like anything else; you got used to it after a while. Soon images of that night began to pester him.

Again and again he recalled the way the umbrella shivered in his hand as it met with the hardness of Don Antonio's skull, and the dull crunching noise it made led him to imagine what the rasp of his own death rattle through a severed windpipe would sound like.

There was no question, it was a stupid thing to do, but he was worried about Signorina Terasatti, so much so that he waited around for a few moments in the rain to make sure she would be all right with her father.

At the time he didn't stop to ask himself why he gave a damn. He simply protected her, the natural thing to do—which as far as he was concerned it wasn't. It's your own ass first in this world; Scarfo had taught him that much, pounded it in time after time, the first rule: Where your life or your living was concerned, you were always more important than the next guy.

So why had he done it? He thought about the way he found himself tongue-tied when she opened the door. He thought about the way his knees suddenly got weak when she took his arm. He thought of all the times he looked for her after making a fool of himself by hanging from his toes forty feet in the air. There was only one explanation for all this stupidity: it had to be love.

The worst kind of love it was, the kind that hit you like lightning. It almost killed you before you realized it had you by the throat, suddenly made you short of breath and dizzy so you couldn't see clearly. It cost you your good judgment, so you would go out and get yourself into all kinds of trouble.

Everybody heard stories of such love, and now he had fallen victim to it. It was a big pain in the ass, but what could you do about it? You did what you had to do, that was all. Nothing else could get in the way.

Scarfo was puffing furiously and the cottage was so stuffy that Giorgio had to gasp a little to catch a full breath.

"You going to smoke that thing all night?" Giorgio's voice gave away his irritation.

"Light up a cigarette if you don't like it. Breathe your own smoke."

"You're going to make my suit smell like that stinking tobacco you buy in town."

"Then hang your precious suit outside and let the rain wash it out."

"You got no damn respect for me, Scarfo."

"I got respect for men, not boys. If you act like one, what kind of respect you think you're going to get?"

"Oh, I'm acting like a kid, eh? And what about you, pacing back and forth, back and forth, like an old blind dog waiting for the butcher to throw him a piece of meat." Giorgio's hands were wildly describing a symphony as he spoke.

"You're a goddamn idiot if you go to see la Terasatti. An idiot. How far are you going to push your luck?"

"Far enough."

"Too far!" Scarfo snatched his pipe from his mouth and poked at the air for emphasis. A little shower of orange sparks leaped out of the bowl and stung his hand. "Son of a bitch! See what you made me do?"

"I didn't make you do nothing. You did it yourself because you want to give me advice I didn't ask for." He beat his chest with the side of his fist. "I am Giorgio Farenza and I don't need your advice."

"So what's that supposed to mean?"

"I got my own brain to think with and my own heart to love with."

"Agh, *fang' gool*. You think with your balls."

"At least I still got a good pair to think with."

The argument fell into frustrated silence. Giorgio didn't want to hear any more and he didn't want to say any more. Why bother arguing with a dried up old man whose greatest pleasure in life was eating a few figs for breakfast?

Giorgio went to his own bed, a platform spring he had found cast off by the side of the road outside the village and a makeshift mattress stuffed with the dried leaves of a corn plant. From behind it took his mandolin. He played tunelessly, as if drunk.

"Another thing," Scarfo said, though Giorgio didn't acknowledge him even with a look. "Don't you never bring that bit of trouble here to my home."

Giorgio snickered. "Here? Why would she ever want to come to a place like this?"

"There's nothing the matter with this place," Scarfo snapped resentfully. "It's been good enough for you all these years."

Giorgio already regretted what he had said. It was wrong to insult the very roof that kept the rain off him. It was like blasphemy. He was ashamed of himself, and he mumbled, "That's not what I meant. You're talking like an old idiot."

"I talk the way I talk, and I say what I want to say, and what I want to say is this: You don't even know this rich signorina, and already she has mixed up your brains. She ain't nothing but trouble, and if you do something dumb because of her again, don't bother me with it, because I ain't going to help you. I'll throw you out on the street like a sick dog for the rats to have a feast."

Giorgio's hand stopped for a moment and the mandolin was silent. He tapped his foot impatiently and closed his eyes. The old man was talking through his hat. His feelings had been hurt and now he was trying to get even. Giorgio had to admit it was working. That last remark had been the words of a real first-class son of a bitch, especially coming from Scarfo, who had always been like a father to him, a mentor, a man to respect and revere.

The argument had taken a bad turn. It was no longer a little shouting and cursing to get the fire inside burning or to make the juices flow better. It was no longer the kind that was good for you the way work and wine were good for you. Instead it was making him feel cold and alone, left with nothing to say.

Without opening his eyes he began to pluck the strings

of his mandolin once more. In between the notes the fire snapped up twigs and branches with a sudden, violent crackling.

From across the room came a noise like the honking of a goose. Giorgio opened his eyes in surprise. Scarfo was blowing on his trumpet so hard his face was turning red. This is more like it, Giorgio thought; he replied by harshly striking the strings of his own instrument.

Scarfo began a rendition of *Santa Lucia*, a song Giorgio despised. In retaliation Giorgio played *Luna de Oro*, a melody he knew always gave Scarfo a headache. The battle standards were raised.

Through song after song they blew and picked until their cheeks and foreheads filmed over with sweat and they lost all concentration. When they ran out of ugly songs, they played pretty ones badly, then annoyed each other with any kind of racket that came into their heads. Finally the fire in the hearth began to die and Scarfo gave up. He put his trumpet back in its place and held up both hands for Giorgio to stop.

"You win," he said. "You play the worst music in Italy. I can't compare with you."

Agh, you son of a bitch, Giorgio thought, but he forced a highly artistic edition of a feckless little boy's smile, then began to play as delicate and lighthearted a rendition of *Funiculi,* as he could force from his fingers. He had a hard time of it, since his fingertips were sore from playing so hard for so long, but he knew Scarfo would overlook bad technique in favor of humor. The old man cackled approvingly and tears formed in his eyes at the peace offering, as Giorgio knew they would.

"I play so ugly I make you cry, eh?"

"That's right," the old man replied, "at least when I'm not too busy laughing. I never heard such ugly playing."

"Then maybe I should stop before it gets so bad it

kills you." Giorgio said, and he laid his instrument down beside him.

"You ain't gonna kill me. I'm tough. Go ahead. Play all you want."

Instead Giorgio said, "It's all your goddamn fault I play so ugly, old man. I play from my heart, and everything that's in my heart I get from you. So if my playing is the worst, or if it's the most beautiful in the world—which it is—it's all your fault."

Scarfo grew thoughtful and silent for a moment, then rubbed his eyes with his thumb and forefinger. "You make me tired, boy."

Giorgio absently plunked at the double strings of the instrument on the bed beside him. "It's late. That's why you're tired." But he knew the old man was pleased, and to please the old man at this moment warmed Giorgio's heart. "Go to sleep. I'll play for you tomorrow night."

Scarfo lay back on his bed and covered his eyes with his forearm. He would be asleep in a moment, snoring comfortably as always. It was a sound that to Giorgio seemed as much a part of the night as the squawking of crows were of the morning.

After a quiet moment Scarfo spoke. "When will you present yourself to the signorina?"

"Tomorrow," Giorgio said, though his plan became definite only as he spoke. "In the morning."

"Maybe we'll both be lucky and she'll laugh in your face."

"Maybe, Scarfo, maybe."

"Be careful of her father."

"I will."

"How will you get in the front door if no one makes the formal arrangements with him? You have no go-between to plead your case. He's rich, and take it from me, rich men love tradition. Anyway, she's already engaged. You ain't got a chance, boy.''

"She ain't gonna marry that guy. She can't bear the sight of him. It was all over her face, how she loathes him."

"What she can bear is whatever her father says she can. I'll tell you what I think. You show up on the front door of the villa and the gardener will have to pick up pieces of you from the front lawn."

"I can't help it. I'm in love." He announced it passionately, the more so because the words had to get by the cold lump of fear in his throat. Scarfo was right. Scarfo was always right, the old bastard. He was wily as a mountain goat and he knew all the angles. Giorgio would never get in to see Signorina Terasatti if he showed up at the front door. He hadn't thought his plan all the way through.

"What do you think I should do?"

"Give up."

"I can't give up."

"Then wait until she comes down to the mausoleum. Talk to her then."

"When I'm working? When my hands are filthy and I'm sweating in my rags? Never. She must see me when I'm at my best. Otherwise how can she respect me?"

The old man sighed. "I don't know what to tell you. Like you said, you're Giorgio Farenza. You got your own brain to think with."

The fire had begun to die, leaving a small mound of orange embers in the hearth. Giorgio's eyes fluttered with sleepiness, but his mind roiled like a lake in a storm as he tried to come up with a plan for making his way into the villa. Most of his ideas—climbing up to a balcony, sneaking past bodyguards, bribing a servant to let him in—were silly, foolish, bound to fail, though they had great style and were worth considering for that reason alone.

What the hell is the matter with my brain, anyway? he thought angrily. What good is it if it can't come up with a practical idea? Run in, barge in, send a note, call out her name, leave flowers, beg the don for mercy—nothing was any good. Finally he was so frustrated, so agitated that despite his tired eyes and aching muscles, he couldn't fall asleep.

He rolled over, adjusted his arms, rolled over again, then sat up abruptly. On a shelf by the door sat four unopened smoky bottles of Chianti. He took one down, uncorked it and began to drink. Scarfo was snoring softly.

Giorgio listened as to a tenor singing an aria. It's a hell of a world, he thought, a hell of a world that tortures a man like me with such feelings while it leaves others sleeping so peacefully, without a care, without a worry. Why couldn't it have been old Scarfo who fell in love with a princess, eh?

He tried to form a picture of his round and wrinkled friend with his whiskers shaved close, with his entire appearance transfigured by a new suit of clothes, with Signorina Terasatti on his arm. When the image came clear, a womanish burst of laughter escaped Giorgio's throat. Of course the old man couldn't understand why Giorgio had to go to meet her. The only pleasures Scarfo knew anymore were cutting hard and heavy stones and eating figs for breakfast.

A sudden pang of compassion overcame Giorgio and he went over to Scarfo's prone form and put his ear to Scarfo's mouth, not so much to hear better as to feel the man's breath upon him, to feel the touch of his life.

"Hey, old friend," he murmured, and because Scarfo didn't answer, more insistently, "Hey!"

Scarfo sputtered and wiped the back of his hand

across his mouth. One eye opened, just barely. "What? Oh, it's you. Now what do you want?"

"I want to tell you I love you, old man. I want to tell you I'm crazy about you."

Scarfo made a grimace and tried to wave Giorgio away. "You been drinking. Get the hell out of my face."

Giorgio wouldn't be put off. "I shouldn't argue with you so much. You been good to me. This is a lovely house. I love it. I love everything about it. I love the walls and the floor and the ceiling and the air inside. I love the table and the fireplace and the chairs and the beds."

"Agh, *stai'te zit'*, shut your mouth and go to bed."

Giorgio frowned. Something occurred to him. Maybe it was silly to think of the old man with a princess now, but he had been married himself. He knew something about love. At least he knew something about women. You couldn't live most of your life with a woman and learn nothing.

"Tell me, lovely old man," he said, "How did you meet your wife? Did you have a go-between to make the arrangements?"

"I didn't need no damn go-between. I make my own traditions," Scarfo muttered.

"And her father didn't shoot you?"

"Her father wasn't a crook like Terasatti. Besides, I know a secret about women and their fathers."

A secret! Of course, there was always a secret. Whenever there was a problem you couldn't solve, you could be sure someone knew a secret that would give the answer. It was the way God had made the world. There were two things you needed to survive: a good brain and a knack for finding out the secrets. "You don't know nothing about women, old Scarfo. You're too ancient. Even though I love you, I know that about you."

"You don't know nothing." Scarfo seemed to drag

himself out of deep slumber to form every answer. His voice was the slow, gravelly voice of a dreamer. "You don't know the power of a young woman's love."

"And what's that supposed to mean? That she's got magic? Eh?" In his drunkenness he went a little too far and nudged the old man, annoying him, but after a brief scowl Scarfo's face relaxed again.

"Listen, Giorgio, if I tell you what you want to know, will you shut up and go to sleep?" he muttered.

"I don't want to know nothing from you." He lied from reflex.

"If the woman is truly in love with you, you don't have to do nothing about her father. She'll take care of him. Don't worry, she'll think of a way. Women are smarter than men."

"But how can I be sure she's truly in love unless I talk to her?"

"Talk—don't worry about talk. You have to be like a thief. You have to steal into her life like a shadow, like the scent of a flower in the air. There are ways to make her love you without ever speaking another word to her."

"I don't understand."

"Agh, the famous Farenza brain." Scarfo allowed himself a chuckle. "A gift, you idiot. Make her a gift."

"What kind of gift?"

"How do I know what kind of gift? A gift she'll like."

"Maybe a little portrait of myself..."

Scarfo shook his head and turned his face away. "*Stupido*," he mumbled.

"If only you'd taught me how to carve like you promised," Giorgio sniffed, "I could make a statue of her."

"I told you once before, you ain't suffered enough."

"What can I give her, then? Tell me."

Scarfo wouldn't answer. Giorgio persisted. Scarfo still wouldn't answer. Giorgio shook him by the shoulder. Scarfo began to snore.

"A gift, then," Giorgio repeated to himself. "Sure, something she'll like. A nice trifle that will make her love me. Sure, no problem." He went to bed, drunk, confused, with no idea of what kind of gift such a woman would care for.

Chapter 10

Giorgio opened his eyes. The sun hadn't risen yet and the embers in the fireplace had died. Only the faint glow of a half moon in the window relieved the blackness. His throat and lips were dry and sore, and the sharp smell of wood-smoke burned in his nose.

His bed was damp with sweat. He shivered. His head was throbbing. All night long he had tossed and turned like an overexcited child on Christmas Eve because an idea had come to him, a simple notion but a brilliant one, he told himself, one that was certain to work. He had discovered a way to steal into the signorina's life.

He sat upright on the edge of the bed and for a moment went dizzy with fatigue. His mind was full of fog and his eyes were scratchy. Maybe he was too tired. Maybe he should wait another day.

He shook his head to clear it. He had to move fast. Scarfo would be up with the sun, and Giorgio didn't want to waste the morning arguing with him. There wasn't even time to shave.

He groped around on the floor until he found his heavy leather work boots, encrusted with dry mortar. He crept with them in his hand through the darkness toward the door, which creaked on its hinges when he opened it. He wanted to curse himself for not oiling it, but he bit his lower lip instead. He took his winter jacket from a hook on the wall and slipped outside. Scarfo didn't stir.

The bare ground was cold, even against his heavy woolen socks. He found a patch of brush to sit on and pushed his feet into his boots.

The tools were kept a under a lean-to made of cast-off plywood and odd bits of slate roofing shingle. He didn't need much—a hammer, a drill and bit, a saw, a long rope and a strong plank.

In the dark he had to search by groping. Again and again he cut and scraped himself against the sharp edges of shovels and trowels and stubbed his fingers on chisels and mallets. As he tried quietly to move a piece of canvas that blocked the floor, a half dozen heavy buckets clattered down from a pile and bruised his shins. He kept from cursing by whispering little prayers of exasperation to the saints, though that didn't seem to satisfy the demands of his pains nearly so well as a nasty oath would have.

He found everything he needed among the scaffolding tools. His weariness was gone now, dispelled by exertion, the cold and the excitement. This was better than leaving a note, he thought, better than singing a song under her balcony or sending her a flower.

The real beauty of it was that the don really couldn't object. He might even take it as homage, a sign of respect. Yes, it was a brilliant idea, the best he'd ever had. He was so proud of himself he felt like slapping his thighs and whistling. He coiled a fifty-foot piece of hemp rope over his shoulder, gathered the rest of his instruments into a long wooden box and started out for the Villa Vicchieri.

It wasn't very far, only five miles, and he was used to the rugged, craggy road that wound up the side of the plateau, but the extra weight of the rope on his shoulder tired him enough to slow his brisk pace to a slow walk after half the distance was covered. By the time he got there, the brilliant stars, cast like carnival glitter across the cloudless sky, had begun to fade in the grey pearl of dawn.

The front gate was open. Giorgio shook his head. The don must be a very arrogant man to leave open such an easy access to his house. It must be wonderful to be so arrogant, so powerful and feared. No doubt there were bodyguards inside—they were always sticking their noses out of corners like termites—but bodyguards could be bought off, just as gates could be breached.

No, The don's real strength, the source of his fearlessness, was his hold on the hearts of the people. Everyone knew the score: If you put so much as a scratch on the skin of a Terasatti, not only would your own life be forfeit, but so might the lives of your children, of your wife, of your parents and brothers. The vendetta was cruel and went far beyond the reach of justice. A man like the don could reach out from the grave to kill you—and anyone else who might bear a grudge on your behalf.

Giorgio moved quietly around the great house and set his tools down under an ash tree beyond the terrazzo. In the back of his own mind these many years had slept the thought of another vendetta, sworn but not yet carried out—to find the murderer of his own parents. What a world, he thought, to ask such things of a man. He had no heart for violence, no taste for bloodshed. As for courage, leave that to the soldiers.

He didn't remember his parents; what were they to him? His blood. This he knew in his soul and could never forget. He was bound by his oath, but fortunately, he had never given himself a deadline. Ha! That was a stroke of luck. There was no need to do anything right away. Maybe someday he would get lucky and be rich like the don.

Then he could hire somebody else to go out and do the dirty work for him.

A noise startled him and he froze. A nightingale chirped in the tree above, but that wasn't it. It was a man's voice. Giorgio crossed himself. Ah, there it was again—two men, maybe more. At first they seemed to come close, but soon they were moving off into the distance toward a wood a few hundred yards to the south.

Giorgio could see them now, two short, wiry figures walking abreast of a tall, broad man who wore a sport hat with a yellow cock's feather stuck in the band; the don, no doubt, and two of his flunkies. He carried a gun, but from this distance Giorgio couldn't tell whether it was a shotgun or a rifle. Never having handled either, he didn't know the difference except that the shotgun looked stubby and mean, like the wrestlers who sometimes came through the village to make money giving demonstrations in the streets.

Most farmers and many craftsmen owned a gun of one sort or another, but through some oddity of personality, Scarfo would never allow one into the house, and Giorgio had no strong objection. Money was better spent on fine shoes or expensive clothing. It was better to be beautiful than deadly as far as he was concerned. About guns he knew only that they killed what they were aimed at, and that was all he needed to know.

A moment after the little party disappeared into the stand of trees a muffled report disturbed the morning quiet. Then came the chaotic squawking of a flock of crows. The don was hunting.

It was a little past the usual season now, but if you could find a bird it was still fair game, and apparently these birds felt themselves under some obligation to make their rookery in Don Antonio's private preserve. Everything came easier to the rich, Giorgio thought wistfully, then set to work.

When he was finished, he would sneak back to work at the wall and catch a little nap under a tarp. The other workers wouldn't begin to arrive for another hour or so, plenty of time for a snooze if he could do this little job quickly and without breaking his neck.

Gabriella Teresatti awoke with the sun; she always had. After making her morning prayers and lighting the votive candle on a little shelf by the door of her room, she put on a brown cotton dress and a woolen shawl and went to breakfast.

As usual, it was waiting for her—thin sticks of very hard bread, a cup of coffee and at this time of year a couple of figs, though she preferred the oranges and tangerines of summer. Her father, his mistress and most of the servants thought she was a little odd, eating a meal before noontime. What kind of digestion was a stomach barely awake capable of? It was bound to lead to trouble.

The nuns insisted that it was a kindness to treat the body to a little nourishment before the work of the day began, and the body, after all, was the temple of the Holy Ghost. Unfortunately for many of the sisters, this dictum simply meant building up spiritual strength by the daily purification through suffering, during which they flayed their own backs with hooked scourges until they bled.

This practice had been instrumental in discouraging Gabriella from entering the convent. Otherwise, to be a bride of Christ, to dedicate one's life to humility and the sacraments, seemed to her noble and worthy. She had never quite understood why this horrified her parents. Of course, there was the obligation to perpetuate the bloodline, the family name, but was not the blood of the family of Christ more precious?

She dipped her bread into the scalding espresso to soften the crust. There were other reasons she hadn't taken her novitiate vows. There was her habit of smoking, a grave sin she had never confessed. Because of it she was also guilty of making bad confessions, hundreds of them. Not only were all her sins unforgiven (thank God most of them were small ones), but she would have to admit all this to a priest before entering the convent.

In her imagination she could hear the man thundering with indignation, preaching and remonstrating with such force and volume that everyone else in the chapel knew the exact state of her soul to the last peccadillo. She had seen it happen to other girls and she could not bring herself to stand for such humiliation. In due time she would make a confession to a priest in the town. They would not dare embarrass her. They knew her father.

Her last reason for choosing the secular life, and the one she understood least, had to do with forbidden curiosity. She wondered what it would be like to have a husband—not just a provider and lord of the house but someone to kiss, to hold, to stroke like a puppy. Somehow that was what she wanted to do to a man.

Oh, not a fellow like Francesco, her fiance. She could barely stand to be in the same room with him. But—and she had a very difficult time admitting this to herself—maybe someone like that workman, the mason, Giorgio Farenza. There was something both kind and rebellious in his manner that she liked. And for some reason she could imagine him chasing his own tail just like a puppy.

The coffee was strong and bitter. She took it in tiny sips, like a bee at a flower, then shuddered and added two large lumps of sugar to the brew. She thought of the taste of his impudent kiss. That too had remained with her for a long time, but there was no way to sweeten it.

It was her first kiss, but not like her dreams of her first. It held no passsion, no tenderness, no violence, nothing—just a quick, dry pushing against her mouth, a clumsy little nibble, and then the feeling of shame. It was stupid and thoughtless of him. Where did these men learn their manners—or for that matter their morals?

She might have blamed it on his poverty, but her own father was no better. He had brought his mistress to his own wife's funeral. She had a fantasy of gathering all the men of the province, rich and poor, farmer, shopkeeper and tradesman, and forcing them to sit through a lecture on how one should conduct oneself as a civilized human being, especially where the sensitivities of a woman are concerned.

"Good morning, Gabriella."

Gabriella started and blushed at the intrusion of Brigetta, embarrassed by her thoughts. "Good morning," she replied, but with too much haste to sound as disinterested as she would have wished.

"Do you mind if I join you?"

Gabriella made an apologetic gesture. "You're welcome to sit, of course, but as you can see, I'm quite finished. I must go and give the servants their orders for the day."

Somewhat to her surprise Brigetta had not challenged her for the household authority. Gabriella had expected a bitter battle, concealed from her father, of course, but with the servants in the middle. However, every morning she selected the menus for the day, discussed laundry, cleaning and entertaining with the housekeeper, and was even making inroads on the upkeep her parents had neglected for so long. She got the roof fixed by the simple expedient of ordering it done without consulting her father. Brigetta, meantime, seemed content to behave as a guest.

"Stay for a moment. I want to talk to you."

"Perhaps later in the day." Gabriella started to rise, but Brigetta's hand stopped her with a firm touch to the forearm.

"There is a matter we should discuss Gabriella. Your father has not been well."

Making a face to show her displeasure, Gabriella sat down and folded her hands in front of her. She kept her gaze fixed firmly on the pink buffed nails of her thumbs. Until now the two women had avoided each other in all circumstances but at dinner, when meeting was inevitable. Even then they kept their conversation terse and unfriendly.

For the signorina to interrupt this most precious part of the day was nearly enough provocation for trading slaps. However, there was nothing to do but listen. If her father's health was really of concern, Gabriella had a duty to hear the hussy out.

"My father seems fit enough to me," Gabriella said. Let her prove her case if she could.

"Yes, he looks well most of the time, but it is not always so. There are moments of great difficulty. At night he becomes very short of breath. Sometimes he clutches at his chest as if he's about to die, as if his heart is about to break."

"He's always done that, at least for the benefit of my mother. It made her sympathetic, and she would treat him like a little boy. Sometimes he likes to be treated that way. Maybe you remind him of my mother, eh?"

The signorina turned pale. "It's not the same. I know him when he wants sympathy, but this is different. Now he's coughing up blood, as if he had been wounded in the chest."

"As if he had consumption, you mean."

"Maybe, yes."

Gabriella thought for a moment. Maybe there really was cause for concern. On the other hand, what was a little blood? Cut your finger and it bleeds. It doesn't mean you're going to die. Sure, sometimes sick people coughed blood, but maybe well people did too sometimes. She said as much to Brigetta.

"Child, you know nothing about these matters. You go to Naples sometime and listen to the beggars cough. I grew up there. I know what such a sound means—death. It is always death."

Gabriella felt herself beginning to grow alarmed, but she controlled the feeling by flattening her hands on the table as if to keep them over a hole to trap her fear inside. "If you think he's sick, call a doctor."

"A doctor? You want to kill him twice as fast?"

Gabriella lost her composure. "So what, then? You say he's dying and there's nothing to do about it, so what do you want from me? You're a stranger in this house. Whatever you have been to my father, you are not mistress here. The only rights you have are the ones you have stolen. So what do you want, eh? My father is dying and you want something from me. What is it?"

It took a long time for Brigetta to answer. She assumed a very grave expression, though her voice remained calm, unabashed. "He has been asking me since before your mother died, but I have turned him down until now. I thought it inappropriate."

"He has asked you what?" Gabriella shouted. She felt a burning in her stomach, a point of pain that began to ooze nausea like oil from a leaking barrel.

"Don't pretend to be softheaded, child. You know what I mean. He wants me to marry him at once, without a waiting period."

"You can't marry him! You must wait the year of mourning!"

"Suppose he doesn't live another year?"

"Yes, suppose he doesn't? What difference will it make if he is married or not?"

"It is his wish."

"It's not my wish. I won't have it."

"He is *dying*. He is your father. Don't you care anything for his feelings?"

"How dare you ask such a question? I have the greatest respect and love for him. As a respectful child, I would not see him throw his name into the street or leave it to someone who would drag it through the mud. I'll see him dead first. I'll kill him myself, in his sleep."

She felt panic making her sicker. It was clear what Brigetta was after—money. Who wouldn't be in her situation? If Gabriella's father died, she would be left with nothing. On the other hand, if she married the don, Gabriella might well end up on the street herself.

There was no doubt that the woman was cunning, and Gabriella didn't feel at all competent in the ways of money and power and property. She knew how to live with them but not how to control them. They were like the weather, like the powerful storms that blew over the hills in the autumn and winter.

This woman, this mistress, this whore, she would know how to seize the reins, and the wealth of the Terasattis would pass on to strangers. Gabriella would become an outcast, without even a good name to call her own.

Brigetta seemed unruffled. This early in the morning her face was a little puffy and her makeup gave her an untrustworthy look, but her deep brown eyes were clear and comprehending.

"If I decide to marry Don Antonio," she said calmly, "I will do so. There is no argument. He is mine. Before, I had to share him. Now I do not. I can make him my husband or I can eat him for breakfast. For whatever I want, he is mine."

Her expression clouded and without warning her voice became strident and her fists clenched. "I have given everything to your father, Gabriella, everything—my honor, my virtue, my soul. For many years I have given all I have. Now I will get something back. I won't be left out in the street.''

She gave Gabriella a calculating look before she went on. ''What do you think, that I waited outside your father's door with a trap and captured him? Is that how you think I got to be his mistress? He took me. I was a village girl no older than you and he saw me on a Sunday morning. He called me over; I knew who and what he was—a Terasatti, a landowner and the son of a landowner.

''Why do you think I went with him? Because he could make life even more miserable than it already was for my family. I dared not resist him then and I love him now, so to hell with you if you think I'm going to let you get in my way. If you want to make a fight, little girl, we'll fight!''

Gabriella covered her eyes with her hands. Her eyes were burning and wet. There was nothing to do, nothing to do, a voice repeated over and over inside her. Everything was lost and gone.

Brigetta was not so far wrong; she needed a roof over her head and food on the table like anyone else. What had she done that was so terrible? Only what she had to do. But now she was like a hungry goat, ready to eat everything in sight, and there was no way to stop her.

Madonna mia, help me, she prayed. She was not strong enough, not wise enough to handle this ravenous woman.

Brigetta gently touched her fingertips to Gabriella's wet cheeks. ''Don't worry, little one,'' she said. ''No one will turn you out of your house. You'll be taken care of until you marry whether your father is alive to see it or not. And you'll have a generous dowry, as well. I don't hate you. I understand why you are afraid and resent me, but there is no need.''

Now what, kindness? She had too many weapons, this bitch, this peasant, this whore. Does she want me to think she's good and just? Yes, that's exactly what she wants me to think, and I won't! I won't believe that. Heavenly Father and all the saints, what am I to do?

"You are a liar, signorina," she said, and without another word Gabriella rose from her seat and rushed out of the house. She didn't want to hear any more. She didn't want to argue anymore. Whatever would happen, let it happen. She wanted only to cry, to let out the steam that was pushing inside her.

She crossed the terrazzo and ran under the trees where there was shade and no one would see her. Her eyes were bleary with tears and she took a handkerchief from her sleeve to dab her nose. When something caught hold of her shoulder and refused to release her, she was at first frightened, then angry. She struck out and twisted to free herself. Wiping her eyes, she spoke out loud. "What's the matter now, eh? What's this?"

When she saw what she had tangled around her arm, she didn't know what to make of it. Where only yesterday there had been nothing, a swing made of rough wood hung from a low bough of the tree above her. Who had made it? One of the servants, perhaps? Why? There were no children here.

Impulsively she sat upon it and took hold of the dry hemp ropes that held it aloft. She pushed off a little and let herself move in a small arc, back and forth, back and forth—who had built the swing and why—what's that?

Her right hand recoiled. There was something on the rope. An insect? Wait, no. She reached out. Ah, a rosary. A clue. She had seen this rosary before, hadn't she? Her brow furrowed. Of course she had. It was her own. It was the rosary she gave to a young boy in the piazza so many years ago.

So that's who built the swing, the man Farenza. He had built it for her. Her heart gladdened. That's what the rosary meant.

What about her father and Brigetta? To the devil with them. What did they matter? Oh, they meant a great deal, she knew, but just now they seemed to disappear in a mist, to become as nothing, because someone had made something only for her. Someone had tried to please her. If he was only a craftsman, so what? He was a man, which was more than she could say for her fiance. He was sweet, and a little stupid too. Perfect!

She pushed herself off hard and grinned with exhilaration as she swung higher and higher. The bough bent a little with her weight and a few dried leaves tumbled like laughter in the air. The morning sun was growing bright and she closed her eyes to the glare, squeezed them tight as she swung, and watched the backs of her lids turn red in the brightness. Though the air was chilly and raised gooseflesh on her exposed arms and neck, she felt warm and not too much alone for the first time in a very long, long time.

Chapter 11

Giorgio smashed his thumb and cursed. Scarfo giggled with self-satisfied pleasure.

"What's the matter, kid? I think you're too tired."

"Your ass is tired from too much thinking," Giorgio retorted sharply.

This made Scarfo laugh even harder. Some of the other masons joined in the teasing.

"You don't rest so good when you sleep out of doors, eh?"

"That's right, Farenza. Why do you think they invented houses if we we're supposed to sleep outside?"

"Agh, shut the hell up, all of you." His reply was mumbled, without heart. He felt fatigued and torpid, as if recovering from a terrible drunk. His eyes were heavy and he forgot things. Tonight there would be nothing but sleep, nothing but rest.

"It ain't so much because he's tired," Scarfo said to the others. "It's because he's in love."

"Sure, with the fairy princess," said one of the ditchdiggers. "He's got a big chance there. A big chance she's gonna laugh so loud they'll hear it in Naples."

Giorgio shook his head, tightened his grip on an inch-thick piece of grey flagstone and struck hard with his mallet. This time he was careful to keep his thumb clear, but his aim was careless and he shattered the stone.

A flying chip struck Scarfo on the cheek. The old man turned sharply, but rather than becoming angry, he seemed even more full of mirth than before.

"This rich little signorina ain't just gonna kill you, little Giorgio," he said, "she's gonna kill the rest of us first."

Giorgio tried to ignore him. If he made too much of a fuss and then Signorina Terasatti really did make a fool of him, he would never live it down. But Scarfo wouldn't let it go.

"Hey, sweetie boy, when are you going to tell us what you were doing here so early in the morning?"

"When you kiss my ass."

"Oh, that's a nice way to talk." Scarfo was laughing so hard he practically lost his balance on the scaffold.

"What do you think, everything's a big joke or something?"

"No, no," Scarfo said, wiping the tears of mirth from his squinting, close-set eyes. "Nothing's a joke. If you don't want to tell us, it's all right."

He realized the laughter wouldn't stop any more than his weariness would go away. It had started when di Tommasi, a common laborer, found him asleep in a dried-out mortar tub with a canvas tarpaulin pulled over him to keep him warm. First he nearly broke his neck climbing the tree to hang the damn swing, and then he scraped his shins and forearms sliding down the trunk. After shivering his way through a few minutes of fitful sleep in the dusty cement tub, he awakened to the noise of di Tommasi laughing like an idiot. How wonderful was falling in love. Maybe falling out of the tree would have been better.

The day went on that way until lunchtime, when many of the workers returned home for a hot meal, and those who didn't took a few sips of wine and ate some fruit and cheese and cold roast lamb from the little sacks they brought with them. Giorgio, in his rush to get out in the morning, had not thought to bring any food, and he wasn't inclined to ask anyone for a handout, so instead of eating, he went for a walk in the garden.

It was a chilly day. Even the sunlight seemed cold in the stiff breeze that had gathered strength since morning. He turned up his collar and thrust his hands into his pockets. Just beyond the garden lay the terrazzo, and over to the left was the tree with the swing.

He wondered if she had discovered it yet. How wonderful it would be to see her come upon it, to watch her fly through the air, maybe even to give her a little push from behind and find out what sort of backside she had. She looked a little skinny, but he didn't mind, though it made him wonder if she knew how to cook.

He wanted to take a look and see if she had been there yet, but he didn't want to get caught nosing around the house. Still, for all his caution he found himself sauntering idly through the rows of neatly trimmed hedges toward the villa. Now and then he would make a little detour, stop to look at a shrub just to fool himself into believing he was wandering without destination, but he was getting closer and closer to the end of the garden, from where it would be simple to step over to the swing.

A scratching sound on the other side of the hedge attracted his attention. Through a break in the greenery he caught a glimpse of old Bobio raking pebbles into order.

Bobio was the gardener. He was a tall man, stooped at the shoulder and lacking upper front teeth as well as pride in the way he dressed. It was said that he hadn't changed his trousers in ten years and that his shirt—a black silk rag that hung off him by threads—was even older.

No one knew anything about him for sure. He had been a hermit most of his life, living up in the hills in a little shack of wood—wood was unfit to live in—and coming down only to do a little work for Don Antonio. The old women in the village said he was a saint, but the common rumor was that he had been treated badly by a northern barbarian, a woman from Genoa, who made a fool of him and cheated him out of a small fortune. Thus he had renounced the world.

Mothers in the streets used him as an object lesson in the hazards of falling in love. Giorgio had always felt a little sorry for him. He never smiled, never spoke, never even seemed to listen. And he was so old that soon his life itself would be gone.

It seemed that most of the men around these days were old—too old to fight in any case. The army was always putting young men into uniform and shipping them off somewhere—those they could catch. Many of them never came back. These days they were going north to fight the Austrians in the Alps. Before that it was the Serbians and before that the Ethiopians.

What did it matter? Giorgio had never met anyone from any of those places. He wanted only to live his life and to be left alone. So far he had been lucky. While those around him fell to the conscription lists, his mallet and chisel still rang in stone. The reason was simple: The government did not know he existed. He wasn't married. He had no parents, no papers, no property, nothing. He had never paid a tax.

No one bothered to turn him in. In fact, most of the people who knew his situation would rather hide him in their houses than let the government take him.

It had been forty years since the government in the north sent troops to put down the rebellions in the south, uprisings led by simple people who wanted only food and relief from outrageous tariffs and corrupt officials. These rebels were the same men who fought alongside Garibaldi to unite all the kingdoms on the Italian peninsula and whose hopes were dashed when the industrial north exploited them until there was nothing left to their children but empty bellies and cholera and malaria. Forty years, but no one had forgotten. The government to the north was still the enemy.

And so Giorgio was safe from conscription. If worst came to worst, if he was ever actually called to duty, there was still another option—fleeing to the hills to make a life among the brigands and highwaymen. It was a hard life, but you could make a name for yourself and the children in the villages would sing songs about you if you got famous enough.

He sauntered down the gravel lane between the hedges. If Bobio heard him it didn't matter. That old guy wouldn't say a word to anyone, and anyway, who would listen? Giorgio felt sorry for him. He must be lonely. Maybe he would like a cigarette. But maybe he didn't like his privacy intruded on either. Better to leave him alone.

When he reached the far end of the garden, Giorgio cast a casual glance toward the villa, then let it wander over the landscape. How nice to be so rich, he thought, to have so much money and land all to oneself. He often wondered what he would do with so much money. Buy a new wardrobe, of course, but then what? A villa, perhaps, but one with a decent face, one you wouldn't be be ashamed to invite your friends to.

His gaze moved over olive trees and ashes and birches, over the soft green thatch of the lawn. Ah, there it was, but had she seen it yet? There was no way to tell from here. If the rosary was gone, then he would know.

He looked around. There was no one in sight, not

even the gardener. He couldn't resist the temptation. He had to see for himself.

He felt as if a thousand eyes were watching him as he ran. If anyone saw him moving so fast, he would look very suspicious, he knew, but he couldn't help himself. When you were sneaking around, you had to move fast, though you might feel like a fox just ahead of the hounds. Speed was a law that had been built into his legs.

It took him only a few seconds to cross the distance, and when he reached the swing, his heart leaped. The rosary was gone. She had found it! Now everything was wonderful—wasn't it? Of course it was, but where was she? Why hadn't she come looking for him? A thousand reasons—maybe this, maybe that.

But *Madonna mia*, suppose it wasn't she who found the rosary. Maybe the old gardener had stumbled on it and kept it for himself. Or worse, perhaps Don Antonio had found it. Giorgio gave his cheek a little slap. What the hell had he done? The don would demand an explanation. The swing might be explained—a little toy, a gift to the villa. But the rosary would be more difficult. Not more difficult, impossible.

He could only hope that it was the signorina who found it after all and that she was waiting for a better moment to meet him, though now he was beginning to think it more likely that she was up in the villa at that very moment having a good laugh over him. He wrung his hands. Of course that's what she's doing, he thought in anguish, because he had made a fool of himself.

Word would get around and he would be the laughing stock of the entire province. How would he ever face Scarfo again? How would he ever face life? A woman like the signorina owned jewels and fine dresses and horses. What did she need with an old piece of wood tied up with construction rope?

He sat on the swing and swayed in little circles as he made scratches in the ground with the toe of his boot. He had behaved like an idiot and now he would pay the price.

Bobio appeared out of the garden across the way and leaned on his rake. He seemed to be staring at Giorgio, but the mason didn't care. The wind rose a little and shook the branches of the tree. It was a chilly wind. Slowly the sky was clouding over. The rains would come again and work would be over for the day.

Giorgio hated work. Giorgio hated everything. The world was clouding up and the breeze was as cold as death. He would never see the signorina again. He couldn't bear to see laughter in her gaze. Old Bobio came off his rake and walked toward Giorgio, who kicked at the grass under his boot.

"What's this thing?" the old man asked, pointing at the swing. His voice was tired and squeaky.

"It's my stupidity," Giorgio mumbled.

"What do you mean? Did you put it there?"

Giorgio sighed. Why was this ancient billygoat bleating at him? "Yes, I put it there."

"Then you got to take it down. Nobody puts nothing around here. I'm the gardener and I say who puts what. Except that ugly goddamn wall over there."

Giorgio didn't rise to the bait. He wasn't in the mood. "You say who puts what? I thought you didn't say anything. I thought you didn't have a tongue."

"Oh yeah, that's what you thought, eh? Because I mind my own buisness, you think I got no pride. Well, just you remember, you little turd, I'm the gardener here and nobody ruins my landscape. I don't bother nobody and nobody bothers me. But these trees are mine. So are them hedges and all the grass and the flowers too, in case you thought I forgot about them."

"Look, you crazy old crow, what do I care about

your landscape? You want the swing down, you take it down.''

Bobio waved his arms up and down like a stick toy and the corners of his sour turned-down mouth were lubricated with tiny flecks of white spittle. "I'm too old. How am I supposed to climb up there, eh? *Signor Terasatti* will have my job if he sees this thing hanging from one of his trees. Then how am I supposed to eat, beg? I got my pride, boy, I got my pride. And I'm too old to rob travelers in the hills, so don't give me that story. And I don't have any other trade, so don't give me that either. Just get this goddamn thing out of my tree.''

"You're a peasant, Bobio.''

"And what are you?'' Bobio shook his fist, white and fragile with grey-blue veins too prominent on the backs and across the knuckles. "Just because you stand on a rich man's land don't mean you got a rich man's money.''

"All right,'' Giorgio shouted, waving his arms to keep a distance between himself and the other. "I'll take the goddamn swing down.''

He stood next to the trunk and looked up to gauge the distance to the lowest branch. He was about to make a leap and shinny when a thought stopped him. "Hey, Bobio,'' he said, "I want to know something.''

Bobio grunted. "That's too bad, cause I don't know nothing.''

"Maybe you do. Maybe you know what happened to some rosary beads that were tied up to the rope here.''

"I know you're full of shit. That's all I know.''

"Bobio,'' Giorgio said in a supplicating voice, "those were valuable beads.''

"Sure, from a rich man like you.''

"They belong to Signorina Terasatti.''

"So how did you get them?''

"Never mind how. I just want to know, did you take them?"

Bobio's face contorted as if he smelled something putrid. "What do you think, I'm a crook? A thief? Is that what you're saying? You call me a crook, you son of a bitch, and I'll kill you. I'll kill you till there ain't nothing left of you." He swung his heavy rake like a scythe, and Giorgio, made clumsy by the weight and size of his boots, just barely escaped losing a hunk of the left side of his head.

"Hey, come on," he shouted as he ducked around the tree. "I just asked a question. That ain't no reason to kill a guy."

Bobio just cursed and came on, digging up divots with every swipe of the rake. Giorgio stayed just out of range, and though he was sure he could outrun the old gardener in the open, he was piqued enough to tease him by leading him in circles, around and around the tree until Bobio had to stop and wipe his forehead and gain his balance. Giorgio laughed and caught his breath; then the game.

There was no laughter in Bobio's eyes, only murder. Not even hatred—he was too tired for that. Only the dumb determination to club his quarry with a weapon. It took a woman's voice to stop him.

"What are you doing here? What is this?"

Bobio's eyes were strained wide with anger. Phlegm and wheezing strangled his voice to a high, garbled whine. "Ask him. He's the one who put it here. I don't know nothing. He called me a thief. Maybe Don Antonio will kill him for me, eh? I swear a vendetta before God—"

"Enough, old man," Brigetta said and touched her hand to her head as if to ease a pain. "How can I think with you going on this way?"

"Signora Terasatti would never have spoken to me in

this way. She showed respect for her elders. She was a good woman, and kind—''

Giorgio bowed his head in embarrassment. As despicable an old broom as Bobio might be, it was a shame to see him make such an ass of himself before a woman of quality. There was only one explanation. Sometimes old people got a little mixed up and forgot themselves. They made trouble. Otherwise why would this fellow, whom nobody had heard speak in sixty years, suddenly have such difficulty shutting up?

Brigetta let him go on for another minute before stopping him again. ''Signor,'' she finally said, ''I will call out one of the don's little friends to encourage your silence if you won't volunteer it.''

''Agh, now you want to beat me up! Sure, I'm an old man. It's easy.''

Giorgio expected him to launch into another screaming tirade, but he fell into a crying heap instead. Then he got to his knees and reached for the signorina's hand. She avoided his grasp, but he went on anyway.

''Why would you want to hurt me, signorina? I haven't harmed you. I've never harmed anyone. I live in the hills and don't bother people. I'm as innocent as a sparrow. I don't eat much; I don't steal; I pray on Sundays—''

''Signor, please tell me who this man is and why you're behaving like such an idiot. That's all I want to hear.''

''Signorina,'' he wheedled, ''I work hard. All of my life is devoted to one thing—to make this a beautiful place for Don Antonio to live. No, not just a beautiful place, but a palace, a paradise. Everything is perfect. Everything is symmetry. Look around. You can see for yourself. But now this peasant, this jackal, this worshipper of ugliness—''

This was too much. Giorgio couldn't let it go by. ''What are you saying, you son of a bitch? If you knew anything about beauty, you could look into my soul and see it there."

Then both men began screaming and waving their arms until the signorina angrily clapped her hands to get their attention. "Stop at once. At once!" she shouted.

Giorgio, who had better hearing than old Bobio, broke off first, giving the old man an opportunity to catch him across the nose with a backhand slap. A little blood trickled out and across his lip, but he stood respectfully waiting for the signorina to speak. He was too embarrassed by his own outburst to do anything else.

She took a swatch of white silk from some secret place in her sleeve and handed it to him. The sight of the blood seemed to make her uncomfortable.

"Signor," she said to Giorgio, "perhaps you can tell me what this is all about without making so much noise."

"He don't like the swing, signorina. What can I say?" He felt his mouth turn up in a little, charming smile. "He's ancient as a ruin, if you know what I mean. Maybe some of the bricks are falling out." Giorgio pointed at his own head, expecting the signorina to be amused. She was not.

"This is ridiculous," she snapped. "You are both ridiculous. If Don Antonio knew there were such disturbances going on near his home he would have you both chased off with a horsewhip."

"You see?" Bobio rasped at Giorgio. "You see what you have done?"

"Silence!" the signorina rapped out. "You," she said to Giorgio, "what's your name?"

Giorgio didn't like this. For the woman to know his name was a great risk, but he had no choice. To refuse to answer might be an even greater risk. "Farenza, Giorgio Farenza."

"All right. Very good." Her pretty face was full of

sternness. "Now what about this swing? How did it get here?"

Giorgio laughed nervously and chewed a little piece of his lower lip. This is where the real trouble starts, he thought. "I put it here," he admitted sheepishly.

"What for? You think the place needs this kind of thing?"

"Eh, there, I told you," Bobio mumbled.

"It was just a thought, signorina, an homage to Don Antonio, to his entire family."

The singorina's eyes narrowed. "What family? His daughter, maybe? Is that your interest?"

Even in the cool air Giorgio began to sweat, and he couldn't seem to focus on anything.

Bobio looked delighted. "Sure, that's it," he cackled. "You call me a thief while you try to steal away a man's daughter. Ha! That's who got the rosary—Signorina Terasatti."

Giorgio turned on him. "You keep her out of your filthy mouth or I'll rip our tongue from your head."

The old man's mouth relaxed into a satisfied smile, and he bobbed his head. "I know, I know, you're all the same, you kids. The mind is always in the same place."

This time the signorina seemed thoughtful rather than angry at the outburst. "Leave us, old man," she commanded. "I will take care of this man. And not a word to anyone. If there is a scandal, Don Antonio will hang your head in the piazza for the pigeons to sit on."

Bobio's eyes flashed with fear and the color left his cheeks. "Not a word, signorina, not a word. I leave this jackal to your most capable, most efficient hands." He went his way, bowing and scraping as if leaving a powerful noble's court.

When Bobio was finally out of sight the signorina

took Giorgio by the arm and walked beside him. "Tell me what's going on here. Be honest with me."

This was going to be difficult. He had to come up with something fast, something convincing, something as honest as he could make it sound. "I have heard that Signorina Terasatti is a beautiful young woman, a Venus, a credit to the entire province—"

That last was stupid, he thought. He could tell by the look on Signorina di Boromeo's face. "To tell you the truth," he said with affected weariness, "I thought that if I made a gift to the daughter of the don, he might look on us kindly when the work stops for the winter and perhaps give everyone a little bonus. It's hard to get by in the cold season and money runs out fast. I'm sorry if I've offended anyone. A wealthy woman like you wouldn't understand."

"I understand perfectly," she said without a pause. "I haven't always been, as you say, a wealthy woman."

A stroke of luck, he thought. Maybe she would be sympathetic enough to believe the story.

"Signor Farenza," she said thoughtfully, "if there is anything I know about men, especially men who are a little frightened, it is that when they sound most convincing, they are inevitably lying. Do you understand?"

He feigned a confused look—too confused. She'll think I'm an imbecile, he thought. There, that's better. Not so twisted around the eyes.

"You do understand, despite the contortions of your face. Now listen to me. Little Gabriella has caught your eye, no?"

He reddened.

"She has. Good. Now, this is more important. Have you caught her eye as well?"

He could feel the blood flushing fire into his cheeks and the signorina's face seemed to brighten visibly. "Excellent. Maybe there's a chance."

"Excuse me, but a chance for what?"

"A chance for you, dear boy, a chance for you."

He would have to show his hand a little. He didn't like it, but there was no other way. "She is already engaged, isn't she?"

"She's engaged to a fool. She despises him, and to tell you the truth, I don't blame her."

They walked for a moment in silence before she spoke again. "It was very sweet to build the swing for her, very romantic. The idea of a child. She would like that."

He wasn't so certain he liked being considered childlike, but he smiled anyway.

"Have you spoken with her about it?"

"No, of course not," he protested. "How could I speak to her without her father's permission, without an introduction, without—"

Brigetta held up her hand. "Perhaps it can be arranged."

"But why? Why should you help me? She's the daughter of a rich and powerful man. I can't give her this kind of life. I can't afford her. I can't do nothing for her."

"If you don't want her, Giorgio, if you think you're not man enough for her, then say so and that will be the end of this."

"I am Giorgio Farenza and man enough for anyone. I just want to know why you care about me."

"Maybe because I haven't always been rich. Maybe because you should have a chance, just as I did."

Yeah, sure, he thought. The rich are always helping everybody else. That's why most people had to live like pigs, because the rich were so kind and so helpful. Even the rich who used to be poor are helpful that way.

Whatever he thought, however, he could not bring himself to turn away from her extended hand. Anything to bring him closer to Gabriella, any chance was worth it. In fact, this woman was probably making a good offer. Why would she lie? Maybe she was lying about her reasons, but so what? Her reasons were her own.

"What must I do, signorina? I don't even know your name."

"You have cement on your trousers. You're a mason? Working on the wall?"

"Yes, but the work won't go on much longer. A few more days at most."

"When the others have gone tonight, wait by the mausoleum. We will see what happens."

"But signorina, what will they think if I don't leave with them?"

"What do you care what they think?" she asked harshly. "For a man with no means you're too cautious. If you want something badly enough, you take it. If you can't get it right away, then you do whatever you have to do to lay your hands on it. You understand? If you want to speak with Gabriella, you do what I say."

"I understand."

"Good. Then you will wait."

"Yes, I will wait. By the mausoleum."

"Stay until an hour after dark. If nothing has happened by then, go home and forget her."

"As you say, signorina."

Chapter 12

Brigetta di Boromeo was pleased with her luck but not surprised. Luck always came her way. What a scandal it caused, for example, when Antonio first plucked her off the street so many years ago and made a kept woman of her, and how the old women clucked and gossiped, but it turned out to be a wonderful stroke of good fortune.

From that day her life changed in ways she never would have imagined. There was no more shameful poverty, no more scrubbing laundry on rippled boards until her fingers were flayed raw or going so hungry her stomach and chest burned.

Yes, it would have been better if Antonio had taken her to wed, but he was already married, and being second in line was better than nothing. As for the old gossips back in Naples, they were full of pity and envy for Brigetta in those days but had long since forgotten her name.

Perhaps God would punish her one day for her sinful life, but so far He had shown her great tolerance, and why should He do otherwise? Look how well He had treated Maria Magdalena.

Now and then things hadn't been quite so easy. Antonio was given to violent rages, and one time he left her with a broken arm because a bouquet of flowers was accidentally delivered to her apartment. He had believed the worst of her, that she had taken another lover.

It was his age, she knew, that lay at the bottom of his tantrums. He was afraid of getting old. For the most part, however, when he could forget his wrinkles and his paunch, he was a gentleman, and perhaps because she had never known another lover, she always found his companionship satisfactory if not exciting. Certainly he provided for her, gave her the life of a princess if measured by the number of dresses and shoes she owned or by the prestige of her address, or by the deference with which she was treated by bureaucrats and hotel clerks.

Now the only obstacle between herself and a comfortable middle age was Gabriella, whom she liked much more than she ever would have admitted, and even that problem seemed to be taking care of itself. Antonio had been struck from behind out near the gatekeeper's quarters on the night of his wife's funeral, though he would never allow himself to admit it. What had happened was obvious.

Gabriella had arranged to meet a man and been caught in the act. Who the man was Brigetta had no idea until she met him in the garden this afternoon. Then the puzzle was solved as easily as if Luck herself were piecing it together.

It would, of course, be difficult to arrange a marriage between Antonio's daughter and this *braccianti*, but a marriage wasn't necessary. It mattered only that Gabriella fall in love, that her fears for her own future be calmed long enough for Brigetta to marry Antonio. Then what would be would be.

If she didn't find herself a husband, Brigetta would care for her. It was the least she could do for the don's only child. She herself would have wanted the same for her children if only she had been able to have any.

She found Gabriella in the study. Brigetta was never very comfortable in this room. The windows were very high and the cretonne draperies, pulled apart and swagged back, let in a barren, glaring light that neither warmed nor illuminated the room, but fell in sinister jigsaw patterns upon the floor.

Two walls were full of books from floor to ceiling, many of them ancient manuscripts that hadn't been touched in generations. All that old paper gave off a musty odor she couldn't get used to. There were secrets here she would never fathom. She had no interest in books, could read only well enough to follow a story in the paper, and these books, peering down like so many faces, frightened her. They were the works of learned men, men of authority who would have no sympathy for a woman like her.

Gabriella sensed Brigetta's discomfort. Perhaps that was why she so often came here, to find sanctuary. Brigetta suspected as much, but she wouldn't be put off so easily today.

Gabriella was sitting at the Florentine desk that stood like an altar beneath the three windows at the far end of the room. She was toying with something, though Brigetta couldn't tell what it was at first.

"I would like to speak to you," Brigetta said.

"We have already spoken today," Gabriella replied, but her voice was no longer full of despair. Instead she seemed bemused, almost unaware that Brigetta was there.

"I have something important to tell you."

"Signorina, that is most unlikely."

"It is about Signor Farenza."

There was a sudden sound like gravel falling on wood as whatever Gabriella had been holding slipped out of her hands and onto the top of the desk. Brigetta inched closer for a better look. A rosary—of course. The mason had said something about a rosary.

To toy with her, Brigetta said, "We can speak later."

Gabriella seemed wary, frightened, cautious of every word as she spoke. "What do you know of him?"

"Not as much as you do, I'm sure."

"I know nothing of him. He works for my father, that's all."

"In that case what I have to say will be of no interest to you."

Gabriella couldn't contain her exasperation. "Please say what you have to say!"

"Only this. He will be waiting for you on the other side of the garden after the workmen leave in the evening. He will wait one hour and no more."

"Why should I care if he's waiting?" Gabriella's frown was most convincing. "He's nothing to me."

"He would be sorry to hear you say it."

"That's too bad for him. Why did he give *you* this message? Why didn't he come himself?"

"Because as you know very well, he would be risking his life if he did."

Gabriella turned her head away sharply as if insulted. "It's nothing to me. Let him wait an hour or a year for all I care."

"I'll tell him not to wait at all if you like."

"No, no, don't waste your time. Let him learn a lesson."

"You're a very hard teacher, Gabriella."

"I'm learning from you."

Brigetta bowed her head slightly and smiled to herself as she left the room. It would be a real surprise if Gabriella didn't go to him that evening. Brigetta sighed. Old men and the young were so predictable. What a shame. It sometimes made life a little boring.

Gabriella could hardly contain herself. He would be waiting for her. In just a few long, long hours—how

would she spend all that time?—they would meet and
speak. "Thank you for my garden swing. It was very
thoughtful of you."

"Not at all. My pleasure. Anything for you."

"You flatter me too much, signor, far too much."

"How could I flatter you too much? You are lovelier
than flattery can say."

She heard it and rehearsed it and turned it a hundred
ways in her mind. She didn't really know him, but that
was how love happened, wasn't it? It wasn't like meeting
someone you were promised to. It didn't have to take a
long time while you got to know each other, too well
maybe, and learned how to put up with each other. Love
wasn't like that. She had discovered much about love in
her eighteen years. It was all in the books there on the
study wall. That was how she recognized it now that it had
come to her.

At first she hadn't known what to call these sensa-
tions that were so new to her. She tried to remember how
she felt about Giorgio that first night in the rain. His kiss
made her angry, but there must have been something
pleasurable, she was sure, because she hadn't told her
father who hit him on the head, and she went to Giorgio's
workplace to inquire after him. Oh, it was love, it was
love, it was grand as water splashing in a fountain. It
made her giddy whenever she thought about it, and she
thought about nothing else.

But how did that witch Brigetta get involved? How
had she come to be Giorgio's messenger? That was
something to think about. Maybe her father would be
waiting and watching from a hiding place. Maybe it was
all a trap. There was no way to know, but if it was a trap,
the bait was too sweet to resist.

She took a bead of the rosary in her hand and absently
said a Hail Mary for luck. *Madonna mia*, she prayed,

protector of young lovers, Star of Heaven and Queen of Hosts, keep my Giorgio safe and curse anyone who would bring harm to him.

Giorgio hadn't decided what to do. He was so weary his eyes seemed swollen and his voice wouldn't rise above a mumble. In fact, he was so dull that the other workers had stopped teasing him. He was no fun if he was too tired to defend himself. How could she love him if she saw him like this? She would think he was simple-minded, and maybe he was. After all, he had entrusted a stranger to make these arrangements for him—not only a stranger, but a woman he knew to be the don's mistress, a woman whose first loyalty lay with the very man who would shoot Giorgio if he found him out. Stupido, stupido, stupido, Giorgio repeated to himself, and tapped his forehead with the palm of his hand.

Several times Scarfo asked him where he had disappeared to at lunchtime, and always Giorgio told the old man to mind his own business. Now Scarfo had stopped asking. He refused even to look Giorgio in the face. There was no doubt he still suspected something. Well, to hell with him, Giorgio thought. Let him suspect. Let him wonder and guess. A man has a right to to keep his own business to himself.

So he kept it to himself and a curious thing began to happen. Giorgio felt a sudden impulse to tell Scarfo everything, not for advice or comment—Scarfo could be a real *cafonn'* at times—but just to have someone to listen, someone who would know what Giorgio was going through. Giorgio found that keeping a secret, especially one that had to do with love, was a terrible torture. If he was unsure, he wanted someone to be unsure with him, and to share his misery and his hopes.

Trapped with his uncertainties, he became wistful,

then luxuriantly depressed. He convinced himself that he would inevitably be the victim of heartbreak. Ah, Signorina Terasatti, he thought, if only you would come to me at the end of the day, but I know you will not come. I will wait for you and hope to hear your footsteps, and I will not hear them. You will stay in your big house laughing at the poor little workman who built a swing for you, and to be honest, not a very beautiful little swing.

If only you came to know me you would not laugh. You would love me. I'm very handsome in a suit. I have one made of silk from Sicily. Yes, you would love me if you saw me in that suit. I should have worn it that night I came to your house, but I was a jackass that night. I don't blame you for laughing. I too would laugh at a jackass. So when you don't come and my heart is broken, I won't think any worse of you. I will remember you always and hold you in my heart as I have worn your rosary next to it for so many years.

Bobio didn't like the idea of these workmen ruining his garden with their hideous wall, but a man had to accept some things he didn't like. Don Antonio was the boss, and you had to listen to the boss. Sometimes that was hard, obeying another man's orders, but life was hard. It required great courage to go from day to day, never knowing what calamity the next moment would bring.

This was a lesson you learned in the hills, where the wind chewed the skin from your face and every cutthroat for miles was ready to grab the food out of your mouth. Years ago Bobio went to the hills to find freedom—from the church and from God always looking over his shoulder, from the taxman always sticking his hands into a man's pockets, from women who as far as he was concerned were worse than the church and God and the taxman put together.

What he found in the hills was servitude—he became a slave to his own belly, since every bite of food he took had to be paid for by sweat and labor and cunning. There was no way out of the miseries of life but death, and he did not want to die, so he learned to serve and to forget about freedom.

Now he served Don Antonio and through him the beauty of this garden, but today he had been reminded of a bitter lesson. A man like himself, old and without property, served everyone and everything. He served the worms who ate the dirt, the birds who ate the worms and the damned paid-for woman, Signorina di Boromeo, who had the birds roasted and braised for her own dinner.

Worst of all was the son of a bitch who put up the swing and scratched off strips of bark from a fine tree with his clumsy boots and dug up divots of the grass that was so difficult to grow in this region. Bobio spat into a hedge. God had finally caught up with him and was making a fool out of him. Not only did he have to serve the beauty of the garden, but he had to serve the bastards who ruined it.

It was no proper life for a man, he told himself, no life at all, and the more he thought about it, the more he was convinced that he should abandon this place and move along. He could go back to the hills and raise a few chickens and live off the eggs.

He wasn't sure what to do about Don Antonio. As far as bosses went, he had been a good one, and he deserved a little loyalty. Not so much that Bobio felt obliged to spend his remaining days here, but a decent boss deserved at least an explanation. Don Antonio would understand. He was a man of the world.

Bobio rehearsed a little speech as he began collecting the garden tools. "I'm sorry signor, but even an old man like me has his pride. I must leave the Villa Vichierri, though it breaks my heart. First-class gardeners are hard to find, I know, but there's nothing to do about it.

"Why—you say why? Because I won't have some stupid jackass of a stonemason building swings all over the landscape, and—please forgive me for this, signor—I don't like having a woman telling me what to do. It's not natural.

"What woman? I would rather not say. Only that she is known to you—in fact, is very close to you. But even if I meant Signorina di Boromeo herself, what would be the difference? A man is a man, and he is not born to take orders from the lower species—not the worms or the birds or the women."

Yes, it was a good speech, he told himself. The don would be moved to pity.

By the end of the day it was raining again. Giorgio stood under the stone eave of the mausoleum for protection, but as the drizzle turned into a shower and then a downpour of slapping sheets, he was forced to open the bronze doors, green and black with verdigris, and to take shelter inside.

Just my luck, he thought. Just my no-good luck. And You, God, You're lucky. You're my friend or I would tell You where to go. Why did You have to choose this minute to make it rain, eh? I'm not gonna do nothing wrong. Just talk to a young lady, that's all.

With the door closed there was no light in the mausoleum. It gave him an eerie feeling and frightened him a little. The only noise was the hiss of the rain against the bronze and the clucking of his tongue against the roof of his mouth. He stood very still, tensed to feel the slightest movement in the damp, chilly air, as though there might be something in the dark watching, listening, about to walk . . .

He quickly blessed himself and mumbled, "I'm sorry, God. I didn't mean nothing. Let it rain. I'm glad for the rain. I love it."

But how am I gonna talk with my signorina in a place like this, with dead people all around listening? he wondered. Then the obvious answer came to him. There was nothing to worry about. No one would be stupid enough to come out in weather like this. He wasn't going to talk to nobody. He was the only person in Italy who was out in this rain.

A sound. What? A little murmur in the rain. Barely a sound at all. Maybe a voice—maybe. Then a different sound, footsteps. And again the murmur—yes, a voice, but such a tiny voice.

"Signor Farenza? Are you here?"

His heart leaped and he nearly threw open the door and called out, but a sudden thought stopped him. How was he to know it was the signorina? He couldn't remember what she sounded like. He'd only heard her speak once. Then he shook his head and said to himself, Agh, Giorgio, who the hell else would it be? You're driving yourself crazy. Stop it right now.

With his heart fluttering like a dove in his breast and his blood burning in his cheeks, he pulled against the heavy weight of the door and opened it wide enough to see out.

"I'm in here," he said.

Her figure looked ghostly in the rain and mist, mysterious and pleasing. She slipped inside. Her head was covered with a brown shawl, which she held together with one hand at her breast. Ringlets of dark wet hair fell like festoons over her forehead, and her clothing, soaked and heavy with rain, made her shiver.

"What do you mean, making me run around in the rain looking for you?" she said petulantly. "If that's what you wanted, just to make me get cold and wet, then you can go home and never come here again—"

The tirade, he knew, would go on for another five minutes if he didn't stop her, so he followed an impulse.

He took her in his arms and kissed her. The wetness made her feel slippery. She didn't fight, but she didn't give in to him either. She stood with her arms at her sides. He tried to make her lips come to life by pressing hard against them, then by brushing them lightly, and then, even though he knew he was taking his life in his hands, by touching them with the tip of his tongue. Still she didn't respond, but she didn't slap him either. It was a beginning.

"You're very brazen. You have no manners," she said when he finally released her, but her protest was meek, halfhearted, and Giorgio was pleased. Maybe there was a little fire lit inside her after all.

"I'm sorry, signorina, but you looked so beautiful with the rain in your lashes, as if you were crying, like the Madonna herself, as she stands over the alcove in the Church of San Martino . . ."

"Ah, I see. Now I have to listen to your boring flattery."

As lovely as she was, as giddy as he felt just being near her, he heard his voice grow thin and sarcastic. "If I bore you, why don't you leave? Go back to your ugly damned villa and forget you ever spoke to me."

"Forget? I never forget anything. I don't forget the way you hit my father over the head with your umbrella."

"Agh, *Madonn'*, you're impossible. I hit him, at the risk of my own life—"

"A worthless life—"

"At the risk of my precious life, to protect you."

"Who are you to protect me from my own father?"

"Signorina Terasatti, in all the years since I met you the very first time, you are still the same. Not a change, not a difference, nothing." He reached to his shirt pocket for his cigarette tobacco. He hoped it hadn't been soaked.

"Why should I change? I like the way I am," Gabriella said, then glanced around furtively. "Don't smoke in here."

"Why not? You think the dead people care?"

"I care. My mother is buried here. Besides, you wouldn't smoke in church, would you?"

"What do you mean?"

"Light a match."

It took half a dozen strikes to get a wooden match lit. She took it from him, and protecting the flame with the cup of her hands, made her way through the dark and lit several votive candles in a golden heart-shaped holder that stood against the wall across the room. Everything became dimly visible. The walls were checkered with engraved plaques that marked the crypts, and at the other end of the tiny building a simple marble altar was watched over by a plain Roman cross. Out of respect Giorgio crossed himself.

"Okay, I won't smoke," he said, but he regretted it because he felt very nervous, very trapped, and a cigarette would calm him, cool his brain a little. After all, here he was with the object of his desires, a woman who captured his every thought, and she had all but spat on him from the first moment. He wanted to run, but he couldn't. He loved her. It was a curse. His feet might as well have been nailed to the floor.

She came up close and looked into his face. Now what? he wondered.

"It was you who made the swing for me," she said.

"Yes, of course. Why? Don't you like it?"

Her lids fluttered and she cast her eyes down. Her voice became a hush. "Yes, it's a very nice swing."

"I thought maybe you didn't like it. Since you don't like nothing else about me."

"No, I like the swing."

Again his heart seemed to jump within him. She loves me after all, he thought. "But you didn't like the rosary."

"It was my rosary to begin with."

Maybe she doesn't love me so much. "I kept it all those years. Does that mean nothing?"

"Maybe it means something. Something small."

So she loves me a little bit. "It made me think of you every day."

She looked up at him brazenly. "You're a liar and a peasant. Who knows why you kept it?"

All right, she hates me then. "I kept it to throw in your face."

She glowered at him but resisted the impulse to strike. "Don't talk to me that way. I'm not a woman of the street." A tear glistened at the corner of her eye.

Now, what the hell? He didn't know what the tear meant, since she had started the argument, but he gently put his arms around her and held her close as if to warm her. "I'm sorry," he said. "They should take me into a field and shoot me and cut me up for the crows and burn what the crows won't eat."

Gabriella sighed. "That's enough, Giorgio. You don't know when to stop." She touched his breast with her fingers and made little figures, as if she were drawing on parchment. "I don't know what's the matter with me. I don't know why I'm being mean to you."

"Me neither. Maybe you got a touch of malaria."

She laughed. It was as beautiful laugh, he thought. It made his skin tingle.

"Maybe I'll go see a doctor," she said. "You know any doctors?"

"You're crazy. The doctors will kill you faster than the malaria."

It was a long time before she spoke again. Giorgio felt vaguely uncomfortable in the silence, but she was settled so snugly in his arms that he didn't want to disturb anything.

"I've never been alone with a man before," she finally said.

"Yeah?" He wondered what she was trying to tell him.

"I don't feel right. I feel hot under the skin."

"Maybe that's why you act so crazy, this heat under the skin."

"Maybe. I liked the swing very much. It was a nice thought."

"Ah, good. You liked it then."

"I just told you that."

"Sure, but I wanted to hear you tell me again."

"It was a wonderful idea. A grand idea. And the rosary too."

"The old gardener wanted me to take the swing down."

Gabriella frowned. "I'll have him fired."

"Your father would do such a thing for you?"

She thought a moment. "No. I suppose not."

"Ah, well then, signorina."

"Please, Giorgio, stop that. Call me Gabriella. That's my name. You make me feel like a stranger."

"You are a stranger."

"You have kissed me twice and built me a swing. How can I be a stranger?"

"All right. I'll call you Gabriella, then. It's a very nice name. Like an angel, eh?"

"Don't make blasphemy."

He laughed nervously. The candles flickered. The hiss of the rain seemed to grow louder. His eyes wandered among the shadows, over the plaques bearing the names of the dead. There must be some other place to meet, he thought.

"Giorgio, tell me something. Why did you give your message to my father's mistress? Weren't you afraid she would give you away?"

"What else could I do? I could not come in to see you myself. And she was the one who saved your swing from the gardener. So I took the chance. Besides, she seemed to know my feelings for you, as if they'd fallen out of my mouth on the ground in front of her.''

"I don't understand. We are not friends, she and I, yet she does this for me. It's curious.''

"Women,'' he muttered. "Who can understand anything they do?''

"But I am a woman!''

"Yes, and what do I understand about you? Nothing.''

"Good. That's the way it should be. A man should be stupid and a woman should be clever and beautiful.''

He stroked her damp hair lightly with his rough hand. "It's true,'' he said, as if reaffirming a remark made elsewhere. "You're the most beautiful woman I've ever seen.''

She took his hand from her hair and held it. "Does that mean you love me, Giorgio?''

The question startled him, and he answered as though defending himself before a judge in a court of law. "Of course I love you. How can you ask? I have loved you from the first with all my heart, all my soul, all my strength. At night I dream about you; during the day I think about you. It's like a sickness. It's worse sometimes because I think of the man I met at the villa, the one who will marry you, and I want to kill the pig. I want to strangle him and crush his bones with the heel of my boot. Do you understand? Of course you don't. No one understands such a love as I have for you.''

Throughout the speech a little smile touched Gabriella's lips. Giorgio wondered what it meant, but it looked like one of those smiles you don't ask a woman about. It had the look of secrecy, of the mysteries women share only with each other. Still, it piqued him enough so that he went on ardently.

"I want to be like a real suitor to you. I want to come to your parlor, and take you through the village in a cart, and walk along the corso dressed in fine clothes so everyone will see you on my arm and be jealous. But you're already promised, and even if you weren't, your father would never let me marry you.''

She looked at him in surprise. ''Marry? Giorgio, how can you talk about marriage yet? I don't know if I want to marry you. It's too soon. I only know that I love you.''

''You do? You love me?''

''Of course. Do you think I would have come here otherwise?''

''No, no. You're right, I should have known. But I'm only being stupid, like you said.''

She looked up at him and shook her head in a gesture of amused exasperation. Then she kissed him, a long kiss that touched his lips as lightly as the brush of a breeze.

If she loved me, why didn't she do this before? he wondered. Then in his euphoria, his thoughts seemed to turn into nothing.

They lingered together in their kiss.

When their lips parted, she seemed to meditate upon his face for a moment, then said, ''Good-bye, Giorgio,'' and she was almost out the door before he could speak.

''When will I see you again?''

''I will send for you. Be patient.''

Bobio delivered his message to Don Antonio exactly as he had planned it. Cicero couldn't have done a better job, he decided proudly. His hands wove a fantastic pattern in the air as he spoke, like a woman at work on a tapestry, but his feet remained together with perfect decorum, like the feet of a real gentleman. The tone of his voice, the choice of his words, the sincerity and passion that exploded from his throat—*mamma mia*, no wonder a storm gathered in the boss' face.

The performance was made in the don's office, a small room covered from floor to ceiling with dark hickory paneling. There was only one window, blocked by heavy blue-velvet curtains, and a thick sculptured maroon rug covered the floor. At first Bobio felt his voice muffled and swallowed up by the place, but his cunning told him to play with the effect, to let intimacy grow in it so that the don would become one with an old man's words.

When the show was over, it took a long time for Don Antonio to speak. He sat at his desk, a large, heavy piece of oak with a top completely unblemished by pen, paper or writing material of any kind, and he folded his hands before him as if in silent prayer.

Bobio grew nervous in the silence. The lid under his left eye began to twitch. He realized for the first time that he feared the man sitting in front of him, though he couldn't explain why. After all, murder was the worst one man could do to another, and Bobio wasn't afraid to die. But to the old man a greater power, almost a divinity, seemed to lurk behind Don Antonio's stern face. Bobio coughed and shifted his feet. The don slowly raised his eyes to the man.

"You don't quit, Bobio. Nobody quits working for me until I'm through with him."

"Signor Terasatti, how can I work with the mason ruining everything I do and women running about giving me orders—I explained to you already."

"I understand and I will take care of everything. You are back on the job tomorrow. Go on now, get out of here."

Well, the old man thought as he bowed and backed out of the room, it won't hurt to come back as long as the don takes care of everything. And of course there was no question that he would. Don Antonio Terasatti was a man of his word.

* * *

What is going on in my house? Don Antonio angrily demanded of himself. He was on his way down a narrow hall that led to Brigetta's private room. At night, when he was asleep, she would leave his bed for her own and spend the night by herself. For some reason it salved her conscience, and if he was honest with himself, he had to admit that it salved his too. After all, his innocent daughter was in the house.

He found Brigetta dozing, as he expected he would. It was her habit to nap in the late afternoon. She lay fully clothed in a dark blue cotton dress, with her hair unpinned so that it spread like a dark corona upon the white linen bedcover. At any other time, finding her looking like that, he would have taken her without hesitation, he would have conquered her sleeping innocence and ruined it, but now he wanted only to slap her and to make her talk. There was something going on in his house, and he did not know what it was, and he did not like it.

"Get the hell out of that bed," he barked as he grabbed her arm and jerked her upward.

For a second she looked dazed and terrified. He shook her violently, but then her eyes became serene. "Antonio, what it? What's happened?"

"Bitch," he snarled and grabbed a handful of her hair, then yanked backward. "You tell me."

She gritted her teeth but refused to give in to him. "Antonio, I don't know what you're talking about."

"The peasant. The workman who's been hanging swings from my trees," he shouted, then began to hack and cough so that he had to let go of her hair.

She did not go to help him, but rather waited for him to finish. He put a handkerchief to his mouth and little bloody spots appeared on it. Then he began to retch, and in a moment the white silk in his hand was soaked in red.

Finally the attack abated and he was left struggling to clear his throat.

"If you work yourself up like this," Brigetta said to him, "You'll die that much faster."

"Don't worry about me dying," he said in a strangled voice. "I'll die when I'm damn good and ready and not a moment before. That's what I got bodyguards for."

"Don't be stupid, Antonio. I don't like you when you're stupid."

"Agh, you don't like me when I'm stupid, eh?" He gave her a weak slap, not enough to hurt her, just enough to warn her. The coughing had taken all the strength out of him. He felt dizzy and less mean, but he was suspicious. It was only a hunch, but his hunches had always been his closest allies. They had never lied to him before.

"What about this swing? Old Bobio says a man has been ruining my trees."

"One of the workmen thought it might be a nice present for Gabriella. That's all."

He looked at her closely. He couldn't see a lie in her eyes. But when it was there, he would know. "Why do the workmen bother with my daughter? She's none of their business."

"It is because of their respect for you, Antonio. What do you think?"

"Yeah, maybe, but what about this rosary?"

"I don't know anything about a rosary. I didn't see a rosary."

"Bobio says the workman accused him of stealing it."

She shook her head and laughed as though in disbelief. "These men are peasants. What do you expect from them? All their lives they grovel in the dirt and steal from each other."

Still he couldn't see the lie. "Why did you send the

old man away? What were you doing alone with this young mason?''

Brigetta looked as if she could barely contain herself from hysterical giggling. "Are you jealous? Don't be a fool, Antonio.''

He growled like an animal. "You remember last time. I broke your arm.''

"Yes, and for no good reason. It was stupid, and do you remember how long it was before I could come to your bed again? If that's what you want, my love, then break my other arm.''

He thought for a moment. It annoyed him when she mocked him this way, but she knew his weakness, she knew how he hated to go without her for long, and he felt tied tight like a gift in a package.

"All right then, suppose I believe you," he said. "What were you talking about to the man?''

"I was trying to get the story from him, Antonio. I was trying to find out what the fuss was all about. Bobio was making so much noise I had to get rid of him before my head split open.''

"It's not your business to order my workmen around. They don't like it.''

She bowed her head, as he expected her to. "I'm sorry, my love, but if the man had shown me the least amount of respect, as anyone should knowing my relationship with you, there would have been no need for orders.''

She was leading Antonio in circles. He sensed it, and he hated it, and he knew there was nothing to do about it. "All right, then," he said, "What was the story? What did the workman tell you?''

"Only what I said before. The swing was for Gabriella.''

Still no lie in her eyes. Maybe he had missed it. Maybe the blood in his chest was fouling his instincts. There was no way to know. He could only accept her word as the truth, at least for now.

If she was telling the truth, if the workman had made the swing for Gabriella, then another thought couldn't be ignored. His daughter had been alone with a workman the night of poor Maria's funeral. Maybe that was her game. Maybe she was fooling around with workmen. She'd better not be. He would break her neck. But just to make sure, he would see that Gabriella was watched more closely.

"I don't want a swing on my property," he said. "We have no children here. I will have it taken down tomorrow. As for the workman—what is his name?"

"I didn't ask him, Antonio."

Ah, there it was! The lie. So there was something to be suspicious about. "As for him, the next time he'll regret giving gifts when they haven't been asked for. I don't want Gabriella exposed to any of this. From now on she goes nowhere without an escort."

"You mean me?"

"No, not you," he said pointedly. "The French maid will do." The maid was loyal, he thought, because she was afraid of him and because she came to his bed at night sometimes after Brigetta had gone. Yes, little Suzette was a good girl. "In fact," he went on, "I don't want my daughter left alone at any part of the day. Do you understand? At night the gate will be locked and dogs set loose on the grounds. No more swings, no more nothing."

"Whatever you wish, Antonio."

There was a look of perplexity and disappointment on her face. It was only a slight cast of the eyes, a quick tremble of the chin, but Don Antonio saw it and he was pleased. Yes, there was something up with the daughter, and it would be stopped, or somebody would pay with their blood.

Although Giorgio promised himself he wouldn't say a word, a single evening hadn't gone by before he blurted out the whole story to Scarfo. He was too excited and confused to keep everything to himself. Gabriella loved him and he wanted everyone to know. To Giorgio Scarfo was everyone.

"It's all very interesting," the old man said. "Aren't you worried?"

"About what?"

"About getting your throat cut."

"If I do, I do. What the hell. I am alive, Scarfo, for the first time in my life. Once you've been alive, what the hell does it matter if you die?"

"You're young, but let me tell you. It matters."

"Is that all you have to say? Don't you think I was clever to make a swing for her? Don't you think I did everything wonderfully?"

"Yeah, sure," Scarfo said, and drank back a glass of wine in one gulp. "You're wonderful all the time. It's nice to be young. Enjoy it. You're right. If you get killed, what the hell. Who will care besides me?"

"Gabriella will care."

"Ah, her. Maybe." He nodded sagely. "Maybe she will care."

"She would. She loves me."

For the rest of the night not another word passed between them.

Chapter 13

For a week Giorgio heard nothing. Every day on the job he waited for some sign—a note slipped into his hand, a word whispered in his ear. He continually scrutinized the hard, weathered faces of the men around him, looking for one that might give him a clue, perhaps one with the sly, satisfied look of a man who had been bribed, but nothing happened.

His hopes, which had been fragile to begin with, dwindled like the body of a starving child. There would be one more week of work, no more. Then he would be trapped in the little house with Scarfo for the rest of the season, doing his best to stay warm and to keep sane.

Time after time he played the scene in the mausoleum in his mind. Sometimes when no one was around, he would speak his own part out loud, changing a little bit here and there, a word, a phrase, a tone of voice, and he would try to guess how she would have answered him differently. When he was at work or Scarfo was in the room, he would drift off into daydreams in which he would try to imagine his next meeting with Gabriella. His feelings kept stirring him just a little, like a leaf in a light breeze, and he would find himself laughing or frowning without knowing why.

Scarfo ignored his mooning. In his mind Giorgio was a goner. Giorgio, for his part, paid no attention to his old friend's fatalism, but he too felt willing to let matters go their own way. Love made fate worth risking.

Only once during that week did any event take his mind off her for even a minute. Giovanni Sticcola, the one they called Gigolo for a joke, a mason's helper and a terrible gossip, brought news on Thursday. A conscription officer had been waylaid four miles outside of Caserta and killed.

This in itself was no surprise. The army was the government and the government was run by strangers from Rome. No town in the south gave up its children easily. Why the hell should the army have the local boys to fight its idiotic wars? Strong arms were needed here to farm the hills, to dig the stone into terraces for planting, to make walls and houses and factories and schools.

No, what was intriguing about the murder was that the man's head had been removed and smuggled into a draft office, where it was placed upon the ink blotter of his very own desk and left there to greet his co-workers in the morning. It was very funny, everyone agreed.

Nonetheless, Giorgio felt uneasy. Every time one of these bastards was killed, a whole gang of them came down and shook out the local farms for evaders. The cry of the government was always the same—Italy has enemies (What the hell was Italy?) and today the enemy is Austria. (What the hell was Austria?)

Friday, having had nothing from Gabriella, not even so much as a wave from her window, Giorgio was beside himself. Either she was ill or she had lost interest in him. Or worse, she had lied to him to begin with.

That made no sense. Why would she go out of her way to tell such a fantastic lie? Why would she try to make a fool of him? He was only a poor mason, hardly worth the trouble. If she were ill, it would have been the talk of the work crew by now.

There was only one likely answer. Her passion had burst into flame for a brief moment and then died out like a candle in the rain. She would marry her fiance after all, and she would forget all about Giorgio—if she hadn't already.

What a life, he moaned to himself over and over again. He tried to resign himself but couldn't. He tried to make excuses for her, but he couldn't do that either. He couldn't even know if he was right. Something had to happen. He had to know for sure.

So he wrote her a note. It was brief; writing was hard for him, and he had to spell the words by sounding them out. It said simply, "Have you forgotten me? I will never forget you. I love you. Giorgio."

He reread the note on Friday night after he'd had too much wine with supper and cried, touched by his own sentiments. Then he folded the paper, a grease-stained little scrap that had been the corner of a fish wrapper, and he put it in his pocket.

Scarfo caught him going out the door. "Hey, kid, where are you going?"

"To the Villa Vichierri, the place where we work, where we sweat and cut stone for a man whose throat we'd like to cut."

"What the hell are you talking about? I don't want to kill nobody. If you're smart, you don't want to kill nobody either. And stay the hell away from the villa at night. I ain't got enough money put away to give you a decent funeral."

"You don't got to give me no funeral. Just feed me to the pigs, like you were going to do the first day I woke up here." He belched and made a face at the rancid smell of

his own breath. He didn't want a lecture tonight. He didn't
want anything but Gabriella.

Oh, Gabriella, who had such sweet lips, and who said
she loved him and then left him alone and lonely to get
drunk on wine...

"To hell with you, old man," he said, though the
words were so badly slurred he wasn't sure Scarfo understood them. "I got mail to deliver. I got a letter for a
lady—a lady who can read, you hear? An educated lady."

Giorgio couldn't tell what Scarfo answered. Suddenly
his head was buzzing so loud inside that he could hardly
hear a thing. He always got this way when he was too
drunk. First his lips went numb, then his nose tingled and
then his hearing went.

He knew Scarfo was yelling, though. The old man's
arms were waving and his face was screwed up into a
scowl and his mouth was moving rapidly. Giorgio answered him soundlessly. He put one hand in the crook of
his elbow, made a fist with his other, and closed his arm
over the first hand. Now the old man knew what he could
do with his lectures. Giorgio stumbled out the door.

The next thing he knew, he was staggering through
the dark on the familiar road to the Villa Vichierri, promis-
ing himself to get his note to Gabriella no matter what the
risk.

"Why don't you leave me alone? Get out. Get out!"
Gabriella took a white porcelain statuette of the Virgin
from her bedside table and threatened to throw it at Suzette,
sitting in a cushionless wooden chair across the room. The
maid held up her hands to protect herself, ducked down a
little to make a show of her fear and began clucking away
in her dialect so quickly that Gabriella hadn't a chance of
understanding her.

"Why don't you learn to speak proper Italian?"

Gabriella sneered. "It's bad enough to have a jailer, but this gibberish is intolerable."

"*Mi dispiache*," Suzette apologized in a voice so labored and precise that it was almost as annoying as her clucking.

Gabriella shook her head. There was no point in taking it further. Suzette was here because her father had put her here. Somehow he had found out about Giorgio.

Brigetta had told him, probably, though what she had gained from doing so Gabriella couldn't say. She expected the worst from her father's mistress, but she didn't expect blind vindictiveness. Brigetta had always seemed too calculating, too practical to be bothered with petty cruelties.

Gabriella lay back on her bed and threw one arm over her eyes to shut out the offensive sight of the maid. She was worried about Giorgio. What would he be thinking? Perhaps he had already given up on her. It was a week now and she had had no chance to communicate with him. Perhaps he had found another to love. He was handsome enough. He could have anyone in the village he wanted, she was sure.

Madonna, she prayed silently, help me. I'm not asking for much, just that my Giorgio love me. Let him come to me and take me far away from here, where I can forget about my father and his mistress. That's all I ask, that you take me away from the sin under this roof. There, Holy Mother, you see? I am requesting deliverance. Surely you cannot refuse me. Surely that would be against the law of heaven.

She sighed as the details of his face drifted back into her mind. Light brown hair, long and soft, blue eyes, a kindly mouth if a little too thin... Oh, why had she treated him the way she did during those first moments? How often she had regretted her behavior since then. She wanted nothing but love, sweetness, joy in those first moments

and instead she did all she could to make poor Giorgio
miserable. Why, why, why?

Giorgio said he didn't understand women, but neither
did she understand herself. It was as if she knew no other
way to talk, no other tone of voice than that of sarcasm
and annoyance. He had said he loved her at least, and they
had been words to dream about for awhile.

Now they had not been together for a whole eternal
week, and most of her memories of her time with him
were of her own truculence. First he kissed her and she
didn't know what to do. She was afraid. It wasn't so bad
this time as the first, that night in the gatehouse, because
he was more tender, though he touched her with his tongue
and she didn't know what to make of that. But she felt—
what? Reluctance? Remorse? It was as though he was
trying to take something precious from her that she didn't
want to give—and yet she did want to give it.

It was all so stupid. She had behaved like a sulky
child. Thank God they had had a little time to be tender.

The maid said something incomprehensible. Gabriella
took her arm from her face and looked up, bleary-eyed.
Now what?

The look she saw in Suzette's eyes was one of
sympathy, she would have thought, of understanding. The
maid came to her and put her hand on Gabriella's cheek,
then bent over and lightly kissed her forehead. Gabriella's
eyes gleamed with tears. The two women embraced and
suddenly Gabriella seemed to love the maid as much as
she had disliked her a moment before. She didn't know
what to think. She didn't know what to feel. It's an
impossible situation, she thought, completely impossible.
The only thing she was sure of was that she was losing her
Giorgio.

Suzette patted her as a nanny would a child, then
turned her around and began to undress her for bed. The

simple care soothed Gabriella and she began to regret the way she had treated her over the past week. There were worse things than not being able to speak proper Italian, and Suzette had never been unkind, only obedient to Gabriella's father, as was everyone in the house.

Her father. More and more he seemed to be at the center of her troubles, and the thought of him did not raise proper daughterly feelings—loyalty, obedience, respect—but rather made her feel hopeless, as if she were buried alive. She wondered if her mother had felt that way, if death had really only been trading one tomb for another.

When Gabriella's nightdress was tied and buttoned down to the floor, Suzette took a brush from the nightstand and began stroking sheen into her mistress' long hair, then braided it loosely down her back. Gabriella turned to Suzette, whose own blond hair was tucked neatly under a black lace cap.

A sudden impulse, formed partly from gratitude and partly from whim, made Gabriella return the favor. She removed the cap, undid the strands of silver-yellow hair by taking out three wooden combs, and began brushing. The maid's face was flushed with embarrassment; Gabriella could guess why. She knew about the French and their attitudes.

A French aristocrat would never speak unnecessarily to a person of lesser station, never mind perform a servant's grooming task, but Suzette's kindness had awakened a sisterly affection in Gabriella that made this small favor pleasurable for her.

"Have you ever been in love, Suzette?" she asked.

"Of course, signorina," the Frenchwoman answered. Or at least so it sounded, more or less, to Gabriella.

"It's a wonderful thing, isn't it? It's all you can think about day and night."

"Sometimes it's wonderful, yes. Not always."

Gabriella frowned and resisted a sudden stinging in her eyes. "Yes. As when the man you love is gone from you and there is no way to see him, to hear his voice, to whisper in his ear at night."

"Or when you catch the man you love with another woman."

The comb stopped. Gabriella felt her lips and gums and neck and cheek burning. "Do you think he's found another woman?"

"Pardon?"

"My Giorgio." Wait, no, what had she done? Now the servant knew his name. Nobody must know his name.

"I don't know your Giorgio. I only know men."

If only she could take back the word, swallow it as if she had never said it. "Suzette, you must never mention that name in this house again. It was a mistake for me to tell you."

"Of course, I understand," Suzette said, then added something Gabriella couldn't quite make out.

For the sake of the maid's feelings, Gabriella nodded her head in agreement.

"I think perhaps I should go to bed now. I'm very tired."

Suzette was obviously disappointed. If Gabriella went to bed, that meant she had to turn in as well, because the don wouldn't allow his daughter a moment alone, even in her sleep.

"Perhaps tomorrow we'll go into town and buy us each a new pair of shoes."

That brightened Suzette's face considerably, and she launched into what Gabriella could only surmise was a speech of gratitude. Gabriella smiled in indulgent incomprehension and let the gabbling go on while the maid put on her own nightclothes. Here and there a word, a phrase, sometimes a whole sentence made sense, but in a short while Gabriella found herself growing impatient again, and rather than lose her temper with her new friend, she said good night and doused the bedside lamp.

It took Giorgio a very long time to find his way to the villa. There was a bright moon that turned the landscape into white and indigo, so the way was clearly visible, but his gait was so staggering and his balance so poor that he found himself sitting down time after time, and twice he made a wrong turn that forced him to backtrack over a mile.

He was aware of how drunk he was, but where he wanted to go and what he wanted to do shone in his mind like bright stars: the villa, the note, Gabriella. Unfortunately, his body, his vision, his hearing, all seemed to have lost their connection with his intentions. His helpless mind was buried in a drunken body. If only he could sober up. If only the fog would go away.

He breathed deeply as he walked and even tried slapping himself in the face, but he couldn't feel it. Only his legs, numb as they were, seemed to obey his will, though crazily. It was through exertion of will, a tremendous sweating exertion, that he finally covered the last mile up the plateau road and came to the gate of the house of Terasatti.

There were windows dimly lit by candles, but the place seemed quiet enough. The gate was locked, of course. They wanted no swing makers trespassing in the night, but he was more than a swing maker, he mumbled to himself. He was a stonemason and a gate climber too—unbeatable combination of talents. A man of unstoppable intentions, that's what he was.

He took what he thought was a running start and

leaped up at the iron bars of the gate. His hands grasped, his feet kicked, and he slid down and landed on his seat.

Try again.

Another running start and this time a little yell of bravado as he jumped. Same result.

The third time he tried a new tack, shinnying up the bars. He knew he was bruising his legs because he could feel the pressure against them, but there was no pain, only somewhere in his mind a small voice of warning that predicted a very uncomfortable pair of shins the next day. He made it to the top of the gate.

Now to the problem of getting over the spearheaded bars without impaling himself and without falling and breaking his neck. It was at least a twelve-foot drop. He managed to get the first leg over, but as he straddled the gate, he had to hold himself slightly above the pointed spears with the failing strength of his arms, and he felt a slight prick in the back of his left thigh. He made as strong an effort as he could, a great, straining push with his arms, and he was over.

But not without cost. He'd heard a rip and now had the vague sensation of coldness on the back of his leg. And he was left dangling by one hand from the top of the gate. He managed to steady himself after a few seconds and slid partway down the bars, but he lost his grip and fell backward the last five feet.

His head banged against the cobblestones of the drive, and for a moment he was too dizzy to move. He closed his eyes and felt for the damage to his trousers. His leg was moist. A shiver of panic went through him. He tasted his fingers. Blood.

Signorina Gabriella, he thought, if only you could know how I'm suffering for you. If only you could see me now you would never forget the vision of a man who loves you giving his blood in order to see you.

A dog barked. A dog? Where the hell did a dog come from? he wondered in amazement. There had never been a dog here before. But it was definitely a dog, and it was coming closer.

Well, now what? If he had known there was a dog, he would have brought along a scrap of meat. Ah, there he was, running toward Giorgio from the house. Not such a big dog. No problem.

The animal, yelping and barking and snapping at the air, stopped a few feet from Giorgio and began to dance little circles around his quarry as if to corral him. Giorgio remained unafraid, though something told him his courage was only the stupidity of drunkenness. He staggered to his feet and held out his hand as if inviting the dog to lick it. This had the effect of quieting the barking to a low, threatening growl.

Giorgio sized the beast up. It wasn't just an ordinary watchdog, this one; it was a terribly angry watchdog. You could see anger in the way it drew its black lips away from its teeth and in the way the fur all along its spine stood up on end. Even its eyes looked afire. Poor dog, Giorgio thought, who has made you so angry?

He began a slow walk forward, making little kissing sounds as he went. The dog was not beguiled. When Giorgio finally reached him, it made a savage snap at his extended hand.

Now it was Giorgio's turn to get angry. The son of a bitch had drawn blood.

"What do you think, I'm going to take this from an animal?" he said out loud. "You're a stupid brute to do this to me. You know why I'm here? Because I love your mistress. There is nothing that can stop a man who loves a woman. His fate is written in the stars. What do you suppose you, an animal, can do about that? God will strike you dead."

The dog tried to rush in and take a piece of his ankle, but Giorgio kicked fiercly and caught its snout with the toe of his boot. Now they were both injured. They stood quietly catching their breath and regarding each other.

They might have stood that way all night if two pairs of human hands hadn't taken Giorgio's arms and forced him toward the villa at a speed he couldn't keep up with.

"What do you think you're doing, eh? Let me go," he yelled, and would have tried to kick them if he hadn't been tripping over his own feet.

"Shut your fucking mouth or I'll shut it for you," said one of his captors.

Even drunk he knew better than to answer. By the merciless way they pushed him along, shoving and delivering short little blows to his kidneys as they went, they gave him the message that he could easily be in for the worst time of his life. Just one wrong move, one wrong word—he could have expected more mercy from the dog.

The don was waiting inside the house. Next to him stood Signorina di Boromeo. Giorgio was thrown at their feet.

"What are you doing on my land, boy?" Don Antonio said quietly. "I don't like strangers on my property."

"I got lost, signor," Giorgio said. "And then your dog, he bit me. Such a price a man has paid for getting lost—"

"Shut up. I don't want your speeches. I want an explanation or you'll want my mercy, you understand?"

As if to underscore the point, one of the two guards kicked him in the ribs. The pain was sharp and nauseating. The numbing effect of the alcohol was wearing off. Even his head was clearing—not to think, but to scream inwardly with the agony of his torn body.

The don would insist upon an explanation and there was no explanation to give. The situation was hopeless.

Giorgio knew he was about to die. It was all so stupid. Scarfo was right. He would be murdered by a crooked landowner, just as his own parents had been murdered.

He thought sadly that he would never see his brother or his sister-in-law again, never look on the face of their child, his nephew. Until that moment he had never realized how he missed them, but now he discovered that somewhere in the back of his mind he had always held the hope of seeing them again.

"Boy, if you want to walk out of here, you better give me an explanation now."

Another kick—Giorgio doubled up and groaned. O God, why are you doing this to me? What have I done to deserve it? I've been a good man. I've missed church, all right, but I've done a few good things too. Don't that count for nothing?

"What's your name, kid?"

He couldn't speak through the pain. Another kick.

"I said, what's your name?"

"Antonio, show a little mercy. What's he done to you that you treat him like an animal?" It was the lady speaking.

The don's eyes became wide and wild and he pointed a stiff trembling finger into Brigetta's face. "Don't you tell me what to do, woman. Don't you question me or you'll find yourself down there with him. You like that, eh?" He built himself into such a rage that he spat as he spoke. "You're only a goddamned woman, don't you forget. You cross me and I'll have you making your living on the street."

Brigetta lowered her eyes in mortification, and even the two toughs who still stood to either side of Giorgio looked embarrassed for her.

Don Antonio turned his wrath on Giorgio. He began to kick him, an activity he usually left to his goons. "I tell you the explanation, kid. You're a pig who got eyes for my daughter, right? Eh? A pig doesn't know what the hell is good for him.''

"Please, signor, please, you're killing me," Giorgio groaned. His stomach retched and cramped and vomit shot from his mouth.

Gabriella started from her sleep in a cold sweat as if awakening from a nightmare, but it was the voices coming from downstairs that had roused her. She hastened to the door of her room without housecoat or slippers, though she didn't know why she felt such urgency. Suzette did not stir.

Intending just a quick peek over the balustrade of the balcony to see what was going on below in the foyer, then a quick retreat to her bed, she recognized the prone, writhing figure on the floor at once.

"Papa, what are you doing?"

Giorgio thought it was Gabriella's voice, but he couldn't be sure. He couldn't be sure of anything. He tried to look up. The candlelight seemed too bright—almost blinding. Someone was running down a flight of steps. Pain exploded in his side again and then everything seemed to turn to smoke.

Barefoot, she ran along the railing to the steps and charged down with a terrified, heart-rending scream, like a child falling from a great height.

He's dead, she thought in panic, my Giorgio is dead, but he can't be dead—if he is, I'll kill my father. I'll take his life with my own hands. Mother of God, forgive me. What has he done to you, my Giorgio?

Her father was there to catch her in his arms, and when she tried to escape, he shook her and screamed ferociously into her face. "You know this man, eh? You know him. How do you know him, you little bitch, you little whore?''

"Papa, how can you do this? Papa, I'll kill you for this, I'll kill you..."

"You gonna kill me, eh? Your father you're going to kill. I'll show you how to kill."

His foot lashed out to catch the side of Giorgio's head. Gabriella's mind raced. Giorgio was moving. He wasn't dead, but her father would kill him yet if he went on this way. She struggled harder and her father held harder, and he screamed louder, and there was nothing she could do. Then he kicked out again, and when he did, he lost his grip on her. She went to her knees and grabbed his leg to stop another attack on the man she loved.

"What's he doing with you, this guy, eh? What's he doing?" Don Antonio tried to shake his daughter loose and tears of rage and sorrow streamed down his face. "He been screwing you? Is that's what's been going on in my house?"

"No, he loves me, Papa, he loves me," she whimpered as she held him. "He didn't do anything to me. He repects me."

"Some goddamn stranger comes into my house and screws my daughter and turns her against me, and now look at you! Look at you on the floor. I should beat some sense into you, you little goddamned piece of nothing." He raised his arm in a wide arc to swat her down, but Brigetta grabbed his elbow with both hands and threw all her weight against it.

"Antonio, she's your daughter. Listen to me! You'll never forgive yourself. Antonio, stop! Stop at once."

"Everyone in my house turns against me to save this peasant, eh? To hell with all of you!"

Gabriella held more tightly to his leg and closed her

eyes tight, murmuring, "no, Papa, no," as he raged and snorted like a penned bull. Then the coughing began.

Gabriella had never seen it before, the uncontrollable hacking, the sound in his chest like cardboard tearing, the dark red paste of blood that stained his lips. The two thugs looked confused and frightened. Gabriella knew them both; they were regular faces around the villa, though she had never heard either speak. She could guess what was in their minds. To see Don Antonio, the big boss, the padrone, so suddenly brought down, to see him bleed, was like witnessing the exposure of a false saint.

Her own terror was for the man lying dazed on the floor with his hands clutched tightly to his gut, his eyes blinking too fast and his breath short and shallow.

Her father's cough grew worse. He was blinded by the tearing in his eyes, and his legs seemed to give way as Gabriella released her hold on him. The two bodyguards came to his aid at once—that is, they held him up, but neither seemed to have any idea what to do for him. He made a feeble attempt to wave them away, but his humiliation and anger seemed almost ludicrous, and they paid him no mind.

"Take him upstairs to his room," Brigetta commanded.

One of them looked to Don Antonio. "What do you want us to do, boss?", he asked, but the don couldn't speak and Brigetta repeated her command. There was nothing to do but obey.

Brigetta waited behind as they dragged him up the marble staircase. Gabriella leaned over Giorgio, trying to clean his face with the corner of her nightdress. She was sobbing and cooing, and at first he seemed not to know she was there, but Brigetta fetched some brandy from a small cabinet in the dining room, and when she touched it to his lips, that seemed to bring him around a little.

His eyes closed for a long moment, and Gabriella

could feel her heart beating so quickly she was sure it was breaking. She was afraid he would never open his eyes again. She blew on his face to cool it while Brigetta slapped the backs of his hands to sting him into consciousness.

Gabriella said prayers not only to the Virgin and to Our Lord Himself, but to every saint she could remember from the litany as well as a few she wasn't sure existed. Finally Giorgio began to mumble and curse under his breath. His lip was stained raspberry, as he had bitten it during the beating. Now his eyes opened, and though they looked very weary, he was obviously conscious.

"Can you walk, Signor Farenza?" Brigetta asked immediately.

Gabriella turned with a snarl. "Walk! How can he walk? Look at him. You must be some kind of a witch to try and make him walk when he's like this."

"Gabriella, hush! This is no time for your damned arguments. If we can get him out of here, your father won't have another chance at him. If we can't, then kiss him good-bye now and wish him well on the trip to heaven."

"They don't want me in heaven yet," Giorgio muttered and began pushing himself to his knees with painful effort. "They only take little babies and men who look dried up like prunes."

"Oh, Giorgio, you can speak, oh my Giorgio—" Gabriella was so beside herself she began to kiss him all over his face and threw her arms around his neck as if she would never let him go.

"Gabriella," Brigetta said gently, "let the poor man get up."

"Oh, I'm so sorry, Giorgio," she said, putting the tips of her fingers to her mouth to cover her gasp of shame,

"Please, let me help you. Can you stand? Are you all right?"

"I'm terrible, my love," he said and forced a smile at her. "I am in terrible pain for you."

"Oh, yes, I know, you are wonderful, the way you suffer for me."

Brigetta began to grow impatient. "Children, please, hurry up."

Giorgio, leaning on Gabriella for support, managed to come all the way to his feet, but he still clutched his side and winced horribly at every movement.

"Signor Farenza, do you think you could ride a horse?"

"I could fly if I had to, believe me. I've had enough of Don Antonio's hospitality for one night."

"Take one of the mares from the stable," Brigetta advised. "The chestnut. She's too old and lazy to give you any trouble, and she hasn't been ridden, so she won't be too tired."

"Brigetta, I don't know why you're doing this for us," Gabriella said without a hint of gratitude, "but thank you and good-bye."

"You're not going with him?"

"Of course I am."

Giorgio seemed to forget his pain for a moment. "You are?"

"You don't think I can remain in this house with a man who would do such a thing to you, do you?"

"No—no, of course not." He laughed a little in confusion.

"Gabriella, you can't," Brigetta said.

"I should think you would be happy."

"It will kill your father."

"Ah, yes, before the wedding. Now I see the problem."

"You see no such thing," Brigetta snapped. "I have

been your father's mistress for many years, my dear. Do you think I have no feelings?''

Gabriella almost snapped back, like an ember suddenly fanned, but she held her tongue. She didn't know anything about Brigetta's feelings and she didn't care. She shook her head and shrugged. "I can't let him go alone. He's in no condition. He'd fall off and kill himself.''

"Then take him to a safe place and come back at once. Please, Gabriella. For your father's sake.''

"I'll do nothing for my father's sake. Not after tonight.''

Brigetta watched silently as the young woman turned away and led Giorgio into the night. From the balcony above came a little cry. Suzette stood at the balustrade with her hand to her mouth. "Where has the signorina gone with that man?''

"Very far away, I'm afraid, Suzette. Very, very far.''

Chapter 14

"Just take me to Scarfo. He'll know what to do." Again and again Giorgio repeated this advice into Gabriella's ear.

"Who is this Scarfo?" she asked him the first time.

"He is my friend. He's very old and not so stupid as I am. We live down the plateau road. Look, I'll show you." He pointed the way as best he could, though he'd never seen the road from atop a horse.

By the time they trotted up to the front door of Scarfo's little house, Giorgio had to lean against Gabriella's back and drape his arms heavily over her shoulders to keep from slipping off. The mare was a gentle animal and easy to ride, but she wasn't particularly strong. Bearing the weight of two riders over steep mountainous roads had tired her to exhaustion, and her gait was so jerking and labored that even Gabriella found it difficult to stay mounted.

Giorgio, who had never ridden a horse before, was thankful for whatever small miracle had kept him from falling, as weak as he was, but every movement of the animal acquainted him with a brand new degree of pain.

The cut on his leg was smarting, the dog bite on his hand burned like a dozen hot needles on his skin, and his head and ribs were roaring and screaming. His only relief

came as he rested his weight against the small sturdy form
of his love and his cheek touched the soft nest of her hair.

Just the feel of her and the sweet musky smell of her
comforted him, and now and then for a second the pain
would seem to drift away. He was reminded of a time
many years ago when he sprained his wrist trying to do a
cartwheel in the street and Teresa dressed the swelling and
sang him a lullaby and hugged him and kissed his fingers.
What a lovely memory; what a lovely woman…

Gabriella pulled up on the reins and the mare slowed
her pace, danced heavily for a moment, then stood still.
Giorgio refused help in dismounting. He didn't want to be
treated like a baby even by Gabriella. He managed to
swing one stiff leg over and slid on his belly down the
horse's flank, but the sudden jolt of hitting the ground
almost made him scream.

He felt split with carving knives, starting from the
ankles and going up both legs to the groin, then through
the ribs and into his head. His breath seemed to singe his
lungs. Barely able to stand, he waited by the door as
Gabriella took the horse around to the back.

What a predicatment he'd gotten himself into, he
thought. Still, he wasn't sorry. A little pain was worth the
prize. Gabriella was his. If only he weren't so damned
dizzy, so damned weak, he would grab her and carry her
into the house like a bride. If only his stupid head would
stop spinning so fast.

Tomorrow he would be better, and how she would
love him then. How she would adore him… He slumped
against the door. A fine man he was turning out to be. He
coudn't even stand on his own two feet.

Gabriella came back to find Giorgio curled into a
tight ball on the ground. Please, Mother of God, please
help him. She tried to rouse him, but he couldn't be

budged. She didn't know if he had fainted or fallen asleep, but she could think of only one way to get him inside. She opened the door behind him, and going down on her knees, extended her hands in front of her like cattle catchers and pushed him over the threshold.

"Who's that?" came a voice, harsh with sleep, from the dark.

"It's Giorgio, signor," Gabriella answered.

"To hell. You don't sound like no Giorgio to me."

"He's hurt, signor. Please help me." Gabriella heard a couple of mumbled curses and complaints, then a the muffled thumping of bare feet and finally the hiss of a wooden match flaring to life. The flame touched the wicks of three fat brown candles and the dull light revealed a pudgy, dog-faced man dressed in a full-length woolen nightshirt that was frayed to tatters at the sleeve hems. When he looked at Gabriella, his eyes were so swollen with sleep she couldn't tell if they were open.

"What's the matter, woman, you got no shame?" he sneered.

She looked down at herself. It was true, she was only wearing a nightdress, but it was very modest. What was the man talking about?

"You should be wearing shoes," came the explanation.

She blushed and drew the pink tips of her toes under her hem, where they couldn't be seen. "Please, signor," she said, "Giorgio has been hurt. You must help me."

"All right, all right, let's have a look." He seemed to sway from side to side when he walked like a mule cart with a bad wheel. "He looks drunk to me. He was drunk when he left here."

"No, signor, my father and his men beat him up. They kicked him in the side and in the head. One of the watchdogs caught him outside the villa and bit his hand."

With an aching effort Scarfo crouched down by Giorgio

and poked and prodded his ribs. Giorgio groaned but didn't open his eyes.

"Please, signor, will he be all right?"

"Why do you call me *signor*? I'm a laborer, not a rich crook like your father." He shook his head. "I told him you ain't nothing but trouble. Maybe next time he'll listen."

"Is he going to die?"

Scarfo snorted derisively. "No, he ain't going to die—no thanks to you."

A tear rolled to her lips. She tasted it, salty and bitter. The old man was right. All this was her fault, and to make matters worse, she had not even considered her own responsibility until now. Who else was to blame? If it hadn't been for her, none of this would ever have happened. With hopeless, inconsolable remorse she sobbed into her hands. "I'm sorry, signor. I know it's my fault, but it's not my fault on purpose."

Scarfo seemed surprised by her quick confession; it was the last thing he expected. He moved his hands in a nervous pantomime of helplessness, then looked around in vain for a rag to wipe her tears. Finally he reached over and patted her tentatively, awkwardly on the knee. "Hey, come on, why don't you stop now, okay? I didn't mean to make you cry."

Her eyes were closed and she heard him as if he'd called from a great distance. Even if it was her fault, she told herself, Giorgio would forgive her. He must. She wouldn't hurt Giorgio for anything in the world. She loved him and love was good. Nothing bad could come from love, but only from the devil.

"Come on, now," Scarfo croaked, trying to keep himself from crying again. "If Giorgio wakes up and sees you like this, he's gonna blame me, and then I gotta listen to his goddamned bullshit for the rest of the night."

"But suppose he never wakes up. Maybe he's hurt so badly he'll die in his sleep. Maybe I've killed him."

"No, no, you didn't kill him. He's gonna be just fine. You wait a little, you'll see for yourself. Anyway, I didn't mean it's your fault. It's his own goddamn fault, excuse my cursing. You're just a woman. What can you do? Nothing. He's the one who should have used his brain instead of getting drunk and going to your father's house in the middle of the night."

"No, I should have used my brain. I should have found a way to escape my house and meet him as I promised, but I'm too stupid. I couldn't find a way."

Just then Giorgio stirred and snorted. Both Gabriella and Scarfo jumped a little. Gabriella went immediately to her knees beside her beloved and put her face close to his. Her tears fell on his lips and he licked them off. This gave her great comfort. Then he grunted, and as if she had watched a wound open up, she gasped and kissed him to heal him.

"Let him sleep for a little while," Scarfo said.

"But is that all it is? Sleep? He fell to the ground outside."

"He been up most of the night, drinking. Besides, after you been kicked around for a while, you get tired."

"I don't know..."

"If he didn't spit up any blood and his eyes didn't look funny—"

"No. None of those things."

"Then he'll be all right. Don't start worrying or you'll keep me up all night. Go on, you get some sleep too. Use my bed."

"What about you?"

"I'll throw a few blankets on the floor. Don't worry about me."

"That's not fair. I'm the intruder. *I* should sleep on the floor."

"Is that the kind of hospitality you think I have? You insult me."

"I'm sorry, signor."

"Damn, will you stop calling me that? My name is Scarfo. That's what people call me. Or if you like, Enrico."

"Enrico is nice."

"Fine. Now go to bed. And cover yourself up. Be a little modest."

Gabriella looked down at herself. Her nightdress revealed nothing, of course, but just the idea of parading around in such intimate clothing would bother the old man, she knew, because now that she realized how she was dressed, she was bothered too. She whispered a word of love in Giorgio's ear, stroked his face once, then went quickly to the other bed and covered herself with the rude patched flannel square that Scarfo had been using to keep himself warm.

Scarfo made a place for himself by the darkened hearth. Gabriella worried for a moment that he might be too uncomfortable there, but he was snoring almost immediately, and so loudly it kept her awake awhile.

She wondered if she would be able to hear Giorgio should he need her. Despite Scarfo's reassurances, she wasn't at all convinced that he was going to be all right, and she wanted to listen for even the slightest change in his breathing, just to make sure he got through the night.

After a while Scarfo turned over on his side and his snoring abated a little, but Gabriella remained wide awake. Though she was ashamed for thinking it, she wondered how clean the bed was. It smelled like a man and it was full of little bits of straw from the mattress that clung and made her itch. This is fine gratitude for a poor man's kindness, Gabriella, she told herself. Why should he sprinkle his bed with rosewater for you? He's already sleeping on the floor so you can stay warm, while he's probably shivering.

As for Giorgio, he seemed to be doing all right. His own snoring was beginning to make a harmony with Scarfo's, and despite the fact that she knew he was in misery, Gabriella was beginning to grow a little annoyed with him for his contribution to the noisemaking.

The sun would be up soon. She needed sleep. Her mind began to wander. What would her father be doing? Maybe he had died of his coughing fit. Never had she seen such a thing. It made her want to turn away and be sick. She hoped he wasn't dead. He was still her father, after all. But he deserved to suffer for what he had done to Giorgio, for what he had done to her. He deserved to suffer terribly, as Giorgio had.

It was difficult to believe a man could behave in such a fashion. She remembered when she was just a little girl and he would open chestnuts for her on Christmas and play with her curls as if she were a doll. She remembered all the sweet things he would say to her, how pretty she was, what a lovely voice she had, how she walked like a true princess. She could not reconcile that man with the one she had lived with since coming back from school.

Well, that was over now. To run off with a man was to cut yourself off from your family, to drive a scandal like a spike between you and all those who had ever claimed to love you. Now there were other questions to be faced.

Where would they live, for example? Certainly not here with the old man. He wasn't Giorgio's father and so it wouldn't be proper to eat the fruits of his orchard, as the saying went. Knowing her own father, she realized that it might be impossible to live anywhere in the region. He could make life hell for them, worse than hell, and he probably would. So if Giorgio lived—

What was she saying? He had to live. If he didn't, what would become of her? In the heat of all that had happened, this hadn't occurred to her before. Her entire life was only a breath away from ruin.

If Giorgio died, she would take her own life too. What was the point of going on without the man you loved? The point, idiot, she scolded herself, was to have a family and bear children. Bearing children was more important than her life or Giorgio's or anything else.

She suddenly seemed to know this more surely than she had ever known anything in her life. But how? Where did she get such knowledge? No one had ever told her that. It was just something she had within her, in the same way she knew she what hunger was or how to dream. She wanted Giorgio more than anything, but if he died she couldn't let that be the end of her life.

She sighed and rolled over. Maybe it wasn't too late. Maybe if she mounted her horse and rode back to the villa, she could still salvage some forgiveness from her father. Maybe she would be beaten, but so what? She would still have a future. There was that nitwit she was engaged to. She could learn to live with him—not to love him, but to live.

Suppose Giorgio lived—of course he would live, what was she thinking—yes, just suppose he did. Then she would have the rest of her years knowing she had left the man she loved at the moment he needed her most, and he would never forgive her. Not only that, her father would surely send her away until she was safely married off. She wondered if he had sent out men to look for her.

He must have, but he would never find her here. They were far from any place a person might want to go to.

Thoughts tumbled in her head like butter in a churn, but her breathing grew shallow and steady, and after a while one thought couldn't be distinguised from another she drifted off to a sound sleep.

"*Managia!*" The voice seemed to sob and moan at the same time.

Gabriella opened her eyes and rubbed them. In front of the hearth was a pile of empty blankets. Scarfo was gone. Across the room on the other bed Giorgio lay wide awake with one hand clutched to his left side. Tears were streaming down his face. Under his hands she could see a few rags had been tightly wrapped around his ribcage.

She jumped out of bed with her blanket wrapped around her and went over to him. "Oh, my Giorgio," she cried out. "Does it hurt so badly?"

He forced a smile that trembled at the corners. "Gabriella, there's never been a pain like this one. It's a wonderful pain. It's all for you. I offer it as an aspiration for the holy souls in purgatory."

"I don't want your pain, Giorgio. No, no, I want your pain to disappear, to go away into the ground like a snake. Oh, my Giorgio . . ." She kissed him again and again, on his brow, his cheeks, his nose, his lips, his chin. She couldn't stop herself.

"Scarfo wrapped me up, see?" He moved his hands and displayed his bandages, uneven strips of linen made from a bedsheet. "Putting them on—that was the worst of all, but I didn't cry out. I didn't want to wake you."

"You're such a fool," she sobbed and kissed him again.

"What are you talking about? I ain't no fool. All this was part of my plan."

Her sobbing stopped at once, as if a valve had been closed. "What are you talking about?"

"I let myself get caught as a way to find you."

She shook her head. "You're not a fool. You're just crazy."

"Crazy because you are beautiful. Crazy with love for you."

"You could have gotten yourself killed."

He winced. "Yes, I'm not only crazy. I'm also pretty brave."

Now her dark eyes blazed. "What do you mean, brave? Suppose you had gotten killed. What would have happened to me, eh?"

"Gabriella, please, what are you saying?"

"I'll tell you what I'm saying. This is what I'm saying. If you get killed, so what? What do you care? You're dead. You don't care about anything. But what about me? I have to spend the rest of my life missing you, wondering what it would have been like to be your wife, to have your babies."

With an effort he took her face in his hands and drew it close. "You want to have my babies?"

What had she said? The words had sneaked into her throat without even whispering to her brain that they were there. Naturally she wanted to have his babies. She loved him, didn't she?

"Yes, Giorgio. Lots of little boys."

"And a few girls to look like their mother, eh?"

"Maybe one or two."

He brought her lips to his and kissed her softly. His lips were dry and cracked and scratched hers a little. His face was rough and unshaven. She didn't care; she was glad to be kissing him. Somehow it comforted her, gave her a future, swept away her past. It turned the disapproving eye of her father out of her mind.

"Hey, come on, you gonna stay in bed all day?" It was Scarfo, standing in the doorway. In his arms was a bundle of dried kindling for a fire, and both the pockets of his worn grey overalls bulged with pieces of coal.

Gabriella blushed and came to her feet. "Here, let me help you carry some of that."

"Oh, very kind, very kind," Scarfo said with a prissy look. Then his voice boomed. "You kids got no shame!"

"Agh, *gool le sor'*," Giorgio muttered. "Mind your own business, old man."

Gabriella's cheeks turned from pink to scarlet.

"I'll smack your face, boy," Scarfo said.

"Come and smack, then. You can't hurt me worse than I already been hurt."

"I'll break another one of your goddamned ribs," Scarfo said and moved threateningly toward the bed.

Giorgio, who had until that moment seemed to be immobile, leaped to his feet. Balancing on the mattress, crouched like a wrestler, he was ready to spring out of Scarfo's reach.

Scarfo didn't come after him. He laughed. "You hurt pretty bad, eh, boy?"

Giorgio coughed. His eyes turned red with the pain, but his answer was haughty. "Don't you worry about my hurt. My hurt ain't none of your business either."

"Come down off there. I'll build a fire." He turned to Gabriella. She almost found herself taking a step backward. There was something about the man that frightened her a little. "You know how to cook?"

"Of course I know how to cook. What do you want?"

"I got some eggs and a piece of pork. As long as you're in my house, you do your share of the work, right? You make the breakfast."

"Leave her alone," Giorgio put in.

"Listen, kid, she ain't complaining, are you?"

"No, Enrico. Of course not. But there's something I

don't understand. How come you want to eat so much in the morning? I've never heard of such a thing.''

"He learned it in America, where everyone ruins their stomach with too much eating," Giorgio put in.

"You've been to America?" she asked.

"Sure," the old man answered. "I been there."

"What's it like?"

"It's a place. What do you mean, what's it like?"

"Well, you know. Is it different from here?"

"Yes, very different."

"Different how?"

"Here it's one way, there it's another."

"But what's that supposed to mean?"

"It means what it means. It ain't supposed to be poetry."

"It's useless talking to him, Gabriella," Giorgio said. "He's too stupid to hold a conversation."

Scarfo gave him a sour look. "That's right. I'm too stupid to talk before I eat. So let's get to it, right?"

Right, Gabriella thought. Now what would she do? She couldn't admit she didn't know how to cook, at least not in front of Giorgio. What man would love a woman who couldn't cook? But it wasn't the kind of thing she'd been taught at school. She could read, sure, and spell and do mathematics. But cook? Well, there was only one thing to do. Try and hope and maybe pray.

Scarfo sensed something was wrong the moment she broke the eggs into his old black iron skillet. She hadn't known to heat it first or to add a little oil. And the whites were speckled with pieces of broken shell. But rather than call her bluff from across the room, he did something that surprised her. He strolled up next to her as if to look into the pan and whispered into her ear.

"Pick the shells out of the whites," he said.

"What?"

"Not so loud. Your ugly boyfriend will hear us. You got to take the white things out of the eggs."

"Why?"

"Just do it before they're cooked in, goddamn it!"

She timidly picked out most of the pieces out with her thumb and forefinger, though she hated the feel of the sticky embryo attaching to her skin.

"Now," Scarfo went on, "when I tell you, take a spatula—"

"What's that?"

"Over there, over there," he pointed impatiently to a wooden utensil hanging from a peg on the wall. "You use that to take the eggs out. Understand? Now pour a little olive oil in the pan and throw in the pork."

This part was easy. When the eggs looked cooked—at least when they looked like the cooked eggs she seen—she slipped the blade of the spatula under them, lifted deftly, accidentally broke the yolks so that they spilled over the whites and cooked hard instantly, then dropped them into three porcelain bowls Scarfo had set out for her.

Giorgio had changed his clothes while her back was turned, and now he sat at the little wooden table to eat. Scarfo sat down opposite him. The two men sullenly stared at each other.

When Gabriella served them their eggs, Giorgio took his first bite without looking into his bowl. The taste and texture of the food brought a startled look to his face. His eyes turned slowly downward to stare at his mangled, overcooked breakfast just as Gabriella brought the pork over with a knife on a wooden slab. Scarfo's mouth twisted crazily as he made an unsubtle effort not to laugh.

"This is very nice, Gabriella," Giorgio said. "Is this a special way you cook them?"

"Don't be an idiot," Scarfo interrupted. "It's the way the aristocrats like their eggs. Everybody knows that."

"Oh, yes, of course. I should have known. How stupid I am sometimes."

"All the time," Scarfo corrected him.

Gabriella sat at her place and tried not to pout. He knew. He had known at once. She couldn't cook and they would starve if he married her. It was useless. She wasn't fit to marry a man like Giorgio or to have his babies. She should give up now and go back to the villa, to her father.

She couldn't go back—that idea had just occurred to her for the first time, not that it mattered. She didn't want to go back. She wanted only Giorgio. What was back there for her, anyway? She hated her father, hated him. She didn't care if he had only been trying to protect her in his crazy way. He was a brute. She had tried to stop him and he wouldn't stop. He might have killed her Giorgio.

It was his pride that made him so violent, she thought, though perhaps he had a right to be proud. After all, he was a lord, not a servant. He owned much land and controlled much money. Sure he was proud—too proud to be anything but a brute animal and so she was happy to leave him. Wasn't she? Of course.

Maybe it was a little frightening to think of her life ahead. No more safe, luxurious villa. No more books. No more room to herself—and of course, no servants. She would dress herself, do the cooking and cleaning like any other woman, shop in the *piazza*, maybe even get a job picking fruit. God, she thought, what have I done?

Giorgio unobtrusively put his spoon down and pushed the remainder of his breakfast away. Scarfo wasn't shy, however. When he had finished his own fare, he ate Giorgio's as well.

"Giorgio," he said when he had sated himself, "where's the coffee?"

"What do mean, where's the coffee? I got broken ribs. I'm supposed to make the coffee?"

"Gabriella," Scarfo said, instantly putting her on her guard when he used her first name, "what do you think? Should little puss-face make the coffee?"

Gabriella thought for a moment. It wasn't a man's place to make coffee, and Giorgio was right, his ribs were broken. But there was something about his sullen, sour look and something about the way he had slid his bowl away as if she wouldn't notice that made her decision for her. "Of course he should make the coffee," she said. "Who else?"

Giorgio didn't argue any further, though his resentment practically seethed through his pores. He made the coffee.

When they had finished, Scarfo brought up the subject Gabriella had been fearing. Her father would have blood in his teeth—he would be looking for her and Giorgio, intending to kill the both of them, maybe. It was time to find a place to hide.

Gabriella objected at once. "I don't even have any clothes. How can I leave here wearing a nightdress?"

"For now you can wrap yourself in a blanket. Later I'll get some clothes for you, but first you get the hell out of here."

For once Giorgio agreed with him. "It won't take your father long to find us. Plenty of people know where I live."

"If he were looking for us, he would have found us by now," she replied. "I know my father."

"You don't think he's going to look for his own daughter after she's been kidnapped by a handsome young man?" Giorgio said in surprise.

"Last night you couldn't kidnap anybody. He knows the condition he left you in, and he also knows I must have helped you. He will disown me and forget I was ever his daughter. You wait and see."

Scarfo shook his head. "Maybe so, maybe not, but he won't forget Giorgio. No matter who kidnapped who, Giorgio is the one who ran off with his daughter and made a scandal of his name. You got to hide."

"Hide where?" Giorgio wanted to know. "Everybody in the country will be looking for me. Don Antonio has friends everywhere, even on the ships that go across the sea from Naples. Where the hell are we supposed to go?"

Scarfo rubbed his chin, then took his pipe from its little hollowed-out stand by his bed and tamped in some stale rope tobacco. "I been thinking about this," he said. "Even in my dreams I was like a bird flying all over Italy. There's a place I know where you'll be safe."

"Forgive me for laughing, Scarfo," Giorgio said, "but where is this place, in the hills? A cave like the last time? I won't make Gabriella live like that."

"No, she don't got to live like that. Maybe you do for a while, but not her."

"What do you mean?"

"I'll show you. You let me take you."

Gabriella found a piece of rope near the door and tied it around her middle like a belt. "There's no need for any of this, I'm telling you. If you want to be really certain he won't bother you, Giorgio, take me to a church and marry me right now, this morning. Even if he disowns me, he wouldn't dare to hurt my husband."

"Gabriella," Giorgio said patiently, "that's a very nice idea, but where are we going to find a priest to marry us without publishing the banns, eh? It would take weeks."

"And the priests are as scared of you father as anyone else," Scarfo put in.

"Maybe, but maybe if we offered a little money to help maintain his church, there might be a priest who would forget the banns and overlook his fear," she suggested.

Scarfo gave Giorgio a smug, self-satisfied look. "Maybe she thinks everybody in the world is rich like her father, eh? Where do you think we're going to get this money?" he asked her.

"Leave her alone, old man. She don't know how it is with us."

Scarfo laughed. "Just let me take you where you'll be safe, all right?"

"Yes, all right," she said uncertainly.

Within a few minutes they were on their way north. Gabriella sat astride her father's horse and the two men walked in front. She watched their strong backs ahead of her, leading the way over a trail hardly ever used by travelers. The old man was having his fun, she supposed, but she wished he had told them where they were going because she doubted there was any place in all of Italy or maybe in the entire world that was truly safe from her father.

She shivered. The sky, as usual, was grey as lead and threatening a storm. The wind was strong and seemed to tumble down like heavy rock from the hills ahead. She drew the blanket more tightly around herself.

North, she thought, north. What did she know about local geography? Ahead there might be anything—farms, villages, or as Giorgio had suggested, caves. To the east was Pozzuoli, where it was said that neither the Camorra nor anyone else had sway, but she didn't believe it, and the coast was not their direction. No, the only thing she knew for certain about traveling north was that there were no cities, but only rude villages and towns—Ariano, Irpino, Campobasso, San Bartolomeo.

Don Antonio dipped a hard breadstick into a cup of strong black coffee and swirled it around for a moment to soften it. He watched the steam rise around it. It was a way he had of trying to control his temper. "All right, Brigetta," he said, "now you tell me again. Why the hell am I waiting here doing nothing when my daughter has run off with some goddamn peasant who ain't gonna be alive five seconds after I get my hands on him?"

Brigetta, sitting across the width of the long dining room table from him, looked haggard about the eyes, but her back was very straight and her voice measured. "If you go beating through the countryside, you will cause a scandal. Everyone in the district will know what has happened and your name will be shamed. Think of your honor, Antonio. Think of the honor of your daughter."

He bit off the end of his breadstick as he might a cigar. "My daughter has no honor. If she doesn't care, why the hell should I?"

"Because she is young and doesn't know any better. She doesn't have the benefit of your wisdom, of your age and experience."

She was trying to flatter him, and though he knew it, it was hard for him to resist. Her respect for him never failed to sound genuine. "When I was Gabriella's age, I was very old," he said.

To this Brigetta said nothing. Smart woman, he thought. I wish I had a few men like her working for me. Knows when to shut up. She'll make a fine wife. "You still think she'll come back on her own?"

"Yes, Antonio, I do. She loves you and honors you. She understands her duty to you."

He again dipped the breadstick. "I think you're wrong, my love."

"I've come to know her, Antonio. She's not a bad girl."

He slammed his fist down. "You don't know nothing. You know what she wants you to know. She hates you."

Brigetta flushed. "Antonio, am I sitting here talking

on behalf of your blood, your only child, so that you can mock me?''

"I don't mock you. I tell you the truth. And I'll tell you another truth. I'm tired of waiting. I'm going to send a few men and dogs after those two. When I find them, I'm going to beat the hell out of my daughter and make him dig his own grave, all right? You understand?''

"Why do you want to kill the boy? That's what I don't understand. He's lovesick, that's all. What's he done to deserve to die?''

"He's got my daughter out there in the bushes, that's why. He's out there screwing my child, making a fool of me.''

"If you hurt him, you'll lose your daughter forever.''

"Ah, you know that, eh?''

"I know that because I am a woman, the same as her.'' Brigetta's voice was growing strident, angry, and this pleased Don Antonio.

"She is not a woman, my dear. She is a girl, a little girl with a memory as long as my little finger.''

Brigetta turned away in disgust. "Then kill him and see for yourself. Marry her off to that idiot you promised her to. And when you die, she'll spit on your grave.''

Her mentioning his death chilled him, and the thought of his own child defiling his coffin brought bile into his throat. "How long am I supposed to wait then, eh? Forever? And what do I do with this kid who took her away, let him go to repeat to everyone in Campania all the stories of what he did with Gabriella?''

"You want to do something? Make him marry her. That's all.''

He passed off her remark with a disgusted motion of his hand and pushed the cup of coffee away from him as if the smell suddenly offended him. "Marry her. What kind of husband would he make? He's a laborer, that's all. A common laborer.''

　　"He's a mason. He's not a laborer."

　　"A mason, all right. What the hell is the difference?"

　　"He has a trade. He has respect."

　　"I don't know him. He's a stranger in my house."

　　"Then get to know him."

　　"Agh, go to hell."

　　"You will go first."

Don Antonio put his forefinger to his lips and chewed along the side of it as he thought. There was something to Brigetta's arguments—not about marriage; that was so much bullshit. But the scandal would be very bad. It was true, his own honor would be sullied, and it would surely be a betrayal of his family's good name.

He couldn't give that little bastard too much more time alone with Gabriella. There was no telling what he might do. Beat up as he was, the kid had the energy to get away. No, there was no telling what a young stallion like that might do alone with a pretty woman who had no experience in the world. Don Antonio would wait one hour. One hour and no more.

Chapter 15

Their journey took most of the day, but in all that long way over back roads and mountain trails, Scarfo, Giorgio and Gabriella passed no one but a few shepherds herding small flocks of bleating emaciated sheep from one mountain knoll to another.

In one way they were lucky, for the rains held off. But the wind didn't. Though it was a warm wind for late November, it had such muscular, billowing power that its streaming and blustering felt like strong currents of water pushing the three travelers off their feet.

Gabriella had never seen such a wind. To her it seemed a curse or an omen, a breath from the devil's mouth, and she was convinced that only her rosary, which she had taken to wearing around her neck, protected her from this evil weather. Still, protected or not, she was enduring her share of suffering.

She was hungry and thirsty and most of all weary from her day on the road. For hours she'd had to lean forward and hug her horse's neck with both arms to keep from being blown off. At times it seemed that walking would have been the better choice, but she had no shoes and the trail was cruel with jagged rocks and brambles. She didn't know how Giorgio could stand it. He had been limping the entire way, but he refused to mount up with her—it would make the horse too tired, he told her. Then nobody would ride.

The mare was nervous and shied a step for every ten forward, so finally Giorgio was forced to take the reins and lead her. Gabriella whispered into her ear every once in a while, urging her on with promises of hay and oats and a nice warm stall. The mare only nickered and sputtered nervously and hooded her eyelids to keep from being blinded by blowing dust.

Giorgio kept grimly quiet the entire way, but Scarfo was almost youthfully playful. Every now and then he would scamper up the trail to scout ahead, then come back taunting and laughing, with his eyes glittering like flint. "Only a little while more," he would say. "Maybe two, three hundred miles." Sometimes he would pick up pebbles and cast them at the horse's hooves. Sometimes he would walk close to Giorgio, sneak a hand up and pinch his earlobe.

Gabriella couldn't quite figure out what he was doing, but she was fast getting annoyed with him, not because he caused her any real discomfort, but because somehow she felt he was making a fool of her. She had placed her life in his rough, grimy hands, and look what he was doing— dancing around like an idiot as if to show her he didn't care a damn what happened to her or to Giorgio. To him all this was a show, a *divertimento*, like listening to the street singers in Naples or the story tellers in Capua.

Madonna mia, she found herself praying, if you make that old man trip and bruise his face, I promise to make Giorgio build a grotto in your honor. However, the Madonna seemed less annoyed with Scarfo than Gabriella was, as he was allowed to go on with his antics until they reached a bend in the road that brought them to rest before a large rusty gate in an ancient granite wall.

"What is this place?" Gabriella asked at once, straining her voice to speak above the wind. She gathered that they had reached their destination.

"A place you will like very much, little signorina," Scarfo called back.

"How can I like any place on a mountain in the middle of nowhere?"

Giorgio looked up at her. His face was strained and haggard. Plainly he was in pain. "It will be all right, little one," he said. "Scarfo is our friend, no matter how much he acts like a pig sometimes."

Scarfo seemed to enjoy this characterization. It made him laugh. Then he said, "Now you better listen, both of you. Let me do the talking, eh? I know these people. You don't."

To keep peace with Giorgio, Gabriella refrained from making any more objections. Instead she affected a smile and let Scarfo lead them inside.

They passed into a small courtyard cobbled with small flat squares of stone and shaded by a large fig tree near the center. To one side was a well pump where a nun dressed in a simple brown habit was filling a clay jug. At the sound of the horse's clopping on the stone, she turned in surprise. She seemed confused and upset to be so suddenly confronted by strangers, but after a moment of indecisive stammering, she consented to take them to the mother superior.

All along the back of the courtyard was what seemed to be the facade of an old villa, going to seed with age and disrepair. The nun, one Sister Immaculata, led them through a pair of heavy oak doors on which the Stations of the Cross were carved in relief. The place was neatly kept, though it was unheated and and seemed haunted with deathly silence. The few nuns walked with their eyes cast down and their hands tucked away into their habits.

Saying their rosaries, Gabriella thought absently. As they must say them hundreds of times a day, thousands of times a week, millions of times a year...oh, what had she gotten herself into?

She knew where Scarfo had brought them, and though maybe it was a good idea—her father would certainly never come to look for her here—she didn't like it. She was young and in love. This was no place for her; it seemed to make a mockery of her love.

Oh, maybe she had thought about taking vows once or twice, but that was before Giorgio. Now she wanted to be alone with him, to go before a priest with him and make another kind of vow. Instead she had been brought to a cloister in the mountains, the Carmelite convent just a few miles south of San Bartolomeo. She had never seen it, but she knew about it, as everybody did. It was a favorite retreat for women who had lost their reputations.

They were taken up a flight of marble steps, then down a short hall paneled with dark pine, at the end of which was a small study where a short, stout woman about Scarfo's size sat at a desk writing with a quill pen by the light of a single candle.

"Yes, Enrico," she said, barely looking up, "why have you come?"

Scarfo bowed his head obsequiously and folded his hands in front of him. "To ask a small favor, Mother Regina Giuseppi."

The nun went on writing for a moment as if deliberately to make him wait. A small look of annoyance passed over his face, and Gabriella said a little prayer of thanks to the Virgin. It wasn't exactly a bruised face, but it would do.

"Yes, a favor," Mother Regina said, and looked up with a kinder expression than Gariella had expected. "What can we do for you, Enrico?"

"As you see, I have a young lady with me."

"Yes, I see that. And a young man as well."

Giorgio nervously shifted his weight from one foot to the other and gave the nun a little bow of the head.

"He's just a kid who mixes mortar for me," Scarfo said. "Not much up here"—he pointed to his head—"but a nice boy. It's the young lady I'm here to talk about."

"I see. But perhaps she can talk for herself."

Gabriella started to answer, but Scarfo cut in. "She don't talk. I don't know why. I think maybe she's a deaf-mute. You see, she's an orphan. I found her wandering around the countryside all by herself with no food and no clothing and no place to sleep. That's why I brought her here. That's the favor I wanted to ask. She needs a place to live and I don't know what to do with her. I would take her into my house, but it would cause a scandal. So I thought maybe you would have a place here for her—"

Giorgio looked as if he had been struck. Gabriella nearly blurted out a curse in anger, but she held her tongue. Maybe the old man knew something she didn't. Maybe he had to lie.

"There are orphanages for cases such as these," said the mother superior. "We don't have the facilities here to care for the afflicted."

"But Mother Regina," Scarfo replied with overworked charm, "to be deaf and mute would not be an affliction in a cloister, would it? That's why I thought she would be perfect for you. And she's very religious, praying all the time. She holds her rosary beads and her lips are always going. Besides"—his voice was supplicant, pitiful—"orphanages are such terrible places for the young. Girls of such a tender age, they need to loved, to be cared for, to be disciplined, to be shown the greater glory of God. Don't you agree, Mother Regina?"

The nun thought for a moment. Her eyes came to rest on Giorgio's face, which looked anxious and unsure. Then she moved her gaze to Gabriella, and wistful serenity seemed to relax the lines of her nut-brown weathered forehead as she came to a decision. The soft brown doe eyes she fixed on Gabriella seemed to understand everything they saw.

Gabriella realized at once she would be accepted here, and she almost panicked. Now what would she do? It was all a trick of the old man's. He would take Giorgio away and she would never see him again. But that was silly, she told herself. Giorgio would return for her no matter what. The old man couldn't tie him up and keep him away.

Still, she didn't want to stay here. She didn't want to keep silence while she longed for the touch of the one she loved, to say prayers when she wanted to moan with passion, to kneel before the eyes of God when Giorgio's eyes would adore her.

"Very well, Scarfo. In honor of the Virgin, whose likeness you carved for us so many years ago, I will grant your favor and take the waif in. What is her name?"

"Gabriella, Mother Superior."

"How do you know?"

"What do you mean how do I know? She told me."

"Ah, then she has not always been a deaf-mute."

Scarfo gave an obligatory embarrassed little laugh, but Giorgio, who had been silent all of this time, drew his breath in sharply, averted his gaze in shame, and spoke. "Why don't you tell her the truth?"

"What do you mean, pie-face? I always tell the truth to a nun."

"Yeah? Is this what you call the truth?"

"Gentlemen, please. I will tell you the truth. Would that be all right?"

Gabriella was intrigued. She wanted to know what was behind that understanding look. "Yes, please, Mother Superior."

"These two are in love and the father disapproves, so your friend kidnapped her. It's an old story."

Giorgio stepped forward meekly and dared for the first time to meet the nun's gaze, though only for a moment. "Does this mean you will turn her out, Mother Superior?"

"Of course not. It means only that I won't waste my time trying to persuade her to take her vows. Otherwise she will be as one of us. She will eat what we eat, dress as we dress, pray as we pray. Is that agreeable to you, Gabriella?"

"Yes, of course, Mother Superior," she said humbly, though inside her heart was screaming. What would happen to Giorgio? He needed a place to hide too. And she wanted so much to keep him nearby. She had hoped Scarfo was taking them to a priest to marry them, maybe some renegade hermit who didn't care about banns and wasn't afraid of men like her father. She had half suspected that all his clowning was the prelude to a surprise— the marriage altar. But now all her fancies were rubble and she was suddenly aware how cold her feet were on the wooden floor. She rubbed the toes of one behind the calf of the other leg.

Mother Regina noticed. She almost came out of her chair as she bent over her desk to see Gabriella's legs. "You're undressed, child."

"Yes, Mother Superior."

"We had no clothes to give her. We are only two men..." Scarfo started to explain, but the nun wasn't listening.

"Sister Immaculata!" she called out. The young nun who had met them in the courtyard appeared from the hallway.

"Yes, Mother Superior?"

"Gabriella will be staying with us awhile. Find her some decent clothes and give her a bed in the novices' quarters."

"Yes, Mother Superior."

Gabriella, tired, cold and defeated, followed the other woman obediently. Only once did she glance back to Giorgio, to give him one last sorrowful look. Let him remember me this way, she thought, and he'll be sure to come back.

The two men slowly walked down the steep mountain path, Scarfo because his age was catching up with him, Giorgio because his body was weeping with agony. Each looked grim and stubborn.

"Why didn't you let me talk?" Giorgio said.

"Because you always say stupid things when you talk. You would have ruined everything."

"Me? Ha! That little story you told didn't fool the mother superior for a second."

"Of course not, idiot. It wasn't supposed to."

"I don't understand."

"Oh, you don't understand. So what do you want me to do? You got your own brain, right? You're Giorgio Farenza. Big deal. If Giorgio Farenza, who has a brain as big as a watermelon, can't understand, how can I, stupid man I that am, explain it to him?"

"Yeah, I didn't think about that. Maybe you're right. Maybe it would be too hard for you."

"Son of a bitch."

"Your face is a son of a bitch."

"Listen to me, smart guy." Scarfo held up his hand and ticked off his fingers. "The Mother Superior is a nun, a Carmelite, a holy woman, right?"

"Yes, right."

"And it's bad luck to make a holy woman angry, whether she's a nun or a witch."

"Sure."

"Okay. Now suppose I had gone to the reverend mother and said, 'This woman has run away from her father because of this young goat who thinks he's in love with her. It's caused a scandal in the village, and to make matters worse, she slept in our house last night.' This from me, a man, and not even a priest. She would have thrown us out, and then what? No place to go and bad luck besides."

"But what's the difference, if she knew anyway?"

"The difference is you don't say that kind of thing to a nun."

"Why not?"

"Because she's a nun!" Scarfo shook his head. "Idiot. A complete idiot."

They walked on awhile without speaking. They had to hunch and squint to protect themselves from the wind, and after they had gone another mile, Giorgio's chest began to make an obvious wheeze as he breathed.

"You hurting real bad, boy?"

"What the hell do you care?"

"I don't."

"Good."

"I'll change the dressing when we get back."

"I'm all right."

Scarfo's hand flew up and cuffed Giorgio on the back of the head. Giorgio, reeling with the blow, gave him a sour look and walked a little farther away.

"Don't tell me what you need. I know what you need," Scarfo said.

"Oh, so now I need you to beat me up, right?"

"Maybe."

"It ain't enough Don Antonio beats me up. Maybe you should go to work for him as a goon."

"You're goddamn lucky I don't. You wouldn't be able to walk nowhere if I did the job on you."

"Tough old guy, eh? I thought you were gonna help me and Gabriella find a place to hide."

"What the hell you think we just did?"

"I think we just took care of Gabriella. What about me?"

Scarfo smiled grimly. "What's the matter, you worried?"

"Yeah, you're goddamn right I'm worried."

"I'll take care of you."

"Where am I gonna hide, then?"

"No place. You ain't gonna hide."

Giorgio rolled his eyes heavenward. *"Madonn'*, just what I need. He's gonna take care of me. What are you gonna do, Scarfo, shovel the dirt on my face real nice when they bury me? Is that how you're gonna take care of me?"

Scarfo put his hands in his pockets and walked a little faster, and Giorgio, who fell a few steps behind, had to strain to hear him. "I told you not to get mixed up with that damn woman."

"Big deal. Anybody could have told me that. I need a place to hide out, not a bunch of bullshit."

"You wanted to be in love. If you want to hide, go back to the cave."

"Oh, very nice idea. Gabriella is in the convent, I'll take my poor beaten malarial body to live in a hole in the rocks, her father will spend the rest of his life trying to find and kill me, and you'll sit home laughing like a goddamn jackass. And all this is falling in love."

"I told you, you don't got to hide."

"Then what am I gonna do?"

Scarfo's eyes took on a sly look. He stopped to wait for Giorgio to catch up. "I'll tell you when we get back."

"Tell me now."

"Not now."

"Why not?"

"Because if I tell you now, you'll say I'm crazy and you won't come with me."

"I think you're crazy already, but I'm coming with you."

"Just wait. Be patient. Remember, I'm your friend."

"Yeah. A real *paisan'*."

"Trust me."

Giorgio made his voice crack like an old woman's. "Trust me, he says. Bullshit."

The rest of the way back Giorgio was taciturn and surly. By the time night fell, he was so petulant that he began to enjoy being in pain, like a martyr, and he exaggerated his wheezing so that Scarfo would feel guilty for having brought him all the way up here just to lead him back empty-handed.

All he wanted was Gabriella, and after having gone through so much to get her, he thought he deserved to have more than that sad little expression she had left him with, but what could she do, especially in front of the nuns? It was Scarfo who put him into that situation, and if he didn't have to depend on the old man for safety, he would abandon him right now, in the dark, in the mountains, leave him to brigands and animals.

Somehow the old man seemed different to him lately, not that Scarfo had really changed, but something between the two of them wasn't the same. Their arguments no longer seemed friendly, and the thing like father and son they both shared and loved so dearly, the stone, cutting and shaping and laying it into place, had become only a coincidence of feeling. At least that's the way it seemed to Giorgio.

He wondered if Scarfo felt the same way, but he wouldn't ask him. He couldn't. It wasn't their way to be so forthright. Even if Giorgio spoke up, Scarfo would pretend he hadn't heard. And with the way things had been lately, Giorgio had no desire to speak up.

He wondered about Gabriella, how she felt about her own father now. She had watched Don Antonio kick him and beat him and bellow like a mule when she tried to stop it. For Giorgio's part, he held no bitterness toward the man. The don had only been protecting his daughter, and fathers had been known to do worse. But sometimes it was easier to take a beating than to watch one, especially when both the people involved are men you love—or so he guessed.

He was very glad for one thing: he had had no opportunity to strike Don Antonio back. He was sure she would have hated him for that. She had never really offered forgiveness for that night when he hit the old man with his umbrella. As it was, this time Giorgio had all her sympathy. Yes, he thought, he was lucky he'd been beaten so badly. But maybe Gabriella hadn't been so lucky. Maybe she had lost a father.

Maybe Scarfo and the don weren't so lucky either. They were both afraid of losing their young, their heirs. And yet with that in common they were enemies, because each was enemy to the other's heir.

He looked at Scarfo up and down. The old man was shuffling as if the weight of his own feet was too much to bear. He looked old and weak, but he was the only man who stood between him and the don. And no matter what had changed between Scarfo and Giorgio, no matter how much Giorgio sometimes wished he could maroon him in the mountains, he was the only man in the world to be trusted now, the only one who would not lead death to the door. So no matter what harebrained scheme he came up with, Giorgio would go along with it. He would trust the old man, no matter how hard it was, until his last breath.

Chapter 16

These kids are so damn stupid, Scarfo thought. If I was like them, I would never have gotten to be such an old man. I would have tripped over my own shoelaces long ago and starved to death waiting for somebody to pick me up.

Giorgio is so damned scared of Don Antonio, but it's not the damned father who's the problem. When you got a man's daughter, you got him by the balls. No, it's the two of them. They're all the problem for each other they'll ever need.

He walked a little ahead of Giorgio again and stood directly in front of him to block him from the full force of the wind. The boy was weak and there was no point in making him suffer more than he had to.

It had been hard for him to watch Giorgio throw his life away like this. He was wasting his time courting a young woman who would bring nothing but trouble no matter what her intentions were. She would at the very least begin to make him lose self-confidence because she was rich. What could a kid like Giorgio do for her or she for him? They would make each other miserable.

He was a mason, and not just a drudge who didn't care a damn about the stone. Even if he was too stupid with love to see it, Giorgio would always be the apple of Scarfo's eye, the product of his own teaching and a man who knew his needs: to keep his muscles strong and his mind clear.

Giorgio knew in his heart that it was better to starve and to go cold than to let anything come between him and the stone. The grip on the chisel had to be tight, the stroke of the hammer exact. These were the only things that separated the fools from the sculptors.

The fools came to work and sweated and picked up their pay. Everything for them was on the dinner plate; you could always tell who they were because they got fat. They talked about nothing but money. And this, Scarfo was sure, was what Gabriella would turn Giorgio into, not because she would want to, but because she could do nothing else.

She didn't know how to suffer, didn't see the value in it. Giorgio, on the other hand, knew suffering to its blood and guts. Look how he took such a beating and still got to his feet to walk into the mountains. It would have been only right for him to ride, but the woman hadn't offered. Her feet were too soft. The right wife for Giorgio would wear shoes only on Sunday and would never dream of riding while he walked.

Scarfo had tried along the entire way to show these children what fools they were by treating them like fools. Lovers who came from different classes never belonged together, and never was there a way to keep them apart; they always had to learn for themselves.

To get the lesson over with as quickly as possible, Scarfo would make it easy for them to join one another. He would show the kid how to take care of the don. The rest was in the hands of the Fates.

He cleared his throat and spit. The wind was losing strength now, but the air was still gritty with blowing dust and it was impossible to breathe without constantly cleaning out the passageways to the chest. He wished he had thought to bring his pipe, or at least a cigar. Nothing cleared the lungs like good strong smoke.

In the chapel of the convent cloister of San Domenico Gabriella knelt before a plaster statue of the Virgin, staring into its sentimentally kind eyes without praying. She kept her hands warm by playing absently with the knots in her cincture. She wore the white habit of a novice, though she wasn't required to put on the crown and bib.

She felt empty, confused, lost. What had happened to her? She had given up her home and everything else for a man, a stranger, a peasant who had somehow touched her heart, and now, too soon and too suddenly, he was gone again. She didn't know where he was or whether she would ever see him again. Her life was ruined. If he didn't return for her, this would be her lot for the rest of her days—silent prayer, silent vigil, silent despair.

It was the swing that had done it, that stupid swing. Her mother would have laughed at her foolish susceptibilities. He had given her one gift and she had fallen under his spell like a halfwit under a heretic's.

Her gaze passed from the Virgin's eyes to the cold wooden floor on the other side of the communion rail. Instead of the simple tabernacle was a golden monstrance, a statue of an angel holding up a radiant sun. In its center was a glass phial that contained the Host, on display for the Forty Hours devotion.

This was a time during which someone must always be present as witness. Forty Hours usually took place in the spring, but for some reason late fall seemed to be the rule here. No one had troubled to explain it to Gabriella. She had simply been called from her cell, an eight-by-eight room shared with a novice from Salerno, and told to kneel in the chapel until she was relieved.

It was very strange, she thought. Even with all this religion around, she felt no desire to speak to God or His Holy Mother. She felt empty inside, as if the cold had found a way in, as if death had discovered a place to settle. She was a little worried and a little angry with herself, but beyond that she felt nothing.

She wanted to miss Giorgio, but every time she thought of him, she began to wonder what life would be like with him even if he did come back for her. She didn't know him well at all. Suppose he turned out to be dull in conversation or stupid in other ways. Suppose smoking cigarettes and building swings and cutting stones was all he was good for.

Why was she thinking these things? She felt mildly guilty, as she did when it had been too long between confessions. He had suffered a great deal for her, and whenever she saw him her heart seemed to strain inside her. Her mother would have laughed at that.

But he left without a word, without a sign that he cared, and so she felt deserted, maybe even more alone than she had ever been at the villa. It was the cold breath of loneliness that had blown out the flame inside her. This she knew, though she couldn't quite put words to it.

Now she knelt before the Virgin, letting thoughts come and go, trying to keep warm, wondering if he was worth waiting for, letting the silence fill her like comforting words from a friend.

The little house in the foothills had been searched. The bedclothes were all over the floor, the table lay on its side, coals and ashes were trampled in everywhere, and worst of all, Scarfo's pipe and Giorgio's mandolin were rubble. Even Scarfo's trumpet had a new set of dents.

When Giorgio came through the door and lit the lamp, he could only shake his head in shock. Then tears came to his eyes. Scarfo couldn't be so tame. He cursed and kicked through the mess and shook his fist toward the villa.

There was no doubt who had done the damage, but it wasn't only Don Antonio whom Scarfo damned that night. He also left no doubt who had brought this calamity upon his house, who through his stupidity and stubbornness and rashness had given birth to misery for everyone.

Through it all Giorgio had neither the heart nor the will to defend himself. It was all his fault, and that was all there was to it. Scarfo had been right all along. Loving Gabriella had brought Giorgio nothing but trouble, and now the trouble was spreading around to other people, but what could he do? He was lost. Everything was lost.

His body hurt so much he could hardly stand it. There was a pain in his head that knocked like a fist on a door, and his leg burned and ached constantly. Even shallow breathing brought agony to his chest.

He didn't even know if Gabriella was worth the trouble. Now that she was gone from him, she seemed to have small importance. He couldn't quite explain it, but he even had trouble remembering her face, and the harder he tried, the more her features seemed to disappear into a haze in his memory. He didn't like the feeling. Somewhere inside him an insistent voice repeated that he loved her, that he was tired and hurt and lonely, but the feeling of love, the delight of having her in his thoughts every moment, seemed to have fled from him.

Scarfo began to clean the place up, and though Giorgio helped him, the old man complained the entire time that everything was on his shoulders, that he had to do everything for everybody because everybody was too stupid to do it for himself. It was too much for Giorgio. He began to weep.

Scarfo straightened the straw mattress on his bed and put his fists to his hips. "What do you think you're doing?"

"Nothing," Giorgio sobbed. "That's what the hell I'm doing."

"This is no way for a man to behave."

"How can you call me a man when you say I've acted like such a jackass?"

Scarfo surprised him; he slapped Giorgio across the face. "Don't talk to me that way, sissy-boy," he said and slapped him again.

Giorgio dumbly put his hand to his cheek, then looked at his fingertips as if he expected to find blood. "Why did you do that?"

"To make you shut up. Who the hell are you, a little baby? That's bullshit, Giorgio. I know you. You think if you cry Scarfo will take care of everything for you. You can't fool me."

"I'm crying because my goddamn head hurts."

"Then make it stop hurting. We got things to do. We got the rest of this place to clean up tonight. Tomorrow we go to see Don Antonio."

Giorgio's brows knitted together, and he leaned slightly backward as if to say he wasn't sure he'd heard correctly. "What are you, crazy?"

"You want to marry his daughter?"

"I don't know what I want."

Scarfo swung and connected with Giorgio's cheek again. "I know what you want. Either you marry her or you put her back in her father's good graces. But no matter what, she's gonna have a family. You ain't gonna make no nun out her, and you ain't gonna make no whore out of her."

Giorgio's anger flared so suddenly he forgot how

much he hurt. "You watch what you say, old man, or I'll break your goddamn face. Nobody's gonna make a whore out of my Gabriella, and don't you talk like that."

The old man smiled with satisfaction. "Maybe you do know what you want, eh?"

"That's right, I do know. I'm the one who got beat up for her, and I'm the one who's gonna go back up into the mountains and make her my wife."

Scarfo laughed again, then went about cleaning up the mess in the cottage, whistling the while, even though Giorgio, steaming with anger, didn't lift a finger to help. He sat on his bed and watched, almost spitefully, until the last of the ashes had been swept back into the hearth. Scarfo turned to him with a big, friendly smile.

"What's the matter with you?" Giorgio asked sullenly.

"What do you mean, kid?"

"What made you so happy all of a sudden?"

Scarfo shrugged. "Just that I know you, that's all. You're a funny kid."

"Yeah? How come?"

"You confuse yourself all the time. One minute you're in love, the next minute you ain't. Then you are again. You just forgot for a minute, so old Scarfo had to remind you. You don't know what the hell you're doing."

"I'm a little tired."

"Listen, Giorgio, just so you don't drive yourself crazy—I remember being in love. I was young once too. I had a wife. It's always the same. Half the time it's like you're gonna bust because you can't think of nothing but the woman. The other half, your brain, it's gotta cool down from too much thinking about her. All of a sudden you say, 'What the hell is the matter with me? Ain't nobody worth this kind of trouble.' It's true, you know. Ain't nobody worth that kind of trouble, but what the hell does that matter when you're in love? Don't worry about nothing.

Listen to your heart, not your brain. Later, she'll break it
for you, and then your brain will come in handy.''

Giorgio didn't know what to make of the lecture. A
few moments before Scarfo was cursing like the devil
himself, and now he was singing like a bird all the praises
of love. "I ain't too sure who's confused, Scarfo," he
said. "Sometimes you sound a little mixed up."

"Yeah? Well, I'm gonna tell you a little secret." He
sat down next to Giorgio on the bed and patted his knee
conspiratorially. "In the morning, when we go to the villa,
I want you to be so much in love with your little butterfly
that you would do anything for her Anything! Like last
night, when you got the shit beat out of you. Otherwise,
maybe you'll run away at the last minute, and then the don
will catch you and cut your balls off. As long as you ain't
scared you'll be okay, and as long as you're in love you
won't be scared."

Giorgio's mind was reeling. He had promised himself
he would go along with any scheme Scarfo came up with,
but this was getting too bizarre. He couldn't follow the old
man's reasoning. Probably nobody could.

"Listen, old man," he said. "How come we're gonna
go right into the lion's den when we already know how
hungry he is?"

"We're gonna ransom his daughter back to him."

"You're crazy. He's gonna make a nice lunch out of
both of us."

"No, no, you take my word."

"Shit on your word. His daughter's been gone two
nights. He don't want her back now. He just wants my
blood."

"Don Antonio got any other kids but this one?"

"No. So what?"

Scarfo threw his hands up. "So everything. Maybe he
don't think he wants his daughter back, but you wait until

you make the offer. He'll change his mind. Men like him don't want to go to the grave without children to cry over them."

"Maybe. Or maybe he won't give us time to make an offer, eh?"

"He'll give us time. We're gonna make sure."

"Good idea. Make sure. *Jesu Christ*'. How the hell are you gonna do that?"

"We're gonna bring the whole village with us."

"What the hell?"

"Don't worry. I got it all figured out."

The don's men went everywhere. They banged on doors until the middle of the night. They pushed people around and scared them into telling fantastic lies, but nobody had any information that proved to be of any use. They found his home, but nobody was in it and there were no clues. In the end the villagers learned more from their interrogators than Don Antonio learned from them.

It was a scandal, a delicious scandal that passed through the town like a flash flood from the hills. So when Giorgio and Scarfo appeared brazenly on the streets late the next morning, the villagers knew they were in for a show.

The sun was brighter than it had been in weeks, and the wind that had blown so savagely the day before was gentle, almost affectionate in the way it caressed the laundry that hung like banners from lines strung over the streets. Scarfo was wearing work clothes: boots, brown overalls, a heavy woolen yellow shirt. He also sported a dark blue beret, which he crushed down squarely on the top of his head. Giorgio, whose limp was becoming less noticeable, wore dress clothes—an olive tweed suit with a wide bow tie and white spats over his shoes.

People began calling out to them, and as soon as their

destination was known, a crowd started forming behind them like a large tail on a tiny fish. They went directly up the corso, through the piazza and down the other side of town. Scarfo made long strides, like a man with a mission, while Giorgio squinted and looked noble with the extra effort he had to make to keep up.

The two men said very little, but the crowd had a wonderful time making slanderous remarks about Don Antonio—more than a few of them had taken bruises the night before—and suggestive comments concerning Giorgio and Gabriella. Giorgio listened with good grace. The villagers always made fun of anyone who caused a scandal, especially when it was romantic and they were of different classes. It was an old story.

The gate to the villa was open and the place seemed quiet, but by the time crowd had made its way down the drive to the portico, the entire house staff along with three bodyguards and Brigetta di Boromeo were outside to see what all these people wanted.

When Brigetta recognized Giorgio, she shook her head in disbelief. "What are you doing here? Don Antonio will have your head on the wall of his study."

Out of respect Scarfo removed his hat and held it to his belly. The wind blew his grey-white hair into dishevelment. "Excuse me, signorina, but we have come to speak with the very man you have mentioned."

"Take my advice and leave while you can."

The bodyguards had the look of hungry wolves, but as long as the don did not give them orders and the signorina was there to stop them, they did nothing. The crowd began to jeer and call for the don to show himself. They cried out that while the very man Don Antonio had been looking for was on his doorstep, he was cowering in his big house, afraid because he had pushed so many people around. The hecklers were all careful to keep their faces hidden.

Giorgio didn't like the looks of things at all. If the don came out under these circumstances, he would come out mad, and that would be to nobody's advantage.

"Please, *signorina*," Scarfo said, "would you be so kind as to call him for us? We have important business to discuss with him."

Another voice answered from the door behind her. "I am here. What is all this racket?" Don Antonio stepped outside and stood next to his mistress. He was wearing a rich burgundy morning coat. From his mouth protruded an oversized black cigar. "Who the hell wants to see me?"

Scarfo nudged Giorgio, then stepped forward. "My friend Giorgio would like to speak with you, sir."

Don Antonio's eyes narrowed and he took his cigar from his mouth as he looked down at Giorgio. "I've been looking for you," he said.

"Yes, I know," said Giorgio. "I have something you want." Scarfo had coached him on what to say, but he found he had trouble making the words now that he was face to face with a man who could kill him as easily as look at him.

"Is that what you think, kid, that you have something I want? You have nothing I want."

This too Giorgio expected. So far Scarfo had been right about everything.

"Signor, excuse me for contradicting you. I have your daughter."

"I have no daughter."

"Excuse me again, but if you have no daughter, who was it who left this house with me two nights ago when you beat me up and nearly killed me?"

Don Antonio frowned. "What are you talking about? I didn't beat anybody up. I'm a peace-loving man. Any woman who leaves my house and sleeps with a young pig has no right to call herself my daughter.''

Now it was Scarfo's turn to speak. ''Don Antonio, are you so sure the young lady slept with this pig?''

Giorgio frowned, but the don seemed to show slight interest.

''Who are you?''

''Enrico Scarfeticcerio is my name. Everyone calls me Scarfo. I'm doing a little work for you. Building the wall behind the mausoleum.'' He gave the signorina a quick glance, but she only smiled ingratiatingly.

''What do you know about all this?''

''I know that there has been no impropriety these past two nights. She has done nothing to put a black mark on your name. This pig here has kidnapped her. She had no choice but to go with him. She has defended her honor in such a way that she would make you proud.''

Don Antonio folded his arms skeptically and chewed on the end of his cigar. The crowd was quiet, but the faces were so rapt that they could have been listening to a symphony. Never in all the history of Santa Barbara had anyone spoken in public this way to a Terasatti.

''How could he kidnap her? You know the condition he was in when he left here.''

''Yes, nearly dead, like I told you,'' Giorgio put in.

Scarfo raised the back of his hand to Giorgio's face. ''Shut up, jackass.'' His frown turned to a sweet smile again for the don. ''Excuse me, but what condition do you mean, Don Antonio?''

''He was drunk, and he fell down and hurt himself. That's how I found him on the lawn.''

Liar! Giorgio thought angrily, but he forced himself not to shout it aloud.

''Signor,'' Scarfo said smoothly, ''it is when Giorgio

is drunk that he is at his strongest. There is something about wine that makes his muscles like those of an ox.''

The crowd seemed impressed with this. A few mothers, the ones with daughters still in their kitchens, wagged their heads knowingly, as if Giorgio's strength was fabled among them. The women themselves strained for a better look at him. The men held their smiles where they couldn't be seen by their wives.

Giorgio, for his part, was impressed with Scarfo's strategy. The don couldn't admit in public he had beaten Giorgio up, at least not now that he had just denied it, so he had to accept Scarfo's explanation. In fact, no matter what the truth of the situation, the don now had a way out of his dilemma. He could accept his daughter back into his home no matter what had gone on between her and Giorgio, since Scarfo's story protected her. Yes, Giorgio thought, that son of a bitch is a smart guy. How come he never acts that smart around me?

The don took the cigar from his mouth and spit. Next to him his mistress averted her eyes from everyone, looking to one side as if something else completely were on her mind.

''All right,'' the don said. ''Tell me about my daughter. Where is she?''

''I'm afraid that's the one thing we cannot tell you,'' Scarfo said. ''We would like to, but sometimes circumstances don't permit.'' He shrugged eloquently.

''Circumstances may cause you to regret it if you don't tell me what I want to know,'' the don replied.

Scarfo spread his hands palm upward, a supplicant before a prince. ''Please, signor, would you threaten me in front of all these people?''

''I own these people,'' Don Antonio replied. It was a challenge. His voice, his eyes, even the way he spread his legs apart and set his feet dared Scarfo to meet it.

Giorgio wasn't so sure Scarfo hadn't made a miscalculation. They had depended on the crowd to protect them from harm. The don wouldn't dare to harm anyone in front of so many witnesses—or so Scarfo maintained. But maybe he would. A man as powerful as that, who could say what he would do?

Giorgio stepped a little in front of his friend. "If you hurt us, Don Antonio, who will lead you to your daughter?"

Don Antonio smiled. "One of you will be left to lead me anywhere I want to go."

"Excuse me, but you're mistaken. Old Scarfo, he don't know where Gabriella is hidden. Only I know."

The don's expression grew dark. Giorgio had used his daughter's familiar name as if he had a perfect right to.

"There are ways to make you talk, boy."

The crowd was tense, expectant, almost eager for something to happen. If Don Antonio's men should make a move, Giorgio realized no one would come to his aid, and he couldn't blame them. Why should anyone risk his neck for him? Still, the don couldn't be sure. If Giorgio had any close friends in the crowd and anything happened to him, a vendetta would be sworn. Then the don would have to be on guard from invisible enemies all around him. That, Giorgio knew, was the only caution that had kept the landowner from violence so far.

"What ways, Don Antonio? Forgive me, but I have already had a taste of your ways. They are very persuasive, but I tell you, if you try them, you will never see your daughter again."

The signorina distracted Don Antonio for a moment. She whispered in his ear and he seemed to consider whatever she said. This surprised Giorgio. He would never have believed the don took any woman's word very seriously. The people at the front of the crowd, who could see plainly, were also very much impressed. The signorina had gained great prestige for herself among the townspeople. She had not been out in the village before. Now she could parade down the corso and every head would bow with respect.

"What is it you want, kid? What price are you asking for my daughter?" Don Antonio finally said.

"I want her hand. I want to court her, to come into your house and pursue the traditions of engagement and matrimony. It is my right and my desire."

Giorgio felt the muscles of chest relax after it had been said. He was back to the plan. Once again all was going as Scarfo predicted. That little speech had been rehearsed a dozen times that morning over breakfast. Scarfo was standing well back now, quite deadpan. Everything must be going very well indeed, Giorgio thought, for Scarfo to shut up for so long.

The don's expression changed ever so slightly. His eyes narrowed a bit and the corner of his mouth turned down in a sneer. He brushed one corner of his mustache with his fingertips, then puffed on his cigar. "You got no rights, kid. All you got is a little time. Now where is my daughter?"

Giorgio started to sweat. What had happened? Suddenly the don seemed in complete control again. Or had he ever lost it? There was only one way to find out, by meeting his challenge. Giorgio thought.

"I have asked for my ransom. It is the tradition, the old way, Don Antonio. I have kidnapped the one I love in order to sue for her hand."

Suddenly the don exploded. "Maybe that's the way they do it in Calabria or Basilicata or Sicily, but the traditions here are what I say they are. Now where the hell is my daughter?"

"I'm terribly sorry, Don Antonio. I can only imagine what a terrible, heart-rending thing it must be to lose a member of your family. You have all my sympathy, but I cannot tell you what you want to know until you promise me before God and all these witnesses that I will have my ransom.''

It was a big chance, but there was nothing else to do. He had come this far. If he died now, so be it.

Giorgio turned his back and started back through the crowd at a slow walk. He imagined he could feel the pressure of two black, savage eyes, hating him with all the violence Don Antonio could muster. His stomach felt nervous and jittery. He prayed to the Virgin to spare him. His lids felt heavy, and he had to strain to keep them open. His fingers twitched with his fear.

The voice came clear and cold as a mourning bell. ''I will give you what you want. Do you hear? Now, where is my daughter?''

Giorgio turned abruptly. ''I will bring her to you by tomorrow night.''

''You will bring her to me at once!''

''I'm sorry, Don Antonio, but that is impossible. She is a day's travel from here.''

The don took a deep breath, then threw down his cigar and stubbed it out. ''All right. You will take one of my men with you for company on the road. Not that I don't trust you. And just to make sure, I'll keep your friend entertained until you get back. Understand?''

Two men stepped away from Don Antonio's side and swiftly took Scarfo by the arms. The crowd moved back. Scarfo remained impassive, but Giorgio thought he could feel the fear in the man's gut.

''By tomorrow, boy.''

''Yes, tomorrow. Don't worry. I'll be here.''

''I ain't worried. I ain't worried at all.''

Chapter 17

All this time and nothing to do but pray—Gabriella sighed and gazed mutely into a beam of dull sunlight that passed through the small square window near the ceiling of her cell. Motes of dust flickered, then disappeared into shadow. Time passing, time passing.

How did they keep from tearing their hair out, these nuns? It was never like this at school, where the sisters spent their time teaching and cooking and sewing—they had a hundred little chores every day to keep them busy. But here—how many Hail Marys could a person say?

Nor were the hours of silent prayer the worst of it. Mealtimes, which should have provided a break from dull routine, turned out to be thoroughly dismal. They ate wheat paste with wooden spoons and washed it down with half a cup of wine, which to be fair was a little dry and nutty, not bad at all. No one spoke except to offer thanksgiving to God in mumbled, half-hearted aspirations. Afterward everyone immediately took her utensils outside, washed them and stored them in her cell.

The first of these meals took place just after *matins*, two hours before sunrise. The early rising made the day so long for Gabriella that now, at midafternoon, she wanted nothing but a few hours' sleep, but though she tried saying the rosary and humming and counting her breaths, nothing could make her comfortable in that bed.

Bed—to call it that was a sacrilege. A board, that was all it was, and as far as she was concerned it was good for only one thing—making discomfort worthy to be offered up for the holy souls in purgatory. The cells were more aptly named, like the little dungeons in a prison, which couldn't be much smaller or draftier than this place.

Life with Giorgio, no matter how poor, would be a thousand times better than this, she decided. She had been here only a day, and already there was nothing in the world she wanted so much as to escape, to breathe the fresh air outside, to walk in her garden, to visit her mother's grave, to swing on her swing that hung from the ash tree—no, her father had taken it down.

She would never go back there. It was Giorgio she must look to now. He was a kind man, a good man. She thought about him a great deal during all her hours here, and she thought she had come to know him, as if studying the picture of him in her mind was like being with him. If at first she had been afraid that he would leave her there forever, he now seemed her only hope.

The wooden handle on her door turned. The intrusion startled Gabriella, like a tap on the shoulder. It was the mother superior, who was simply called by her first name, Regina, when there was no protocol to follow for the sake of strangers. In fact, all of the nuns used each other's first names, and that familiarity surprised and disappointed her. It made them seem less dignified, less like the saints she wanted them to be and more like someone you might meet on a village street.

Her mother had disappointed her in the same way once, by admitting that there were times when she would rather do anything than remain the wife of a Terasatti, that she was tired of the class distance between her and her neighbors. It made her feel lonely all the time.

Gabriella had never been able to understand that. A woman's husband and family were her fulfillment. What did it matter how other people treated her? She was the heart of the home, an ideal. Her station placed her beyond the ordinary feelings of other people, like a madonna, like a saint, like these nuns were supposed to be.

For her own part Gabriella swore she would never allow herself such a moment of weakness as her mother had shown, and she wouldn't tolerate anything less than the ideal from these sisters either. She would never call them by anything but their proper titles.

"Yes, Mother Regina? Is it time for devotions?"

"No, not yet. I've come to talk with you a little."

The mother superior sat down at the foot of the bed. Her hands were tucked into her billowing sleeves so that the only visible part of her body was her face from her eyes to her chin. Her voice was soft and low, seductive of the spirit. It had the quality of praying even in conversation, and her silences were like those of a church.

Never before had Gabriella met such a woman. She seemed to have none of the gaiety of other religious women Gabriella knew, nor their sternness nor their flighty love of gossip. Instead she had almost frightening serenity.

"Is there something wrong?" Gabriella asked timidly.

"Pray with me, child," the mother superior said. "Then we'll talk together. Let us begin the *Angelus*." She bowed her head and made the first declaration of the prayer. "The angel of the Lord declared unto Mary . . ."

Gabriella folded her hands and made the response. "And she conceived of the Holy Spirit."

As the prayer went on, she found herself so overwhelmed by the older woman's piety that she began making mistakes, jumbling the words or sometimes leaving out entire phrases. The nun was of no help in these circumstances. Instead of prompting, she would doggedly wait for Gabriella to find her place and then go on as if the rhythms of the chant had never been lost. By the time they reached the end Gabriella was stammering through every syllable.

"Do I upset you for some reason, child?"

"No, Mother Regina."

"I'm glad to hear it. You don't look silly and I would be saddened to learn that you were."

"You don't upset me at all, Mother Regina, not at all," Gabriella said and aspirated her breath, choking and coughing for a moment.

"Can I get you some water?"

"No. I'm quite all right."

The nun nodded without smiling. "Gabriella, I won't mince words with you. What about this boy?"

"What boy is that?"

Mother Regina raised one eyebrow. "I thought you weren't going to be a silly child."

"Oh, you mean Giorgio. Giorgio Farenza."

Now a slight turn of the mouth did brighten the nun's face. "It's a nice name. Without pretension."

"Oh, yes, completely without pretension," Gabriella agreed.

"Have you known him long?"

The drift of the conversation was becoming annoying. What right did this stranger have to ask such personal questions? Well, perhaps she had the right after all. She was a bride of Christ and obviously very religious. But even if she had the right, how dare she?

"We are from the same town, mother superior."

"Ah, childhood sweethearts, then."

Gabriella did not answer.

"Why does your father not approve of him? Is he a thief or an atheist?"

"No, Mother Regina. He's a very nice boy. He's a stonemason and a hard worker. But my father . . ."

"Yes?"

"My father had another fellow in mind for me. We were promised at birth. He's rather shy and a little stupid, but . . . well . . ."

"Yes, go on, I'm listening."

"He is of my class."

The nun's brow seemed to darken. "What is your class? What do you mean?"

"My father is a wealthy man, a landowner."

"Well educated?"

Gabriella's hand went to her mouth to stiffle a giggle. "Oh, no. I mean, he hasn't read many books, and his speech isn't very refined."

Now the nun's face had lost its calm to a righteous scowl. "There are no classes before the Lord and Holy Mother Church."

"Yes, I know. But you will never convince my father."

"Who is this man, I'd like to know," the mother superior demanded.

Now Gabriella hesitated, then decided not to answer. The name Terasatti was well known even this far from home. To say there are no classes is one thing. To rebel in the face of Don Antonio Pietro de Brindisi Terasatti was quite another, and no one, not even this pious churchwoman, could be trusted to keep his daughter from him.

The mother superior seemed slightly hurt. "All right, if you don't want to tell me it doesn't matter. I came in here with the idea of talking you out of this nonsense with your young man, of showing you what a foolish fellow he was to go against the wishes of your father. But your father is a dunce. I can tell by the way you describe him.

"My father was the same way. He was a silversmith in Florence. I wanted to marry a Neapolitan. That's all he had to hear. So I ended up taking my vows—not that I'm unhappy, you understand.

"Here, take the veil from your hair and come with me. I have something to show you."

Gabriella, confused and curious, did as she was told. The nun led her out of the cell and up to the little office on the second floor. Mother Regina looked taller and plumper when she was walking than when she was sitting down, and she had a long athletic stride that Gabriella found difficult to keep up with, so by the time they had climbed the stairs, the younger woman was out of breath and panting slightly. She could feel the dew on her upper lip. That was the way she looked when she walked through the door and found Giorgio waiting for her.

Dio mio, she looks like an angel all dressed in white, he thought in exquisite anguish. He wanted to throw his arms around her, to crush her against him, to taste her lips, to kiss her hands—but what was he thinking? That was no way to treat an angel. Ah, if only that old leather bag of a nun weren't looking on, he would find a way to treat an angel. He would ravage her with dignity, his little Gabriella.

Of course there was Litello, the ugly beast Don Antonio had sent along, always looking on. He was a big man, six inches taller than Giorgio, and the broad pie that was his face was covered with violet blotches and scarlet webbing. Yes, a horror, Giorgio thought, and stupid as well, but still not so frightening as the stone-faced mother superior.

"As you can see, your young man has come for you, Gabriella," said Mother Regina.

Gabriella looked uncomfortable at the sight of Litello,

but she said nothing to or about him. Instead she bowed her head demurely. "Hello, Giorgio," she murmured.

"Hello, Gabriella," he replied. "Everything has been taken care of. I've come to take you back."

"Where is Enrico?" she asked innocently. "I'm surprised he didn't come with you."

"He was detained. He is very busy these days. He has much work to do."

Giorgio was worried about his old friend. If they mistreated Scarfo the way they had him, the old man wouldn't last long. Still, everyone had seen him taken by the don's men, and everyone knew there was no reason to punish him. If Don Antonio cared anything about his own reputation—and even crooks had their honor—nothing would happen as long as Gabriella was returned safely and on time.

"We can leave at once if you like," Giorgio said.

The nun intervened. "You will leave after you have seen a priest and not one moment before. If you want to take her, you will either marry her or come back when you have a trustworthy chaperone, not some fellow without a brain in his head like this one."

Litello glanced at the floor without saying a word. Mother Regina had cowed him in an instant. But Giorgio couldn't remain silent. If he married Gabriella now, who knew what might happen to Scarfo? The don was as man who was used to getting his way. No, there could be no wedding now, and there could be no delay.

"Mother Regina, I promise before God in heaven and all His angels, before the church and the Communion of Saints, that she will be safe with me. I will not lay a hand on her."

"Agh, and why should I believe you? You're a man, and to make matters worse, just a boy of a man. I know how you think. You don't think. A young lady to you is just a thing to play with, right? You think I don't know?''

''I promise you, I can't marry her and I can't touch her either. Something stronger than stone will hold my hand.''

''Oh, and what is that?'' the nun asked sarcastically.

The same question was written across Gabriella's face, but she kept her silence. He could see she was unsure what was going on, waiting to learn a little more.

''This man works for her father,'' he said, indicating Litello. ''As stupid as he is, if I touched her, he would cut my ears off. It's true, he's not really a chaperone. He's a work animal, like an ox. But his job is to bring Gabriella home, and he ain't going to let any funny business go on.''

''You mean you want to take her home to her father, the aristocratic pig who thinks he's better than everyone else in the country? The very man who think's he so much better than you?''

Gabriella spoke up. ''Giorgio, you're crazy. I won't go back to him. Not after what he did to you. Anyway, how can I? I've run away. I've shamed myself.''

Litello made his contribution. ''Your father says come home now, Signorina. No arguments. That's all.''

''You can take her if you think you can get past me,'' Mother Regina countered.

Giorgio tried to calm the situation. ''Mother Regina, please. It's true he's an aristocrat, but only half true, because he's also a violent man who will hurt my friend Scarfo if I don't take Gabriella home.''

''Scarfo?'' The mother superior looked at Gabriella with horror. ''Who is your father to do this thing, girl? Who would threaten the life of that dear old man?''

Gabriella stepped around the question. ''I'm not going anywhere. I'm not leaving this place until I'm married, as you said before. Don't believe all this nonsense, Mother Regina. I know this man Litello who stands before you. He doesn't work for my father. He's the village idiot.''

Mother Regina moved bruskly around her desk and sat down like a judge holding court. "I'm tired of all these stories and lies. I'm not used to such nonsense. It makes my head spin. I want to know the truth. Who is this dangerous father?''

"Her father is Don Antonio Terasatti," Giorgio finally admitted. Now let's see what happens, he thought.

The nun's expression did not change, but her tone of voice became calmer. "Is this true, Gabriella?''

"Yes, ma'am, but I can not help who my father is. You mustn't blame me for that.''

"No one blames, you, my dear, but we must think of Enrico's safety. He is an old friend of this convent. Do you understand? Your father has a reputation for cruelty.''

Giorgio's heart broke as Gabriella nodded in resignation. "Please, Gabriella, you must understand," he said, "I'm not taking you back without getting a good price. He has consented to our marriage.''

She turned on him and in a voice savage with hurt said, "He will never let us marry. I know my father. He would say anything to get his way, but he would as soon kill me as let me marry you. You're a fool, Giorgio, a fool. You must have gone back for him to find you. Why didn't you hide? Why?''

"Sure, very nice. Then what was I supposed to do, wait in a cave in the hills until your father died? He's got more protection than any other man in Italy. He'll live to be a hundred and ten.''

"You don't know what you've done, Giorgio. You just don't know." She turned her face away from him to hide her tears.

Giorgio, tears streaming down his own face, said without hope, "I've done a good thing for us, Gabriella. You'll see. Don't worry about nothing."

Despite Litello's objections Mother Regina insisted that the little party remain at the convent overnight, but as soon as the sun rose the next morning, they set off on foot for Santa Barbara. The mare Gabriella had ridden up the mountain was left as a gift for the sisters. Gabriella had shoes now and she didn't mind walking. Neither of the men was mounted because Don Antonio didn't trust anyone with his horses.

The weather was calm and cold and the travel easy. Giorgio tried to convince himself that his beloved was wrong, that he would come to court her and that after a decent time they would marry and have children like anybody else. Persuading himself was difficult. She was right when she said her father was a ruthless man, and it wasn't at all unlikely that he would go back on his word, but there was nothing to do about it. He had Scarfo, and Scarfo's safety was the most important thing now.

Gabriella spoke not a word during the journey, but kept her eyes always downcast on the trail ahead and her hands folded inside the woolen cape Mother Regina had provided. Giorgio tried to speak with her many times, but she stubbornly ignored him.

He was afraid she had come to hate him for his stupidity and he couldn't blame her. He should have thought all this out. He shouldn't have trusted so easily in Scarfo's plan. After all, Scarfo was old, and not all old men were wise. Oh, Giorgio, he said to himself, you should have done a thousand things. You should have done everything but what you did. Of course she hates you. I would hate you too if I were her.

So his mood became darker and more desperate as

they crossed the valley beneath the plateau, then began the climb up to the villa. Perhaps this was the last he would ever see of her. Even if her father kept his promise, why should she want to marry a man like him, Giorgio?

They hadn't stopped along the way to eat, and they had brought along only a little wine in a gourd to drink, so when they passed over a little stream that ran under a lemon tree on the plateau road, Giorgio stopped to scoop some water into his mouth with the palm of his hand. As he bent over he had a curious sensation of instinctual fear, as if he had exposed his back to a predator. He turned. Litello was standing above him, tall and solid as an obelisk.

"Hey, what are you gonna do?" Giorgio said faintly. He couldn't figure any way to quickly come to his feet from his knees. There was no escape.

"Hurry up, drink your water. I want to get back."

To drink Giorgio would have to turn his back again, and this he did not wish to do. Not that he could have stopped the man from hurting him in any case, but he didn't want to make it too easy for him either. This way, if he saw a blow coming, at least he could try to duck.

"You supposed to keep me from getting back with you, Litello?"

"I don't know what the hell you're talking about. I just don't like standing around waiting. The boss don't like it either."

Throughout this exchange Gabriella seemed not to notice what was going on. Her sad gaze was always turned in another direction. When Giorgio came to his feet, though, she faced him squarely and with relief in her eyes. Yes, she had noticed, he thought, and had the same fear he had.

So it was not imagination. Litello had maybe been thinking something over, like how the boss might like it if this stonemason weren't around to cause any more trouble, how it might mean a little bonus at the end of the month, but in the end, like any soldier, he didn't want to risk his neck. Maybe the boss had something else in mind for this kid. Giorgio said a little prayer of thanksgiving and was careful to keep an eye on the big man the rest of the way back.

Gabriella was confined to her room without an audience. Giorgio was detained in the dining room with the old man. Only Litello saw the don upon their return, and the don was not happy.

"Why the hell didn't you kill him when you had the chance?"

"Because your daughter was looking on, Don Antonio. I didn't think that would please you."

The don made an obscene sign with his left hand. "All right. I got another way to deal with him. Send them in, then get the hell out of my sight."

Like an obedient dog grateful for any attention, Litello made a servile bow and did as he was told without a second thought for Don Antonio's contempt. The two prisoners were led into the study and stood before their don like slaves on a block.

"I should have both your throats cut like pigs," he said to them. "Just so the people of the village will have an example."

"Don Antonio," Giorgio said, "forgive me for reminding you, but you are a man of honor and you have given your word."

"It is true, Don Antonio," Scarfo added. "Everyone in Santa Barbara heard you. What kind of example would you make of this kid? Only that he was the victim of a lie."

"They would learn to keep their place, that's what kind of example!" the don exploded. "They would learn to keep their filthy hands off what does not belong to them.'' Then he forced himself to be calm by folding his hands on his desk and holding his head very still—though his chin still trembled when he talked. ''Nevertheless, I am a man of honor. I made a promise, even though you forced it out of me. You may come to visit my daughter. But not for a week. I've seen enough of you for the time being. And be sure I never find you alone with her or I will kill you on the spot, do you understand?''

''Of course I understand. You're her father. What else could you be expected to say? If I had a daughter—''

''Shut up,'' Scarfo said and nudged him in the ribs. Then he addressed the don. ''I wish to thank you for your hospitality and kindness, Don Antonio. I hope someday I may repay you equally.''

Don Antonio glared at him. ''Yeah? And what's that supposed to mean?''

Scarfo became instantly apologetic. ''Only what I said, signor. Please. I meant no offense.''

It was a long moment before Don Antonio let Scarfo relax his nervous smile. ''Very well. Get going, both of you. And don't let me see your face around here for a week, kid, or I'll make it pretty for you.''

Giorgio left feeling more at ease than he had in a long time. Everything was looking pretty good. How come he'd been afraid, anyway? The don was a man of honor. Everybody on the plateau knew that. That's what he deserved for listening too much to Gabriella. He had begun thinking like a woman. Well, to hell with that. He would think for himself from now on. After all, he was Giorgio Farenza.

Scarfo returned to work the next day. The wall was finished. Just some cleanup work had to be done—some sweeping and lifting, moving out the work equipment, a little pointing here and there—so Giorgio didn't get out of bed. In fact, he slept the entire day and night and halfway through the next.

He would have slept even longer had not the village baker, Luigi Pranzo, awakened him with a loud knock on the door. For some reason Pranzo received all the mail for the town and delivered it twice a week. He'd probably bribed a bureaucrat somewhere, some Roman maybe, or else he'd been granted the favor by Don Antonio. It was impossible to guess and he wouldn't tell. For his trouble he charged a hundred lire per letter. If you didn't pay, you didn't get your mail. Giorgio paid.

He'd never received a letter before, but he could tell from all the marks on the front of the envelope that this one was special. There was no particular address on it. It was simply marked. "S. Giorgio Farenza, Santa Barbara, Campania, Italy."

"It's from your brother," Pranzo said.

"How can you tell?" It annoyed Giorgio when men like this one, little and fat and smug, knew too much about too many things.

"I can tell, that's all. Who else you know in America?"

"America, eh?"

"Sure, look here. U—S—A."

"Hey, Pranzo, don't try to make a fool of me. I know how to read, and that don't say America."

"How could I make a fool of a man who comes to the door in the middle of the day wearing his underwear?" Pranzo said with a laugh.

Giorgio looked down at the worn cotton of his longjohns and rubbed his unshaven face with his hand. "What do you care what I'm wearing? You a sissy or something?"

Pranzo's head bobbed up and down with contemptuous annoyance. "Just give me my money and let me get the hell out of here, Farenza."

It took a few minutes to find enough to pay him, but getting rid of him was worth the money. Giorgio had never liked Pranzo. His baked goods always looked grimy, as if they had been made by unwashed hands, and his manner, always peppered with sarcasm and contempt, was irritating at best.

When Giorgio was alone again, he put the letter down on the table. He watched it suspiciously for a moment as if he expected it to jump. Then he picked it up and examined it, and for no particular reason put it to his nose and sniffed at it.

He wasn't sure whether he should open it now or wait for Scarfo to return. Everything he owned he shared with Scarfo, and something as momentous as a letter—well, it was too grand a thing to approach by himself. Still, his curiosity was playing with his fingers, saying, come on, Giorgio, pick it up, open it. If you don't, you'll go crazy wondering if Pranzo was right, if it really is from your brother. It didn't take long for curiosity to have its way. After all, he told himself, he wasn't a saint.

When he unfolded the little packet of papers, he knew at once the letter did not come from Sebastiano. The script was round and careful, completely unlike his brother's heavy hand. He wasn't surprised. Sebastiano wasn't a man to write letters. What did surprise him was that the letter wasn't from Teresa either. It was from a young girl who called herself Sophia Farenza and who claimed to be the eldest child of Giorgio's brother and sister-in-law.

So, he thought with amusement, Sebastiano's son turned out to be a daughter. Good. A man like that needed two women to run his life. But as Giorgio read on, he discovered there were three more girls and two boys in the brood as well. He shook his head with disbelief. Learning so suddenly that he had such a large family somewhere in

the world was like waking from a long sleep during which
the world had become unrecognizable.

The child went on for another page, talking about her
school and her family and America, and in particular about
one brother, Franco, who she said was a troublemaker and
in her father's words cursed with a stubbornness worthy of
his uncle Giorgio. Then came her signature and after that a
postscript written in a more mature hand.

> Dear Giorgio,
> I hope you are well. I have thought of you
> often over these past years, but I couldn't bring
> myself to write. I think I've been angry with you
> for disappearing as you did, but with all the
> news of the war in the north, I have grown very
> worried about your safety. If this letter finds
> you, please know that all is forgiven. You were
> always a good boy, like a little brother to me.
> Sebastiano is doing well, though he drinks a
> little too much wine sometimes. He works for
> the railroad now, here in Philadelphia.
> You wouldn't believe this place, Giorgio.
> It's nothing like Santa Barbara. There are build-
> ings ten, twelve stories high, and a river goes
> through the city—just like in Rome if you have
> ever been there. See? I'm learning geography from
> my kids. They are wonderful children, very well
> educated. Maybe one day you'll come to America
> and meet them. I've told them all about you.
> Well, I must go now. Little Favia, the
> smallest, is crying for the breast. Please write
> when you have a chance. Both Sophia and I are
> looking forward to it.

>   Love,
>   Teresa

Giorgio read through the last passage again. He tried to hear it in his sister-in-law's voice, but to his surprise, he had difficulty remembering what she sounded like. It had been a long time—eight years.

The line about his brother worried him. If Teresa said he was drinking a little too much wine, that meant he was probably drunk most of the time, and Giorgio wondered what had happened to make him that way. He had always been a hard man, fiery and full of anger, but sober and energetic. America must be a hard place for a man to live, he thought.

There was a very nice part in that letter too. Teresa said she was worried about him, Giorgio. Of course, there was nothing to worry about. The war in the north had nothing to do with him. But knowing that she thought about him gave him a giddy pleasureful feeling in his stomach, as though he had suddenly found himself to be a very important man.

He spent the rest of the afternoon trying to recall incidents from his childhood, not big things, obvious things, but little kindnesses and shows of affection his sister-in-law gave him when he was too young to be grateful. Sometimes when she was cooking she would give him a strand of *linguini* fresh and steaming from the pot, without sauce but a little salty and tender and comfortable to chew upon. At night she would kiss him on the forehead, tuck his covers all around him like a cocoon and listen to his prayers.

The best moments, the ones he never understood, were when he did something stupid like putting his shoes on the wrong feet and she would suddenly smile with delight, then hug him tight or stroke his face. From so many years' perspective those were lovely times, and he spent a wonderful afternoon under the perfect blue skies of his memory.

* * *

Scarfo showed no interest in the letter. He was surly
and taciturn; after he did so much work on the garden
wall, after everyone rushed to complete the job before
winter, Don Antonio had decided not to come down and
look things over. "Why kill yourself to please a man when
he doesn't give a damn?" Scarfo grumbled. To make
matters worse, everyone was told that the last payroll
would be delayed a week.

Giorgio hardly listened to the complaints. It was so
long since he had been on the job that he didn't care
anymore. He hadn't even thought about the job since he
first saw Gabriella. That was strange. It was as if he had
been married to the stone and the one love had stolen
away the other. There was no reason he couldn't love both
at the same time. Loving his work and loving a woman
weren't the same thing at all, and yet he couldn't seem to
concentrate on one without forgetting the other. Yes, very
strange indeed.

Gabriella, Gabriella, Gabriella. He wondered if Teresa would approve of her. Probably not. Teresa was full
of traditions, loaded down with the old ways, and falling
in love with someone not of your class was forbidden. It
was considered as foolish as marrying someone much
older or younger. At the wedding the peasants of the
village would line the streets and call out insults and
obscenities at the bride and groom.

Still, Teresa knew something about love. Maybe she
wouldn't approve, but she would understand. Of course
she would. Teresa was a hell of a good woman. The best.
That much he could remember.

Just after sunset the two men ate a quiet dinner of
white beans cooked in oil, hard bread and half a bottle of
wine. There would be many days like this now. The rains
would soon be pouring for weeks on end. The valleys

would flood and the winds would blow and he and Scarfo would wile away hour after hour, day after day, week after week, in bored silence or forced conversation.

Once in a while a friend would come for a visit, and there would be trips to the village, but for the most part the winter would be a long battle against tedium, and if the money didn't hold out, against hunger. It was like this every year.

After dinner, after they both had settled into meditation, lying on their beds and letting their thoughts wander, the quiet was interrupted by a strange mechanical whine outside, followed by a squeak, then a sharp knock at the door.

"What do you want? Who's there?" Scarfo called out. Giorgio hesitated to answer the door. "Who's there?" Scarfo asked again.

"Open up in the name of the government!" a voice cried back.

Giorgio felt his hackles go up. He didn't like the sound of the voice. It spoke in a strange dialect.

"Open up or I'll break your door down. I'm not alone out here."

Scarfo motioned to the door with his head. "Open it," he said.

"Open it yourself," Giorgio replied sulkily.

"It ain't for me, boy."

A loud thud made the door shudder. Whoever was outside had begun to batter it with something.

"All right, wait a minute, I'm coming!" Giorgio cried out in anger. Another thud. "Wait. I'm coming, I tell you."

He didn't want to open the door. There was nothing, he knew, but trouble on the other side, but he had no choice. If there was more than one of them outside, then they would be watching the windows, waiting for him. But before he lifted the latch, he put his ear close to listen through the boards, and then said, "Who are you looking for?"

"We're looking for you kid, who do you think? You're name is Farenza, ain't it?"

"What if it ain't?"

"How old are you?"

"What the hell do you care? I'm old enough."

"If you're old enough, it don't matter what your name is."

The door shuddered again, this time with two quick thuds, almost like the sound of a horse's hooves coming down one after another. His head too close, Giorgio's ear rang with the blows. After another thud and another he heard a cracking sound. Something was giving way. Giorgio's heart beat hard and his hands shook. A sliver of wood came away.

"Open it before they tear down my house," Scarfo shouted angrily.

There was no use in stalling. Giorgio lifted the latch and made way for the visitors to enter. There were three of them, all dressed in military uniform. The first one had loops of gold braid hanging from one shoulder and a mustache so overtrimmed that it looked slightly too small under his hawk nose.

The two men with him were tall and serious looking. Both carried bayoneted rifles. It was the butts of those weapons, Giorgio realized, that had been used against the door. All three were so neatly tailored and their shoes so shiny that somehow the temperature in the room seemed to fall a few degrees at their cold perfection.

Giorgio was impressed. "How do you do, gentlemen? I am Giorgio Farenza. What can I do for you?"

The leader gave Scarfo a suspicious look. "Who's the old bird?"

"My grandfather. Don't worry about him. He's mixed up and can't hear too good."

Scarfo jumped to his feet. "I ain't your grandfather, you little pig. How the hell old do you think I am?"

Giorgio shook his head and smiled conspiratorially. "You see what I mean?" He touched his forefinger to his temple. "Confused."

"I ain't confused about nothing," Scarfo shouted, starting forward, but one of the taller men shoved him back to his bed with a rifle butt.

Giorgio rushed over and bent over the old man, whose hands clutched his chest where the blow had come. "Scarfo," he whispered, "are you all right?"

"Yeah, I'm all right," he gasped, "but you better get the hell out of here. They're gonna take you away, boy. That's why they came."

"Yeah, I know. I know why they came."

"Hey, Farenza, leave him alone. He'll be all right," the man in charge ordered.

Giorgio forced a smile and turned. "Sure, he'll be fine. He's a tough old man, my grandfather."

"You got any guns in this place?" the soldier wanted to know.

"Guns?" Giorgio managed a laugh. "I'm a stone-mason. What the hell do I need a gun for?"

"Maybe to hunt for birds," the soldier said, arrogantly poking behind the utensils in the small pantry near the fireplace. "Or maybe to hunt conscription officers."

"No, I don't hunt nothing."

"That's good, Farenza. It's good you don't hunt nothing, because I don't like the idea of a goddamn igno- rant stupid southerner carrying a gun around, not unless the army gives it to you and shows you where to point it."

It was becoming almost impossible for Giorgio to

smile. "Why do you say I'm stupid and ignorant when you don't even know me?"

"Because you live south of Rome, right? In *Afrika*. You're a stupid monkey, like everybody else around this goddamn place."

Fucking pig, Giorgio snarled to himself. I'll cut his throat if he gives me the chance.

Scarfo was still quiet but alert. He must have read the look on Giorgio's face; he touched his arm to calm him.

"You know why we're here, Farenza?"

"You tell me," he invited, though he perfectly well knew why.

"We're gonna make a soldier out of you. We need more soldiers up north. The Austrians kill them too fast. We can hardly keep up with the demand." He laughed. "You got a good friend around here, you know that? Yeah, some guy who knows you wanted to meet your responsibility and fight for Italy."

Italy, Giorgio thought in disgust. Screw Italy. Italy is north of Rome.

"Some big shot, this friend of yours," the soldier went on. "Name of Terasatti. He must know a few people high up. We were all sent here just for you. That's a real honor, you know, Farenza?"

"Sure. I'm real honored," Giorgio mumbled. He wasn't smiling now. He felt beaten, smothered, humiliated. The don had made a fool of him and there was nothing to do. He could try to make a run for it, but they would stop him, maybe kill him before he got ten yards.

"I got time to pack?" he asked them bitterly.

"You don't need nothing. The army's got everything you need."

Giorgio nodded in resignation and turned to Scarfo. The old man got to his feet. There were tears in his eyes. "Don't let them kill you, kid," he said. "When you're done in the army, you come back here to old Scarfo. This is your home, you remember that, and I'm your family. Here, take this." He scrambled down to his knees and took his old trumpet from under his bed. "Take this with you and play the notes that I taught you. It will remind you where your home is."

Giorgio tried to give it back. "Scarfo, I can't take this away from you. It's yours."

"I ain't giving it to you, idiot," Scarfo snarled. "I'm lending it. You better bring it the hell back when you're finished being a soldier for these bastards."

"Agh, *fan' gool*. All right, if you're that stubborn, I'll take the goddamn thing."

With that they exchanged a long embrace and kissed each other on both cheeks.

"Get word to Gabriella for me," Giorgio whispered in his ear.

Scarfo nodded but did not speak.

In a few moments Giorgio was sitting in the back of a truck, the first such vehicle he had ever seen, bouncing and jostling his way off the plateau to the foreign war in the north.

Chapter 18

A week went by, then two. Gabriella's hopes, dim to begin with, faded completely. Something had happened to Giorgio, though what it was she could only guess. Perhaps he had come to see her and her father found a way to put him off—threats or money or both, though she hated to believe he could be so easily frightened or bought.

She questioned her father about it, but he denied knowing anything. He even went on to imply that Giorgio might have found someone else, one of the village girls maybe, or a spinster with a dowry.

Gabriella knew better, or at least she hoped she did. After all Giorgio had been through for her, she doubted his head would be turned by the cobbler's daughter. On the other hand, a man would get tired after so *much* punishment, after a beating and two cross-country hikes and endless waiting, and when a man got tired, there were always women around to comfort him. That was the way of the world, and that was what worried Gabriella through sleepless nights.

It was Brigetta who finally brought news, learned from a maid who had heard it from a woman selling lemons in the marketplace at the center of town. Giorgio had been drafted and gone gone off to fight in the war up north.

No one knew where the information came from. Old Scarfo never said a word. Though he was seen from time to time buying salt and feed among the stalls along the corso, he never spoke to anyone. He was much changed lately. He looked old and beaten, and he seemed almost feeble the way he doddered. This whetted everyone's curiosity and gave rise to a hundred stories about a falling-out between the old man and the young one, but there was nothing of any substance.

When Gabriella heard the news, she was dumbstruck. Of all the possibilities she had considered, this one had never entered her head. Giorgio in the army? She couldn't conceive of such a thing. He didn't even own a gun. How could it have happened? The conscription officers might have found him, but surely he would have sent word to her if that had happened.

There was another obvious possibility, even a probablility, that nagged and gnawed at her, and she asked Brigetta point blank about it. "Did my father have anything to do with this?"

They were sitting in the tea room in the west wing of the villa. Brigetta looked much more distressed than Gabriella expected.

"I don't know. He's told me nothing. You know Antonio. He can keep his mouth shut as tight as a bishop's purse when he wants to."

"But how about the gossip? What have you heard?"

"Nothing worth listening to. A thousand stories and all of them ridiculous."

So then maybe there would never be an explanation. Gabriella seethed with anger, but whom should she blame? Her father? Brigetta? Herself? Everything was leading in circles, but in the center of every circle was the same name—Giorgio, Giorgio, Giorgio! Whatever had happened, he should have written to her. She was entitled to an explanation at the very least. The army!

For Brigetta Gabriella could only feel kindness and gratitude, and she almost laughed out loud at herself when she realized it. The world was turning backward.

"If only Giorgio would write to me." Gabriella sighed. "I don't know what to think. Maybe I was a fool to expect more from a peasant."

Brigetta made a scornful face. "Listen to you. Now you *are* being a fool. You don't know what happened. Maybe your father *did* have something to do with it."

Gabriella grew suddenly vicious. "If he did, I'll hate him for the rest of my life! I'll spit on his grave."

"Gabriella, hold your tongue. He's still your father."

"So what? What does that mean?"

"It means you must respect him."

"I can't respect him anymore. Everyone knows him for what he is—a big-shot crook and that's all. I don't know how you could want to marry him, even for money."

Brigetta cast her eyes down. "Gabriella, there's something you don't understand. I'll try to explain.

"Life is hell when you're poor. Maybe you have a few laughs, and maybe you have to keep plenty busy, but mostly it's hunger in the belly and fever in the head. Your father saved me from that. It was not kindness on his part, I know. It was a business arrangement. If he saved me from poverty, he has made a thousand poorer with his crooked government deals and the way he steals the profits from the little farms of the *contadini*. But to me he has always been loyal and for the most part generous.

"I have come to love him, Gabriella—maybe because there has never been anyone else for me to love. I don't know. But I want to be his wife. I want to carry his name, and I will carry it proudly. When he dies, I'll dress him for the burial and weep for him. You think I want only money, but I could have all the money from him I ever need without marrying him.

"Or maybe you think I want respectability." Brigetta nodded sadly. "Yes, maybe I do, but don't I deserve just a little in my life, Gabriella? I don't want it for nothing. I'll give Don Antonio a good life for the little bit of time he has left."

She stopped for a long moment, as if she had caught herself talking too much. When she spoke again, her voice was tentative. "Gabriella, do you still stand in the way of my marriage to your father?"

Gabriella looked down. She couldn't bring herself to meet Brigetta's eyes. "You have been good to me, Brigetta, in spite of the way I have treated you. I didn't trust you. For all I know I still shouldn't, but I'm tired of all this. Giorgio is gone and there's nothing left for me to care about. Marry whoever you want."

Brigetta reached across the little round table and took Gabriella's hands in her own. Gabriella's soft, full mouth turned up in a sad smile. "I'll say a novena for you. Maybe the Virgin will give you better luck than she's given me."

Don Antonio made a little collection of the letters that Giorgio Farenza sent to his daughter, but he didn't read them. He kept them in a safe behind a copy of a Giotto painting in the wall of his bedroom. He wasn't sure why he kept them. Somehow it seemed like less of a betrayal of his daughter. Or maybe he was beginning to get soft-hearted about the Farenza boy.

He had nothing against the kid. Farenza was impulsive and he took some stupid chances, but he was likable in a way. At least he had guts; unlike some of these bastards who called themselves men, he did more than talk about what he wanted. He went after it.

Unfortunately, what he wanted was Gabriella, and there was no circumstance in which Don Antonio would allow her to marry a poor local boy. It wasn't just a matter of money or class. Those things could be overlooked or taken care of. But for a kid from the streets to marry a Terasatti might give ideas to the peasants.

Once they had one of their own roosters in the henhouse, they'd want a few eggs in return. How long before they started asking for favors or trying to get special terms on their land-lease contracts or requesting dispensation for outstanding loans? Besides, there was another problem.

From the very first that name, Farenza, had bothered Antonio, niggled at his memory like a worm at an apple, but he couldn't quite attach a face to it until the morning the kid and the old man came to his front door. That day, in the bright sunlight and at a certain angle he suddenly saw in Giorgio's face the face of another man.

That other one and his wife had been killed more than twenty years before for being mixed up in the murder of one of Terasatti's men. He himself gave the order. He thought nothing of it at the time, but now their ghosts had come back to haunt him, and in his most private moments it was this more than anything else that bothered him.

So there was nothing to do. The boy had to be gotten rid of, and Don Antonio had handled it the best way he could. If for the sake of Gabriella's feelings Farenza couldn't be killed outright, then he could be put out of the way long enough for her to come to her senses. A little money in the right hand had taken care of that. With just a little luck the Austrians would do the rest. And if they didn't, by the time the war was over, Gabriella could be safely married off to Francesco Speranza.

Don Antonio had no illusions about that one. He was neither smart nor tough, but he was selfish and nervous, and those two qualities might be enough to see him through. Such weakness would turn to ruthlessness in the face of such power as Speranza stood to inherit.

As for Gabriella, perhaps she wouldn't be the happiest of women, but she would have a rich, secure life, and if she desired a taste of the lower classes now and then, why, without a father around to stop her she could have any stonemason she wanted.

Don Antonio patted his stomach as if he had just eaten a grand meal. He hadn't long to live, he knew, but life still treated him sweetly. As always, things were working out his way.

Old Scarfo puttered around outside of his house during the day, cleaning his tools, gathering wood, feeding the pigs, wandering without purpose. In a way Giorgio's leaving had been worse than the day his wife died. She had provided him with comfort and routine and a good time when the lights were out, and when she left him forever, he found life a little empty, a little still. They had enjoyed as many good years together as two people are entitled to—that's what he told himself.

However, when Giorgio was so violently taken away, in his place there remained a great void, a chasm of loneliness; Giorgio had been a son to Scarfo and brought life and youth and vitality into the old man's days. Now that he had been taken away, there was no extra strength to fend off decrepitude.

It was easy to forget things now. Sometimes he would leave his pipe burning for hours without knowing it. Sometimes he would prepare food and forget to eat it. If only Giorgio were here to help me, he would think, but sometimes the worst thing of all would happen—he would forget Giorgio's name.

There was one thing, however, that he never allowed himself to forget, and that was Giorgio's instruction to give a message to Gabriella. He held onto that memory in the same way he planned to hold tight to his scapular medal at the hour of his death so that his salvation would be assured.

Someday he would find a way to deliver that message, but not now. If Gabriella found out what the don did not want her to know, Giorgio might be the one to pay for it. After all, who knew how far the don's power extended? No, it was better to wait, to bide one's time.

There was no chance for those two anyway, never had been. For all his love of Giorgio, he knew his protege for a fool. Scarfo's only hope and prayer was that Giorgio would return from the army safe and sound.

It was a prayer for Giorgio's safety that was on Scarfo's mind the first time he felt a twinge in the center of his chest such as he had never felt before. It happened on a Tuesday. It happened again the following Friday, but for a longer time, and he found himself out of breath and confused a little. He began to ask that Giorgio be allowed to come home soon. Very soon.

No time was wasted turning Giorgio into a soldier. They put a hat on his head, a uniform on his back, boots on his feet and a rifle in his hands. They took him by train from Caserta to a place called Fort San Gabriello just north of Turin. The irony of the name wasn't lost on him.

They made him march for hours on end with a full pack on his back. They made him learn to dig a trench, to clean his weapon, to shoot. They made him eat until he could eat no more and then they made him march again.

So far north the weather was cold and miserable.

Twice there had been light snowfall. He hated the weather
and the army and the training and the government. He
longed for Gabriella and Santa Barbara.

He was put in a platoon with some boys from Naples.
They were roughnecks who liked to fight with knives, so
Giorgio tried to stay away from them, but they wouldn't
let him. They liked his looks and they were determined to
make friends. Their charm consisted in stealing his boots
before reveille, goosing him in the shower and cutting off
locks of his hair when he was sleeping; they were fond of
practical jokes as a way of testing a fellow's mettle.

They thought he would laugh. He didn't laugh, but he
didn't object too strenuously either, so they made a habit
of tormenting him at every opportunity. Their names were
Gino Forza, Pasquale Marino and Mario (the Snake)
Luccarinni.

It was through their efforts that Giorgio found himself
appointed company bugler. One evening he took Scarfo's
trumpet from his duffel bag, not to play it but to polish it
and to hold it in his hands as a reminder of his old friend.
The sudden sight of shiny metal was too much for the
three Neapolitans to resist. Gino Forza, a slightly built
man with tight, kinky black hair, whizzed past like a
housefly and snatched the instrument from Giorgio's grasp.

A chase ensued. Around the barracks, over beds,
down a dilapidated flight of wooden steps they ran. They
wound up outside, fleeing along a dusty old horsepath that
led to the infirmary. Pasquale and Mario ran close behind,
yelling encouragement to both men. Their cries and laughter attracted the attention of their platoon sergeant, who
found them standing happily over Gino and Giorgio, scuf-
fling in the dust next to an ambulance wagon.

The sergeant, a man named Pocatello, confiscated

Giorgio's trumpet and made all four men march in close drill for the rest of the afternoon.

Giorgio was fit to kill Gino Forza and might have taken advantage of his first opportunity to do so had not Sergeant Pocatello interviewed him first. The meeting took place in a large office in the administration building at the center of the fort. Seargeant Pocatello was seated behind a rather luxurious red maple desk; everywhere the place was hung with flags and swords and portraits of distinguished generals with big mustaches. Giorgio wondered how a mere sergeant had managed to secure such a prize office for himself.

"Farenza, does this belong to you?" he asked, holding up the trumpet for Giorgio to examine.

It took all Giorgio's fortitude not to reach out and grab it from the sergeant's rough hands. "Yes, sir. It's mine."

"Can you play it?"

"Sure I can play it. Why would I own it if I couldn't play it? I'm the best trumpet player in all the Campania." This was the answer he suspected the sergeant wanted to hear.

"Here." Pocatello handed the instrument over. "Play."

"Right now?"

"Sure, why not?"

"It's not the right atmosphere, sergeant, sir."

"What do you need for the right atmosphere, an opera hall?"

"No, sir. But I'm just not—my lips feel too tight. I haven't played for a long time and I wouldn't want to offend the sergeant's discriminating ears."

"Play, Farenza, or I'll throw you into a stockade and keep you there until the war is over. The sergeant had bushy eyebrows that gave him a very tough look. He wasn't the sort of man Giorgio was going to take too much of a gamble on. Better to do as he asked.

He licked his lips to relieve the nervous dryness, then kissed the mouthpiece of the trumpet. He played a few notes, or what he hoped would be notes until they escaped from him like screeching, wounded birds. He cringed apologetically, but the sergeant didn't flinch.

"Play again, Farenza."

"I'm a little nervous. You heard yourself."

"Play again."

Giorgio did as he was told, but this time restrained his breath a little to keep his playing under better control. This time the trumpet made a long, sorrowful, honking sneeze.

"Not so good as the first time," said the sergeant, "but good enough." He held out one hand.

Giorgio, incredulous, gave the instrument back. "Forgive me for contradicting you, sergeant, but the playing was perhaps not the best it could have been either time. The notes were a little bit sour."

Pocatello scowled. "Sour don't matter. This is the army. Loud matters. You can practice so you won't be so sour. Just blow hard."

"Blow hard for what, if you don't mind my asking?"

"I'm gonna make you a bugler."

"But I ain't got a bugle. Just a trumpet."

"I'll get you a bugle. Don't worry about it."

"But what about my trumpet?"

"You leave it here at the fort. Come back for it after the war."

"But Sergeant, somebody will steal it."

"What do you think them three guys will do if I let you keep it?"

"I can take care of those three guys."

"Oh, yeah? Tough guy, eh? Well, I'm telling you to leave the trumpet here, and I'm a tougher guy than you."

He laughed ironically. "Anyway, what the hell does it matter if somebody steals it? A guy with a bugle never lasts more than a few minutes on the battlefield. You're as good as dead, Farenza."

Blowing the bugle did have its good points. He was given extra time to practice and a private room in which to do it, so he was excused from most marching and guard duty and he had time away from his three friends.

In his off hours he lost money playing pinochle. As many as a hundred men at a time would gather in the canteen to play after dinner every night, forming little covens around a good view of somebody else's hand, shouting and cursing and accusing with every turn of the cards.

What Giorgio quickly came to understand, though he didn't seem to have the knack for doing anything about it, was that cheating was almost as fine an art among these men as playing the game. So inevitably he would see his funds dwindle night after night, and only a certain natural frugality that made him limit the amount he was willing to lose kept him from going broke the day after payday.

Still, he played on. It was his only relief from boredom, his only salve against the loss of Gabriella and Scarfo and everything of his past life.

He thought about Gabriella often, but there was little he could do to change things. He wrote her nearly every day, a tiring effort for a man who wrote or read so rarely, but he knew she hadn't received his letters. Only recently he had received his first word from her, and she complained in her message that he had never once written a line to her to explain his sudden departure. There was only one explanation. His letters were being intercepted and she had not been told of his conscription. Somehow Scarfo had failed him. To make matters worse,

Scarfo couldn't read, so it was impossible to find out any
more from him either.

At first Giorgio fell into depression, then was simply
resigned. What could he do? He went on writing letters
and sending them off, hoping one might find its way into
Gabriella's hands, but it was a useless, frustrating little
ceremony, like throwing seeds on a bed of rock.

By the time he left Fort San Gabriello his bugle
playing was passable. His notes would sometimes crack
like a young man's voice and his breath would run out
occasionally—something to do with smoking too much, he
guessed—but his battle calls were recognizable and loud.

He wished he could go home and show off for Scarfo,
but that proved to be impossible. He expected to get leave
for a few days before moving up to the front, but as it
turned out only volunteers were allowed any free time.
Draftees were too likely to desert. So the morning after his
basic training was finished, he found himself on a troop
train headed north.

It was a long ride, nearly a full day, and his three
friends never shut up. They were unhappy. It was better to
be poor than dead. A soldier's pay wasn't worth the risk.
They invented a thousand variations on this theme and
repeated the variations over and over.

Giorgio couldn't blame them for their fear. He felt the
same way. He felt it as a tightening in his gut, as a
trembling in his chest and along his arms, as a quiver in
his voice when he tried to speak. Their chatter made him
feel worse. How he wished they would shut up, even for
five minutes . . . for three . . . for one! He tried to tell them,
but they wouldn't listen. They couldn't. Their fear had made
them deaf. If only it had made them dumb.

The train took them to a place called Piave. Giorgio
had never heard of it. He knew only that it was so far

north that the cold, once he had left the train car and been assigned to a truck to take him to the front, made him shiver so badly he couldn't distinguish it from his fear.

The skies were grey as slate from horizon to horizon. Just to the north and east mountains were visible—such mountains as he had never seen. Some were so high they poked through the clouds, and their peaks were covered with snow, which made him wonder how they could be so close to the sun without melting off.

The mountains, however, were not where they would be fighting. He was taken with a thousand other men in a convoy of rickety trucks to a gently rolling plain thick with green and brown grass and dotted with boulders. There was no sign of war at first, only the dark scars of trenches marring the landscape. It was a place that might be pleasant in the springtime, when the peonies grew and the goats chased each other over the countryside.

It was not so harsh a scene as the craggy plateaus of the south made, and Giorgio found himself wondering why God was so much kinder to some places than to others. Perhaps it was a matter of devotion. Perhaps the people here were more pious than those in the south, though he didn't think so. Soldiers from the north had come into his land often enough to slaughter the peasants when the government didn't get its way.

That wasn't the work of pious men, but who knew the thoughts of God? Maybe a priest would have the answer. Or Scarfo. Scarfo had an answer for everything. Sometimes he even had the right answer.

On his first night in the field he was put among strangers in a trench. He had no idea what had happened to his three friends, nor did he much care. He liked the silence of the men who manned the sandbag walls, who sat behind the water-cooled machine guns, who joylessly fingered the triggers of their bayonetted rifles. It was not a comforting silence, not serenity but nervous tension that kept everyone awake and alert. That was exactly the way he wanted his fellows to be. If they were attacked in the middle of the night, he wanted trigger-happy men around him, men who were as fearful as he was.

There was no attack that night. Someone with a gruff whisper offered him a piece of candy. There was no smoking allowed in the dark. The little red coal would shine like a beacon for the Austrians. Giorgio accepted a stale piece of caramel. It sweetened the dryness in his mouth.

He managed to catch a snatch of murmured conversation now and then. There was talk of ghosts; there was always talk of ghosts at night on a battlefield. Sergeant Pocatello had told the recruits to expect this. There would be stories about friends who had disappeared in flame and smoke and who returned to bid farewell under the light of the stars. There would be stories about demons sent by the enemy to destroy the artillery or to steal ammunition or to make the minds of all the Italians crazy.

Everyone, the sergeant said, knew these stories were bullshit, but at night you believed them anyway, and you were lucky if you didn't die of a heart attack from fear.

When dawn came, a gray mist rolled over the plain. A few weary heads peaked up over the lip of the trench, but nothing could be seen. The artillery started. Both from behind and from ahead came constant battering and pounding as though someone were beating on the bottom of a cement-mixing tub with a board, only not so regular, not so benign. Explosions began to kick up dirt nearby, but no one could make out exactly where the shells were landing.

Sometimes Giorgio could hear them whistle, but curiously, that sound always came after the blast, as if it had arrived a little late.

He looked over the men in the trench. He could see

their faces clearly now. There was no bravery in them, no fire, no hope. There wasn't even the kind of gnawing fear he knew must be shaping his own expression. Instead he saw resignation and weariness in every eye.

Someone shouted an order to move out. Giorgio felt himself propelled over the wall of the trench by the strong thrust of his own legs, though he had not realized his legs were moving. He crouched and crept along behind the vaguely described silhouette in front of him.

Who were these men he was fighting beside, and who were the enemy? He would have to kill them, yet he did not even know what they looked like except for a few pictures he had been made to study at Fort San Gabriello. What was he doing here? a voice screamed inside of him. It had never seemed real until now. What was he doing here?

"Hey, where's the new bugler?" a voice said from the mist.

The bugle! Had he remembered it? He reached down to his side and felt for the cold tin bell that hung by a clip from his ammunition belt. Yes, it was there. He gritted his teeth. His fear was making him stupid.

"Bugler," the voice said again.

"Here," Giorgio replied. "Who are you?"

"I'm Captain Sorrelli, idiot. Don't ask stupid questions. You ready to blow the attack?"

Attack? What were they doing? The enemy was in front and that's the way everyone was going.

"What's the matter, you deaf too?" the captain hissed. "I asked you a question."

Now Giorgio could make the man out. He was tall and had a lean jaw and broad shoulders. Instead of a rifle he carried only a revolver in his right hand. "Sure, whatever you say, Captain."

They crept along endlessly. The mist began to clear.

The cold was chilling him through his clothing. If only he could have a cigarette, if only he could take a piss, if only he could do anything, be anywhere but where he was. Oh Lord, he prayed, if only you would give me a little miracle right now—not that I deserve one, but I don't deserve this either.

"Blow, bugler, blow!"

"All right, I'm blowing." It took a few seconds of fumbling to get the instrument free of his belt.

"I said blow!"

Giorgio bruised his lips he put the mouthpiece to them so quickly, then sounded the charge. The men around him began to run. What the hell were they doing? Who were they charging?

Up ahead there was a sudden crackling like a string of firecrackers suddenly going off. Cries of pain and of savagery mixed with the clanking of metal. As if from nowhere the throbbing and chugging of engines nearby filled the air. Tanks; he knew the sound, even if he did not know where the beasts were coming from.

What was that in front of him? Bayonets pointing to the sky, clashing together. Men were fighting hand to hand, yelling, screaming, shooting—din, tumult, confusion.

The mist was clearing rapidly now, and in the cold cloudy grey of the day he could see men dying, and he watched as if from a distance as his legs carried him closer and closer to the carnage. He was running and blowing mightily on his bugle, like Gabriel, he thought, like the angel of God come to announce the end of the world.

What was he doing? Why was he running? Something seemed to have taken him over—lust, foolishness. Men began to fall around him. Pieces of cheek and nose suddenly spurted from the face of a man running not three feet to Giorgio's left, but the man kept charging. Then a little geyser of blood erupted from his chest and he fell to the ground with a grunt.

The firing was ferocious and limbs were cut off. Heads were blown away. Sudden blossoms of explosives erupted from the earth all around. Mines or artillery? He couldn't tell. He ran and ran.

A figure with a point-crowned helmet stepped out of nowhere. Then there were more of them, hundreds of them. Austrians. Bayonets up, parry and thrust! Someone cut at him viciously. He felt a pull at the belly of his coat, but he wasn't cut.

Again the explosions—who were the fools sending in artillery and cutting down their own troops? The Italians or the Austrians? Who cared? He tripped and fell. The grass was cold and sharp stiff needles of hay poked his face. He wanted to cry but couldn't.

"Retreat," someone shouted, "sound the retreat!"

Giorgio raised his head from the ground, put his bugle to his lips and tried to blow, but nothing came out. He had to wipe the grass from his lips. He blew again. This time he made the sound, the blessed sound that let the men flee what they feared. He came to his feet and blew harder. The dead had fallen so thick around him that he had to step on them to run. He didn't care now. What the hell was he doing here? Gabriella, he thought, Gabriella, look what your father has done to me!

There was something to the left—what? A sound? An explosion? No, it couldn't be. He would know an explosion. But how had he come to be on his back? His arm hurt and he was sleepy. This is no time to go to sleep. It's time to retreat.

But he could do nothing but sleep, even here in the midst of the blood and smoke, even with all the pain in his arm. Yes, a sweet sleep as if he were lying among the flowers.

* * *

It was nearly nightfall before he was found by two corporals with a stretcher, though he had awakened an hour before. He was bleeding badly and too weak and dizzy to stand. Among the bodies of the dead and badly wounded all around him roamed the scavengers—not only the jackals and buzzards, but pigs and goats too, pushing their snouts into sweet bloody wounds and stirring away the flies. When any came too close, he blew weakly on his bugle to frighten them away, but they were getting used to the sound now and it was only the voices of the young men with the stretcher that saved him from attack.

He was placed on the canvas gently, then lifted and carried off under a dark sky. He had to sleep again. He heard a bugle calling from somewhere. Men jostled passed him. They were going to the fight again. Good. Let them go. To hell with them, he thought. I've had my fighting for the day. And then he was gone into the blackness.

Chapter 19

Giorgio spent two long weeks in a field hospital before they moved him back to Rome. The army didn't want to give up on him too easily. He was a trained bugler, and it would be a shame to let him go after his first battle.

By the end of December, though, the fighting had stopped because of a paralyzing snowstorm that rolled down from the Alps, and the French and the English had sent in troops to help the Italians. The odd man here and there didn't count for so much now.

Giorgio had suffered wounds both to his head and to his right arm. The head wound was slight, though it caused a concussion that sometimes made it very difficult for Giorgio to keep his balance. The other wound was serious. A piece of shrapnel had embedded itself in his forearm, causing the loss of much blood and severing the nerve. He would not be able to move his hand for a long time.

The doctors were brusque about it and the nurses didn't seem to care a damn, which threw Giorgio into despondency. The army owed him a little sympathy, he thought, maybe more than a little. There was no sympathy, not from anyone. He had to live alone with the constant pain in his arm and the dizziness in his head, knowing he would not work again with a chisel and mallet until he healed—if he ever healed. They wouldn't promise anything.

When he was well enough to walk, he was given furlough pay and discharged. He wandered the streets of Rome in a black mood, staring ahead without looking left or right; even children ran out of his way because of the dead look in his eyes.

What would he do now? A man who couldn't work was worthless. Gabriella might have married him before even though he was not wealthy, but now he was a cripple, and there was nothing ahead for a cripple but begging and poverty and the handouts of the church.

It seemed that everywhere he went in Rome there were carvings and statues and reliefs, and they seemed to mock him. He often thought about asking Scarfo to teach him to sculp and how Scarfo said that he, Giorgio, hadn't suffered enough. Giorgio laughed bitterly to himself. He'd suffered plenty now, but he still couldn't sculp, not without a hand.

He felt at his neck for the rosary he had carried around for so many years. That rosary was his good luck, he told himself, and he had been stupid to give it up, even for love. Well, it was too late to worry about now. The damage had been done.

As for the trumpet, who knew when he would get it back? He made the short ride to Turin the first day, but Sergeant Pocatello was no longer at the fort and a requisition would have to be approved by a dozen bureaucrats before the instrument could be given back to its owner. There was no use in waiting for it. The process might take weeks, months or—if he knew the army—forever.

He came back to Rome and visited St. Peter's, but the presence of God was no comfort to him. Neither did the sights of the city, the ruins, the fountains, the churches, the piazzi, have an affect on his mood. He was out of work. Though he had plenty of money in his pocket, he didn't rent a room, but slept on the walls of public fountains for three nights in a row. His big army coat kept him warm enough to survive.

By the fourth day he'd had enough of the city. There was nowhere to go but home, even though home was the one place he was afraid of, the last stop where he would have to face a future of—what? Of nothing. Of no place. His love would be gone from him, his work would as well. To hell with it all. Let the world give him a living for a while. He would go back to the orphanage and ask for a handout. The nuns were always good for a lira or two.

He took the train to Caserta and walked to Santa Barbara. He had come to like walking. It made him think about his legs instead of the useless appendage that hung from his right elbow.

He walked past the villa but did not stop there to claim his prize, his right to court Gabriella Terasatti. She would forget him, if she hadn't already, he told himself. It would better for them both when she did.

He walked through the center of the town, and when the people there recognized him, they looked at him strangely, as if he carried a curse upon his head. No one spoke to him. He didn't care. Whatever was bothering them, they would get over it in time. Something had happened to estrange them from him. Good. He didn't want to talk anyway.

But when he reached the little cottage on the other side of town, when he opened the door expecting to see old Scarfo waiting there for him with a bottle of wine, he found instead an empty shell. It was dark and cold. The hearth had not been recently lit. The floor was cluttered with rags and soot and the beds were gone, as was everything else of the slightest value. Either Scarfo had moved out or the place had been looted.

Giorgio shook his head. Now, what the hell? Was fate laughing at him again? Not only was his future gone, but his past had somehow disappeared as well. There had been a home here. Now there was nothing.

He had to find Scarfo. He went back to the town. First he asked an old fool named Maglio, also called Mouse, who sold lemons in the piazza. Maglio only bowed his head and mumbled incomprehensibly. Maglio had not been Scarfo's friend, but he had sold him lemons twice a week.

Giorgio began to get worried. He asked up and down the corso and was met with shrugs or puzzled looks. Now what? Now where to go?

The other masons would know. The work at the villa was finished, but he knew where many of them lived. He turned on his heel and started toward the west end of town, but he didn't have to go the entire way.

An old hag whose face he didn't recognize leaned over the rail of her balcony and stopped him with her cracked, smug voice. "Hey, who you looking for, boy?"

"Nobody you know, old woman."

"No? I know everybody, that's who I know."

Giorgio squinted to get a better look at her. She was ugly enough. Maybe she was a witch.

A few heads turned to get an earful of the conversation. Everyone on the street seemed a little too interested for Giorgio's comfort.

"I'm looking for old Scarfo, Enrico Scarfeticcerio. You know him?"

"I told you, I know everybody. Even the dead."

Giorgio's heart beat faster and a sharp burning taste filled his mouth. "What do you mean? What are you telling me?" he cried out.

The old woman cackled. "If you were his friend, all that he left is yours, boy."

A scream escaped Giorgio's throat. He held his good hand up and it trembled before his eyes. What had happened to the world? Where had it gone? The army took him from one place and left him in another, a place of dreams, of nightmares from which he must wake up. Oh, Scarfo, Scarfo—

He fell to his knees on the hard stone of the street and bowed down in grief, face buried in his hands. He wanted to shut the light of day out of his eyes, to make the truth disappear. How could Scarfo be dead? How? He had always been around, and he always would.

Passers-by skirted around the inconvenient sobbing fellow in the street. Not many of them recognized him, but the few who did gathered around him to soothe him. He needed nothing so much as soothing, the laying on of kindly hands.

He knelt upright and looked to the sky in despair. "*Madonna mia*," he cried, "why have you let this happen? I have always shown you the greatest respect." There was a pause. "I will wait until you answer me."

The people stole fearful glances upward, but there was no reply to the blasphemy, only the gray winter sky with no face, the impenetrable clouds that would again bring the cold rains.

Giorgio knelt there a very long time, and no one could persuade him to go home. At last when night began to fall, he finally bowed his head and came to his feet, beaten by the silent sky.

"He is home," Brigetta said, "here in Santa Barbara, but your father doesn't want you to know."

Gabriella felt tears stinging her eyes. The moment had come and she could bear up no longer. No longer could she hold in her heartbreak. "Why should I care if he's home? I hate him, Brigetta. I hate him!"

Brigetta took Gabriella into her arms and tried to comfort her. "I know, little one. I know."

"In all this time he's never written to me, not even once, not even after I wrote to him. How could he do this to me, Brigetta? How? And then to come back so boldly and to spurn me this way. I know he's home. You're not the first to tell me. The maids gossip, you know. He's been home for a long time, and he has yet to show himself here."

"He doesn't show himself to anyone, Gabriella. Not since he learned the old man died."

"What do you mean, since he learned? The old man has been dead for weeks."

"There was no one to write to him. He learned it in the street on the day he came back to Santa Barbara. They say it was terrible. They say he beat his head on the street and tore his clothing off and cut his breast open with a knife."

"What do you mean? No one told me this." Despite herself Gabriella felt her sympathy rising. "Is he all right now? Has anyone looked after him?"

Brigetta shrugged. "He has no family. You know that. Who is there to look after him?"

"No one," Gabriella spat bitterly. "So let him look after himself." But then she cried harder, saying, "Poor Giorgio. What will he do now?"

"He will suffer alone unless someone goes to him."

"Go to him? How can I go to him now, after all that's happened?"

"And what's happened? Nothing, as far as I can see. He went into the army and you don't know why. He didn't answer your letter and you don't know why. That's all."

"I have my pride, Brigetta," she said through her tears.

"Tell your pride to go to hell," Brigetta replied acidly. "It will get you nothing and nowhere. Gabriella, do you want to go the rest of your life wondering what happened to your love? You want your head in the dark forever?"

Gabriella sniffled. Brigetta was right. Yes, there was one obvious thing to do, and she must do it now, when Giorgio was suffering so.

"I will go to him," she said, "but what about my father?"

"Leave your father to me. As long as he doesn't suspect anything, he'll be easy to distract."

Gabriella nodded. "Brigetta, thank you."

The two women embraced. Within the half hour Gabriella was on her way to the little cottage where Giorgio lived alone with his despair.

Giorgio tried getting drunk and that didn't work, so he got drunker. That didn't work either. It only made him cry more easily, but it didn't change anything and it didn't make him forget. So now he remained alone in the dark with cheesecloth pinned up over the windows to keep out the light.

He ate a little bread now and then and sometimes drank a little wine. He had not shaved or washed in days. At first he felt vile with grime but didn't care. Anyway, the feeling passed quickly enough. Now he felt nothing. There was only the sound of his own movements to disturb him, and those sounds didn't disturb him much. He was grateful for the stillness, for the darkness. They were the only comforts, the only friends he had these days.

The only one who had come to visit was Pranzo, the foul-smelling baker, and he only to gloat. He brought with him the story of Scarfo's death. No one knew exactly how it happened, but the old man's body was found on the plateau road, still fresh because it hadn't grown cold yet. His hands were clutched to his chest. Everyone in town interpreted this to mean that he had died of a broken heart, probably because Giorgio had gone off to join the army.

"But I didn't go off to join!" Giorgio shouted in anger. "They came and took me away in the night. Scarfo saw it all happen."

"Ah, then maybe that was why his heart was broken." Pranzo seemed happy about it all. "It's too bad you couldn't run away from the army and come back like some others have."

"I'm not some others. I didn't have a chance to run away. They would have shot me."

"You were afraid of the guns, then?"

"Of course I was afraid. I ain't stupid."

"Then he died of shame at your cowardice. I am beginning to understand."

"You don't understand nothing. I ain't no coward. I went to war, remember. The Austrians were shooting at me."

"So then you're not afraid of guns?"

Giorgio grabbed his guest by the shirt. "Pranzo, get out. Don't come back. Think what you want. They can all think what they want. I don't care. Just leave me the hell alone."

"Don't you want to know where he's buried, Giorgio?"

"No. Now get out."

So the man left and there were no more visitors and Giorgio was left not knowing where his old friend had been interred. He wondered if anybody had been decent enough to put a marker on the grave. The masons, perhaps. Yes, the masons. They would have carved him a beautiful one with his name and dates on the front—if anybody knew the date of his birth.

Well, there would be time enough to visit the grave. Giorgio's life was nothing now. It was only time and sitting in the dark.

He wondered about Gabriella. In those few moments when he allowed himself to feel anything, he ached for her. She had been his hope, his light, his family, his future. When he slept he dreamed of her. Awake, he pictured her in his mind, but the pictures only tantalized him, made him suffer for his efforts. He wanted her badly and knew she would never be his.

Pranzo was right about one thing, Giorgio thought. He was a coward, not in the army but now, when he should go Gabriella and hold up his limp hand, his ruined life, and show her why he could not marry her.

Oh, Scarfo, he thought miserably, you warned me. I have to admit it. You told me she was nothing but trouble, but you know me. I don't listen. The only thing, Scarfo, is that it ain't her fault. It was her father and the goddamned army and maybe a little bit of the devil that did this to him.

Giorgio was sitting on the floor with his thoughts. His arms were wrapped around his knees. Without a bed he lived most of his life on the floor these days.

A gentle knock at the door interrupted the silence. Who the hell could that be, he thought angrily, Pranzo again? Well, let him knock. I ain't gonna answer the damn door.

The knock came again, and along with it a voice, but not Pranzo's. "Giorgio? Please, Giorgio, I know you're there. You must let me in."

Gabriella! Oh, God, what was he to do? He was filthy. Besides, he didn't want to see her. He didn't want to face the shame of showing her he was a cripple, of seeing the look of disgust and disappointment on her face. Why did she have to come? Why couldn't she leave him alone, like everybody else?

"Giorgio, please." Gabriella's voice grew harsh. "Open the door at once, or by the power of the Holy Virgin, I'll kick it in. I have strong legs, you know."

There was a thud at the door, and then another.

"Don't!" he cried out. "You'll hurt your foot."

"Yes, I will!" she cried back. "I'll hurt it terribly and then I'll be crippled and ugly."

Her words stung him, and he shook his head as if to dislodge a pain. "Go away. Go away at once."

"I won't. Let me in."

"You don't know what you're doing."

"I know what I'm doing." Thud. "Don't tell me I don't know. Open the door." Thud.

"All right!" he hollered. "All right, I'll let you in and we'll see how much you know."

He got to his feet, pulled the latch and swung the door wide. The sudden light hurt his eyes and he squinted to see her.

"Giorgio, look at yourself. Look at this place," he heard her say, though he didn't have enough vision back to see her mouth. "Have you turned into a pig?"

"Ah, so this is why you come to see me, to insult me, right? I should send you the hell back up the road on the end of my boot."

"Watch your mouth, Giorgio. It's as filthy as the rest of you."

"Agh, *fang' gool*'," he spat and turned back to the darkness in the cottage.

Enraged like a teased cat, Gabriella made two fists, and bursting in after him, pounded on his back with all her might. The blows surprised more than hurt him, and he spun about to catch her fists, forgetting for a moment that his right arm was practically useless. A fist flew toward his nose. He put his hand up to stop it, but his hand would not work. The fist made contact and came away bloody.

Gabriella glanced at her bloodied hand, then looked with horror upon what she had done. "Oh, Giorgio, Giorgio, I'm sorry. What have I done? Oh, my Giorgio . . ."

"It's all right, it's all right," he grumbled. "What can you do to me, anyway? You're only a woman."

But she clucked and cooed and with the sleeve of her coat wiped as much blood off him as she could. "You should never curse at me. Don't you know that by now? I don't like it, Giorgio. I'm sorry I punched you, but why didn't you stop me?"

"Because I chose not to stop you," he said sullenly.

She stared at him a long moment, as if trying to find something hidden in his eyes. "What's wrong? What is it?"

"It's nothing. What do you want? Why have you come here?"

She held her anger in check. Instead of answering she cast around briefly to size the place up, then went to the windows, tore away the cheesecloth and looked for something to sit on.

"Where is your bed? What happened to the chairs?"

"Everything was gone when I got here."

"Very well," she said, and sat on the floor near the corner where he slept. "This will do."

Giorgio didn't sit. It made him uncomfortable to see her there on the ground; she looked as if she was planning to stay for a long time.

"You came to see how I'm living, right? You came to see how I'm getting along," he said. "Well, look. Now you see. If there ain't nothing else, go back to your big ugly house and leave me be."

She wagged a finger at him. "Don't you speak to me

that way, Giorgio Farenza. What do you think, I'm just going to walk out the door without an explanation?''

''An explanation for what?''

''For what you did to me.''

''What did I do to you?''

''You left in the middle of the night without a good-bye or explanation or anything else. After everything we went through together for each other—poof, up and away you go, like smoke out of the chimney.''

''Sure, up and away I went, with a bunch of soldiers pointing guns at my back. What did you think, that I deserted you?''

''What else was I supposed to think? You never sent a letter, not a word.''

''I sent letters, plenty of letters. If you never got them, it ain't my fault, but I wrote them. By the hundred, by the thousand, by the million—''

''Giorgio, please.''

''All right, then, not millions, but plenty.''

''If you sent them, I never got them.''

''Sure you never got them. Your father, who gave my name to the goddamned conscription officer, probably kept them from you.''

''No. Brigetta would have known.''

''Brigetta thinks she knows a hell of a lot more than she does. You think your old man is stupid? Brigetta knows what he wants her to know.''

Gabriella looked long and pensively out a window. ''My father has done all this to us?'' Suddenly a small tear appeared at the corner of one eye.

''He was only being a father. It's what they do—protect their daughters.''

The single tear moved slowly down her pale cheek. Giorgio was touched by it, but he did not go to her. He did not want to torture himself.

"Only being a father. Look what he has done to you. Look at the way you live."

"This has nothing to do with him. It's my choice to live the way I want."

She looked at him resentfully. "Why have you chosen to live this way and to spurn me since you returned?"

"Because Scarfo died, that's why."

"Giorgio, Scarfo died, and it broke my heart when I heard it, but you could have come to me. I would have given you comfort."

Giorgio turned his back on her. "To hell with comfort. I don't need comfort."

She thought for a moment. "All right, then. If he didn't do this to you, look at what he's done to us."

Giorgio felt a sudden welling up within him as grief took hold. "Things are as they are. We can't do anything about them." He bowed his head to stifle his sobs.

"Tell me," she said quietly, almost in a whisper. "Don't you love me anymore?"

He took a deep breath, turned and went down on one knee before her. "I want to say I don't. Look at me. I can't have you. But I do. I do love you."

She was on her feet in a second, wearing a fierce look, a woman protecting her own. "Then we'll go to my father at once. I don't know why you say you can't have me. My father has broken too many promises, but he won't break this one, Giorgio. He said he would give you my hand, and he will."

She started toward the door, but he resisted. "No. It's no good," he said.

"Why not?" Her voice challenged him to convince her.

"I can't."

"Are you afraid?"

"Yes," he muttered. "I'm very much afraid."

"Why? You've been face to ugly face with my father before."

"Not of your father. Of you."

She frowned, perplexed. "What are you talking about? Just because I gave you a bloody nose?"

"You didn't give me no bloody nose," he asserted.

"No? Find a looking glass if you don't think so."

"I got a bloody nose because of this. He held up his right hand in his left and steeled himself for her reaction.

"Because of what? I don't know what you're talking about."

"Because of this! This!" He shook it around for her to see how limp it was. "My hand is dead. I can't work. I can't make a living. I can't use it to caress you."

"Giorgio, be careful what you say."

"Oh, what the hell does it matter what I say? Look, Gabriella. I'm a cripple."

She reached out and took the damaged hand in her own. She brought it to her lips and kissed it. "How did this happen?"

"A piece of shrapnel cut it. Look, you can see the scar."

She traced the length of the scar with her finger. "This is a terrible thing to happen to a man," she said, "but it will make no difference between us. The only thing I care about is that you wash it a little. Look at the fingernails. They're disgusting."

"You don't understand! I can't cut stone anymore."

She looked at him seriously, intently. "Then don't. My father will give me a generous dowry. I will see to it. You won't have to cut stone for a living."

What was she talking about now? Women were such idiots sometimes. "Cutting stone is my pride. Without his pride a man is nothing."

"I will give you babies, and there will be your pride," she said with determination.

And those words on her lips seemed to make everything else disappear, all the difficulties, all the obstacles, all his grief. "You still want to marry me?" he ventured timidly.

"Come. We're going to see my father," she said. Giving him no opportunity to answer, she took his hand and led him to the door.

Don Antonio received them coolly. He was sitting behind his desk in his study. In the hallway he had posted a bodyguard, so somehow he must have known Giorgio was coming. He made them wait nearly twenty minutes before admitting them, and when he spoke to his daughter, it was as if she were a stranger.

"What do you want?" he said.

"I want to know why you lied to me," she replied, unabashed.

Giorgio looked on dumbly. There was something between father and daughter his instincts told him not to interrupt.

Don Antonio slammed the side of his fist on the table. "Are you calling me a liar? Remember, I am more than just your father. I am the padrone here, the father of the land and the people on the land. Be careful what you say."

"Why? What will you do, send the conscription officers after me?"

He half rose, seething, out of his chair. "I don't know what lies this filthy pig has been telling you, but they have nothing to do with me."

Giorgio blushed. For the first time in many days his appearance began to embarrass him.

"Where are the letters, Father?"

"What letters?"

"I know there are letters from Giorgio."

Rather than irritating him more, her insistence seemed to make him thoughtful. "I burned them."

"Why would you do such a thing?"

"To make you forget him."

She was at once outraged and confused. How could he be so bold as to admit to such a thing? "Well, as you can see, Don Antonio," she said, "I've forgotten nothing. And I won't let you forget either. You made a promise of my hand to Giorgio, and you're going to keep it."

"Impossible."

"I say it's not impossible! I say it's very possible!"

Don Antonio looked Giorgio in the eyes. "It's impossible because Giorgio has to kill me. Don't you, Giorgio? Tell my daughter how you are honor bound to kill me."

Giorgio felt confused. He glanced back and forth between father and daughter as they waited for his answer. "Why should I want to kill you?"

A smirk touched the don's lips. "Don't you know? Isn't your name Farenza?"

"What's that got to do with anything?" Gabiella said impatiently.

Giorgio was getting suspicious, and his heart was sinking. "Go on, Don Antonio. Say what you have to say."

"I knew your parents, boy. Do I have to say anything else?"

The grief and anger he felt was not for the memory of his parents, for he had none. Nevertheless he had once made a promise, and a man's promise is his honor. He had sworn to kill his parents' murderer as he was bound to do by tradition.

In all the land there was nothing more precious than a man's family. It ran in the blood. Though he had been lucky enough to find someone like old Scarfo, Giorgio felt with an aching emptiness the place where his blood parents should have been. If he could not know them, he had always yearned for them.

He was seized with rage, and he started for the don. The older man was ready for him, his arms up, his yellow teeth bared in a hungry smile as if to say, come on, Farenza, come and get your death.

Gabriella let out a little squeal of fear, but there was no need. Giorgio could not make a fist. He held his hand up to Don Antonio to strike him, but the limpness in his fingers made him ashamed. The don looked bemused, as if he didn't know what to make of the boy's strange behavior but found it pleasing.

"What is it, Giorgio? What's going on?" Gabriella said worriedly.

"Your father has the blood of my parents on his hands."

"Oh, no," she moaned. "Please, Holy Mother of God, no!" She tried to put her arms around him, but he would not allow it.

"Now do you see why you cannot marry him?" the don said simply.

Gabriella spoke only to Giorgio. "It makes no difference to us, my darling. What my father has done is not my sin."

Giorgio made his voice hard. He didn't want to speak to her this way, but there was nothing else to do. "I can't stay here unless I kill him. It's my sworn vendetta. But I have a useless hand, and I can't kill him."

"You couldn't kill me anyway, Farenza." Don Antonio pointed at the door, where a goon stood with pistol at the ready.

"Anyway, he's your father," Giorgio went on. "How could I kill your father?"

"Giorgio," she pleaded. "It's all in the past. There's nothing we can do. Forget about it. Marry me. Give me children."

"No. Not here. Not on this filthy soil, this dirt your father owns. This place has never done me any damn good. If you want to marry me, come away with me."

"Come away where?"

"To America," he heard himself say. "I have a brother there. He'll help me find some kind of job, maybe. A job for a man with one hand."

"But Giorgio, how can I leave? This is my home."

He knew he had asked too much of her and regretted it the instant he had said it. Gabriella had never gotten on by herself, had always been cared for in comfortable circumstances. Why should she go to America?

"There's no life for me here," he repeated.

"Go to America with him, Gabriella," her father said. "Live like an animal with the immigrants. I know about these things. I have friends who have gone and returned."

"Giorgio," she said, fear and trembling in her voice, "I can't. Please don't make me."

Giorgio calculated that she would go if he insisted, and he knew just as surely that they would have a bitter life together if she did.

"I'll come back for you," he finally managed to say. "When I have money in my pocket and your father is dead. You told me he spits up blood."

This angered the don. "Don't worry about me, you little son of a bitch. I'll live forever."

Gabriella took Giorgio's arm. "I don't want you to go. You've already been gone from me too long, Giorgio. I can't stand it anymore."

"If I stay, I will kill your father or he will kill me. I

can't. Come on. Walk me back to my place. We'll talk it over.''

Without another word Giorgio turned, pushed his way past the bodyguard and headed down the hall.

Before she left to follow, she found one more thing to say to her father. "I will never forgive you for this. I will hate you and the name of your family for the rest of my life.''

"You will do as I say, Gabriella," the don said sadly, as if he had anticipated her declaration.

But Gabriella did not hear the sadness in his voice. She was already gone.

BOOK III
THE PROMISED LAND

Chapter 20

The railroad station smelled of coal fire and creosote, sweat and apples and stogies. Four tall windows, hazy with dust and smoke, were set in each pale green plaster wall, and between them hung posters advertising mustache wax, chewing gum, iron nails and boot polish.

A trainman, stiffly dressed in a billed cap and a black suit with gold buttons, rang a brass handbell and announced in a twangy voice arrival of each train. A fat old Greek gentleman wearing a shoemaker's leather apron followed him around and registered a confused look with every announcement.

All of the Farenzas, Sebastiano and Teresa, Sophia, Franco, Tina and Favia, the baby, moved in a huddle through the crowd. The girls all wore wide-brimmed hats with feathers, the boys, knickerbockers and buckle-top shoes. Everyone wore a long, heavy coat, sewn by Teresa without a pattern, that gave them approximate uniformity, like a street choir of evangelists.

Sebastiano, stern and determined, led the way, while Teresa hollered and smacked and nudged the rest together. The children were excited and noisy. They craned their heads back as they walked to see the high, buttressed ceiling twenty feet above them.

Franco, eight now and in his own opinion too old to be called little, affected an arrogant sneer whenever anyone looked his way. He liked to think of himself as the second lieutenant of the group. His father was top banana and he was number two.

They made their way through the door to the southbound platform. Despite the cold there were vendors selling candy and tobacco and fruit. Favia, three, began to whine that she was hungry. For her trouble she received a smack from her mother. And just for good measure Franco gave her a dirty look. He liked to keep the other kids under his thumb, just like Pop did. Nobody messed with Pop. Even the policemen said good morning to him. That's the way Franco wanted to be when he grew up.

He wasn't so sure about this uncle who was coming on the train. The only things he knew for sure were that the guy's name was Giorgio and that he was a greenhorn, straight off the boat from Italy.

Franco had seen plenty of recent immigrants and to him they all seemed kind of stupid. Of course a few of them were okay in the brain department—the crooks, his father called them. These were the same guys that the kids in the neighborhood down on Front Street said were dangerous, and bad Italians too, but Franco admired them for their toughness.

The trainman stepped into the frigid air and announced the Sweet Molly, arriving on time from New York. The Greek gentleman was still following him around. Down the track the great black nipple of a locomotive's boiler became discernible in the cold light of late afternoon.

As it drew closer, its sharp, loud bell and whistle made the air shiver, and when it finally pulled into the station, jets of steam hissed over the platform as the screech of brakes became deafening. The children put their hands over their ears—all but Franco, who was too proud of his toughness. Even their mother made a sour face at the noise, though Sebastiano, like his son, refused to notice.

When the passengers began to disembark, Teresa stood out in front of her husband, straining to catch sight of a familiar face, but Giorgio was almost upon her before she saw him, and even then it took a long moment to recognize him. She squinted at him as if to correct her vision. This wasn't the Giorgio she had known. Of course he was older, taller, but there was more to the change than the years. And it wasn't just the serious, grim look that so many of the immgrants had. His skin was waxy and yellow and his eyes seemed sunken under his brow. He walked feebly, like an old man out for his last constitutional. He reminded her of death, of bones, of the drying of flesh.

He extended his arms to her and said her name in a croak. Before she could stop herself, she drew back a little. The children, when they saw that, took fright.

Sebastiano corrected the situation at once. He stepped forward and offered Giorgio an arm to hold. Giorgio accepted the help with a weak smile, and when he took hold with his left hand, Sebstiano patted his fingers as he might to reassure a blind man.

"What the hell happened to you?" Sebstiano said under his breath in a dialect so peppered with some foreign influence that he was difficult to understand.

"It's the malaria," Giorgio replied. "It came back on the ship."

"What malaria?" Sebastiano said like a stern father to a wayward son.

"My malaria," Giorgio grumbled testily. "The malaria I got because you went to America."

Sebastiano replied without looking at his brother, "You

haven't changed a goddamn bit. How can it be my fault you got the malaria? You're crazy."

"Yeah, because you make me crazy."

"Shut up, both of you," Teresa put in. "You're scaring the kids." Then she turned to her brood. "Everyone come up and pay your respects to your Uncle Giorgio. He has come a long way to see us."

She ushered the little ones up to her brother-in-law, though none of them, not even Franco, seemed very brave about it. She couldn't blame them. How ugly he was, but ugly face or not, the man inside was still her little Giorgio as far as she was concerned. Nothing could change that, not time, not distance, not age, not sickness—nothing.

As Giorgio let each of them take his hand, he gave a little smile, though it seemed an effort for him. Once or twice Teresa caught him stealing a glance at her with his pitiful eyes, which were tinged with the color of unripe oranges. She shuddered and told herself once more that this was the same Giorgio she had held in her arms and rocked and sung to so many years before, though the more she saw of him, the harder it was to believe.

Sebastiano was the only one among them who seemed not to think much about Giorgio's condition, but Teresa wasn't surprised. He didn't think much at all anymore. Half the time he was drunk and the other half he was quiet or mean. Ever since the boat ride over from Italy he had been different from the man she married—surly, taciturn, always turning his eyes away, always looking for an excuse to act like a son of a bitch.

She kept the children away from him as much as she could, because he was sometimes too quick to use the back of his hand across their faces, even Favia's, and Teresa was afraid he would really hurt one of them. She had already lost one baby, Dominic, to influenza. He was a sweet boy, her favorite in fact, though she would never admit that to anyone. Now the remaining children were twice as precious, and she wouldn't let any harm come to them, not even from their own father.

She also feared his influence on their only remaining son. Franco worshipped his father, imitated him in every way, talked about no one else. Sometimes he was a little *duce*, a chief, who pushed his sisters around until they screamed and pulled his hair. This only made him laugh and push harder.

There were other moments too, when he was his mama's boy, wide-eyed, gentle, easy to take as a little breeze, more like his older sister Sophia. But even that concerned Teresa. She didn't dare try to exert too much affect on him for fear he would turn into a sissy. All in all, ever since receiving her brother-in-law's letter a month before, Teresa had been hoping Giorgio would have a good influence on Franco.

It was a strange letter. She remembered it well. It said only, "I will be arriving in your village on February 24, 1918. I hope can you put me up for a little while," and after that, his name was affixed.

It would be difficult to find room for another adult in their three-room house, but he was family, so sacrifices would have to be made. And, of course, she was delighted that he had finally decided to come. Even after so many years she thought about him every day, wondered how he was doing, worried about his health and his safety. And when she thought about him, she often wished her own little Franco could be more like him.

Now, with Giorgio himself so nearby, maybe Franco would change. Maybe he would find another hero to worship. But she hadn't counted on this malaria business. She was shocked at the change in the wild face she remembered so well from Santa Barbara.

They hired a hansom cab to take them home. They

would have walked, but Teresa feared it would be too much strain on her brother-in-law, and for once Sebastiano agreed with her. Maybe he wasn't so dense after all, she thought, though she knew he would prove her wrong again a hundred times. It was his way.

They lived in a small row house just opposite the Delaware River, about ten miles south of Philadelphia. They had lived with Sebastiano's old friend Morretti and his shrew of a wife, Gina, for only a few months after arriving in America, a few months of hell and heartbreak.

First there was the baby—a girl instead of the son Sebastiano had always wanted. Then the complaints about the noise started; Gina and her fat, loud-mouthed husband didn't like the sound of a baby crying even though their own six kids never shut up.

The last straw was the accusation that Sebastiano cheated at cards—a stupid business, since he and Morretti and the other pinochle players at the Italian American Brotherhood hall never bet on their games—but Sebastiano's honor was offended.

The Farenzas spent days and days looking for a place that wasn't too dirty for human habitation. They found one on Catherine Street, in a Polish neighborhood. There they lived for three years. Franco was born only eleven months after Sophia, but the other two waited until their father had enough money to buy a little place in the small town of Chester before they slid out of the womb.

Front Street was always cracked and caked with mud because the river flooded with heavy rains and sometimes even rose up over their front stoop to deluge their kitchen. The cellar, of course, was almost always filled with green brackish water, but they only used it after the grape harvest, when the fruit had to be pressed for the wine. All in all it was a comfortable house in a mostly Italian neighborhood, though there were a few Irish and Jewish families as well.

Teresa could tell Sebastiano wanted Giorgio to be impressed by the way he named everything he owned: "This is my house, and that is my stoop, and over there is my bed," but Giorgio seemed too tired to care about any of it. The children were eager to tear off their dress clothes so they could play in the street with the other urchins.

Their mother sent them out and Giorgio was shown his bed, a military cot wedged into a corner of the children's room. He wasted no time, but bid his brother and sister-in-law good night and lay down for a nap.

"Maybe I should make him something to eat," Teresa fretted to her husband, though Giorgio was already snoring.

"Leave him alone. He'll be all right."

"He don't look too good, Sebastiano."

"What are you talking about? How do you know what he's supposed to look like, eh? You ain't seen him in years. Maybe he looks like that all the time."

"Don't be stupid. He's twenty-three years old and he looks seventy-three."

"So? Maybe when he's seventy-three he'll look twenty-three."

Teresa sighed with exasperation. "Okay, you're right, as always. But we gotta do something about his sickness."

Sebatiano grunted, then went to a small cabinet in the kitchen and took down a bottle of American whiskey. He poured a bit into a coffee cup, then made himself at home on the midnight blue stuffed sofa in the living room.

"Maybe my brother's contagious. You ever think of that?"

"*Madonna mia*," Teresa said and crossed herself. "God forbid. But I don't think Giorgio would give his sickness to us. He's always been a good boy." She knew she was talking nonsense, but if her children were in danger, there was nothing to do about it now but try to live with it. And sometimes the best way to live with something was to lie to yourself about it.

"We got to get him some quinine, right? That's for malaria. I remember from the old country."

"You know something, Sebastiano? Ever since we came here, I've never seen anybody get malaria. Everybody who's got it brought it over with him."

"So what's that supposed to mean?"

"Maybe it's something you can't get over here. Maybe you only get it in the old country."

Sebastiano shrugged. "Maybe." It was as good an explanation as any. "You want me to go to the apothecary?"

"Maybe you better," she said after a long moment's thought, though she didn't like sending him out with money in his pocket. There was never any way to tell when he would come home again. Sometimes he would disappear for a day and a night.

She couldn't guess how much the quinine would cost, so she gave him a dollar and a half. That should cover even the most expensive medicine. Sebastiano took it without a word, swallowed the remainder of his whiskey and left.

Teresa hesitated, then went to the door of the bedroom to look in on her brother-in-law. Even in the innocence of sleep she could see little of the boy she had known, but if she looked just right, there was something familiar, vague but definite. Ah, well, she thought. At least he ain't dead.

Franco stood with a group of boys on a street corner three blocks north of his house. One of the boys had a jackknife, and he was playing mumbly-peg so dangerously that the others were cheering, but Franco couldn't pay much attention to the game. He was still disturbed by the sight of his uncle.

He had hoped for another man like his father, someone who could show him the ropes, teach him how to take care of himself. Even if the guy was a greenhorn, he was still a Farenza, so he had to have some brains. But this Giorgio didn't look like much of anything when it came to knowing his way around. He was a little scary, sure, but not because he was tough. That was just his looks, like something from a bad dream. What the hell was it all about, this malaria? He knew other people, parents and grandparents, in the neighborhood who claimed to have it, but none of them looked like his uncle.

And there was something else odd about him. When Franco took his hand, it felt limp and cold in his grasp. The feeling made him shiver, as if he'd grabbed hold of something dead where something alive should have been. He found himself hoping Uncle Giorgio wouldn't be hanging around too long.

"Hey, Franco, you just going to stand there all day with that stupid look on your face?" It was one of the other boys, a freckle-faced Irish kid with a perpetual sneer. His name was Pat McIntyre and he was the only one in the group intrepid enough to challenge Franco. He held the jackknife in his hand, then suddenly pitched it in Franco's direction.

Franco cut himself catching it, but he grinned and said, "You do that again, I'll punch your nose."

The sneer remained on Pat's face, but he didn't take the challenge. He knew better even though he was big for his age. Franco was pleased. They knew he was tough. He wasn't afraid of anything, not a big kid, not a knife, not even his ugly uncle. He just didn't like newcomers, he told himself. That was all.

Sebastiano bought two bottles of quinine and had plenty of change left over, but he didn't go out for a drink.

He was too curious about his brother, the stranger who was his blood kin and who had come to live in his house. He wondered what had brought the kid to America and what had happened to him over all these years. He had questions about the old country, about old faces he still remembered, about the war and politics. But most of all he had the need for another man in the family, someone he could trust, someone he could confide in.

Sebastiano had many regrets now. America was not all he had hoped it would be. His first months here were full of hope, even though he and Teresa had to live in a filthy rat-infested tenement with the Morrettis. He had never seen such conditions even in Italy, and he had been forced to swallow his pride to consider living in such a place.

Now things were better. Sebastiano was making a living wage working for the Baltimore Ohio Company down at the railyard at Twenty-fourth and Chestnut, earning more than many of the long-timers because of his talent with a hammer and saw. He had also made three dining room suites for stockholders, which of course, they bought at cost.

A living wage wasn't riches. He had been making a living wage in Santa Barbara. And there was something else at the back of his mind that brought him to crisis every time he thought about it. He had killed a man.

Sometimes he was surprised at how long he could go without thinking about it, but always that night on the ship came back to him in his dreams, and he would wake up in a sweat, hearing the man's terrified whimper as he plunged to his death. It was wrong to kill, no matter what the man had done. And after all, what had he done? Nothing. Made a little conversation with Teresa, that's all.

It was strange. Other men, men Sebastiano knew, would kill for any reason without thinking twice about it, even for money, God forbid, but for him it was different. Always he found himself looking through that fellow's eyes as he dropped through the air into the black ocean, knowing his end was at hand and able to do nothing about it. It was terrifying to see another man's doom, and such imaginings made Sebastiano's guilt more and more oppressive.

Religion was helpful at first. God would balance all things in the end. But the longer he lived in America, the less important and dependable God seemed, so Sebastiano started getting drunk all the time. Nothing much mattered when there was whiskey in your belly. But his guilt was sly and didn't like to be locked out of the house. It turned itself into loneliness, and even liquor couldn't close the door on that.

Drunkenness worked less and less of the time these days. What he needed, what he yearned for, was someone to talk to. Not Teresa, who was a woman and so couldn't know much about anything but cooking and making babies. Not a priest either. Even though you were supposed to able to talk to the collar without worrying, those guys were all in the business of making you feel worse than you had to begin with. No, he needed a brother, and a brother had come to him.

Sophia, a pretty girl with auburn hair and black eyes, waited a long time for her mother to busy herself with cooking dinner. She wanted to see more of her uncle, who had so startled everyone when he appeared at the train station, but she didn't want her mother hanging over her shoulder, pestering her.

She managed to slip into the bedroom unnoticed, then stood by the long, prone form on the old cot and with a thrilling sort of dread reached out her hand and lightly brushed his discolored cheeks with her fingertips. He snorted and startled her back a step, but then she tried again.

If his skin looked funny, it didn't feel very different. She stroked along his cheek so lightly she could barely feel his whiskers. A little smile teased nervously like a tic at the corners of his mouth.

It wasn't such a bad face, she told herself. In fact it might even be a kindly one, at least when he was sleeping. If only it weren't so ugly. Sometimes ugliness wasn't so terrible, only pitiful.

She thought of the old huckster who brought his wagon around twice a week in the warmer weather and sold fruit and vegetables off the back. He had no upper lip, so his speech was always lisping and his pink tongue stuck out at odd moments. But he had always been very generous to her and very polite. He gave her free plums when they were in season, and sometimes he would tell her stories about the old country that would keep her spellbound for hours. She liked him very much and she pitied his ugliness.

She touched her uncle's brow. She didn't know if he was generous or polite, but she decided to feel sorry for him rather than fear him. This time her touch awakened him, but not abruptly. His eyes opened slowly and he let out his breath in a long sigh. At first Sophia was ashamed, standing over him with her fingers upon him, but as he sat upright, there was nothing but curiosity in his eyes.

"What were you looking at?" he said.

"I don't know. Nothing."

He shook his head slowly. "Then I hope you weren't looking at me, because I am more than nothing."

She flustered. "That's not what I meant, Zio Giorgio."

This seemed to startle him. "Nobody ever called me uncle before. It makes me feel like I'm somebody else."

"I'm sorry if I offended you," she said quickly, but he reassured her.

"No, I'm not offended. It's very nice to be an uncle."

Before Sophia could reply, her mother appeared at the door with a stern look on her face. "Your uncle is tired," she said in English. "Leave him alone."

"What?" Giorgio said with annoyance. "Speak so I can understand you."

"I'm sorry, Giorgio," Teresa said. "I forgot. Living in America, you learn to speak half and half most of the time."

Giorgio looked displeased at this. "It's an ugly language, this English. It sounds like a drainage pipe sucking up water."

"Agh, sure, brother-in-law, I hear that all the time from people who won't learn, even the ones who have been here for thirty years. But when it comes time to buy food, I can haggle over the price, I can find out what I'm paying for. If I need directions, I can ask anybody for them. And I can recite the Pledge of Allegiance."

"So what's that to me?"

"You'll learn when you apply to become a citizen."

Giorgio found this amusing. "To hell with becoming a citizen. I just came to make a little money, then I'm going back to Italy."

"I would love to go to Italy," Sophia piped up.

"Sophia, go out to the kitchen and stir the sauce," her mother said.

"But Mama, I want to talk some more with Uncle Giorgio," she said.

"Go out at once before I slap your face, you hear?"

"Mama, you never slap my face."

"I will this time if you don't do what I say."

The girl turned away dejectedly, but Giorgio spoke up

to make her feel better. "You and me, we'll have plenty of time to talk. Don't worry about it. Okay?"

Sophia brightened. "Sure, Uncle Giorgio. And you can tell me all about Italy."

When her daughter was gone, Teresa's tone grew serious, thoughtful. "Giorgio, why have you come here? If you still feel the same about America, I don't understand what you want."

"I told you, I came to make a little money."

"There's not so much money in America as you might think. Anyway, you got a trade. Ain't you been making money in Italy?"

"In Italy I been making war."

"You been in the army?" Her voice was suddenly full of concern. "Did they make you fight?"

"Sure they made me fight. That's why they gave me a gun. Here, you want to see what the army did for me?"

He pulled back the long sleeve of his cotton shirt and showed her the angry scar on his forearm. "A piece of metal kissed me here, and now I can't move my hand. It's like it's dead."

Teresa's hands joined at her heart. "Oh, my Giorgio, such suffering. All that, and now this illness. You don't need to work. You need someone to care for you."

He stared at her quizzically and suddenly she thought she understood. That was why he was here. For her to take care of him. After so long he remembered how she used to made medicinal tea for him and say the rosary with him in the afternoon. He had come all this way for her. She blushed.

"Teresa, what is it? You look funny."

"Nothing. Just a thought came into my head."

"What kind of thought?"

"No kind of thought. What's it your business?"

Giorgio shook his head in consternation. "I don't understand."

"I don't understand," Teresa repeated in a nasal mocking imitation. "Because you ain't supposed to understand."

He smiled. "You make me crazy sometimes, Teresa. I remember. Even when I was a kid you made me crazy."

"You're still a kid. What are you talking about?" she teased back, and despite the look of his illness, she found herself recognizing him once again.

When Sebastiano brought the quinine home, he poured a glass of wine for Giorgio and one for himself and made his brother sit at the table with him in the kitchen as Sophia put out the forks and spoons. There was no opportunity for intimate conversation, but the subject of a job came up, as did that of Giorgio's hand.

"Don't worry about the hand. I'll find you work."

"What kind of work?" Giorgio wanted to know.

"What do you care, what kind of work? Work, that's all. You can be my helper."

Giorgio frowned and his face wrinkled like parchment. "Why should I be your helper? I don't know nothing about carpentry and I don't want to know nothing."

The old argument was aflame again, but this time Sebastiano wasn't interested. "Giorgio, if you want a job, I'll get you one. If you want a miracle, go to St. Anthony."

Giorgio thought for a long moment. "What kind of work can I do with one hand?"

"You can saw planks and sweep the floor. I'll find ways to keep you busy."

"I don't want no charity job. If I want charity, I'll ask for money, not work."

"No charity job," Sebastiano promised. He understood pride. He understood dignity. Sometimes when he felt he had none left of his own, when he was full of whiskey and stumbling around helplessly, he thought he understood dignity better than anybody.

"All right, then," Giorgio said. "I'll work."

"Thank you."

"You're welcome."

Franco didn't like any of this conversation. He didn't like anybody talking to his father that way. After all, who was this Uncle Giorgio, a big shot? He was nothing, nobody. What right did he have to get off the boat and start right away insulting somebody's father? He shook his head but ate his meal without comment. He didn't think he was much going to like this Uncle Giorgio.

Chapter 21

It didn't take long for the quinine to take effect. Within a week Giorgio began to lose his yellow pallor and his strength returned to him. Teresa's cooking put meat on his bones, and he was even looking forward to the job his brother had arranged for him.

Something else was happening too, something he hadn't expected, at least not so soon. He had regained a little feeling in his hand. Not much, just a tingle in the wrist and middle finger and occasionally a cramp in the forearm, but it was enough to give him hope. He couldn't move anything yet, but just the feeling was enough to give rise to a prayer of gratitude, though not a prayer exactly.

He was angry with God. After all, Who had given him all this trouble in the first place? Oh, sure, Don Antonio and the army and maybe even he himself something to do with it, but Giorgio was sure God had a hand in it. He could tell by the way the malaria struck so suddenly. It was a turn of luck only God could manage. And how about the piece of shrapnel? Another couple of inches and maybe it would have missed him altogether.

No, all this was the work of Somebody Big, so Giorgio wasn't speaking to Him for the time being. His prayer of gratitude was whispered "to Whom it may concern."

As for America, he liked it more than he had thought he would. There were so many buildings, so much action, so many people it was like nothing he had ever known. Even Rome, itself a very large place, didn't seem so crowded, so full of life.

Of course, there were problems, plenty of them. Teresa, though he hated to admit it, was right about the language. It was very difficult here unless you learned to speak like a barbarian, but as he didn't plan to be here that long—only until Don Antonio managed to die—there was no point in wasting his time on English. Then there was the problem of strangeness. There were no friendly faces, nothing familiar, nothing he knew he could trust.

The worst problem, however, was the ache inside he felt for Gabriella. She had pleaded with him, practically begged on her knees—or so he remembered it—for him not to leave, though she knew there was no choice. Every day she came to visit him at the cottage, presumably with Brigetta's connivance—and every day she cried with him.

Yes, he cried too, especially as the departure day came nearer. As a pledge of faith to her he made a day trip to Caserta and spent half of his remaining furlough pay to buy her a ring with a very small ruby in it. That seemed to make her feel easier, and it certainly helped him. In return she gave him the crucifix from the same rosary he had kept for so many years.

"We will unite the cross with the beads when you come back to me," she said, and he was so touched that he kissed her deep and long, and boldly put his hand upon her breast, which he had never done before. Instead of pushing it away, she held it there for a long moment like a keepsake, then suddenly with a teasing smile stepped away from him.

Ah, how he desired her then. He felt his face flushing with the memory of it. But she would not allow more. No matter what she felt for him, she would hold the reins of passion tightly and pull up on them when she had to. It was the woman's job, and she knew her job well. Now he thought about her continually and yearned for the day when he could return to take her hand.

There was something funny going on his heart, though, something about Teresa. When he didn't feel too shamed to admit it, he realized his eyes had been wandering over her strong figure in a rather admiring way, just as they had when he was a boy. Sometimes he thought she noticed him doing it; she would turn red and make a sarcastic remark to put him off. It made him feel disloyal to Gabriella, but he couldn't help himself. He just did his best to keep his hungry eyes under control.

Otherwise, life in the house was comfortable if not quiet, and the food was good, though sometimes he wondered why Teresa made so much pasta. In the old country it was a side dish. Here they ate bowls of it. To him it was like making a meal of an appetizer. He couldn't quite understand why they ate that way, but he didn't ask. It would have been rude.

The kids were something else again. The two little ones hardly seemed to notice him, but Sophia spent as much time with him as she could, while Franco, who reminded Giorgio of a street urchin, was rebellious and smart-mouthed in a way that even he, Giorgio, would have been ashamed of.

It was one thing to argue, to show a little passion, to rebel. It was another to challenge, to sneer, to disrespect. Yet that was the way Franco treated his mother, and when Giorgio raised some objection, the boy told him to go to hell. Go to hell! If Giorgio had been strong and fast enough to catch him, he would have broken the little creep's head, but lucky for Franco, Giorgio was still recovering from his illness. That one was going to be trouble when he got older, Giorgio thought. Big trouble.

Two weeks went by while he lay in bed or puttered about the house. He had his first letter from Gabriella then. Teresa was curious, almost nosy about it, but Giorgio didn't want her to know about Gabriella. In fact he said nothing about his situation in Italy because he didn't want anyone's advice or comments. It was his affair, and it was complicated enough already. Besides, it made him seem a little mysterious, and he liked that.

He did talk about Scarfo, whom neither Teresa nor Sebastiano had known, and he found that talking made the great knot of his sorrow unravel and dwindle. It didn't matter whether they listened to him. Sebastiano, for one, said very little, while Teresa couldn't express her regrets enough.

Sophia was a different matter altogether. She seemed to take the name of Scarfo into her heart like the hero of a legend. She treasured every story about him and asked to be told special ones again and again. Giorgio enjoyed her company in a way he did no other. She was a friend, interested in what he had to say, and because of her he felt he had a little importance in the household.

He had to admit, everyone was a little kinder to him now that he was recovering. As his looks returned to normal, they all seemed to feel easier around him, though Franco took to staring boldly when Giorgio had trouble with his hand. The boy obviously found something intriguing about it, but when Giorgio brought the subject up one night after dinner—he had accidentally knocked a place setting off the table because he couldn't always tell exactly where that hand was—Franco scorned the entire subject.

Teresa made him apologize, but Sebastiano, though

wise enough not to interfere with his wife's discipline, still made his displeasure with her obvious by his tight-lipped downcast face. Giorgio knew his brother didn't necessarily approve of Franco's behavior, but neither did Sebastiano care to see him embarrassed in front of his sisters. Justice was supposed to be simple and straightforward: a slap across the face, a kick in the ass, and forget it.

The next day was Giorgio's first on the job. He had to get out of bed by five, as it was a long trip into town, but at least it was an interesting one. He and his brother had to make three cable-car transfers along Philadelphia Pike, which led all the way from Wilmington, Delaware, in the south, through the city of Chester and into the heart of Philadelphia.

Most of the way between the cities was marshland, though a few factories had sprung up, including a large shipyard and an electric power plant, but as they traveled downtown, they saw shops of every kind, people of every color, noises of every texture—and the smells! Some could send you to heaven, while others could only kill you.

The trainyard was a tangle of tracks and buildings and cars and locomotives, punctuated here and there with piles of wooden ties or scrap iron and gangs of men laying rail in every conceivable cranny. Giorgio remembered seeing it when he first came through the city from New York.

Sebastiano was making sawhorses for the maintenance crews. Giorgio was to help in whatever way he could manage. The work turned out to be easy and boring. Giorgio would hold down a piece of two-by-four with his knee and saw off a measured piece and Sebastiano would take the piece and nail it to another.

New sawhorses were stored outside the little workshed. When several were finished, the two brothers would carry them across the yard through all the clanking, rushing, chugging and steaming of engines, freight cars, flatbeds and machinery, over tracks and around small buildings, and then deposit them with the various foremen, all of whom seemed to be on good terms with Sebastiano. All but one.

There was an incident with a man named Morgan, a rail boss who didn't like Italians and especially didn't like Sebastiano because it "wasn't right for no damned dago to be pulling down that kind of salary when there were real human beings out of work."

Giorgio didn't understand what went on between them, but the shouting told most of the story. Morgan accused his brother of something. His brother made a denial. An argument ensued, which got hotter and hotter until Morgan picked up a sledgehammer and threatened Sebastiano with it.

"Son of a bitch," Sebastiano said and started to go for him, but his brother got in the way.

"What's the matter," Giorgio hollered, "you want to get killed? What did you do to make him so mad?"

"I didn't do nothing," Sebastiano snorted, trying to get past his brother. The other man taunted and glared and held his weapon ready to swing. "He accused me of stealing some tools," he went on. "This is the third time he's done this. He's trying to make me lose my goddamn job."

"What's the matter," Morgan sneered, "the other dago don't speak nothing but dago?"

"Don't you worry about my brother, you son of a bitch," Sebastiano spat back in English. "My brother will fuck your wife after I break your neck."

Morgan swung the hammer, but short and halfheartedly, as if afraid to make contact with one man while the other was still free. He was a big man, almost Sebastiano's size, with a bald head and heavy black sideburns, but he wasn't big enough to handle them both at once.

Nevertheless, the two Italians dashed out of the workshack for safety, and when Morgan came out swinging behind them, yelling, "I'll teach you to talk about a man's wife that way, you dago wops," a crowd of laborers surrounded him and held him back.

Morgan wasn't well liked out in the yard, where most of the men were immigrants—not that the various ethnic groups were in love with each other, but they all held resentment in common against Americans who tried to push them around. Maybe these white boys, as the Italians called them, could keep you out of their homes and their churches, away from their daughters and maybe even out of their neighborhoods, but it wasn't prudent for one of them to get out of line when too many of your own people were nearby.

Morgan was lucky. The hammer was taken away from him, but nobody thought to use it on him. Sebastiano and Giorgio never looked back.

"Come on, let's get some lunch," Sebastiano said as he caught his breath. "Someday I'm gonna get that son of a bitch alone and I'm gonna push his pig nose through the back of his head."

"Tell me, brother," Giorgio said casually. "What does this word 'dago' mean?"

Sebastiano shrugged noncommittally. "It's a word people use. It means something like jackass or pig, only they only use it to mean Italians."

"What kind of Italians, Sicilian?"

"Sure, and Calabrians and Neapolitans and Abruzzians—everybody."

"I don't understand. What the hell do I have to do with the Abruzzians?"

"To them everybody from the *mezzogiorno* is the same. They hate us all. They're like the pigs from

Alta Italia, like the Romans, only maybe not so bad. At least here they don't shoot you if you don't pay your land taxes to the goddamn government.''

"No," Giorgio said sarcastically, "instead they try to smash in your head with a hammer for no reason at all.''

"Maybe not for no reason. I insulted his wife.''

"What do you mean? What did you say?''

Sebastiano told him.

"So it was my head and not yours he wanted to smash, eh? Thank you very much, my charming brother.''

Abashed, Sebastiano laughed nervously. "Don't worry about Morgan. I'll take care of you.''

The carpentry shed was too cold for them to sit inside and eat lunch. There was no heat and enough boards were missing from the sides so the wind blew through unobstructed. Instead Sebastiano found them an abandoned yellow caboose where they could sit and enjoy their food in privacy. Teresa had packed lunch for them both—cold slices of pork and thick pieces of home-baked bread.

Giorgio didn't care much for the meat. There was something about eating pork, especially after what he had seen on the battlefield near Piave, that made him lose his appetite, but for the sake of peace he didn't complain. Besides, there was more to do than eat. Sebastiano wanted to talk. "That guy scare you back there?" he asked.

Giorgio needed no time to ponder. "Sure he scared me. You think I'm crazy?''

Sebastiano rubbed his chin, then reached into his jacket and pulled out a small metal flask. When he took off the cap, the unmistakable smell of grain alcohol escaped. "What I mean is—" He took a swig and offered some to Giorgio, who refused "—you were in the army, right?''

"Sure.''

"There was people shooting at you, wasn't there?''

"Everybody was shooting at everybody. So what?''

"I thought that after you been though such a big deal, a guy with a little hammer ain't gonna bother you so much."

"Shows how much you know. A hammer can kill you just as dead as a cannon."

"Maybe so." Sebastiano took a swig.

"What are you drinking that stuff for?"

"Because it's cold outside. Why do you think?"

Giorgio shrugged. "Shows how much I know too."

Sebastiano pondered a moment. "Anyway, it keeps my gut awake," he said.

"How can you stand the taste of it? It smells like poison."

"I can stand it because I got hair on my chest, kid."

Giorgio shook his head and rubbed the back of his neck. It bothered him to see his brother drinking all the time, and it obviously drove Teresa crazy, but Sebastiano didn't seem to care who he bothered these days. It didn't make sense to Giorgio. What made him drink so much? The guy had a family, a job, a house—what more could he want? Maybe he was trying to kill something inside, a passion or a sorrow or a hunger, but Giorgio couldn't figure out what it might be. Who knew what a man carried in his soul?

Sebastiano's eyes looked rheumy and bloodshot and his speech was becoming slurred, almost stuporous, but the more he drank, it seemed, the more he wanted to talk. "Tell me more about the army, Giorgio. They were going to take me from my family and put me in the American army, but I had too many kids. The Americans fought over there too, you know."

"Not in the old country."

"No, not there. In France."

"Over the mountains up north."

"That's right."

"That's not so far, Sebastiano. At least you could have gotten yourself killed close to home."

Sebastiano chewed on a crust of bread like a ruminating cow. "You ever kill anybody, kid?"

"No. Never even shot my rifle. I was a bugler."

"Ah." Sebastiano made an exaggerated sage nod of the head. "You made music."

"Like a bird."

"Let me tell you something. You're lucky you never killed nobody. There ain't no worse feeling than that."

Giorgio narrowed his eyes, at work on a riddle. "How do you know? You said you didn't go in the army."

"Never mind how I know. I know. It's something you never forget, not for as long as you live."

Giorgio put his good hand on his brother's shoulder with fraternal affection. Maybe this was why he drank so much. "You kill somebody, Sebastiano?" he asked simply. Killing was a terrible crime, but common in the south of Italy. Between the brigands in the hills, the gangsters in the cities and anybody anywhere who happened to have a vendetta to fulfill, there were more funerals for murdered men than for cholera victims. Yes, it was a terrible crime, but it could be forgiven by a man's own brother.

Sebastiano, however, was looking at him suspiciously. Maybe he had shown too much curiosity for his brother's comfort.

"Who told you I killed somebody?" he demanded to know in a voice that was sharp as a straight razor.

"Nobody. You did. Just now."

"I didn't tell you nothing. What do you think, that I'm stupid? I know what I said."

"Hey, Sebastiano, eat shit, all right? I thought you wanted to talk about this guy."

"What guy?" The big man shouted so forcefully that tiny droplets of whiskey fell from his huge mustache.

"The guy you killed!" Giorgio shouted back, just as loud.

"You better watch yourself or maybe I'll kill you too."

Giorgio took a breath and looked away. "You're impossible. I never knew nobody so impossible as you in all my life."

"I'm the only one you gotta know."

There was a long silence during which each tried to spite the other by folding his arms and staring at the ceiling. Giorgio was the first to break it.

"I almost killed someone once," he said.

Sebastiano was immediately hooked. "Yeah? Who?" He took a swig of whiskey.

"The man who killed Mama and Papa," Giorgio said simply.

Sebastiano spit his whiskey over his chin. "You found the son of a bitch? How the hell did you know it was him?"

"He told me, that's how I know."

"He just came out and said, I'm the one who murdered your parents? That was very good of him."

"Yes, very good."

"Why didn't you do it then?"

"Because he would have killed me too. That and some other reasons."

"What other reasons?"

"Other reasons, that's all."

"Okay," Sebastiano said, "other reasons. What was his name?"

"What was the name of the man you killed?"

"Forget it."

"You too. Forget it."

Rather than insisting Sebastiano seemed relieved that he didn't have to hear it, but he added, "It's a good thing you didn't kill him, even if he really was the murderer of our parents.''

"Yes. It's a very good thing."

After that afternoon Sebastiano seemed to make an unusual effort to show friendship to his brother. He even demanded on Giorgio's behalf a measure of respect from Franco, who resented his uncle all the more for it. He felt insulted and left out as his father and uncle talked together, went for walks together, smoked together, ate and worked together.

Teresa didn't know what to make of any of it, but she was glad to see them behaving as she imagined brothers were supposed to, without yelling or cursing or threatening each other. She was also very pleased to notice that even though Sebastiano still drank, he more often managed to keep his temper under control.

As for Giorgio, she enjoyed having him around. He was looking more like himself every day so that now she could recognize the face of the boy in him. To tell the truth she liked that face. It was a little pretty with its high cheekbones and rather severe with its very straight nose, but his light blue eyes would melt the heart of any young woman, and his lean strong shoulders seemed made to carry the burdens of a family. The idea to find a girl for her brother-in-law came as naturally as clover in May.

First, without telling anyone, she invited Constanzia Corretti, whose family owned a little candy shop on Third Street, over for dinner. Everyone, including Constanzia, a shy girl of sixteen with long red hair and green eyes, was embarrassed when she was seated next to Giorgio and he spoke not a word to her all evening.

Teresa wasn't about to give up, however. At least once a week for the next four she found a new match for Giorgio, and with each one her raised hopes were dashed by the end of the meal. Oddly, Sophia seemed delighted at the exit of each crestfallen maiden. Maybe she was a little jealous? Teresa wondered. A girl of nine wasn't too young for infatuation.

Franco also had fun describing each new prospect in blistering, hilarious detail, displaying an unnaturally keen eye for the worst faults of a person, no matter how minute—this one's nose was reaching for her lip, that one had feet big enough to float on, another picked her teeth when she thought no one was looking.

Sebastiano pretended he didn't notice what was going on. Why should he notice, after all? It was none of his business.

Giorgio refused to explain not only his lack of interest but his lack of manners as well. Teresa would get so frustrated with him sometimes that she growled and made two fists at him, but he would only smile charmingly and shrug his shoulders. There was no way to stay angry with him after that, but she was determined to find him a wife.

She was tempted to open his mail, since she was convinced his behavior had something to do with the letters he received regularly, but she couldn't bring herself to invade his privacy that way, at least not so soon. In a way he was still a stranger in their house, and if he found out she had been tampering with his property, there was no telling what he might do.

Six weeks after Giorgio's arrival he and his brother had a run-in with Morgan again. It was after lunch. This time, however, there were no histrionics, no yelling, no swinging of hammers, only a flash of movement that meant more than all those other things.

The two brothers had just finished lunch, and as usual, Sebastiano was drunk, but not just routinely drunk. He was reeling and holding his ribs because he couldn't stop giggling. During their meal he had talked about Teresa in terms so personal, so lurid, that Giorgio finally had to tell him to shut up. He'd heard enough of the details of his brother's love life to last him a long time. That was what started Sebastiano's laughter.

Morgan was standing across the yard. His hands were on his hips, and he looked like he was waiting for a victim. Sebastiano was a natural. Morgan watched him carefully, without apparent emotion, until he was certain Sebastiano was looking in his direction. Then he raised his fist in the air. Sebastiano, unsure what to make of the gesture, kept laughing until Morgan's middle finger raised from his fist.

"Son of a bitch," Sebastiano said, setting out for him.

"Hey, where are you going?" his brother yelled, trying to grab Sebastiano by the jacket, but he felt its heavy denim slip out of his grasp; he had forgotten and used his bad hand. What happened next was a scene that would play itself over and over again in Giorgio's nightmares for years to come.

Sebastiano stumbled toward Morgan without looking right or left. He was determined to have blood for the man's insult. A sharp whistle broke the air, then another blew from the opposite direction. Two freights on parallel tracks were rolling toward a common pass-point. Giorgio could tell even before they converged that Sebastiano would be caught between them. It often happened, but there was always three feet of clearance between passing trains, and under normal circumstances no one got hurt.

Today circumstances were not normal. Sebastiano was too drunk. As the locomotive behind him passed, it jetted a spray of steam, which startled him. He lurched backward and his right arm was caught on a spar that protruded from a flatbed car. He was flipped into the air and he landed half on his shoulder and half on his head.

Giorgio screamed and lay down flat to see under the moving carriages. Sebastiano's momentum carried him forward in half a somersault, and his legs, hips and stomach rolled under the second train. It looked to Giorgio as if his brother was already unconscious when the wheels of the train rolled over him with a little lurch and cut him in two.

Chapter 22

The news came from Giorgio's lips, though he did not tell the details; Teresa did not want to know them. It was enough to hear that Sebastiano was gone forever. At first she refused to believe it.

She panted a little and her eyes opened in a wide stare of frenzy and despair. Mother of God, how could this happen to her? She tore at her clothes and clawed her own skin as if to tear open a hole and let out her grief.

When Giorgio tried to stop her from hurting herself, she slapped his face and spat at him, then slapped him again and again. He realized she didn't know what she was doing, and he tried to hold her close to comfort her, but she pushed him away and keened like the damned. "He's gone, he's gone," she cried, "he's gone away from me."

The children, seeing their mother so distraught, began to cry with her even before they knew why. When Teresa tried to tell them, she choked with tears, so Giorgio did it for her. At first they didn't understand, so he had to explain several times. Finally it sank in and they huddled together like kittens in the cold, shivering with shock until Franco, with a shriek of rage, suddenly broke their ranks and flew out of the house.

Giorgio took Sophia aside. "You must help your

mother," he said. "I know you are upset, but you must be the woman of the house for a little while now and take care of your mother and the little ones."

Sophia threw her arms around him and sobbed into his shoulder, but after a moment he managed to make her listen. Pointing at the bedroom, where Teresa had gone, he said, "Don't leave her alone now. She needs her children with her." He called the two little ones over. "All of you, go in and help her."

"But what can we do?" Tina asked. "Our father never died before."

"Don't do nothing. Just go in and stay with her."

"But what about you?" Sophia sniffled. "Why don't you comfort her?"

"She don't want me now. I'm nothing to her, a stranger. Besides, I got to go after your brother. The way he looked, who the hell knows what he might do?"

The three girls, sorrowful and obedient, marched into the bedroom and timidly touched their mother as Giorgio went out to look for Franco.

Neighbors were already on their way to the house, ready to offer help and consolation if they could. It was always the way with a birth, a marriage or a death, the same as in the villages back home. A few people would come out of curiosity, a few out of spite, but most out of kindness. Many brought food, knowing from experience that a large crowd would gather and would have to be offered hospitality.

Giorgio asked around after Franco until somebody remembered seeing him running south along the street and ducking up an alleyway. That was where Giorgio found him, in the dead end of the alley, curled up like a baby in a dark corner, biting at the back of his thumb and crying.

"Franco," he said quietly, "come home with me."

His nephew refused to answer or even to look at him.

"Do you hear me?" Giorgio repeated. "I said come home with me. Your mother needs you."

He reached out to take the boy's arm, but Franco swiped at the extended hand like a cornered cat. "Leave me alone," he said in English.

"I don't understand. What did you say?"

All of a sudden Franco was hysterical with rage. "Why don't you learn English, you stupid immigrant?" he screamed in Italian.

Giorgio stood back helplessly for a moment. At first he was furious and wanted to smack Franco one to quiet him, but Franco was only a boy with big sad eyes and dark pouting lips, and he found himself wanting to take his nephew into his arms to comfort him. Franco would never stand for it, but Giorgio understood.

This was his first real lesson in life, and lessons were always hard. Giorgio had been given enough of them himself to know. Franco lost everything when he lost his father, and now to him the world was a hateful place, a place to despise. If there was nothing else to do for him, then Giorgio would stand by and let him weep.

He had cried himself, but only a little. The manner of Sebastiano's death was horrible, but he had not suffered at all, Giorgio was convinced of that, and now he was in the hands of God or the devil. There was nothing to do.

In fact, Giorgio felt very little grief, and that pestered his conscience, but after the death of old Scarfo, the loss of someone he hardly knew, brother or not, seemed almost insignificant. After all, not so long before he had never expected to see Sebastiano again, so the brief time they had together was no cause for regret.

On the other hand, it was a wasted death. There was no reason for it but a bottle and a man who hated Italians. Maybe it all could have been avoided, though the more he thought about it, the more he doubted things could have turned out any differently, because nothing ever seemed capable of turning out for the best. Lately it seemed to him that matters like these weren't even in the hands of God, but in those of Chaos.

Giorgio realized the most difficult times still lay ahead. Sebastiano was his brother and there was no other kin, so responsibility for the care of his wife and children now fell to Giorgio.

At first he resisted the idea. It was only a tradition, and what the hell did tradition matter in a country full of barbarians? Besides, he had a life of his own to worry about. Gabriella was still waiting for him, and he ached so much for her he thought about little else these days.

However, the moment he brought home the news, he learned something terrible about himself—he had a conscience. He realized at once that he could never leave his sister-in-law and her children to charity or the poorhouse. They were his family.

After nearly half an hour, Franco suddenly came to his feet and started out of the alley.

"Hey, where you going?" Giorgio said, rushing to catch up to him.

"You said my mother needs me. I'm going to my mother. I am the man of the house now."

His face looked too grim, too hard-edged for a boy of his age, but Giorgio admired his sudden stoicism. Franco managed to tame his own sorrow in order to do his duty to his family. Not many grown men could do as well, Giorgio thought, but why allow him to feel all the burden?

"We will both be the men of the family for a little while, all right, Franco? You and me, we'll make a good house for the women."

"To hell with you!" Franco spat. "I don't want you in my house. What can you do with your crippled hand? Go back to where you came from. Go back to Italy."

Giorgio's breath hissed between his teeth. He had had enough. "Listen, little boy, don't talk like that to me or you'll swallow a few teeth. I'm a grownup, I'm your uncle and I'm bigger than you. I don't want no more bullshit out of you."

Franco wouldn't be stopped. "Sure, go ahead," he said, "punch me in the face. I can take it. I ain't afraid of you."

Giorgio could feel the blood rushing to his cheeks. "I don't care if you're afraid of me, but you better show some respect."

"Why? Because my father's dead I got to listen to you? I don't know you. You're not my family. I got plenty of family already. I don't need no stupid *greenhorn* telling me what to do."

He suddenly turned on Giorgio and tried to punch him in the stomach. Giorgio managed to catch his hand and twist his arm around gently, but Franco thrashed and grimaced with hatred.

"Let me go. Leave me alone."

"I'm taking you home, Franco. Stop fighting. I don't want to hurt you."

Giorgio's heart nearly broke when he saw Franco's look of anger, hatred, accusation. Franco blamed him for Sebastiano's death; it was obvious. Giorgio was there to see it happen, and that meant to Franco's young mind that Giorgio could have prevented it. After all, Giorgio was not just anyone. He was a Farenza. It was his duty to protect his brother, just as it was Franco's to protect his sisters and mother. If only there were a way to explain to him. If only.

Franco didn't stop his struggling the whole way back, so it was a slow, painful process to get him up the street and into the house, but once inside, he gave up his thrashing and turned docile and morose.

*   *   *

The next day, though she still cried and beat her chest with sorrow, Teresa managed to gain some control over her emotions. There were other things to think about now. There were the children and the house and food and clothing and a thousand other things to pay for—but no money. Sebastiano left no will, no insurance, nothing—they had only the little bit Teresa had put aside every week from Sebastiano's paycheck, and half of that would go to pay the undertaker.

Giorgio was very kind, very helpful, though she knew she had treated him miserably when he brought the news to her. He understood, she was sure of it. When the right moment came, she would apologize to him.

Sebastiano's death, she was convinced, was his own doing. Doubtless he had been drunk. Nobody said so, but they didn't have to. He took a flask of odorless grain alcohol with him to work every day, and he was usually a little woozy when he came home at night. All the evidence was there. Besides, how else could such a stupid accident happen?

The thought of his drinking roused furious anger in her. "You stupid son of a bitch," she cried out, "why did you do this to me? Why did you do this to the children? I loved you and cared for you and gave you a family and look what you did to me—left me with a family and bills to pay. Now what the hell am I supposed to do? Tell me! What?"

She wept standing in her kitchen with neighbors bustling all about her. An arm went around her shoulders to comfort her. She didn't know whose—she could see nothing through her tears—but it didn't matter. Six months from now where would the comforting arms be? Everyone would be back to business as usual, but her problems would still be there, and Lord Jesus, Sebastiano would still be dead. He would be dead forever.

"It's all right, Teresa. Everything will be all right." It was Giorgio's voice. It was he who held her.

"What am I going to do, Giorgio?" she demanded. "I'm all alone with these kids. What am I going to do?"

"I'll take care of everything. Sebastiano was my brother. You're my responsibility. You don't have to worry."

She knew she did have to worry. How nice it would be to believe him, she thought bitterly, but he was too young to make such promises. Young people were never as good as their word. When they meant to be sincere, they were only cruel, because being young, they would promise anything to make you feel good, and then they would forget all about you and have a merry life of their own.

Anyway, even if Giorgio did try to help, he had only one good hand. What could he do? His promises were worthless, just like his brother's. Sebastiano, you promised to spend a lifetime with me. Now look what happened to your promsises.

She almost pushed Giorgio away, but then he patted her gently and held her close and she smelled the sour scent of him. She let herself trust him in spite of herself, because no matter how young or incapable he might be, there was no one else to trust.

My loneliness is making me stupid, she thought, but she didn't care. It was better to be foolish than lonely. Let Giorgio make his promises. Let him hold her and comfort her. After all, there would be enough time when no one would hold her. From now on there would be no one to warm her bed at night, no one to throw his big arms around her and make her feel safe. No one to do what one did in the marriage bed . . .

* * *

"*Sanctus, sanctus, sanctus,*" the priest intoned like an incantation. In response an altar boy jingled a small brass bell three times. At each ringing the Roman Catholics in the congregation struck their breasts with balled right hands. Others who had come to pay their respects looked around uncertainly, as if they would find an explanation hiding among the grieving faces.

The priest was Father Bruno, the pastor of St. Anthony's, and he was dressed in a black stole and chasuble for the requiem mass. He was elderly and he had witnessed many scenes like this one—the women in black lace crying into handkerchiefs; the men, dressed up in dark ill-fitting suits, trying to comfort their wives; the children, innocent and respectful; the infants, babbling and gurgling happily while death hovered so close by. When he turned to bring the smoking censer down from the altar, swinging it in front of him by a two-foot chain as he walked around the coffin in the center aisle of the church, he abandoned the rituals for a moment and stopped to comfort Teresa.

He whispered into her ear and she answered him with loud moans, like a young child who cannot be comforted. Many people were weeping, but hers was the only audible voice. This was traditional. Only the widow had the right of abandonment to grief in the silent air of the church, and the singlular sound of her in the huge, crowded, quiet room had an eerie quality like a dance tune sung with no accompaniment.

Giorgio sat next to Teresa. The children were one pew back. Again, tradition. When the priest stopped to whisper to his sister-in-law, Giorgio had the sudden urge to put his hand in his trouser pocket. He kept the little crucifix there, the one Gabriella had given him from her rosary.

The feel of it reassured him. Whenever he touched it

and closed his eyes, her face would appear before him, and her lovely forlorn brown velvet eyes would beg him to hurry back to her. He wondered about her father's health. He could not return until the old man was dead, of that he was sure, and though he knew Don Antonio was sick with consumption, sometimes these matters took years.

At least that would give him time to get matters settled here. Somehow he would have to make enough money to support Teresa until she could find herself another husband—if she was willing to. Like most new widows, she had repeatedly made an oath never to marry again. What worried Giorgio was that Teresa was so stubborn she just might keep her word.

"Are you all right, my son?"

Giorgio opened his eyes, startled.

"You look pale. Are you ill?" It was Father Bruno.

"No, Father, I'm fine, thank you." He made an embarrassed little smile and put his hand to the small of Teresa's back.

"Take care of your sister-in-law," the pastor commanded. He was very bald on top with a fringe of white hair over his ears, and he had a strong Roman nose that made him look as dignified as a judge. "She has no one else now, so she becomes your responsibility."

"I know," Giorgio agreed with several nervous little bobs of his head. "I'll take good care of her."

Father Bruno raised one eyebrow to show doubt. "See that you do," he said, then went off swinging pungent puffs of incense over the coffin and the heads of the people. Inevitably much coughing followed.

Without looking at him Teresa took Giorgio's hand in her own. He squeezed affectionately, but it was an effort for him because at that moment it seemed like just another demand for filial duty. For the past few days people had been reminding him over and over of his filial duties, and he was tired of it. Right now he wanted nothing so much as to be left alone for a little peace and quiet.

Thank you very much, he knew quite well what he had to do. He had to provide for his brother's family, make certain the children didn't go out and get themselves killed in the street, protect the widow's virtue, make a living for himself, earn enough money to go back to Italy, marry Gabriella, make a new family, provide for them and make sure they didn't get killed in the streets. . . . Yes, he could make a very nice list without reminders from strangers.

He looked at the coffin the way a drowning man might look at a lifeboat floating away from him. Sebastiano, he thought, I wish you had never come to America.

"*Requiescat in pace.*" At these words from the priest, six pallbearers came up the aisle and lifted the casket off its gurney, then started out of the church.

As Giorgio came to his feet to follow Teresa out of the pew, something in an alcove to his left caught his eye. There above a little side altar was a statue of the Virgin that had been cast in plaster and had suffered badly from water damage because of a leak in the ceiling above. She might have had a pretty face once, but now the eyes were gone, and half of one cheek as well as most of her left shoulder.

He thought of the crucifix in the shepherd's chapel that had given him comfort so many years ago. He remembered how haunting those eyes were, and how he had longed to carve such beauty in stone, and now he had an idea.

His hand was still of no use, but the feeling was coming back faster than he had hoped, and until he was healed, he could use his left hand to make the preliminary drawings. The only problem was finding a place to work, and that was settled as if by providence at the cemetery. After everyone had thrown a white rose on the casket and

the crowd was beginning to disperse, Father Bruno took
him aside.

"What are you going to do about work?" he asked
bluntly. "Can you go back to the trainyard?"

Giorgio shrugged. "For what? They hired me as my
brother's helper, as a favor to him. Now he's dead. But
don't worry, Father. I'll find something."

"You don't have to. You'll come to work at the
church."

"That's very kind, Father, but what can I do around
here? I have only one good hand, and I'm not a priest."

"You can keep the place clean and repaired. I need a
custodian. Mr. Califrongio, who does the work now, is
sick and the doctor says he's not going to get better. It's
very sad, but I must retire him. Holy Mother Church will
care for him in his remaining days, but I need someone to
take his place. Would you be willing?"

"I can try, Father, but as I told you, my hand—"

Father Bruno's voice became stern. "You can have
patience and try, can't you?"

"Of course, Father. I can try."

"Very good. You'll start tomorrow then. Be here at
seven o'clock."

"Seven, yes, but excuse me. There's a matter we
haven't discussed yet."

The priest wrinkled his forehead with perplexity. "What
matter is that?"

"The small matter of wages," Giorgio said.

Father Bruno thought it over for a moment. His eyes
turned sly and his manner evasive. "Two dollars a day,
six days a week. Twelve dollars a week," he offered.

Giorgio was affronted. "Father, if I am not mistaken,
you have offered me this job for the sake of my sister-in-
law and her children. How can a man, a woman and five
children survive on twelve dollars a week? Sophia would

have to leave school and take a job in a mill. Franco would have to find work too. Even then there might not be enough. Children can't earn very much pay. I would rather pack my clothes and go back to Italy than stay here and witness such a tragedy, especially if such a terrible thing were on the head of the church.''

Giorgio knew about the plight of children in the mills. The streets were full of little ones so badly injured from machinery that they had to beg for a living.

The priest scowled, then relented a bit. ''How much do you want?''

''My brother was making forty dollars a week at the trainyard.''

After a brief fit of choking Father Bruno managed to repeat the sum as if it were a vile curse. ''Forty dollars! Sometimes we don't see that much in the collection basket on Sunday.''

Giorgio believed him. The Italian parishoners here were almost as poor as the peasants back home. ''All right then, Father. Twenty dollars a week for five days' work.''

The priest grew red with anger. ''Five days! What can you do in five days? You have only one good hand.''

Giorgio was insistent. ''Five days, and on the sixth, I would like a place in the church basement to do some other work.''

''What kind of work?''

''Private work, but for the church.''

''You must tell me what it is.''

''Only when I'm ready.''

''Oh? And when will that be?''

''Soon enough, but not too soon.''

''Suppose I insist.''

''Suppose I go back to Italy.''

Father Bruno sighed. ''Very well. I'll meet your terms even though you're worse than a pirate. You should be ashamed to steal from the church. But as long as it's for Mrs. Farenza and the children, I suppose I have to agree."

Giorgio smiled modestly. "You're a very kind man, Father. May God Almighty give you a place at His right hand in heaven," he said, then added quickly, "but not too soon." And under his breath, "just soon enough."

Teresa knew there would be trouble. Franco had not taken to his uncle from the beginning, and now, lopsided as the contest might be, there would be a struggle for power in the house until the question of mastery was settled.

With the father gone it was traditional for the eldest son to sit in his father's place, and the mother had a duty to treat her son as her master whenever they were among outsiders. This ensured that the family would be respected by the community. When they were alone, of course, it was a different matter. Then she was mother and he was son, and woe to him who should forget it.

When it became clear that Giorgio had found a job and would provide for the family, however, the situation was complicated. He was older and a member of the family, so he had to be respected. On the other hand, he was not Teresa's husband and therefore not truly father of the house, so she wasn't surprised when only a few nights after her husband's funeral there was an eruption at the dinner table.

It was over a small matter. Franco came to the table early and seated himself at its head. Sophia, finding him there, scolded him at once. "That place is for Uncle Giorgio. Get up at once."

"Go to hell," Franco muttered and turned away to let her know she would be ignored.

Sophia turned into a spitfire. She grabbed his thick black hair and scratched at his cheeks and tried to pull him to the floor. In turn he made two fists and tried to punch his way free. Giorgio and Teresa came at the same time from opposite sides of the room.

"Stop it, both of you!" Teresa hollered, while Giorgio, tangling his arms with Franco's, managed to separate the children. Tina and Favia, screaming with delight, ran in from the other room to watch the ruckus.

"Get your hands off me!" Franco hissed, turning his wrath on his uncle.

"Behave yourself," Giorgio grunted, "or I'll break your neck."

"Mama, listen to him. You heard him. He wants to break my neck."

Teresa had a firm grip on Sophia's ear. "So what?" she said tiredly. "How many times did your father offer to break your neck, eh?"

"He's not my father!"

"He's your uncle," Sophia put in, "and it's practically the same thing."

"It ain't the same thing," Franco shot back. "Mama, tell her it ain't."

"You just shut up, you," Teresa said to avoid the issue. "I don't have to tell your sister nothing."

"What the hell is all this about, anyway?" Giorgio demanded. He released Franco's arms to wait for an answer, but as soon as he did, Franco was after him, punching and kicking and biting with the fury of a cyclone. To stop him, Giorgio made his left hand as flat as a paddle and smacked him across the back of the head. "There now, you satisfied?"

Franco screamed like a small girl, which shocked Giorgio, and before anyone realized what had happened, Teresa was in the fray, clawing at her brother-in-law's cheeks. "You don't hit my son, you bastard, you hear me? You don't hit my little boy!"

Giorgio had no more patience left. He shoved her roughly back with his shoulder and grabbed the howling Franco by an ear. "You better shut up, boy, and shut up right now, you hear me?"

This only made Franco get louder, and now Teresa was coming after him again. He released her son and faced her nose to nose when she came up to him.

"Nobody hits my kids, nobody, you tyrant!" she snarled. "I'll cut your throat with a kitchen knife if you lay another hand on him."

"If he don't learn some respect, Teresa, I'll put my foot up his ass, so you don't got to worry about him."

Sophia was crying openly now, and the two little ones held on to each other and stood back in a corner in terror. Franco was smugly sulking at the table, still seated in Giorgio's chair.

"You ain't gonna point your foot nowhere," Teresa shouted, "because this ain't your house, and you get the hell out of here."

Giorgio almost took her at her word. To hell with them all. Why should he care what happened to them, any of them? She wasn't his wife and they weren't his children. But the sight of Sophia, trying hard not to shed a tear and failing with drop after drop, touched his heart, and instead of turning around and walking out, he drew himself up as if to make a proclamation.

"I am Sebastiano's brother. By tradition and by right all that was his belongs to me. This house is mine, this food is mine, this table is mine. You are here only because I let you stay."

"Nothing is yours," Teresa said, shivering with anger.

"We will go to the judge and see. You think the American judges are any different than the Italian ones? You're a woman. All that belongs to you are the fruit of your womb."

She made no answer this time, but glowered at him and waited for him to continue. "I work for you, I slave for you, I sweat for you at the church, making money to keep you alive. What do you think, I like doing it? You think I love all of you so much I can't wait to get up before dark and go to work for that slave-driving priest of the devil?"

As it had turned out, Father Bruno rarely spoke a word to Giorgio and was quite an easy taskmaster, but this was no time to mention that to his family of disrespectful crazy people.

"I do it because I have an obligation before God and Holy Mother Church and before the ghost of my brother, Sebastiano, your husband and their father, to make sure you don't die before you've had a few years to suffer in the world. I ask nothing in return but a little respect and a little peace. I don't care if you love me, I don't care if you fear me, I don't care if you hate me. But you're gonna respect me and leave me in peace or I'll have to teach you some respect, and that includes you, Franco, and you, Teresa, and if it takes a good hard smack now and then, I'll be glad to hand it out. You hear?"

No one answered.

"You hear me?" he repeated, looking directly at Teresa.

"I'm older than you. Don't you talk to me this way," she said, but weakly.

"Agh!" he barked and raised his hand as if to slap her. Holy Mother of Intervention, he prayed, don't let her challenge me; I'll never be able to make myself hit her.

For once the Blessed Virgin favored him. Teresa didn't flinch under his threat, but neither did she venture another remark.

Giorgio turned to Franco. "What about you?"

Franco said nothing.

"What about you, boy? Speak civily for once."

"You ain't my father," his nephew sneered, "and I ain't ever gonna treat you like my father. I don't care if you kill me just like you did him."

"I didn't kill nobody," Giorgio bellowed. "It was an accident."

"I know what you did, and I'm gonna hate you until I'm big enough to get the hell out of here."

Teresa, to Giorgio's surprise, intervened. "Franco, that's enough. If you say another word, Uncle Giorgio has my permission to beat you and lock you in the cellar."

The young boy's lower lip made a vulgar pout and he looked at his mother like the worst kind of traitor, but he said nothing more that night—not a word.

Dinner was quiet and tense, but Giorgio sat at the head of the table and there was no more arguing about it. Afterward everyone turned in early.

As she lay quietly in the dark, Teresa thought about what had happened before dinner that night but could make no sense of it. Giorgio had been well within his rights to slap Franco a good one for his behavior, yet a tiger had jumped out of her to protect her little cub.

Then Giorgio made his ridiculous speech. At first she had to force herself not to laugh at him, but by the time he was finished, he had from her exactly what he wanted— respect. She no longer thought of him as a boy but as a young man who was the master of the house.

As she drifted off, she wondered why he hadn't asked for her hand after Sebastiano died. It wasn't required, but most single brothers would have done exactly that in this situation. It almost went without saying.

Then she started to wonder what it would be like to have a husband who was younger than she, who was as different from Sebastiano as Giorgio was. Faced with tonight's scene, Sebastiano would have drawn blood. Giorgio had been gentle in a way, as a woman or priest might be. She liked that about him. Maybe he wouldn't be such a bad catch, now that she thought about it.

It made her feel funny inside to think about it, as if she had stirred up a broth in her stomach, warm and slightly salty. The feeling brought her back to wakefulness, and from a sudden impulse she went to the bedroom door and latched it.

Chapter 23

Franco was as good as his word. As the rest of the household settled into normal activities, he became more and more of a nuisance, finally a problem that couldn't be ignored. He would go for weeks on end without speaking, then suddenly overturn dishes at the dinner table or throw a coffee cup across a room. He continually skipped school and he ran away from home three times, coming home only when he was dangerously weak with hunger.

Giorgio shouted, begged and slapped him around. His mother did the same. Sophia, complaining that he smelled bad, avoided him, while the other two girls were perplexed, fascinated and frightened by him.

On the anniversary of his father's death two constables brought him home in the afternoon, while Giorgio was still at work.

His mother answered the loud knock at the door, and when she saw who stood there, her hand went to her mouth. "*Dio mio*, what have you done?" she cried out when she saw her manacled son unceremoniously shoved through the door.

"Are you Mrs. Sebastiano Ferenza?" one of the policemen asked. He was tall and fat with sparse red hair under his crushed blue cap.

"Yes. What are you doing with Franco?"

"We're bringing him home to place him in the custody of his parents, madam. He was caught running out of del Sorlo's Specialty Shop with his pockets stuffed full of these." He held out his hand and revealed half a dozen jawbreakers, each the size of a small hen's egg.

Teresa looked over the merchandise. "You put my boy in handcuffs for stealing candy?"

"Mr. del Sorlo threatened to press charges. We had to do something to calm him down."

Teresa knew Joe del Sorlo. He was first-generation American, a mean, stingy son of a bitch who didn't go to church and who sold novels by the filthy-minded swine, D'Annunzio, under the counter to children, even to girls.

"Will you please leave Franco to me, then?" she asked quietly. "I will take care of this."

The redheaded man fumbled for keys while his partner, a shorter fellow with a square jaw and a mole over his left cheekbone, looked contemptuously up and down the street. He obviously didn't like the neighborhood, but he had sense enough to keep quiet while he was here.

"I'm sorry to trouble you this way, but you've got to keep Frankie out of del Sorlo's for a while or we'll have to lock him up overnight."

Teresa nodded. "Yes, of course. Thank you for your kindness."

The tall man tipped his hat. The other, the unfriendly one, did not. Franco was turned over to his mother and they were left alone. She led him by the ear from the porch to the parlor.

"Stay here," she said. "If you move one step out of this house while I'm gone, I'll kill you."

She went to the tiny pantry in the kitchen and returned with a stiff broom, then marched toward the front door.

"Mama, where are you going?" Franco ventured.

"Shut up," she said and made Roman paces out of the door, down the steps, up the sidewalk, around the corner and into del Sorlo's Specialty Shop.

Joe del Sorlo stood behind a glass counter filled with licorice sticks, pistachios, marshmallow peanuts, jaw-breakers, gumballs, jelly beans and a dozen other kinds of candy. For a moment Teresa wondered how Franco had managed to get back there to steal anything. Amazing, that boy sometimes. Too smart for his own good.

Del Sorlo himself was not so appetizing as his candy. His head was shaped like a bell gourd, he had yellow-grey hair that swelled out over his ears, and he was skinny as a snake. His neck, thin and crooked forward like a turkey's, was speckled with red from razor cuts, and his pointed nose was webbed with spider veins.

No wonder he's so miserable, she speculated. Any-body would be if they looked like him. But that didn't excuse him for what he had done to Franco.

"Mr. del Sorlo," she said in English, as it seemed more appropriate to talk to him in the tongue of a savage.

"You want to buy something here, lady?" he asked her insolently. " 'Cause if you don't, I don't want you in my store."

"Yes," she said calmly. "I want to buy a piece of candy."

Another customer, a teenage boy, probably from the Polish neighborhood over in the west end, snapped his chewing gum and stood patiently beside Teresa to wait his turn.

"What kind of candy you want?" del Sorlo asked her.

"You decide."

The Polish boy looked with uncertainty into the Italian

woman's face; he had heard the threat in her voice. His eyes shifted nervously to the door.

"How about a couple of nice jawbreakers? That's the kind of stuff your kid likes, isn't it?"

"A jawbreaker is fine," she said.

Del Sorlo smiled sourly and bent over to reach into the case. Teresa caught the teenager's eye and signaled for him to leave. He wasted no time and the door slammed shut behind him.

"Damn kids," del Sorlo mumbled, "they're all the same." He stood up to put her merchandise on the counter. As his hand came down, so did the heavy handle of the broom. She didn't smash hard enough to break his fingers, but hard enough so that he would know she meant business.

"Hey, lady," he cried, "What the hell do you think you're doing?"

"Now, you son of a bitch, what's the big idea of siccing the cops on my boy?"

"Your son's a thief."

She reversed the broom, drew it back and this time made a full swing at his head. He managed to step back just in time.

"Cut it out, will you?" he yelled, more with annoyance than fear.

"I'll teach you to call the cops on my kid." She beat him over the shoulders until he was finally smart enough to turn tail and run through a curtained door into a back room. She followed him and found herself in his bedroom. Ignoring this circumstance in her frenzy, she continued to pound at him. With every blow she had something to say.

"You don't call the cops." She gave him a wallop to the head. "My boy acts up, you don't call any *American*." Wham, wham. He turned his back and put his arms up to protect himself. Dimly realizing the danger of hitting him too hard in the head, she shifted to his shoulders.

"The Americans are idiots, like you." Wanting him to hurt all over, she shifted to his back. "You call me, you hear? Me, me, me." Working down over his buttocks and on to his legs, she continued to shriek. "I'll take care of my son the thief."

Throughout the entire scene he made a screaming racket, cursing and calling for help in both English and Italian, but nobody from the neighborhood cared to come to his aid. He wasn't well liked.

When Teresa was satisfied that he understood her message, she went home and gave her son another message in the same language, then went into her room and closed the door, because there was a serious matter to consider. She had learned something back at the store.

Amidst all the filth and howling that came out of del Sorlo's mouth as she beat on him, he accused her of living a life of shame with her brother-in-law. She knew what this meant. A scandal had started in the neighborhood. It had been almost inevitable, of course, but she hadn't allowed herself to think about it until now.

Something would have to be done, but she didn't know what. She couldn't ask Giorgio to leave. He had been so kind to them, and he had nowhere to go. On the other hand, he had shown no inclination to propose to her, though it was the custom. If nothing was done, not only would she become an outcast, a pariah, but her children would as well. Yes, something would have to be done, but she didn't know what.

Giorgio sat on the floor next to the coal bin in the basement of St. Anthony's. From his trouser pocket he pulled a neatly folded rectangular piece of stationery. It was a letter from Gabriella.

It wasn't new, but it was the last he had received

from her. It had come two weeks before. By now he had read it so many times that he knew the contents by heart.

My Darling Giorgio,

It has finally happened. My father is dead. I am here with Brigetta, and together we are managing the estate.

He played a trick on that dear woman, Giorgio. He put off marrying her again and again until it was too late. He died without giving her his name and without naming her in his will. I believe this had something to do with you and me, that he learned she had given us aid and so plotted against him. Of course, I could not turn her out. I have promised that as long as she remains unmarried, she will have a place here, and I have settled some money on her as well. She is a fine woman, Giorgio.

So I am left with wealth and lands and all the headaches of managing them. There are some legal questions, of course. It isn't simple for a woman to hold property here. But I think with a little money put into the right hands, everything will be all right.

The most difficult problem now is refusing the daily proposales of Francesco. There is a certain legality involved here also. My father, after all, promised my hand to him, but perhaps some arrangement can be made to satisfy his ardor with a few *lire* as well, although not too many, I hope. While our estate is wealthy in property and produce, there isn't much cash.

I'm not nearly so happy at my father's death as I thought I would be, though I'm not sure why. Perhaps losing a father is always difficult,

no matter what kind of man he's been. You
know, I don't remember him being so cruel when
I was younger. In fact, he doted on me. It was
only when he realized that I was becoming a
woman that his temperament changed. I don't
know. I don't want to judge him too harshly.
This must sound foolish to the son of two of his
victims, but I cannot help it. He was my father.

Oh, Giorgio, there is only one thing more to
say. I ache for you. I long for the day of your
return. My bed is cold and I am lonely. Please
come back to me soon. I'm waiting as patiently
as I can, but please, don't make me wait any
longer. Never once have I removed the ring you
gave me from my finger, and the rosary awaits
the cross' return. You are my heart and my love,
and I wish more than anything to be your
betrothed.

Lovingly and faithfully yours,
Gabriella

Giorgio kissed the signature, then carefully folded the
letter and slipped it back into his pocket. He sighed. What
was he to do? The father was dead and his hand was
almost completely better again. It pained him occasionally,
and sometimes there were small tasks he could not
accomplish—picking up a penny from a table, for example—
but he could hold a mallet again, and strike with precision.

He had in fact built a short stairway of flagstone to a
side entrance of the rectory and just that week repaired the
shrine of St. Anthony, a small granite alcove that stood in
front of the church. There was nothing standing between
him and the trip home but one woman and four children.

No matter how hard he had tried over the past twelve
months, no matter what he denied himself or the others,

there was never enough money to put away. The fare home was cheap enough, thirty dollars or so. He could manage that. But if he left tomorrow, Teresa would be in the same predicament she had been in the day Sebastiano died.

He supposed the church would provide something for her. Father Bruno was a good man at heart. He could manage a stipend for her, surely, but another custodian would have to be paid as well, and the church's coffers were not very full.

There was also the matter of the children. Without a father to guide and protect them, there was no telling what would happen to them.

Giorgio laughed at himself. He had used the word father, though to the children themselves he was always careful to point out that he was not their father, but only their uncle and guardian. Still, he had come to feel so close to them, or at least to the girls, that sometimes he thought he would very much like to be their father.

Franco was trouble, but Giorgio liked to believe that he would come around as he got older. If only I could be here when he grows up, Giorgio thought, we might even get to like each other a little.

As for Teresa, he didn't allow himself to think about her much. It was hard enough to keep his eyes off her. She had very round curves and ample hips, hair as black as coffee and eyes as sly as her walk. God and Gabriella forgive him, but sometimes he wanted to grab her and to make love to her on the spot. He felt a little disloyal to Gabriella, but not much. After all, he had lived with Teresa for an entire year, and he was only human.

As always when he thought about Teresa, he made himself put his mind on other things. Across the basement, a large dark room with a low ceiling, was the small private work area Father Bruno had promised him. Not that Giorgio didn't trust the fellow, but the first thing he had done when he came on the job a year before was to make a few simple room dividers out of rope and sheets and block his workshop off. He could only hope that the pastor had too much conscience to peek through the sheets.

He sauntered back there now to sneak in a little time on his project. This was what had kept him from going crazy since coming to work at the church. Here in America he had no passion to make the blood boil, no obsession to make him feel the life tingling in his flesh.

Even death, which in Italy seemed like a constant companion that followed you everywhere to make you quicken your step, here felt like something vague, abstract, an idea to be thought about behind closed doors. In the Campania there were almost as many murders every year as deaths by disease, accident and starvation.

In America it was much harder to see the dangers, so it was much harder to give a damn about them. The *Stati Uniti*, the land of opportunity, had given him nothing to love or fear with all his heart. So the idea that occurred to him in the church on the day of his brother's funeral began to take on more and more importance for Giorgio. It was a simple idea—to build a statue, to carve it from stone, to create eyes lovelier than those on a crucifix in a shepherd's chapel on the outskirts of Santa Barbara.

The project took much patience, and the first cut into stone had yet to be made. With only one hand there was little he could do by himself, and he was too proud ask the help of another stonemason, though there were a few in the neighborhood, most of whom made their living sculpting gravestones. Instead Giorgio first trained his left hand to control a pencil, which took nearly four months, and then he began to draw.

Sketch after sketch of the Virgin's face, her clothes, her hands, her feet piled up on his worktable, and with

each new drawing he would discover a design problem
unsolved, an impossible technical demand or a vague conviction that he had produced something not true enough.

After his right hand regained some control, he began
using a small knife to whittle models of the statue, first in
bars of soap, then in soft wood. His first efforts were
disastrous. Carving the head was difficult, but the arms
were almost impossible, and the hands—the poor Virgin
rarely ended up with any. But eventually he learned how
to be careful, how to be patient, and finally he had a
miniature of the final work that satisfied him.

The design was far from the usual sentimental cliche
of a woman standing with her hands outstretched or folded
and her head tilted sadly toward heaven. Instead it was of
a heartbroken figure, kneeling and holding her hands near
her face in a clawed, terrible plea to heaven. To Giorgio
she was praying for sinners, begging mercy for the idiots
and unlucky people who lived in this world from a Son
who had left her for the glories of life in heaven.

It was his dream that in her face, modeled after
Gabriella, the most beautiful woman in the world, the
people of St. Anthony's would see all their own hopes and
all their own suffering. He wished to show the Virgin to
whom so many of them prayed as one who listened because she was one of them and not a goddess. Holy Mary,
Compassionate Mother—that's how he thought of his work.

He had still to find the eyes he would give her. Even
Gabriella's lovely ones were not worthy of the Virgin, and
none his imagination produced were sad enough, virtuous
enough, kind enough or tortured enough. But he would
think about them and pray for inspiration, and maybe with
luck they would appear to him.

Somewhere in the back of his mind, however, he
doubted that he would ever finish the statue. In fact, he
hoped he wouldn't. Such a project would take time, much

time, and as important as it had become to him, he realized he would have to give it up the moment it became possible for him to return home to Santa Barbara.

O God, he would sometimes pray, do not grant me too much time to complete this work. Maybe just enough to get started. Just enough to do the eyes. It had already been a year—an entire year without Gabriella. How much longer would he have to wait? He was sick of waiting. Sick of it.

Giorgio came home from work just before dark. The moment he walked in the door, Teresa told him the entire day's events from the arrival of the police to the confrontation with del Sorlo. The three girls were sitting at the table awaiting dinner. Franco was not.

"Where is the boy now?" Giorgio asked.

"In the bedroom sulking," Sophia said spitefully.

"I think you should talk to him," Teresa suggested.

"I think I should beat him," Giorgio replied half-heartedly. "We can't let him get away with this bullshit."

"I already beat him," Teresa said. "You don't have to. You can talk."

Giorgio thought it over for a minute. He and Franco had talked before, and nothing had ever come of it but hard feelings and bitterness.

"There's nothing I can say. He knows he's done wrong."

Teresa stared at Giorgio for a long minute. "Something is troubling you," she said.

"No, nothing. Just the boy. I don't know what to do about him."

"It's not Franco. I can tell. If it were Franco, you would be in there with him now."

Giorgio sat at the table, and without bidding any of the girls hello, he poured himself a glass of wine and sipped at it quietly. He was thinking of the letter in his pocket.

"What's the matter, Giorgio? You seem half asleep," Teresa said in a kindly voice.

"I don't know. Maybe I'm a little tired."

"Tired! How can a young man like you be tired?"

Giorgio couldn't even force a polite laugh. "You're right," he said. "I shouldn't be tired. I should be talking to Franco. I'll do it right now."

With that he pushed his chair back and dragged his feet into the bedroom. Teresa shook her head in confusion.

Franco sat on his bed occupying himself by staring at a portrait of Christ on the wall. It was a poorly painted likeness, but the eyes seemed to follow one around the room. Giorgio himself had noticed that when he first saw it. It was an unnerving and annoying characteristic.

"Franco," he said gruffly, "your mother tells me there was trouble today."

"My trouble, not yours. It's none of your business."

"It is my business when American policemen come to my front door with my nephew in chains."

"They weren't chains, they were handcuffs. I stole some candy. Big deal."

"Today candy, sure. Tomorrow maybe a little money, eh? And then a lot of money. And then what? You want to grow up to be a crook?"

Franco looked over at his uncle with eyes that didn't give a damn about anything. "So what if I do? All Italians belong to the Black Hand."

"The Americans are stupid," Giorgio said, touching his head.

"Then maybe that's what's wrong with me," Franco said, "because I'm an American. Don't forget, I was born here."

Giorgio suddenly found the energy for passion. "Let me tell you something, kid. As long as you live in this house, you ain't American, you're Farenza. If you trust the Americans, you're a goddamn fool. Their ways are not our ways. Their traditions are made by the government, the bureaucrats, the police. I know about the goddamn government, believe me. Italy got a government too. They steal your money and send you to war, that's all they're good for."

"That's Italy's government," Franco replied heatedly. "What do you know about Americans or their government? You've only been here a year and you're not even a citizen yet."

"What makes you think I want to be a citizen? The only reason I'm hanging around here is to take care of the family, to take care of you. To make sure you don't grow up to be a goddamn crook. Sure, I know about the crooks too, Franco. I knew one of the biggest and worst in all of Italy. I know the Mafia and the Camorra—you know those names? Eh? Cross them and they cut your throat. They throw you into a pit of lime and burn you up, just like what happened to your grandparents."

A frown passed over Franco's face. "My grandparents?"

"Sure. Don't you think your father and I had parents? You think maybe somebody pissed on the ground and we grew up like tomatoes?"

"I thought you were orphans."

"Sure, because some damn crook made us orphans."

Franco looked shaken by this revelation. It was the first thing Giorgio had ever said to him that seemed to have an effect.

"Who was this crook?"

"None of your business, that's who."

"Did you find him and kill him?"

"Nobody killed him. You don't kill a man like that. He kills you."

Franco rubbed his hands together and rocked back and forth for a moment. "If that's the way Italians really are, I'm glad I'm not Italian. Americans don't do things like that. They don't just murder a guy's parents. And if they do, they get arrested and they go to the electric chair."

Giorgio laughed derisively. "Oh, yeah? Like this guy Morgan who tricked your father into falling under a train?"

Now Franco's face turned crimson with fire. He came to his feet. "What are you talking about?"

"Don't worry about what I'm talking about. You just stay away from the Americans and keep your nose clean. I want no goddamn policemen hanging around here."

"But you said somebody named Morgan killed my father."

"I didn't say nothing. Forget what I said. And don't say nothing to your mother, either. Keep your voice down." Giorgio knew the look of vendetta, even on a nine-year-old face. Once that lust took hold of him, nothing would shake it free. It was a disease, and he didn't want his nephew to catch it, but he had a hopeless feeling that it was already too late.

"Who is this Morgan?" Franco persisted. "What did he have to do with my father?"

"He's a guy who didn't like Italians, that's all. Like all the Americans. I told you, forget it."

"I won't forget nothing. He did a crime."

"Oh, yeah? And what are you gonna do about it? You're a kid. You can't do nothing."

"I'll wait til I grow up and then do something about it!"

"Agh, *fang' gool*. You're talking stupid."

"And you're talking like a coward. You should have

had him arrested, but you didn't. Now it's my job to take care of things."

"Oh, now you're gonna be the man of the house again, right?"

"That's right!"

"You got a job to pay for the food and to buy clothes for your sisters?"

"Maybe not, but I don't make a whore out of my mother, either."

Giorgio's hand shot out and slapped the boy hard. "Don't talk about your mother that way."

Franco's cheek turned red, and his eyes glistened, but he didn't allow a tear to fall. His voice grew loud so everyone in the house would hear. "It ain't me who talks that way. It's the whole damn neighborhood. They say you been living in this house a whole year, and there ain't no way for a man to live with a woman like my mother without—"

"Without what?" Giorgio was hot with embarrassment and shame.

"I can't say it! But you know what I mean. Ask my mother. She'll tell you."

Giorgio shook his head like a wounded bull. "Oh, *Dio mio*, what have I done? There's been a scandal and it's my fault."

"That's right, so why don't you just go back to Italy where you came from and don't worry about us Americans? We'll get along just fine."

Giorgio rushed back into the kitchen. All mouths were silent. All eyes were cast down. They had heard, the children and Teresa.

"Is this true?" Giorgio demanded. "Have I caused a scandal?"

Teresa looked at him with brave eyes. "What does it matter? Who cares what people think?"

Giorgio knew it wouldn't be all right. People would whisper behind her back and spurn her and forbid her children to come into their homes. They would become strangers to everyone. Outsiders. Cast off, like old clothes thrown into a heap of trash. No man would ever marry her for fear of looking like a fool to everyone in the community.

Oh, God, God, God, what have you done to me? his mind screamed in an agony of realization. I will never be free of this family. If I leave, who will take them? Who will care for them? They will live their lives in the shame that I caused them.

His eyes filled with tears. There was only one thing to do, only one thing that could rectify the wrong that had been done. What he said next he did not want to say, but he had no choice. There was no other answer. As he spoke, he felt all his hopes of the past year, all his hopes for the future crumble within him, and he heard a voice from his soul cry out, Gabriella, forgive me, forgive me and remember me.

"Teresa, you were my brother's wife. I have not done my duty by you. I took the burden of your family on my back, but that was only half the burden. Because of my stupidity your name has been dishonored. Now I will make right what I have done. You will become my wife."

Teresa answered with a small nod. There was nothing else to say between them.

Only Sophia cried as if her heart was broken. Giorgio went to her and knelt next to her. "What is it, little girl? What's wrong?"

"I wanted you to marry me," she whispered in his ear.

The nuptials were celebrated without a mass in the rectory of St. Anthony's. No guests were invited but the children and one couple from the parish to act as witnesses.

Franco didn't want to attend, but Giorgio forced him. Sophia didn't want to attend, but Teresa forced her. Tina and Favia were in tears the whole time because there would be no cake and no reception.

The wedding night was worse. At first they were awkward together. She waited for his advances, but he was so unsure of himself and so heartbroken at the turn of events that the advances didn't come.

Finally Teresa touched him and rubbed his belly and petted between his legs, and she kissed his chest and his nipples and—God forbid, what was she doing? He thought for a moment in horror that she would take his member into her mouth as he had heard the prostitutes sometimes did, and then, when she didn't, he felt vaguely disappointed.

After a while his timidity turned to resentment. Why was she doing these things to him as if she were the man and he the woman? He remembered that last conversation with his brother and how Teresa's sexual ardor had been described in such annoying detail. Lord, what had he gotten himself into? A lifetime of this.

He rolled over on top of his new wife to perform his conjugal duty. Her duty as a wife was to lie there and not object. Her body felt warm and firm and very strong under him, but he refused to let such vile thoughts stay in his mind for long. If she were a whore, it would be different. Or if she were the one he loved, that would be different too. But in this impersonal coming together between brother and sister-in-law, now husband and wife, there was no place for excitement, but only duty.

When he entered her, the bed creaked under their weight, so he was careful to go slowly. He didn't want the children to hear. He didn't want them to know what he was doing. She must have been thinking the same thing, because she didn't move very much at all. When it was over, neither said a word. Each hugged a side of the bed and turned away from the other to conceal the tears.

The next afternoon Teresa sat in a small rocker near the front window of her house and said a prayer, as she did every day, only today she prayed for something different. "Holy Mother of God, I don't know what will happen to us now. I have affection for my husband, but I don't think he has much for me. His mind is elsewhere, back in Italy. I suspect he has made a very great sacrifice to marry me."

Tears came to her eyes. "Please forgive me if I have ruined his life by this marriage, and let him forgive me. It isn't my fault, really. I didn't trick him into the wedding, but how could I turn him down? Could I allow my children to suffer with a sullied name? Please, Oh Mary, help me to give Giorgio a decent life so he will not hate me too much for what has happened. And give my children a good life too. As for me, I speak directly to your Son, Our Lord Jesus, and I say, Thy will be done on earth as it is in heaven."

It took Giorgio a long time to compose his letter to Gabriella, and he stained the ink with his tears as he wrote. Finally it was done. He read it over once before sealing it.

My darling,

There are some things for which a man will never be forgiven, and perhaps this is one of them. Still, I must do what I must do. I love you with all my heart, Gabriella, and now more than ever, but I cannot return to you. We cannot marry.

Fate has been unkind to us in many ways, but this is the cruelest I have ever seen her.

When my brother died, as I've told you before,
the responsibility for all of his family fell to me.
I lived here and cared for them as best I could,
but my presence in the house caused a scandal.
The good name and honor not only of my sister-
in-law but of my entire family was at stake. I
had no choice.

Yesterday we were married. I beg of you to
forgive me and to try to understand. There was
nothing else to do. Also, you must believe that I
have never been unfaithful to you, not since the
day we fell in love. In my heart I will never be
unfaithful to you.

Please, keep the ring to remember me by.
And I will keep the little crucifix from the rosary.
No matter what has happened, I will love you
forever, Gabriella. Forever even past the day I
die.

With all my heart
I am yours,
Giorgio

He sealed the envelope and addressed it. He would
put it in the post and it would be on its way that night. He
felt as if he had sealed the lid to his own tomb.

Chapter 23

Giorgio didn't hear from Gabriella, not in all the eight years it took him to complete the statue of the Virgin for the church, but it was her lovely, innocent face that he engraved in the white marble, her features racked with longing pain, because he wanted God to look down from His altar and bear witness to a poor man's heartbreak.

Today that face would be unveiled and blessed at a special high mass celebrated by Father Joseph Cressida, the new pastor. Father Bruno had been forced into retirement three years before and had returned to Basilicata in Italy to spend the rest of his days in peace.

Peace, thought Giorgio with envy. How long he had wanted it for himself—the simple life, as he had called it in the old days. A life without complication that had a beginning, a middle and an end and no detours here and there along the way. This would be paradise for a man, but he had learned that for him it was not meant to be.

What had he done to deserve such suffering? He often knelt at the communion rail of the church at night, staring into the flames of the votive candles on the altar and asking God as politely as he could why so many troubles had befallen him, but the answer was always a silence deeper than death. There was nothing to do but accept and struggle along as best he could. America was supposed to be the land of opportunity, but opportunity for whom?

Oh, sure, you could make money here. One of the parishioners, Guy Papano, who owned a little construction company specializing in private homes and small government buildings, had given Giorgio a job at seventy-five dollars a week not a year after he married Teresa. But even when you made a good living the problems didn't get any easier.

First, of course, was Teresa. She was a goodhearted woman and smart when she wanted to be, but she could be stingy to the penny, even now that there was plenty of money, and always with her it was family, family, family.

How did he know if he loved her? They never spoke of love. They spoke of the children, and now they would be speaking about even more children, because finally, after a such a long time, she was pregnant.

The midwife, Mrs. Costellino, who lived up the street, had not been excited when she heard the news. Teresa was a bit old to be having babies and it had been a long time since her last, but Teresa insisted that it was Giorgio's right to have offspring and it was her duty to bear them.

Giorgio wanted to be pleased and proud, but in private moments he was uncertain. If his reluctant marrying had made him feel like a boat stopped in the water, the coming of a child was like letting down the anchor into deep mud. Sure, he had four stepchildren, but it wasn't the same. It wasn't the same at all. Suppose this child was cursed with the same bad luck as Giorgio? He would bear all the reponsibility for another ruined life.

Still, whatever other feelings he bore for Teresa, this child bound them together tighter than any embrace of passion. He found himself suddenly anxious over her health, and when they walked together on the street, he always insisted on walking on the side near the traffic. There were too many motor cars on the road these days, and Giorgio didn't trust them to stay on their own side of the curb.

For the most part Teresa was easy enough to get along with, though she could have the temper of a hellcat with its tail pulled when someone insulted any member of her family, including him. As for family decisions, ever since they got married, his word had been law in almost all matters—disciplining the children, deciding political affiliations, enforcing school attendance—everything but finances.

Teresa controlled the coffers. She demanded that he hand over his wages every week and she hid the money away in a place he had never managed to stumble upon in all his years of living in that house. Some of it, of course, went to pay for food and clothing, and some of it was given back to him so that he would have a little spending money, but some of it just seemed to disappear. This, he assumed, was money she put away for some unnamed catastrophe in the future.

In addition she insisted on spending ten cents every week on a life insurance policy on herself. It had been sold to her by a polite Irishman named Mr. Page who came around for coffee and the premium payment on Mondays.

She gave a mite to the charities that collected from door to door. The only one she ever turned away was a local preacher who came to convert her to something or other and tried to buy her faith with a promise of food assistance. She was so deeply offended that she refused him with her infamous broom and continued refusing him for three blocks north up Front Street.

All in all, Giorgio had to admit, Teresa had turned out to be the least of his problems, and in some ways—no, in many ways—she had turned out to be a pleasure, even in the bedroom.

If he was uncertain and afraid of her during their first

year together, now he bit his thumbnail hard just thinking
about her ardor. Of course, he had to stay away now that
she was pregnant. If not, and the baby was a boy, he
might grow up to be a sissy.

No, his greatest difficulties were with the children—
not the little ones, who kept themselves busy. Favia loved
to sing like a diva and Tina loved to eat.

Sophia and Franco were another story. Sophia was
only now returning to his good graces. At the age of
sixteen she eloped with a British stevedore from Marcus
Hook, a port a few miles down the river. His name was
Bobby Stewart, though Favia insisted on calling him Mr.
Stuarti out of sheer perversity. Franco was the one who
introduced them, naturally. He was nothing but trouble,
that boy.

From the time of his marriage Sophia talked about
nothing but getting married and having babies, and she
didn't seem to care who the groom might be; she just
watched Giorgio and speculated. Maybe she was trying to
make him jealous. He didn't know. He didn't understand
women any better now than he ever had.

Whatever her reasons, the previous December she had
made good on her dreams and disappeared from her bedroom in the middle of the night. She left no note and
didn't show up again for six weeks. At first he feared that
she had been kidnapped by white slavers. She was a pretty
girl with auburn hair, a cherubic face and a lush figure for
her age, and it wasn't unheard of for such girls to be
snatched for the brothel trade in Europe, the Far East, even
the American West.

Even white slavers were businessmen, though, and it
was usual for them to send a ransom note before going to
other markets. Since they got no note, Teresa decided her
daughter had been murdered and thrown into the river,

though she had no explanation for someone's stealing into her room and dragging the body out.

It was Franco who finally cleared up the mystery. His mother's grief was too much even for him. Teresa pined away until she was drawn and thin like a little old lady. One day Franco came home from a week's unexplained absence and was so shocked at her appearance that he broke down and admitted the truth. His friend Stewart had been seeing Sophia for several months and they had planned to run away to Elkton, Maryland, where the marriage age was sixteen and there was was only a three-day residency law. He assumed they had been lying low ever since to avoid the wrath of her stepfather.

"Ah, she thought I would be mad?" Giorgio said in a reasonable, detached way.

"Yeah, funny, ain't it?" Franco replied with an unsure smile that died in a nervous laugh.

Teresa stood by with her lips pressed tight as though forcing herself to withhold her reaction. She yielded the right of first explosion to Giorgio.

"You're goddamn right, it's funny," he bellowed in his best English—even the Poles could understand his English these days. "I ain't mad. I'm just gonna break her goddamn neck, that's all. But not because I'm mad." Franco noted with well-concealed awe that his arms were doing the strangling at that very moment. "I'm thrilled to death for her. Only the death is gonna be hers."

At this point Teresa began delivering stinging little slaps across the back of Franco's head. He was a tall and strong young man with a mane of curly shining black hair, but for all his size he endured his mother's abuse with the meekness of a schoolboy.

"You bring that son of a bitch into my house and he eats my food—a *stranger*, a bum. A stevedore from the docks who don't know nothing but how to work like a bull and eat like a pig.''

"Mama," Franco tried to explain, "he's a nice guy. He's gonna go to trade school to learn to be an electrician. Sophia'll be all right.''

"*Traitor*," she shrilled, "you set your sister up with a stevedore and he isn't even Italian!''

At that he bridled. "What's wrong with being a stevedore? I'm a stevedore. I do all right. I make good money.''

"You're what's wrong with being stevedore," she said.

"What's that supposed to mean?''

"It means your mother knows what you do down there," Giorgio put in. "You work for a big syndicate boss, and for this favor he does you, for letting you do the work of a jackass, one of these days he's gonna ask a little payment—like maybe you do a job for him, right?''

"You don't know what the hell you're talking about!'' Franco snapped viciously. "I listen to Mama, but I don't got to listen to you. You're nothin' to me.''

This part of the argument had been going on for a long time, but now Franco was old enough to fight back physically, and he showed he wasn't afraid to by raising a clenched fist at his stepfather. The subject of Sophia and her new husband was forgotten for this more important one.

"What do you think, you're gonna beat me up, kid? Eh? Come on, let's see.''

Franco stood and kicked away his chair, then crouched and with little waves of his fingers urged Giorgio to come at him. "You been a tough guy for a real long time, *Zio*. Let's see what you can do. Come on.''

"Franco!'' Teresa's voice was a whipcrack. "He's

your father. Sit down and stop at once!'' She was too late. Giorgio was already going for his nephew.

The scuffle was brief. They clinched like boxers and Franco threw little rabbit punches to Giorgio's kidneys. Giorgio winced with the wrenching pain and freed one arm long enough to backhand the boy mightily across the face. Franco went sprawling. Giorgio was on top of him at once, but only for a moment. Teresa tried to separate them.

Later they couldn't figure out who accidentally hit her, but one of them tapped her on the mouth with a knuckle, broke a front tooth and knocked her out.

Both men were on the floor at once, Franco trying to revive her by patting her hand while Giorgio cleaned the blood from a cut on her lip. When she came around, fluttering her eyes and shaking her head with dizziness, both apologized profusely, but not to each other.

Giorgio eventually forgave Sophia, and though it took a little longer, he even came to accept her husband, a nice-looking towheaded fellow. He wasn't pleased when the couple decided to move to Trenton, New Jersey, but there was nothing he could do about that. At least they were close enough to make day trips.

Franco was another matter. That day hadn't been his first run-in with his stepfather and it wouldn't be his last nor his worst.

Franco never forgot the name Morgan. He hated the man, though he had never laid eyes on him, hated him and wanted revenge. A boyhood without Sebastiano made him bitter, but knowing the name of his father's murderer made him a little crazy.

While other neighborhood boys of his age were hot to take their first dives into sex, even if they had to pay for it, he was eager only to swim in the blood of another man.

They wanted to copulate; he wanted to kill. Everybody was frustrated.

His temper was worn raw by his obsession, and though he liked to imagine himself as a killer without feeling, a man without conscience, a rush of cold air that would bring death to a stranger named Morgan, in fact he was often ferociously, extravagantly violent. He never fought only to win, but mauled his opponents. Then he would scream curses in their ears on their mothers and the saints who protected their mothers until his throat turned raw.

Afterward, when he could find a place to be alone, he would bury his hands in his face and cry. He hated himself for what he had done.

He often wondered when the time would come to realize his daydream, when he would go to the trainyard, find his victim and send him to the devil. After his fight with Giorgio he felt released from constraint. He had fought a grown man, a man much stronger than himself, and though he had known Giorgio would beat the hell out of him if not for the accident to his mother, he was not afraid.

Now he knew he could do it. He was tough enough and he had enough guts. He would find Morgan and kill him.

The choice of weapons was easy. A gun was effective from far off and the noises of the trainyard would cover the shot. Buying a gun, however, was much more difficult than he had imagined it would be. The *padron'* at the dock, Mr. Bonatti, turned him down flat. He said he didn't want "no damn fool kid running around with a dangerous weapon he didn't know how to use."

Christ, thought Franco, how hard can it be to shoot a pistol? Point it in the right direction and pull the trigger. But Mr. Bonatti wasn't to be argued with. When he began to ask discreetly among his friends, they began to get nervous if not frightened. He had a reputation, after all. When he offered big money, however, fear started not to matter so much. Angelo Marronozzi, whose father was a big shot in the syndicate, somehow managed to find a big army forty-five revolver, probably left over from the war.

As Franco left the house early one Thursday morning with the pistol shoved into his waistband, Tina and Favia caught a glimpse of the handle when a flap of Franco's jacket slipped over it. Giorgio had already left for work, but Teresa was standing over the kitchen basin wiping down a cast iron skillet. She allowed her children the American custom of eating breakfast, though her flapjacks were were more like cakes, an inch thick and smothered in oversweet Karo syrup.

"Mama," Tina said as the screen door slammed shut after her brother, "what does Franco have sticking out of his pants?"

Teresa turned red, misunderstanding her daughter's meaning. The things children said these days—absolutely brazen! She turned, about to scold, when Favia spoke up.

"Don't be stupid," the eleven-year-old said. "It was a gun like the policemen and the soldiers have."

"What are you talking about?" Teresa demanded, going from crimson to white.

"Maybe it was a gun," Tina agreed, "but where would he get such a thing?"

"From a gun store," Favia replied matter-of-factly.

Teresa was already on her way out the door, and she screamed after her son, but he disappeared around the corner without looking back. She went after him. *Managia*, she thought, what's he doing with a gun? It's those crooks he works for . . .

She turned the corner just in time to see the north-bound trolley stop, then go on with Franco aboard. He's going into town, she thought in confusion, but why? What's he going to do with a gun in Philadelphia? He'll get himself killed.

There was no way to catch and stop him now, but Giorgio had to be told. If there was trouble coming, they all had to be prepared.

She ran home and in her panic threw over her shoulders a half-finished crocheted shawl she had been working on in the afternoons as she silently said her daily prayers. Giorgio was at a construction site halfway across town, all the way up on 20th Street, so she had to catch a trolley four blocks north from her house and make a change at Ninth. The trip took forty minutes.

She found Giorgio waiting impatiently for a young helper, no more than Franco's age, she thought, to finish mixing a batch of mortar, so he didn't see her at first. She could identify her husband from very far away—he always wore a grey felt hat for protection from the sun and except when the weather was extremely warm, he wore a beat-up jacket of cowhide.

He rarely got very dirty at work. That, he insisted, was what the helpers got paid for. They did the labor and he did the "beauty" work.

When she was close enough to be heard, she called out his name. He turned and put his hands to his hips. He would immediately know something was wrong. Teresa had never come to see him on a work site before.

"Giorgio," she said as she came puffing up to him, "Franco is in trouble."

Giorgio led her away from the other workers. Family business had nothing to do with them.

"What's he done now?"

"He got a gun someplace. The girls saw it. He was carrying it this morning."

"*Stonat'*," Giorgio grunted and kicked at the ground in agitation. "Where did he go, to the docks?"

Teresa shrugged. "He took the Third Street trolley like he was going to the city."

Giorgio thought for a moment. "All right, don't worry," he said, looking worried, "I know where he went."

"Where?"

To spare her feelings Giorgio had withheld the details of Sebastiano's death. "Never mind where. I'll take care of it, but I got to make a phone call."

The East End was a pleasant, prosperous neighborhood with friendly people, and after knocking at only seven doors, they found someone who had a phone and was pleased to let them use it.

Franco had to sit slightly hunched in the trolley seat so no one would notice the great bulge at his waist, but he managed to make it into town without getting caught. Finding his way around the trainyard without attracting attention was a little more difficult, however. He had to keep an elbow tucked into one side and walk with a limp.

Naturally, a young fellow who had so much trouble getting around had no business hanging around dangerous equipment, so plenty of disapproving stares followed him as he stumbled over tracks and wondered aimlessly while he tried to figure out where to find Morgan.

"Hey, you, kid," an American voice said from behind him. He turned and saw a short, stout, sandy-haired man with a broken nose waiting to be acknowledged.

"Yes, sir?" Franco said politely.

"You looking for something special around here?"

"Yes, sir. A man named Morgan, sir."

"Morgan? What do you want with that s.o.b.?"

Franco thought fast. "I have an important message from his wife, sir. She paid me to bring it to him."

The short man rubbed his jaw as if considering the boy's story. "I thought Maggie left him a year ago."

Franco's heart pounded frantically in his chest, but he kept his composure. "I don't know about that, sir," he said. "I only know she paid me twenty-five cents to deliver a message to him."

"All right. He's in the shed with the tin roof—you see it over there behind the turnstile?"

Franco followed the man's pointing finger and nodded.

"Well, he'll be there, boy, if he ain't on one of his four-hour coffee breaks."

Franco thanked the man and turned to go, but he didn't get away without hearing a word of warning.

"You watch your p's and q's around that guy, sonny. He don't take much to eye-talians."

"Thank you, sir. I'll remember, sir."

He was so close now he could taste death on his tongue. It burned and cloyed like hot oil. Outside the shack a big man with a bald head was stacking empty kerosene drums. He didn't even notice Franco come up behind him.

Franco pulled the heavy gun out from the waist of his trousers. The hammer caught on his suspender and he had a moment of panic as he struggled to free it.

"Hey, what are you doing there?" The bald man said.

"Is your name Morgan?" Franco asked him, trying to keep his voice steady, though he could feel it strain and crack in his throat.

"Maybe it is..." he saw the gun. "Hey, what the hell is that?"

"It's a message from Sebastiano Farenza."

The man looked not only frightened but confused as well. "I don't know anybody named Sebastiano Farenza. There used to be a Farenza who worked here, but he's dead . . ."

"He was my father, you murderer!"

Franco lifted the heavy pistol and it wavered in his

grip. Morgan put his hands up as if to stop the bullet, but it didn't matter. He would shoot until the man was dead.

Then something hit him from the side. The gun went off and Morgan fell to the ground, howling and holding his leg. Franco also went down; someone had tackled him. He struggled and punched blindly to free himself, but now there was more than one pair of hands to hold him. He was manhandled onto a canvas tarp by three men, wrapped up and carried away.

A few moments later help came for Morgan.

"Why didn't you let me kill him," Franco cried, "like he killed my father?"

The three men had taken him to a warehouse and unwrapped him from his cocoon. Freight shipments were stacked to the ceiling all around. He didn't like being outnumbered by three grown men this way, but he had already been disarmed. Whatever they wanted from him he would have to give them.

One of the men spit, a skinny little guy who Franco noticed had a habit of constantly petting back his slick black hair. He spoke in American street Italian, a combination of old country dialects and English. "Your stepfather called us on the telephone and warned us you was coming."

"My stepfather! He's next!" Franco shrieked. "I'll get him too, the filthy coward." Tears of frustration streamed down his face.

"You ain't gonna get nobody," another of the men, a bruiser with lips like sausages, said to him. "You're lucky you only got Morgan in the leg. The cops'd be beating up on half the yard workers by now, and then they'd all be after you."

"Why, he some kind of big shot?"

"He ain't Italian and we are. That's all the big shot he's got to be."

Franco hung his head. It was over for the time being. The man had been warned and he would be on the lookout now. "Who are you, anyway?" he asked them. "What the hell business of yours is it what I do or who I kill? I had a vendetta."

The third man laughed and tipped his crushed porkpie hat. "We're friends of your old man, railroad workers, just like him."

"If you're his friends, you shouldn't have stopped me."

The first man spoke up. "You don't know the whole story, kid. What do you think, Morgan pushed your father under a train? Ask your uncle. He'll tell you what happened."

"Don't you worry about my uncle," Franco raged. "I'll take care of him, all right. Just let me the hell out of here."

"Sure," the third man said. "We'll let you out. Just wait until things cool down a little. We don't want the American police getting ahold of you, do we?"

Franco wasn't sure if he liked the idea of staying with these guys any more than he liked the idea of spending a little time with the police, but he wasn't given the choice.

Franco hadn't been seen since that day. His absence was the only shadow over this sunniest of days, the day of the unveiling, but to tell the truth, Giorgio didn't mind. Only the sadness in his wife's face touched his heart a little. Otherwise he didn't care if Franco never came home again. He had been through enough with that budding gangster.

Today was Giorgio's day, and he didn't want any troubles from his family. Eight years of hard labor would soon show fruit. The world would see the face and the form he had sweated over, toiled over, worried over, wept over, the face of the Madonna, the face of Gabriella.

The statue had come to mean everything to Giorgio. It dominated his every thought, his every feeling, his every dream. He lived and ate and breathed it. If the family caused him problems, if he still suffered a little from the sorrow of losing the woman he loved, all those matters had become peripheral to the completion that face. To learn the use of the chisels he had gone to watch sculptors, though he never asked their advice.

To learn the characteristics of his chosen material he bought nearly a ton of cheap marble from the local quarry to practice on. He didn't want to ruin the white block imported all the way from Latium.

When he finally made the first cut, he begged Scarfo, if he was listening, to guide his hand. Of course he knew what Scarfo would have said. "You ain't suffered enough, kid, and you ain't loved enough."

Only in his darkest, most unsure moments, when he didn't know which way to cut, how hard to strike, did he wonder if perhaps Scarfo was right—but no, Scarfo was wrong. The statue was finished and today it would see the world. He was certain the world would like it, having fallen in love with it himself. Gabriella was gone, so he loved her image instead.

Giorgio had been given a place of honor, a seat in the sanctuary, from which to observe the mass. Prayers were sung by the priest and the responses by a men's choir in the back of the church.

After the last words were said, the choir burst into four Latin choruses of *Tantum Ergo*. Next a children's procession brought flowers to side altar of Our Lady. A little speech was made to praise Giorgio and his efforts and to ask the blessing of the Holy Virgin on the work. When the linen veil was pulled off the piece, the great pipe organ at the back of the church played "Ave Maria" and the priest made the sign of the cross over the statue and doused it with holy water.

The congregation was transfixed. It was a wonderful piece of work, they whispered to each other, exactly how Our Lady must have looked when her only Son was taken down from the cross and carried away to the burial place. Look at the mouth—how tortured the cry from it must have been. And the hands, how they were pleading to heaven for comfort. Mr. Farenza, he must be a saint to have carved such a statue, since he had obviously been granted a miraculous vision.

For a moment Giorgio himself was satisfied. He looked at the face of the Virgin and thought, here is the peace I have longed for. At last I've made something with my hands and my heart that even bad luck ain't gonna ruin. A man could spend a lifetime making such things.

After the mass there was a picnic in front of the church, a picnic with chairs and tables instead of blankets because there was no lawn, only a terrace and many steps. The women admired Teresa for her luck in ending up with such a fine husband, which made her a little arrogant, and gossiped about her, which was also just fine with her since there was no scandal they could gloat over.

The men smoked cigars and played *more*, a game in which two players held up one to five fingers while yelling out a number they thought would be the sum of both hands. There was wine and tortolini and all types of spaghetti covered with sauce that had been stewing with meats for half the day.

Everyone was joyous but Giorgio, and something bothered him. It was the eyes; they weren't quite what he wanted. In fact, they weren't what he wanted at all.

Franco was never very far from home. He slept at the docks sometimes, and sometimes he would make his way into the countryside and sleep in the woods. He wasn't afraid of Morgan or the police. The three men at the railroad yard had assured him there wouldn't be any trouble there. Morgan, who was extremely unpopular, knew that if he talked, he would pay dearly.

No, Franco was hiding for a different reason. He wanted to be away from Giorgio, the man he hated, the man who had tried to take his father's place without love, without caring. He wanted respect because he bought food for the house, because he married Franco's mother without loving her, because he called himself father to children he cared nothing about. And then he let his own brother's death go unavenged.

Now there would be payment. During the day's celebration at the church Franco was only a block away, sitting in an alleyway killing time, daydreaming and performing an odd little shadow play with a heavy hammer he had stolen from a hardware store a week before.

The celebrations were over, the sun had gone down, and the church was dark and empty. He climbed the steps to St. Anthony's two at a time. He was in an ebullient mood. When he reached the red front doors, he found the handles chained together, but he took his hammer and broke the chain. Then he entered the church and lit a match to see his way up the center aisle. Yes, there it was, the statue. He burned his fingertips, threw down the spent match, and struck another. With this one he lit a few votive candles so he could see.

The statue stood white and bloodless on a new altar that had been especially built to hold the great weight of the stone. Franco crossed himself. It was only a statue, but you never knew if the Blessed Mother would be hovering nearby. Not that it really mattered. He would go to confession next Saturday and the whole matter of what he was about to do would be forgiven.

He swung over the brass communion rail, then climbed up on the altar itself. His hand touched the marble. It was very cold. He looked into the statue's face. For a moment he hesitated. It was such a lovely face—how could such features have ever been conceived by his uncle's unfeeling heart? Franco unconsciously turned his mouth down in a sneer. Of course his uncle had conceived it. Even the devil knew beauty.

He took a breath, listened to the harsh hiss of his own laughter echo in the empty cavern of the church, and began to swing his heavy hammer into the Virgin's face.

An hour later at the house on Front Street a voice broke the stillness of the night. "Hey, wake up! Wake up in there!"

"What the hell is going on?" Giorgio sat up in bed and Teresa rolled over.

"Wake up! It's me, your beautiful stepson, Franco!"

"Agh, *Jesu Christe*, I'm gonna kill him," Giorgio grumbled, groping around on the dark floor for his trousers.

Teresa sputtered, then came awake. "What is it?" she mumbled.

"Your son," Giorgio complained, "He's back. He sounds drunk."

"Hey, Papa Giorgio, look what I got!"

Giorgio pulled up his trousers and went to the window. The street was dark, but he could make out a figure holding his arms up, perhaps brandishing something.

"I better get him inside," Giorgio said. "If the police don't pick him up, somebody will shoot him."

He went into the front room to light the lights, while Teresa slipped on a heavy housecoat. Tina and Favia were awake as well. Dressed in white cotton Mother Hubbards, they stood rubbing their eyes by their bedroom doorway.

"Hey, *stupido*, come on in here," Giorgio shouted out the front door. "What's the matter with you, anyway?"

"I got something for you, Papa," he spat, "you coward."

Lights were coming on in houses all over the neighborhood.

"All right, if you got something for me, bring it here!"

"I'm coming, Papa."

Teresa was stood behind Giorgio at the door. "What's he got? Can you see?"

"Who the hell knows? Maybe he killed a cat for pleasure. You know your son."

Franco reached the door and smiled. He stank of wine and sweat. In his right hand he held a hammer, in the left a piece of something white, but Giorgio didn't recognize it until Franco came inside and held up a marble shard with a mouth and part of a nose carved into it.

"Look, Papa, I'm a sculptor too," Franco said happily. "Just like you're my father. And I love this marble Virgin the same way you love this family."

Giorgio said nothing for a long time. Teresa's hand went to her mouth and tears came to her eyes. She clutched at her husband's arm in pity for him.

Favia and Tina, bewildered and lonely, came out of their bedroom and ventured across the room.

"You done enough to me, kid . . ." he started to say, but Franco laughed and interrupted him.

"What the hell do you mean? I'm just getting started, Papa."

Giorgio drew his hand back and slapped his stepson so hard that Franco went down on his back, his mouth bloody.

"I said I had enough of you, boy. I gave up my life for you. I did everything for you and this family, but it wasn't no goddamn good because you ain't no goddamn good. You destroy me. You murder my heart. You strangle my soul. Eight years of my life you hold in your hand, and for that I'm gonna kill you."

"What the hell did you give me?" the boy snarled.

"A little part of your paycheck. You let Morgan kill my father and then you try to pay me in pennies!" He started to get up, but Giorgio smashed him back down with a foot.

Tears of anger were streaming over Giorgio's reddened cheeks, and he snorted to catch his breath. "You're father was drunk. That's why he died, because he was too goddamn drunk to watch where he was going. Just like you were too goddamn stupid to know what you were doing with that hammer!" Giorgio fell to his knees, sinking them into Franco's stomach. The weight of the blow forced the sour, cheap Chianti the boy was so full of to spew out of his mouth and all over his mother's cherished carpet.

Franco, gagging and wincing in pain, brandished his hammer to protect himself, but Giorgio tore the tool from his hand and raised it above his head. "I'm gonna take care of you for good."

"Mama," Franco squealed like a little child, "Mama, no!"

Teresa could not speak. She turned her head away and closed her eyes.

"Mama!"

Giorgio held his weapon high. "He's your son." His voice trembled bitterly. "Kiss him before he dies. It is his right and yours."

Still she didn't speak, but she opened her eyes and looked down at her husband. Oh, dear God, what he saw in those eyes, the love, the sweet foolish love only a woman could know, for her husband as well as for her

son. And then he saw compassion and pity and heartbreak,
not only for her son, who would be crushed under the
hammer, but for him, Giorgio, too.

His past, his great work, had been destroyed, and
now he would destroy his future, his family, with the
death of this boy. How deep and rending were her eyes,
full of suffering and love—the ones he wanted to carve, to
make immortal, the eyes that had haunted him all his life.

Scarfo was right. He had never loved or suffered
enough, not until now.

Giorgio lowered the hammer and placed it to one
side. Then he let Franco free and put his hands to his face
and wept.

Franco was confused. He looked this way and that.
The two girls also cried. Teresa touched his cheek, then
guided him gently to Giorgio.

"Comfort him, boy," she said. "He is your father."

She stroked the hair of the two men and kissed their
heads tenderly. Franco, without knowing why, held Giorgio
tight and wept with him.

The girls stood behind their elders and embraced them
from behind. The five of them made a tight circle of *la
famiglia*, the family.

Epilogue

Sgt. Franco Farenza, Third Corps, Army Engineers, was in Naples to rebuild. Italy was in ruins. What the Germans hadn't destroyed, the Allies had. There were thousands of refugees, mostly children, starving in the streets, stealing to survive, gambling, murdering—it wasn't the Italy his stepfather recalled.

True, the palace at Caserta was impressive, and Vesuvius still steamed over the Campania as she always had—there had been a recent eruption. A few hundred people were killed and a couple of villages destroyed. No worse than a mild day of battle.

But here, in the Villa Vichierri, the past remained as if the war had never come. Of course, there was the superficial pandemonium caused by some roughneck colonel who'd taken the place over as his command post for a few months—posters, pin-ups, paperwork, some broken furniture, nail holes where the American flags had been tacked up, but otherwise the place had a peculiar antique charm about it. His stepfather had been right about something else—the place was ugly as sin.

The woman who sat across the parlor from him was

severely handsome, with pale skin and very dark hair. She seemed quiet by nature and a little nervous. Franco recognized her face at once. He and Pop, as he thought of Giorgio these days, had made the new statue for St. Anthony's together—at least Franco was allowed to hold the tools and sweep the floor.

This lady's was the face of the Virgin. The eyes were not hers, however. They were more familiar, more like the eyes of his mother.

Franco was here at his father's request. "Just look in on Signorina Terasatti," he had said. "We used to be friends."

So now he was taking tea with this Signorina Terasatti. Another woman, a shadowy figure, thin and fatigued-looking, twice passed through and smiled but did not stop to speak.

"You must excuse Brigetta," the signorina said. "She doesn't speak to men very often these days. She hasn't been treated so well by them." She made a little gesture of apology.

"Oh, sure," Franco replied. "I understand." He didn't, of course, but he knew how to be polite.

"So, you must tell me all about Giorgio. Is he happy?"

Franco smiled. "He was doing fine the last time I saw him. Before the war we started our own little construction company. Guess I'll be getting back to it when I'm discharged."

Gabriella sipped at her tea. "It sounds very nice. I'm glad for him."

There was a moment of awkward silence.

"Tell me," she went on. "Does he have any children of his own?"

"Two girls, Dora and Gilda. Real cute kids, too. Are you married? Pop seemed real curious to know."

The question brought a cloud to her face. "Signor, I

know this is an imposition, but I would like you to take a message to your father. Tell him I am happy, and so are my husband and children. But tell him also, I keep the rosary always next to my heart. He will understand.''

Franco nodded. ''Sure, ma'am. Whatever you like. I'll tell him. Anything else?''

''No, nothing . . .'' she stopped for a moment and seemed to lose herself in reverie. ''If you don't mind, I'm very tired now. It was nice of you to come, but I must have a little afternoon rest. It's an indulgent habit, but one I've never been able to break, I'm afraid.''

''Of course. Thanks for seeing me. I'll give Pop your message. I'm sure he'll be glad to hear you're doing so well.''

She led Franco to the door, and he wondered what had caused the sad, faraway look in her eyes. Of course, she was Pop's old girlfriend. That was obvious. But there was something else. Oh, well. He shrugged. He supposed he would never know.

''What did you tell him?'' Brigetta asked when Franco was gone.

''That I'm married and have many children.''

Brigetta shook her head. ''Why, Gabriella? Why did you lie?''

Gabriella reached to her neck, lifted the beads of her rosary and kissed them. ''Brigetta, that is what my Giorgio wanted to hear. And I would have him hear nothing else.''